Also by June Faver

FOREVER
MY COWBOY

JUNE FAVER

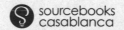

sourcebooks
casablanca

Published by Sourcebooks Casablanca, an imprint of Sourcebooks
P.O. Box 4410, Naperville, Illinois 60567-4410
(630) 961-3900
sourcebooks.com

Printed and bound in the United States of America.
SB 10 9 8 7 6 5 4 3 2 1

Dedicated to all the cowboys I've loved before...

Chapter 1

"OH MAN! THIS IS GONNA KILL CADE!" TYLER GARRETT STARED at the television screen in disbelief. He felt as though he'd been sucker-punched.

Big Jim Garrett came into the den of his sprawling ranch house. "What's up, Son?"

Ty gestured to the video rolling across the screen. "It's bad, Dad. It's the—the airstrip. There was an accident."

Big Jim's jaw tightened as his gaze fell on the wreckage of a small plane. "The Canyon?" But in his heart, he knew the answer.

The nearby Palo Duro Canyon was where Jason LaChance, his niece's husband, often flew tourists over the nation's second-largest canyon for an aerial tour.

Jason owned a small airstrip just east of town. Mostly, he rented space to locals who owned small planes. A couple of companies that did crop-dusting also leased hangar space.

Big Jim prayed someone else had been flying the small plane, crushed like a toy at the bottom of the canyon, but somewhere in his heart, he knew the answer.

It was a prayer with no words but playing over and over in her head. There had been words, but now it was more like a scream of pain playing through every atom of her being. *Please…please… Please, God… Where are they? Please…*

But there were no answers yet. She had called every institution she could think of but had no substantive responses.

Maybe the Garrett family... Social Services over in Amarillo... Someone from the church, surely...

Where are they? The babies... My babies now...

Jennifer LaChance stood in line at the airport, waiting for the TSA to search her person. She had been relieved of her small suitcase but clutched her purse and a fold-over garment bag close to her chest.

"Next!" The security man waved her forward.

She placed her handbag, shoes, and garment bag into bins to be scanned on the conveyor belt, and then stepped up to be scanned herself.

"Raise your arms over your head."

She followed instructions like a robot, then stepped down and collected her items. It seemed as though everything was moving at warp speed except Jennifer LaChance.

Once on the plane, she donned her dark glasses and leaned her head back to indicate to her fellow passengers that she did not want to chat. *Please leave me alone. I'm bleeding from every pore. Can't you see?*

When she closed her eyes, puffy from endless tears, her brain was bombarded with images of Jason, her wonderful brother. The big brother who had led her on endless adventures, protected her and teased her... Her hero was gone forever. And Sara, his fun-loving wife...the mother of his children. They were dead, crushed at the bottom of a canyon. Pain sliced through her, causing her to wince. She opened her eyes to find the person in the seat next to her had drawn back and was giving her a derisive look.

She swallowed hard, hoping the flight attendant could bring her a water. Surely, given all the tears she'd shed, there was no more liquid left in her body.

She hadn't thought it possible that pain this great could hold her in its grip. Her mind and spirit were in ashes, while her body was in a state of rigor. Every muscle was tensed and ready to spring. When she tried to unclench her fists, they curled right back up again.

Jennifer exhaled and closed her eyes again. *Please let the kids be okay.*

―⁓―

Cade Garrett carried his niece and nephew from his truck up to his ranch house. Lissy's head was on his shoulder, while Leo gazed around with wide eyes. "We're home, kids."

Mrs. Reynolds opened the front door for them and stood back while he strode inside with his double armload. "I got their room ready."

"You're a blessing, Mrs. R."

"Here, let me take the little one." She reached for Lissy, and Cade let her ease the young girl from his arm. "Sweet angels," she murmured.

Cade watched her carry the sleepy one-year-old down the hallway to the room she had prepared for them.

"Hey, Leo. Are you hungry? Would you like a snack?"

Leo didn't respond but stared at him with his incredible blue eyes, almost turquoise and ringed with black lashes.

Yeah, your last name may be LaChance, but you're a Garrett through and through.

"Okay, let's see what's in the fridge. Maybe some ice cream. You like ice cream, don't you?"

The little head bobbed up and down.

"Okay, buddy. You sit right here and I'll get the ice cream." Cade placed Leo on top of the counter, fetched a half-gallon tub of vanilla from the freezer, and grabbed two spoons from the utensil drawer. "Here we go." He handed a spoon to Leo and removed the lid. "Dig in." He scooped a spoonful for himself to demonstrate.

Leo followed Cade's actions, as he scooped a much smaller

spoonful and got most of it into his mouth. He swallowed and licked the spoon. "My mommy puts my ice cweam in a bowl."

Cade's heart squeezed with sorrow. These were the first words Leo had spoken since the accident. Cade had no idea how he was going to take Sara's place. His baby sister had been a great mom to her two little ones and had mastered the art of dishing ice cream into a bowl.

Hell, he had no idea how he was going to tell the children that their parents were dead. He swallowed the wad of tears lodged in the back of his throat.

Cade had his own ranch to run, and now he would have to figure out what to do with the small airport Sara and Jason had owned. They rented storage space to a few area ranchers who owned their own planes, and they gave regular flyover tours of the nearby Palo Duro Canyon…the canyon where their own small plane had crashed, taking their lives and leaving behind two small children and their totally ill-equipped uncle.

He scooped some ice cream into a small plastic dish for Leo and put away the tub. Leaning against the counter to protect his young nephew from falling off, he reflected on how his own life had been shattered in the past twenty-four hours.

The minute Cade heard the accident involved his baby sister, he had jumped in his truck to drive to the County Coroner's office for the grisly task of identifying her remains. Tears running down his face all the way to Amarillo, he then had to track down the children. Social Services had taken them from their home, where a neighborhood teenager was doing her best to keep it together, to a children's facility in Amarillo. He had to prove his relationship and get a reference from the pastor and the sheriff before he was deemed worthy and they were remanded to his care.

The social worker would not release them until Cade purchased appropriate car seats, but finally, he was allowed to bring the children home.

He loved the kids, but he had been, up till now, a confirmed bachelor, and he didn't have a clue as to how he would become a substitute father. All the while, his own grief was burning up his heart. *Not a problem, Leo. Uncle Cade is here for you and Lissy.*

———

Jennifer LaChance checked in at the small bed-and-breakfast, the Langston Inn. Her head throbbed, her eyes burned from crying so much. She felt exhausted and almost numb. Shoving her sunglasses up on her nose, she surrendered her charge card.

The woman at the desk was gracious enough, but Jenn just wanted to get settled and find out what happened to her niece and nephew.

"My name is Ollie Sue Enloe," the woman said proudly. "That's short for Olivia Susan. This is my bed-and-breakfast." She beamed at Jenn. "I call myself the innkeeper."

"Good to meet you, Ms. Enloe." Jenn adjusted Minnie in her arms, pretty sure dog hair was all over her jacket.

"Please, call me Ollie." One eyebrow rose as she glared at the dog. "Your dog is housebroken, isn't he?"

Jenn clutched Minnie closer to her chest. "Of course she is."

Ollie looked unconvinced but turned to run the card. "So you're from Dallas, huh? Big city?"

"Yes." Jenn tucked her credit card back in her purse and picked up her suitcase to follow the woman up a flight of stairs to a room across the hall from the bathroom.

"Um, are other people using this bathroom?"

"We don't have any other guests at this time," the woman said.

Jenn was relieved. She wasn't quite a germaphobe...but then again, maybe she was. She carried a small packet of sanitizing wipes in her purse and a larger tub of them in her suitcase.

She entered the room and set her suitcase on the bed. At least the room smelled like fresh linen. This was a corner room, so she had windows on two sides. Thankfully, the sun was setting, so she wasn't blinded by the light. Her eyes felt bruised from all the tears she'd shed over the previous forty-eight hours. She closed the drapes on the west side and went to stare out the back window at the scene below. She felt out of place, here in this rural town where her brother had made a home. She had visited once, after the wedding, but could not for the life of her figure out what the attraction was. It was probably what all of small-town America looked like, but Jenn had spent her whole life in cities and studying at various universities—a very well educated woman with too many degrees. She couldn't seem to find a way to make a living with those degrees, and she feared she would be slinging hash in a diner soon.

Jason had loved to fly, and there was plenty of wide-open airspace out here in North Texas. Miles and miles of nothing but miles and miles...or so Jason used to tell her.

And then there was Sara. Apparently, the small-town beauty had been just what Jason was looking for because they meshed perfectly soon after he hit town. Of course, it was the opportunity to buy the airfield that had drawn him here. Jason loved to fly, and this was his idea of heaven.

Jenn swallowed a bitter taste in her mouth. "Well, I'm sure you really are in heaven, Jason. And now I'm here. I'm going to find out where the hell your kids are, and I promise to take them back to Dallas and raise them as my own." She brushed off a tear as it rolled down her cheek.

Sucking in a ragged breath, she leaned her forehead against the window frame and examined the scene below.

A sweet little yard contained a conversation area, a barbecue grill, and a gazebo, plus some neatly maintained landscaping. Gazing over the fence, she spied the spire of a church a block away. It looked like a painting. So peaceful.

A wave of nostalgia washed over her. When she was growing up, her family had always spent Sundays lying around in their pajamas, reading the Sunday papers and enjoying a late breakfast.

But Jason had turned over a new leaf when he moved to Langston. Jenn had teased him, calling him "Saint Jason." He had gone to church on Sundays with Sara, and they had married in the church.

Jenn had attended their storybook wedding, meeting all of Sara's enormous clan. Apparently, marrying a Garrett meant you were annexed into this large and loving family.

Jenn heaved a sigh and turned around, ready to unpack and try to relax. She opened her suitcase and pulled everything out, arranging it on the bed. She shook out the garments and put them on hangers: one nice dress to wear to the funeral and a couple of more casual dresses. She arranged her shoes in the bottom of the closet: two pairs of heels and a pair of rubber flip-flops. She had packed hurriedly, anxious to find her niece and nephew, but at the moment had no idea what she had really brought with her.

She hadn't planned to stay in Langston that long, but she hadn't rationally been able to decide what was appropriate to take with her. She wondered how her whole family had evaporated in such a short time and how her own life had gotten so lost.

After she had earned her second master's degree, her parents' health had taken a downturn, or perhaps she had finally looked up from her studies to notice they needed her help. Jenn had dutifully moved back into the home she and Jason had grown up in and taken over the household duties, making sure her parents got to doctors' appointments and ate well-balanced meals. Now she was rattling around that big house all by herself, with very little in the way of funds to support it.

Her mother had passed away on hospice care just a few months ago, and her father had followed within weeks. It seemed he didn't want to live without his life mate.

Jenn huffed out a sigh. "Very romantic." But now Jenn felt even more abandoned. Her parents had small life insurance policies that paid off debts and burial costs. Now Jenn needed to find a job to pay the household expenses and support her brother's children…as soon as she could locate them.

Her savings were running out fast and her phone was not ringing with job offers.

Something will turn up. Surely there is a job for a girl with a couple of fine arts degrees and absolutely zero experience. She had to stay positive. Otherwise, she might miss out on the great opportunity she knew was just around the corner.

In the meantime, she needed to get something to eat. Ollie had told her there were three restaurants in town, plus a Dairy Queen. There was the Mexican restaurant, a steakhouse, and, across from the courthouse, a small family-style diner with 1950s decor.

She locked Minnie in the room and went down the stairs. That she was the only lodger at the Langston Inn didn't bother her at all. Crowds bothered her.

Once in her car, she headed for the main street and decided on the Mexican place. Jason had taken her and his family to eat there a couple of times and she recalled that the food was excellent. Tio's appeared to be doing well, if one could judge by the number of cars outside. The parking lot was filled with vehicles, most of them pickup trucks.

She parked between two large double dually trucks and went inside. A sea of faces turned to stare at her. *Yes, folks. Jason LaChance's baby sister has arrived in town.* She held her head high and straightened her spine.

"Table or booth?" the hostess asked.

"Some quiet nook." Jenn followed the hostess to a back corner and slid onto the plastic seat of a booth.

The hostess placed a menu on the table and brought her a glass of ice water.

"I'll have the senorita plate." Jenn closed the menu and handed it back to the woman. She sipped her ice water and surreptitiously scanned the patrons. A few were still gaping at her, but most had resumed their conversations and gone back to stuffing their faces.

When the woman came back, she was bearing a platter of food that would have fed a small family.

"Oh my!" Jenn stared at the mammoth amount of food. "I forgot how huge your portions are."

"You've come in here before, haven't you?" The waitress was a pretty Hispanic woman in her early thirties. "I'm Milita Rios. This is my papa's restaurant. Are you visiting or just passing through?"

Jenn felt a rush of tears but managed to head them off with a paper napkin. "I'm just here to bury my brother, Jason. He brought me here a few times to eat with his family. It was always his favorite."

Milita's face morphed into sadness. "I'm so sorry about your brother. He was a great guy."

A clutch of pain prevented Jenn from responding.

"Such a lovely family." Milita walked away, shaking her head.

Jenn reached for her water and took a sip. Yes, Jason was a wonderful brother, and now he was gone, but where were the children? She ate as quickly as possible, and when Milita returned, she brought a Styrofoam takeout container. Jenn hadn't thought about taking the leftovers home, but Milita was scooping the food remaining on the platter into the divided container. The Spanish rice. The refried beans. And two enchiladas, one beef and one chicken.

"Aww, you weren't very hungry, were you?" Milita snapped the lid on the container. "I understand. Perhaps your appetite will return later."

"That was a huge plate. I ate two tacos and the guacamole." Jenn heard the defensiveness in her own voice. She sighed. "Sorry. My stomach has been in a knot since I first heard about Jason... The food was delicious."

"Glad you liked it. Hope to see you again soon." Milita put the Styrofoam container into a paper bag and slid the check onto the table.

Jenn did some quick math in her head to figure out the tip. Although she was low on funds, she couldn't bear not to leave an adequate tip for Milita. Jenn hated to be chintzy, but there was only so much money left in her account, and she had to stretch that until she got a decent job. Maybe something clerical or even retail. *I am not skilled in pole dancing.* She sighed. *Or much of anything, for that matter.*

Being an artist had only prepared her for being an artist.

Jenn paid the check at the cash register near the door. She was an object of interest again as she passed by. Gathering her credit card, she left without looking back and carried her leftovers to the car. Maybe there was a refrigerator at the inn. Maybe she would eat Mexican food again tomorrow.

Cade didn't sleep well. Hell, he hardly slept at all. Mrs. Reynolds made dinner and left. It consisted of things she thought the children would eat: macaroni and cheese and hot dogs. Just to be sure, she made scrambled eggs.

Tomorrow, Cade would have to shop for groceries...food the kids would like. And he needed to go by Sara's house to pick up clothing for the children.

Lissy sat on Cade's lap and he scooped in bites of mashed pasta, while she held a hot dog firmly in her fist. Her other hand was grasping the front of his Western shirt, grinding in the cheesy grease.

Leo sat on a chair at the table beside Cade. He was too short to reach the table, so Cade had placed a cushion from the sofa onto the chair to give him a little lift.

"How ya doin' there, buddy?" Cade asked, but Leo just looked at him. He was spooning food into his mouth though.

When the children finished eating, Cade had to get them cleaned up and ready for bed. He dressed both in his own T-shirts and tucked them into the bed in his guest room. Lissy whimpered, and he had to rub her back until she fell asleep. Just when he was tiptoeing out of the room, Leo's small voice cut through the silence.

"Unca Cade, where is my mommy an' my daddy?"

Cade froze in his tracks. He had no idea how to tell a three-year-old that his mother and father were dead...that he would never see them again.

"Um, your mommy and daddy had to take a trip, and I'm going to take care of you until—until they come back." Unable to speak the truth, Cade's chest tightened as he uttered the lie.

Leo's large blue eyes examined him carefully.

"Now, you get some sleep. Here, snuggle down." Cade pulled the quilt up under Leo's chin and gave him a pat. "Night, Leo."

Cade left the door open a bit and went to the kitchen. He grabbed a beer out of the refrigerator and carried it to his man cave: the den where his giant curved-screen television dominated one wall. He found the remote and flipped on the television, turning the sound way down. He was desperate to find something to occupy his brain besides the image of Sara lying in the coroner's office.

He watched a show without seeing it, and then the news came on. The anchor did a recap of the terrible accident that had occurred when a small plane took a nosedive into the Palo Duro State Park, killing both occupants. Just as the news anchor was wrapping up and the weatherman made an appearance, he heard a small voice.

"Unca Cade?"

He sat up and swiveled in his recliner. "Leo? What's wrong?"

A tear rolled down his cheek. "Lissy, she made pee-pee in the bed."

Cade stripped the sheets and bedding. He found an old plastic tablecloth and put it down over the soggy mattress. Then he made the bed with fresh sheets, put the children back to bed, and flung himself down on top of his own bed, exhausted but too tired to sleep. He lay awake in the dark, staring up at the ceiling, hoping the kids didn't wake up until morning.

There was a void in his chest. Every time he thought about Sara and her crumpled remnants lying in the coroner's office, he felt as though someone had ripped the heart out of his body.

Chapter 2

TYLER GARRETT CLIMBED OUT OF HIS BIG DOUBLE DUALLY truck and rounded the cab to open the door for his lovely wife. He took the containers out of her hands and helped her slip down to the ground.

"Is he expecting us?" she asked.

Ty shook his head. "You know Cade doesn't stand on ceremony. Cade is all about family." He gave her a kiss on the cheek.

"Poor man," she said. "I haven't really accepted the fact that Sara is gone. I can't imagine how he feels."

Ty gestured toward the house. "Sara was a little brat when we were young, always tagging along…but she was sweet. Turned out to be really smart in school. When she and Jason LaChance got married, it was what everyone expected. She fell in love with the flyboy as soon as she set eyes on him." He shook his head. "Great couple. I guess I never thought anything could happen to them. I haven't really kept up with them lately, but they always looked so happy together when I saw them in church."

Leah made a scoffing noise. "You've been so wrapped up in your music, it's a wonder you keep up with anything."

He leaned against the doorbell. "I just try to keep up with you."

The door opened and Cade Garrett stood inside, appearing to be exhausted. He had always been a big, good-looking man, but sorrow was etched deeply on his face. Without speaking, he stepped back and gestured them inside.

"It's just me and Leah," Ty said, ushering her inside.

She took in Cade's appearance, obviously sympathetic. "Um, we brought you a little something."

"Hey, Leah. That's very kind." He shook his head. "I'm just overwhelmed at the moment."

"We're all just devastated about Sara and Jason." Ty reached out to Cade, wrapping his arms around him and holding him for a long moment. He felt a tremor ripple through Cade's body.

Cade drew back, his eyes lowered and lips pressed together. "Thanks, Ty. Let's go back to the kitchen." He led the way but turned and put his finger to his mouth. "The kids are here."

Ty and Leah followed Cade as quietly as possible. Ty set the container on top of the counter and Leah placed a paper bag next to it.

The kitchen occupied one end of a sizable combination family room and casual dining area. A large television was mounted above the fireplace mantel, and a big yellow SpongeBob image cavorted across the screen. On Cade's sofa, a tiny, diapered girl slept on her stomach, drooling. Fortunately, there was a small blanket under her.

Leah smiled. "Aw, Lissy's so pretty."

Leo had wedged himself under the coffee table, lying on his side with his knees folded up. He gazed at them with large blue eyes…as sad as Cade's own.

"That's where Leo has holed up," Cade said. "He's pretty confused right now." He shrugged his wide shoulders. "I guess I am too."

Ty felt his cousin's aching grief. "Dad wanted us to tell you, he's got your back. Anything you need." He spread his hands. "He figured you didn't need the entire Garrett clan to cluster around you right now, but we're all here for you."

"Thanks, Ty. Did you draw the short straw?" A wry smile lifted one corner of his mouth.

Ty grinned in return. "No, asshole. I got to come because you and I were in the same grade all the way through school. We're more than cousins, bro."

"I know, bud. Just giving you a hard time. What did you do with your kids, Ty?"

Ty removed his Stetson and tossed it on a side table. "Leah's grandmother is taking care of the kids. Gracie is helping." He had to smile when he thought about how much Gracie loved her brand-new baby brother. "She loves playing big sister."

Cade nodded, seemingly wrapped in emotion. "I hope I can be good enough to raise Sara's kids without screwing them up. That's my biggest fear."

Ty gave him a slap on the shoulder. "Oh, get over yourself. I've never known you to lack confidence about anything. In school you did okay, and you were a leader in sports."

Cade raked his fingers through his thick, dark hair. "I know, but this is different. More important."

"You can always lean on your family if you need a break. I know Leah and I can keep the kids for you."

Leah nodded, adding her support.

Cade took a wide stance and hooked his thumbs through his belt loops. "Thanks, man. That means a lot...but I think, right now, I need to keep them as close as possible. They need to know I'm doing what Sara would want me to do. I'm going to raise her children as she would want them to be brought up."

Ty realized Cade was just speaking through his grief. "You and the children are going to need all the family you can get. The Garrett clan is a formidable force around here." He turned to see his beautiful wife doing what Leah would always be doing: leading with her heart.

Leah was sitting on the floor, her back against the sofa. Leo had crawled out from under the coffee table and was plastered against her like a baby monkey clinging to his mom.

Ty swallowed hard, while Cade stared at her, openmouthed. "It's okay. She has that effect on kids... Heck! She has that effect on everyone."

When Jenn returned to the bed-and-breakfast from her outing, she tiptoed into the kitchen to place her takeout container in the refrigerator. The house was dark and the innkeeper had gone to bed. It was kind of eerie, but she managed to creep up the stairs to her assigned room.

First, she gave Minnie half a cup of dog food and took her for a quick walk. Then she climbed the stairs again, this time with Minnie tucked under her arm. The children and her small dog were the only ones she would be responsible for now. She didn't have that much left to lose.

She was tired but probably much of her exhaustion resulted from her emotional chaos. This would pass, but in the meantime, she thought she would take a bath and relax. The bathroom sported a real claw-foot bathtub and she wanted to try it out.

Gathering shampoo, bath gel, and her robe, she locked herself in the bathroom with only Minnie for company. She turned on the water and sprinkled in a handful of bath beads, while Minnie made herself comfortable on the bath mat.

While the tub was filling, Jenn placed a washcloth and a bottle of water on the bath tray that spanned the tub. She slathered an oatmeal mask on her face and slipped off the robe.

Jenn stepped into the tub and sank down into the warm, fragrant water. In a few moments, she could feel the tension ebb and her body relax. She laid her head back and slid lower until only her neck and head were above the surface. She reached for the water bottle again, grasping it carefully so it didn't slip from her wet fingers. The ice-cold liquid rolled down her throat, cauterizing a path to her gut, numbing her in the process. Exhaustion began to set in, easing the tension from her tight muscles. Her head throbbed in time with her heartbeat.

The next day she would have to show up at the funeral and watch the community mourn her brother and his wife. They would bury him in the dirt...forever entombed here.

A man who loved to fly would be interred in the earth. Grounded forever.

She had seen her brother in person as often as possible for the past couple of years. Most of their conversations had to do with finding someone to care for their parents and also the cost of such services. But they talked on the phone often and exchanged emails on a daily basis. Sometimes they Skyped. When she was down in the dumps, he was the one who could cheer her up, sharing a photo of the children or telling her about something they had done that day. He was also the one who would transfer money into her account when things were really dire. Now, she had no one. At least their parents had passed on and didn't have to mourn the death of their beloved son and his wife.

A tear rolled down her cheek. *How did I screw up so badly?*

Just a few years ago, Jenn LaChance thought she had the world by the tail. As a brand-new graduate with a master of fine arts, her future was bright. It had seemed like such a wonderful career path when ensconced in the comfort of the educational womb. However, in the real world, there didn't seem to be an abundance of eager employers waving job offers at her.

She expelled a deep breath and sank deeper into the water.

Now she had an ocean of educational loans to repay and no means to readily deal with her debt, although she had been able to earn a few scholarships and grants to lighten the burden.

"They can't squeeze blood out of a turnip, Minnie."

Minnie stretched and put her paws on the side of the tub.

"Sorry, kiddo. You have to stay out there." She reached out her wet hand to pat at the dog's little round head and received an affectionate lick in return. "I guess we're on our own. We have to be big girls now."

It wasn't that she expected Jason to bail her out. She just expected him to lift her spirits.

She accepted that she had been sheltered by the world of

academia, but now she was getting acquainted with the real world, and it was not being kind. Okay, she had been wide-eyed, wanting to be an educated and sophisticated woman, her future firmly within her grasp. She wished she had been able to fight the aching loneliness instead of burying her head in her studies and the accolades from her professors.

For all the letters after her name, Jennifer LaChance was just a naive girl, ill prepared for the hard-edged reality of her new life.

But, oddly, it was her big, brash brother who had kept her on the straight and narrow. No matter what time of the day or night, Jenn knew her brother was always happy to take her calls or respond to her texts.

Having Jason available to FaceTime with gave her the confidence to get through whatever the day held.

We're all proud of you, kiddo, Jason would say. *Just stay positive and keep your sunny side up.* Yes, it was corny but remarkably comforting.

"No, Jason, I was an idiot with no idea how to live in the real world."

Minnie whined, gazing at her with an adoring expression.

"Now I have to find Leo and Lissy and figure out how to support us…and how to live without my guardian angel, Jason." A single tear rolled down to moisten the oatmeal mask. She scrubbed off the gummy mess, all the while wishing she had been able to learn the children's whereabouts. She would do whatever it took to provide for them.

She sank further down into the warm and comforting water. The forgiving water. The headache had eased a bit. She felt moderately cheered that at least she could provide her own consolation.

She closed her eyes and inhaled the fragrance of the bath beads. Lilac…

She took another long drink of the bottled water.

The next thing she knew, she felt someone dragging her out of the water by her hair.

Minnie was yapping rhythmically.

"Are you all right?" It was the innkeeper. "My goodness gracious! I thought you were dead." She was holding both hands over her heaving bosom.

Minnie's paws were on the edge of the tub, and she was whining.

"I—I must have fallen asleep." Jenn was flustered and she was suddenly aware of her own nakedness and tried to cover herself with her hands.

"I see." The innkeeper's lips formed a thin line. "Your dog was barking up a storm. You should get out of the tub right now."

Minnie gave a yip of agreement.

Jenn felt a little shaky. This woman was frowning ferociously, and her disapproval was evident. "Um, Ollie, isn't it? Could you turn around, please?"

Ollie huffed out an impatient breath but turned away. She took a towel off the rack and tucked it under her arm. "Now please get out of the tub. The water's cold and you're all pruney."

Jenn glanced at her fingertips, and indeed, they were wrinkled as prunes. She reached to pull the plug and tried to stand up, but the tub was slippery, probably due to the bath beads. A little whiny sound escaped her throat, causing Ollie to turn.

Ollie held out her hand and steadied Jenn when she attempted to stand. Jenn gave up and allowed the woman to help her climb out over the edge of the tub and then handed her the bath towel.

"Thanks." Jenn wrapped the towel around her torso and then took a second towel to drape around her dripping wet hair. She managed a weak smile. "Thanks again. I can take it from here. Guess I was just really tired."

Ollie crossed her arms over her chest, her face a picture of disapproval. "Tired?" she echoed.

"Look, my brother and sister-in-law were killed in an accident. I'm just here for their funeral." She paused as tears flooded her eyes. "It—it's hard."

Ollie's face morphed into an expression of concern. "Oh, you poor dear. Your brother was Jason LaChance? Such a nice young man. He and Sara were members of our church." She clucked her tongue a few times.

Jenn nodded, wiping her eyes on the edge of the towel. "I just need to get through the next couple of days. I need to find the children."

Ollie frowned. "The children? I understood a social worker had taken them to Amarillo."

"Oh, great," Jenn said. "I'm sure I won't be able to find them until they open on Monday. Poor kids."

"I'm going to the funeral... The whole town will be there. Everyone loved Jason and Sara."

Jenn nodded. "I'm just going to dry my hair now and go to bed."

"Yes. Yes, of course. You get some rest. I'll see you tomorrow." She patted Jenn's damp shoulder and left the bathroom.

Jenn still felt more than a little shaky. "Tomorrow," she whispered.

She wiped the steam off the mirror and peered at herself. Her eyes were red, but that was probably from the tears and getting no sleep. She slathered several layers of skin products on her face, neck, and body, hoping it would make up for her lack of rest.

She slipped her robe back on and tied the sash. Although she was twenty-six years old, she had never held a real job outside of academia, where she had acted as TA and tutor occasionally. She hoped to be able to get her butt in gear and find a job. Any job.

When she tiptoed across the hall to the room, she felt pleasantly relaxed. She locked the door behind her and let the robe slip to the floor before falling across the bed naked and instantly descending into a deep slumber with Minnie nestled against her side.

Chapter 3

CADE WOKE UP TO FIND TWO PAIRS OF EYES GAZING AT HIM. Garrett-blue eyes.

Or perhaps it was the smell of urine that roused him.

Cade opened his own eyes fully and stared back at the two children, at least one of whom needed to be changed. "Morning," he mumbled.

Leo looked somber, and Lissy was sucking on her index finger. "Are you kids hungry?" he asked.

There was no response other than an occasional blink of the eyes.

"Mmph," Cade said. "Let me get up, and I'll fix your breakfast." He struggled to sit up and swing his legs over the side of the bed.

"Lissy do poo-poo." Leo pointed at his sister, who continued to munch her finger with even greater enthusiasm.

Cade raked his fingers through his hair. *I can do this. Sara would have wanted me to raise the kids.* He hoisted himself to his feet and surveyed his two miniature responsibilities. "C'mon."

He shuffled down the hall to the bathroom, lowered the lid on the throne, and took a seat. "Okay, let me figure this out." He leaned over to turn on the water in the bathtub. "I think this situation calls for a significant amount of bath time." He adjusted the temperature and turned back to the children.

"Um, let's get those clothes off." He gestured to Leo and helped him strip off the oversize T-shirt and underpants. He eased Leo over the side of the tub and told him to sit down.

Heaving a sigh, he pulled the T-shirt over Lissy's head. Her diaper was wet and contained a full load in back. Cade's gag reflex was working overtime. He turned off the bathwater and handed Leo a washcloth and a bar of soap. "Go ahead and get started, Leo. I think you're going to want to wash up and get out while you can."

He took a moment to center himself, reminding himself that he was able to geld young animals on the ranch. He should be able to de-poop his young niece.

After a great deal of wiping down with toilet paper and wet wipes, Lissy was howling but clean enough to take a turn in the tub.

Cade helped Leo out, wrapping him in a towel, before easing Lissy into the water. He lathered a washcloth and gave her a quick once-over. When she was also wrapped in a towel, he heaved a sigh. This parenting thing was definitely more difficult than he had thought.

Sara and Jason had made it look easy. Well, there were two of them. Cade just needed reinforcements.

Thankfully, Mrs. Reynolds arrived early.

"I thought I would get a head start on breakfast today." She was breaking eggs into a bowl.

"Thank God!" he murmured fervently. "I have no clothes for these children. I don't have a key to their house, and they didn't have anything other than the clothes on their backs when Social Services took them. Can you watch them while I run to the store? I have to hurry and get them outfitted, so I can get dressed for the funeral this afternoon." He shook his head. "I'm so glad you're going to be here with them, Mrs. R."

She smiled and gave him a long, somewhat pitying look. "Do you even know what size to purchase? Or what to have on hand for children this age?"

"Um, no. I have no idea." He sank onto one of the chairs at the dinette table.

"In that case, I will whip up these eggs and run to Walmart."

She arched an eyebrow. "Just fork over that Visa card, cowboy, and I'll get you fixed right up."

"Deal!" Cade surrendered the plastic and went to wrap Lissy with a small towel around her lower half. He hoped that would be absorbent enough to get her through the meal.

Mrs. Reynolds had breakfast on the table and gave him a sassy salute as she headed out the door. In a remarkably short time, she returned, flipped him the card and a receipt. She plopped down on a chair across the table from Cade. "I have a degree in power shopping." She displayed two large plastic bags.

Cade heaved a sigh. "Obviously." The process of getting food into the two youngsters had proven to be frustrating, but he had managed the task. He sat in a semi-stupefied state as he watched the industrious Mrs. R remove tags and get the clothing items ready to be slipped on the children.

Leo looked interested, but Lissy was sniveling and, once again, had the forefinger inserted in her mouth.

Cade made a deal with Mrs. Reynolds, who would wrangle the little ones while he grabbed a shower and got himself dressed.

Once in the shower, he let the hot water soothe him and calm his frazzled nerves. He hadn't considered that taking over for his baby sister would be so grueling, but surely he was up to the job. "I'm a Garrett. We don't back down."

—⁓—

Jenn was awakened by the sound of a message arriving on her cell phone. She raised her head, flinching when the pain caught up with her, but stretched out to grasp the device. "Please...please... please..."

She retrieved the email message, sitting on the edge of the bed.

Sorry, Ms. LaChance. The position has been filled. Thank you for your interest. Your résumé will be kept on file for a period of three months. Please check back for future openings.

She reeled back on the bed, flinging her arms and legs out and lying spread-eagle to stare up at the ceiling. *Oh no! How can I have become so worthless…at least to employers?*

Jenn gave in to tears, silently allowing them to roll back into her hairline and tickle their way through to her scalp. She whimpered a bit and tried to imagine how she would support two young children with no income. She had seen on the news that people were living on the streets in big cities and tucked up under overpasses, but she couldn't imagine how they were subsisting.

No! She would find a way to survive and thrive. She had to— for the children.

She thought about selling the house in Dallas…the house where she had hoped to raise her niece and nephew in relative comfort and security. That thought brought her renewed pain. She sucked in a deep breath and blew it out. *I'll find a way.*

Jenn sat up and walked, nude, to where her large handbag hung on a hook inside the closet. She rooted around until she found what she was looking for. Her last link with Jason. It was a card he had sent with a family photograph. She stared at his kind face and those of his now-deceased wife, sweet baby girl, and young boy with very blue eyes. She swallowed hard, hoping that someone nice was caring for them. The children's fate was gnawing at her gut. *Where are Leo and Lissy?*

———

"You look fine. Stop fussing." Mrs. Reynolds straightened Cade's tie and went back to arranging Lissy's hair. Mrs. R had tied it up in two ponytails on either side of her head and now brushed the curls into ringlets around her finger. Lissy looked angelic.

Cade swallowed hard. He couldn't imagine how his

housekeeper had transformed the finger-sucking tot into this little doll, but he was extremely grateful.

Leo had been easy. Getting him dressed in his new clothes had been a breeze. What had not been easy was dodging his questions as to where his parents were and when were they coming to pick him up.

"I'll see you after the service. People have been dropping off food, so I presume they will show up here. I'll have everything ready," Mrs. Reynolds called as Cade sailed out the door, leaving her to care for the children and evade the questions Leo was asking.

It was early, but Mrs. R had assured him he should be on hand well before the service began. As Sara's closest relative, the congregation would want to express their condolences to him, so he owed it to her to present a solemn facade and look as though he was able to provide a responsible upbringing for the surviving children.

"Miss LaChance! Miss LaChance!" It was Ollie, the innkeeper, beating on the door.

Jenn was sitting on the edge of the bed, dreading the event to come.

She had dreamed she was painting. Standing on some beach, with her easel in the sand, adding strokes of paint to the canvas. A seascape with a white sand beach.

She awakened with renewed pain. She had lost her brother and her father...perhaps the only two men who would ever love her.

More frantic beating on the door.

"Yes?" she shouted.

"Miss LaChance. The funeral is going to start in a short time. You need to get to the church right away."

Jenn stood up quickly. It felt as though all the blood had drained from her head. *To the church*. Her mouth was dry. Her tongue was glued to the roof of her mouth.

The funeral. Jason's funeral.

More knocking. "You know where the church is?" Ollie asked.

Jenn reached for her handbag. "I think so. It's the one with the tall, white spire on the street a block over. The one I can see out the rear window, right?"

"Oh, you're so right. I'm leaving then. See you there."

Jenn heard her clomping down the stairs and then silence.

She hurried to run a brush through her hair and took a second look at herself in the mirror. Her eyes were bloodshot and red-rimmed. They were so puffy she looked like Mr. Magoo's little sister.

"Oh no!" she wailed. Running cold water over a washcloth, she made a compress for her eyes, but it didn't help much.

"Can't be helped." She dashed downstairs and recoiled as the first stab of blinding sunlight assaulted her. Blinking, she felt her way to her car and, once inside, groped in her bag for her giant sunglasses. She let out a sigh of relief and started the vehicle, turning the air conditioner up to full blast. For a moment, she sat in the idling car, inhaling cold air, but then, resigned to her fate, drove the few blocks to say goodbye forever to the one man who had never let her down…until now.

The church parking area was overflowing, and she had to park in the street almost a block away. It was impossible to run in her heels, but she managed to make headway doing a mincing little trot.

The church doors were closed, and she heard organ music as she rushed up the steps. She was perspiring and out of breath when she threw the door open and stepped inside.

People were standing and had been singing some kind of mournful song, but they stopped and turned to stare at her. The organist carried on, but the singers fell silent.

Jenn swallowed, looking around for a place to sit.

Then, Ollie Enloe strode down the center aisle with her arms outstretched. "Right this way, honey. Come sit by me up front."

Jenn started to demur, but with Ollie in charge, there didn't seem to be any choice. She allowed herself to be escorted to the front pew, where she was seated next to a big, irritable-looking man. She didn't know how his face could get any grimmer.

She sat down and determinedly kept her face averted. She could feel his warmth through both of their clothing. His man-sprawl caused him to be pressed against Jenn on the thigh until she edged away.

The sister.

Cade couldn't believe this woman was late to her own brother's funeral…and she looked like she'd just crawled out of bed before bothering to make her appearance.

At least she was dressed in mourning. When she scooted away, he glimpsed a pair of nice-looking legs. She crossed them, giving a view of slim but well-toned calves.

He adjusted his jacket, holding his Stetson in his other hand. Some fragrance this woman was wearing had invaded his space. Something sensuous. Not at all appropriate, he thought, although he couldn't say what scent would be more appropriate for a funeral.

The preacher took his place behind the pulpit looking properly somber. He read a Bible verse and went on to extol the virtues of Sara and Jason LaChance, the young local couple who had been ripped from the arms of their loved ones by virtue of an unfortunate accident. He offered a prayer and then a woman sang a very mournful song.

The woman to his right groped for a tissue and blotted her eyes under the ridiculously large sunglasses. Her hands were shaking, and she gripped them together.

Cade felt a pang of sympathy for this woman who seemed to be in the throes of sincere grief. Cade himself was of the "stiff upper lip" camp, preferring not to put his grief on public display.

Ollie Enloe sat on the other side of this woman. Ollie placed an arm around the woman's shoulder and patted her.

Cade knew Ollie. She was a good woman, and she seemed to have taken Jason's sister under her wing. But how well did she know this stranger?

When the preacher asked if anyone would like to say a few words, Cade stood. He was prepared. He knew that Sara was well thought of in this small community, but he wanted to let them know how special she had always been. He talked about their childhood, growing up on the sprawling ranch, about her scholastic achievements, and about her marriage and the subsequent birth of their two children. He talked about her beautiful spirit and how she had always seen the best in her fellow man.

When he finished, the preacher shook his hand, and he returned to his seat. He glanced at the woman sitting beside him.

Okay, he admitted she looked pretty good in spite of her late arrival. She was tall and slender, with very shapely legs.

One of Jason LaChance's in-laws took a turn on the dais. Tyler Garrett affirmed that Jason had been the best person on the planet, telling stories about Jason's love of family, loyalty to friends, and business acumen, having acquired the small airfield and running it with the help of his wife, Sara.

Ollie nudged the sister, hoarsely whispering, "Go on up there. You need to tell them about your brother."

The woman shook her head and gasped, "Oh, no...I couldn't."

More whispering, and finally, the woman stood and walked hesitantly up onto the dais. She took a deep breath, the picture of anguish.

"M-my brother, Jason..." Her voice wobbled. She cleared her throat and started again. "My big brother, Jason, was always my hero."

Cade frowned, reluctantly acknowledging her bereavement. She had tons of long hair cascading down over her shoulders. It seemed to be several different colors, so he wasn't sure if she had light-brown hair or dark blond, but there were some light strands close to her face. She was talking, but he stopped listening when Ollie Enloe groped for a tissue and let out a loud sniffle.

The sister returned to her seat. She sank onto the pew beside him and hung her head.

At the end of the service, the two coffins were carried from the church by friends of the deceased.

Cade stood and gripped his Stetson, looking around at the packed interior of the church...the church he had attended all of his life—Sara's church. This was the last time she would be here, at least physically.

Jason's sister rose and stared up at him for a moment. At least that's what he thought, since her huge sunglasses were still in place. Then Ollie took her in hand and gestured that she was supposed to follow the caskets.

She heaved her shoulders in a huge, dejected sigh and stepped into the aisle.

Cade followed behind her.

She held Ollie's arm, so that anchor must have been helping her not to fall over in a heap. Her head was held high, and she looked neither right nor left.

Cade stomped down church steps behind them.

The coffins had been loaded into two identical hearses.

Cade looked around, intending to climb into his truck for the trek out to the cemetery, but a neighbor grabbed his sleeve, pointing to the vehicle behind the second hearse.

"There! The family is supposed to be driven to the graveside ceremony."

Cade thanked him and started walking behind Ollie and the sister, heading toward the long, shiny, black vehicle. A stretch limousine. A funeral home employee held the doors open and helped her inside.

Cade had no choice but to follow. He stooped to get into the interior.

"Over here, Cade," Ollie Sue instructed. She patted the seat beside her.

The interior of the vehicle had seats facing forward and seats facing backward. Unfortunately, the forward-facing seats were occupied by Jason's sister and Ollie.

Cade sat on the rear-facing seat and stared at Jason's mournful sister and Ollie Enloe, sitting across from him.

"Hello, Cade." It was Ollie who broke the ice.

He waggled his fingers in response.

"You may not know Jason's sister." Ollie patted the sister on the arm. "This is Jennifer LaChance." She gestured to the large man sitting across from her. "That big, good-lookin' guy is Cade Garrett."

Jennifer nodded her head and spoke in a throaty voice. "Nice to meet you, even under these circumstances. I just can't believe Jason is gone." Her sensuous lips trembled. "I'm sure you feel the same way about your sister."

Cade's jaw worked as he struggled to keep his temper under control. How could she make such a statement? Of course he was mourning his sister. He just wasn't bawling or hiding behind sunglasses. "Of course I do." He couldn't keep the contempt out of his voice.

Jennifer closed her mouth, and there was a slight twitch of her lips.

Ollie put a protective arm around Jennifer's shoulders. "Your brother was always talking about you. He said you were real smart and would always tell us what you were up to. Lots of honors, young lady. He said you were going for a doctorate." She chuckled. "He called you the brains of the family."

The Jennifer person heaved a sigh. "Yeah, that's me, except I dropped out after the Master of Arts degree."

"Your brother sure was proud of you," Ollie asserted. "Your paintings were all over their house."

"Jason was one in a million, all right. I don't know what I'll do without him." Jennifer's voice sounded a little bitter, which struck Cade as strange.

He had seen the many paintings on the walls of Sara and Jason's house. They were mostly landscapes, and he had to admit they were pretty good. However, he didn't recall his sister ever saying anything much about her sister-in-law except that she was a student. *Must be quite a scholar.*

"Well, I'm glad you could make it back for the funeral," Ollie offered.

"Yeah, well…I wouldn't miss my brother's funeral, and I have to take the children with me. They need my care."

Cade felt as though she had punched him in the gut. He had not considered that anyone else would want to be the children's guardian. He was horrified but remained silent. This was not the place to hash it out with her. *Not taking my kids.*

The procession had come to a stop at the small cemetery just west of town. The long limousine rolled to a smooth stop, and in a few minutes, the driver opened both doors wide and held out a hand to this Jennifer person. She glanced at Ollie before accepting the hand and stepping out.

Ollie followed, then motioned for him to unfold his long legs and emerge into the bright sunlight.

Cade crawled out and jammed his Stetson on his head, adjusting the brim to shade his eyes. "Come on. Let's get this over with."

Jennifer, escorted by the limo driver, led the morose parade, and Cade brought up the rear.

Their destination was an area near a grove of trees. There, a pop-up tarp with folding chairs was arranged underneath, and more chairs on the other side of two open graves. Both of the coffins were being arranged over the gaping voids.

Jennifer's escort led her to the front row of the chairs under the tarp and handed her off to Ollie.

Cade noted that Jennifer was shaking. It seemed she had not come to terms with the fact that her brother was really dead.

Chapter 4

BIG JIM GARRETT FOLLOWED THE HEARSES AND THE BIG BLACK limo containing the victims' next of kin. He trailed a respectful distance behind in his large, silver double dually truck. His youngest son, Beau, rode beside him, and Beau's pretty redheaded wife, Dixie, and young daughter, Ava, were in the back seat. The adults were suitably grim, as befitting the family of the deceased. Even little Ava was uncharacteristically silent, perhaps as a result of parental guidance, but thankfully, she remained unaware of the sad purpose of their outing.

Sara Garrett LaChance was Big Jim's niece. He remembered her as a beautiful little girl with a winning smile and lyrical laugh. Cade Garrett's little sister. It was hard to believe such a beautiful life force had been snuffed out.

Big Jim huffed out a sigh. He knew things like this happened... to other people. True, he had lost his beloved Elizabeth when the church bus in which she was riding was involved in a rollover accident. Revisiting that event still caused him great pain, but somehow, he had been able to raise their three boys as he thought Elizabeth would have wanted.

Now he was driving down the highway, following the remains of his beloved niece and her husband, pondering the fairness of life and agony of death. As a Christian, he believed in life after death but, in his heart, knew he was not ready to let Sara go.

It seemed totally unfair that a young couple with as much going for them as Sara and Jason had met such a cruel and untimely end.

He pulled into the cemetery and brought the truck to a stop. He sat, letting it idle for a moment, while Dixie freed Ava from her car seat.

"Now you need to be really quiet for a while, honey," she said. "Something sad happened, and we want to be respectful."

Ava looked at her uncertainly.

"It's okay, Ava. Daddy's going to carry you." Beau opened the door and held out his arms. Ava immediately threw herself at him, only to be enveloped in a bear hug.

Big Jim turned off the engine. "You kids go on ahead. I'll bring up the rear."

He watched them join the crowd of people converging on the spot where the young couple would be interred.

Dixie's admonition echoed in his ears. *We want to be respectful.* What he really wanted was to scream and throw things. How could he have lost a young member of the family? A lovely young woman and her husband, a thoroughly likable fellow, had been ripped from the people who loved them...and now Big Jim Garret had to be respectful and not shake his fist.

~~~

Jenn sat down on the folding chair. It was hard and unforgiving. She stared at the two caskets, being readied to go down into the earth eternally. A shudder wracked her body, and she sucked in a gasp of the thick warm air. It was baking, and there was no breeze to stir the heat. She felt as though she had been packed in a plastic bag. It wasn't officially summer yet, but North Texas could be brutally hot in the spring.

Jason is in that box. He's gone from me forever.

Her mouth felt dry. She tried to swallow but couldn't.

That man, Cade Garrett, came to sit on the hard chairs. He didn't sit next to her but left a chair between. Maybe he thought he was being respectful. Mostly, it felt as if he was rejecting her very presence at this event.

She stole a glance at him. *Grim.* That best described his demeanor.

"I—I'm sorry you lost your sister. She was very nice." Jenn stared at the two coffins, wondering which one contained whatever was left of her beloved brother.

He shot a hard glance at her. "Yes, she was the best." His voice was gruff. He cleared his throat. "I, uh...I'm sorry about Jason. He was a great guy. He and Sara were very much in love." He heaved out a deep sigh. "I thought they had the perfect relationship...the perfect little family." He removed his headgear and fell silent.

The preacher came to offer his condolences to both relatives and then took his place near the two caskets. He spoke some words meant to be comforting, but Jenn could hardly hear them.

She felt as though something precious was being ripped away from her. Sorrow was all that was left. Now she was completely alone in the world.

Her parents were dead, and Jenn had many responsibilities now that they had passed on. Only her brother had been her ally. He had always been there for her.

What will I do, Jason? What will I do without you?

The preacher was winding up his spiel. After a few more miserable minutes, Jenn was urged by Ollie to place a long-stemmed red rose on each of the coffins before they were lowered into the ground. She stood up, feeling queasy, gripping the roses.

That's the last thing she remembered before she passed out at the graveside.

When she woke up, she was in the limousine, propped up against Ollie, who was dabbing at her face with a damp cloth. "There you go. She's coming around now."

Jenn's head was throbbing, and she felt nauseous. Her sunglasses seemed to be missing.

A strange woman was sitting on the other side of her, taking her pulse. "Here. Drink this." The woman offered a bottle of water.

"Thanks," Jenn whispered. She took a big swig of the water and tried not to throw it up. "Who are you?"

"I'm Dr. Ryan. Camryn Ryan. How are you feeling now?"

"What happened to me?" Jenn asked.

"You were lucky." Ollie shook her head. "You almost took a header into the open grave. Cade saved you and carried you to the car." She smiled and heaved a huge sigh.

Jenn remembered feeling weak, as though her legs could no longer support her. Her head was throbbing and she was afraid she might throw up at any moment.

"It was probably just heightened emotion," Dr. Ryan pronounced. "And the heat. Why don't you take her home so she can rest and relax?" The doctor looked at Cade when she said it, but Ollie spoke up.

"Sure, I can take her right back to the inn." She smiled encouragingly.

Jenn nodded. "My—my car. I left it at the church." She blinked, but even that hurt. "I parked it about a block from the church. There were so many cars already there."

"I'll bring your car to the inn. Don't worry about it," a deep male voice growled out.

Jenn opened her eyes, noticing that Sara's grumpy brother was sitting in the limo seat opposite her. She had to squint to bring him into focus. "Thank you," she whispered.

Dr. Ryan pressed her business card into Jenn's hand. "Rest tonight and come see me tomorrow. I want to follow up and make sure you're feeling better." She patted Jenn's hand and crawled out of the limousine. "It's better to check you out and make sure it's not something more serious."

Jenn felt an immediate sense of loss. The doctor had seemed to be genuinely in charge, and that meant that Jenn didn't have to be.

"Let's get you back to the inn," Ollie said.

"The driver can drop me at the church. I'll figure out how to get your car back to you." The man named Cade held out his hand.

She stared at the hand for a moment before she realized he was asking for her keys. She fumbled in her handbag and gave them to him. "Thanks...thanks so much for everything."

The driver closed the doors with Jenn and Ollie on one seat, and on the other, Cade Garrett, staring at her with the most intense, almost turquoise blue eyes.

Cade found the car and got in—that is, he tried to get in. He uttered a swear word when he whacked his kneecap against the steering column. He adjusted the seat, sliding it all the way back so his knees weren't under his chin, and closed the door. He huffed out an impatient sigh.

He was still reeling over her statement that she would be taking the children. He would just see about that. There was no way that was going to happen. He would meet with his attorney as soon as possible to see what could be done to prevent her from taking any such action.

This Jennifer woman irked the living daylights out of him. There was just something about her. It wasn't that she wasn't a pretty woman. She was actually quite nice-looking, once the big, dark glasses had come off. Her eyes were puffy and a little red, but he could tell that she was quite attractive anyway. But there was no way he would hand over the children to her.

He shoved the key in the ignition and started the vehicle, giving it a satisfying rev. It had been years since he had driven a sedan, but he managed to get it in gear and moving in the general direction of the Langston Inn.

He parked the car in front of the inn and went inside, pausing at the front desk. There was an old-fashioned bell, so he dinged it a couple of times. In a matter of seconds, Ollie appeared.

"I was coming down. You don't need to make a scene."

"Scene?" Cade felt irritated by this statement. "I just came to drop off Her Highness's keys." He raised the keys and jangled them. "Give them to Jason's sister. Good night." He plopped the keys on the desk and turned to leave.

"Wait! Don't you want to see Jennifer? I'm sure she'll want to thank you herself."

"Not especially." Cade made a break for the door. He stepped through but made the mistake of glancing back to see Ollie's disapproving glare.

He didn't want to bother Mrs. Reynolds or have to make her drag the children out to pick him up after what had been a very rough day, so Cade started walking to his truck, which was parked in the church parking lot. Perhaps he could walk off some of his anger and apprehension over the possibility of losing the children. He had only gotten a short way when he heard a horn toot.

"Hey, Cade. Where are you going? Need a ride?"

He turned to see Big Jim Garrett driving slowly. He braked the big silver double dually truck.

"Hey, Big Jim. Thanks, but I don't need a ride. I was just heading to my truck."

"Aw, get on in and I'll drive you the rest of the way." Big Jim Garrett gestured for Cade to join him.

He climbed into the truck, thankful that he was in the company of a man much like himself, his uncle and a fellow rancher.

Big Jim looked him over and turned the truck toward the church. "You doing okay, boy? You know that the whole Garrett clan is behind you. Whatever you need. I saw you at the funeral, but when that one little lady fell over, I just took Beau and his family back to the ranch. I didn't want Ava to have any more questions. How's the little lady doin'?"

Cade felt his back teeth grind together. "That was Jason LaChance's little sister, Jennifer. She's some kind of city girl, I guess. At least, she appears to be."

Big Jim let out a hearty snort. "Pretty little thing." A muscle in his jaw tightened. "Too bad about Jason and Sara. They were just too young to die."

Cade shook his head. "Apparently not."

———

Jenn had gone to sleep immediately after being delivered back to the inn. Her sleep had been deep and actually restful. Probably due to the fact that her previous couple of nights' sleep had been restless and filled with disturbing dreams.

When she woke up, she was intensely hungry. She had no idea what time it was, but the sun seemed to have gone down while she'd been out of it.

Tomorrow she would contact social services for the county and make it known that she was going to pick up her brother's children.

She lay in the darkened room, staring up at the ceiling, her brain considering the possibilities of finding food as easily as possible. *Maybe delivery? Surely they have pizza here.*

Then she remembered that she had stowed some leftovers in Ollie's fridge. She couldn't recall what exactly was in the Styrofoam container, but it was food.

With a little difficulty, she managed to sit up and find her shoes, which Minnie was lying atop. With a little more difficulty, she managed to make it down the stairs without doing a header, but she did grip the banister with both hands.

"How are you feeling, dear?" Ollie sailed into the lobby, appearing to be deeply concerned about Jenn's condition.

"I—I'm better." She clung to the newel post at the bottom of the stairs, her head throbbing out a tempo of its own.

Ollie smiled brightly.

Ollie told her that a lawyer named Breckenridge T. Ryan had stopped by to see her and left his card. She searched around behind the desk and came up with the card, which she handed over.

Jenn grasped the card, trying to focus on the squiggly writing on the back.

"He said for you to be at his office tomorrow afternoon at three p.m. for the reading of the will."

This might be it. Something to save her. Maybe Jason had remembered his baby sister in his will. Maybe something to tide her over until she got a real job. "Thank you. Do you know where his office is?" She squinted at the card again.

"Right on Main Street, down the street from his wife's office."

"His wife?" Jenn could not imagine why this should be important.

Ollie laughed and shook her head. "You must remember the doctor who took care of you when you fainted. Dr. Camryn Ryan, she's Breck's wife. She wanted you to go in for a follow-up."

Jenn sucked in a deep gasp of air. The lovely blond female doctor who had been so kind. She was married to an attorney who might hold her life in a document...and she would find out all about it the next afternoon.

"Nice... Um, I'll make an appointment."

"This is a small town. Just go into her office. It's first come, first served."

Waiting in a waiting room didn't sound at all appealing. "I put a takeout container in your fridge, and I thought I would see if I could maybe heat it up..." Her voice trailed off.

"Is that what's in the bag? I'll heat it up for you. Want to come with me to the kitchen? I have a little nook with a small table." She smiled and gestured toward the back of the building.

Jenn smiled back. "Thanks." She followed Ollie to a cheery-looking kitchen decorated in delft blue and white. Some ceramic transferware sat about on countertops or hung on walls. *Very quaint. Very retro. And very Ollie.*

Jenn seated herself at the table and watched as Ollie moved confidently around her domain.

Ollie scooped the contents of the Styrofoam container out

onto a plate and placed it in the microwave. While it was heating, she rinsed the container and set it in a bin. She caught Jenn's expression and gave a little laugh. "Yes, I'm one of those tree-hugging manic recyclers. I take paper, plastic, aluminum, and glass to the recycling center every few weeks."

"Hmm…that's pretty nice."

"Just trying to make the world a better place."

This was a new concept in Jenn's throwaway life, where everything and everyone seemed to be disposable. She wondered if she had it in her to become a more grounded person, to take on responsibilities as Ollie had.

The microwave dinged, and Ollie removed the plate with a pair of crocheted potholders in matching blue and white. She set it in front of Jenn and then brought her utensils and a blue-and-white-patterned cloth napkin. "Sweet tea?"

Although the thought of something sweet and cloying held no appeal, Jenn found herself nodding. "Yes, please."

Ollie took two glasses out of an overhead cabinet, filled them with ice and tea. She sat across the small table from Jenn and slid one glass over to her.

"Thanks. I appreciate this. Would you like to share this food? It's pretty good."

"Land sakes, no. I ate a while ago. Just thought I would keep you company." She took a healthy swig of tea. "I was really worried about you when you passed out at the graveside ceremony."

"Yeah, well…it was hot." Jenn took a bite of one of the enchiladas. The one with brown sauce on it. Her taste buds were suddenly alive. She emitted a moan of ecstasy. "Oh, this is delicious." She poked at the enchilada, apparently beef, covered with a chili-type sauce and cheese.

Ollie appeared to be unimpressed. "Yeah, Tio's is the place for good Mexican food. Glad you're enjoying it."

"Mmph!" Jenn made quick work of the first enchilada before

moving on to the other one. This was chicken, covered in a cheesy white sauce with chopped jalapenos. A little spicy, but delicious nonetheless. The Spanish rice was good, but she avoided the refried beans, thinking that her stomach had been in enough distress.

Ollie rinsed the plate and placed it in the dishwasher. "Want a beer?"

"Um, no, thanks. I… How about another glass of tea?" It had been much tastier and more refreshing than she had imagined.

Ollie refilled Jenn's tea and motioned with her head. "Let's go outside."

Jenn thought that she wasn't exactly dressed to go outside and be seen in public, but Ollie was heading for the front of the building. On the one hand glad to have a somewhat pushy friend, on the other wishing she could just go hide in the darkened bedroom, Jenn heaved a sigh and followed Ollie out to the front porch.

It was dark and somewhat humid. Ollie had not turned on the outside lights, so they sat on the porch swing, protected by the porch railing with an ornate cut-out design.

Jenn tucked her feet up under her, content to let Ollie manage the movement of the swing.

"This is a pretty nice town," Ollie commented. "Do you think you might want to settle down here?"

"Jason loved it here," Jenn said. She thought that Langston looked pretty good. It was a clean, small town in North Texas. She had never seen land so flat, but Jason had informed her that it was considered prime pastureland, and since most of the inhabitants were involved in ranching, she supposed he was right. He'd said that the area residents mostly raised cattle and grew crops to feed said cattle. He had wanted her to move to Langston, telling her she could have a new start here, that she could meet a nice local man and settle down.

But by becoming an academic superstar, she was able to meet her own goals and aspirations of furthering her painting abilities and gaining the credentials so she might become a university-level teacher herself.

Jenn grasped the wooden arm of the swing. "I—I don't know if I could live here. I mean, without my brother, it would be very hard for me to settle in. I don't know anyone here."

Ollie reached over and patted her on the arm. "You know me. I'm your friend. That's a start."

Jenn covered Ollie's hand with her own. "Thanks." She found that sitting on a swing on the front porch of the Langston Inn was somehow comforting—especially since she was swinging with her very first real friend in a long time.

Chapter 5

"Miss LaChance, will you be able to come in for the reading of your brother's will this afternoon? It's been tentatively scheduled for 3:00 p.m." Misty Garrett sounded way too perky. She had called Jenn promptly when the law offices of Breckenridge T. Ryan opened.

"Sure, I can make that." Jenn's voice was decidedly raspy. It was her morning voice. She hung up, feeling a tiny bit of hope that Jason might have left her enough to tide her over until she was able to support herself and his children. She was certain there would be a job eventually...whatever that might be.

Yes, she had the talent, but why had she thought she could make a living as an artist? She'd realized that being a bright star in the sheltered world of academia had little value in the outside world. She had hoped that earning her doctorate in art education might help her snag a teaching job at a university, but when her parents had become ill, she had not been able to finish the degree.

Considering the way her luck had been running lately, Jason may have left her the checkerboard they used to play on.

"Good news?" Ollie had gone up to awaken her for the phone call and stood by as though prepared for any eventuality.

"I guess. I'm supposed to go to the lawyer's office this afternoon. He's going to read the will." She sucked in a painful breath and let it out slowly. "That makes it so...so final."

Ollie nodded wisely. "That's what happens. You get to close a door on some things and move on to the rest of your life." She reached out to pat Jenn on the shoulder. "I'm sure your brother wouldn't want you moping around. You're young and need to be thinking about where you go from here."

Jenn swallowed something that felt like a boulder in the back of her throat. "Um, yes, I have been thinking…"

"Well, I hope you're thinking about sticking around here. You got family here…and friends." She gave Jenn a bright smile.

"Family? I lost the last person in my family." Jenn felt the taste of bile rise up in her throat.

Ollie gave her a disappointed look. "But what about the children? You have a niece and nephew, Jason's children. Don't you care about them?"

"I—I adore them, but I don't know where they are. I feel so anxious about them." She felt a shiver coiling around her spine. "They seem to have grown so fast. I was sorry I couldn't come to visit because of Mom's and Dad's health issues, but Jason sent me pictures and we Skyped. They are really cute, and I intend to make a great home for them."

"The most important thing that children need is just someone to love 'em." Ollie's brow furrowed. "And those little ones ain't got nobody else."

Jenn shook her head. "I worked so hard to care for my parents, and I'm determined to give the kids a good life, like Jason and Sara would want." She gave Ollie an extremely lame excuse for a smile and hurried back upstairs.

Jenn got ready to leave, hoping the doctor didn't require payment in advance. She didn't look forward to waiting in a room full of germy strangers, but she planned to sit as far away from other patients as possible and to try not to touch anything.

She got in her car and followed Ollie's directions to the doctor's office. She parked outside, relieved that only a couple of other cars were parked in front.

When she went inside, she was greeted by a cheery-looking, fortysomething woman whose head was barely visible above the counter. "Come right on in here, young lady." She waved her over.

There was only one other patient—an elderly man sitting across the room, reading a magazine.

Jenn approached the desk warily. "I—I'm Jennifer LaChance. The doctor told me to come in today."

"I saw you at the funeral when you passed out and Cade Garrett caught you." She gave a conspiratorial wink. "That was so romantic. I mean, he is a hunk and a half."

Jenn felt her lips tremble and caught the lower one in her teeth. "Well, I, uh… It was really hot."

The woman's face morphed into an encouraging smile. "Of course. I was sweating my fanny off. I'm Dr. Cami's office manager. Just call me Loretta." She handed Jenn a clipboard with some papers to fill out. Loretta offered her a pen, but Jenn shook her head.

"I have a pen." She was convinced that using other people's pens just spread germs, so she was always prepared. She accepted the clipboard and took a seat on the opposite side of the room from the elderly man to fill out the papers.

She jumped when another woman stepped out into the waiting room.

"Mr. Hanson? Come on back." The woman gazed at Jenn intently, as though assessing her. Had she also seen Jenn pass out at the funeral?

Loretta smiled at her. "That's Reba. She's Dr. Cami's nurse."

Jenn pressed her lips together, nodding.

In a short time, Reba returned and gestured to Jenn. She took the clipboard and flipped through the papers Jenn had filled out. "Let's get you set up."

Jenn rose obediently, hoping that getting set up wasn't too painful.

In the hallway, Reba gestured for Jenn to step up onto a balance beam scale. She nudged the sliders back and forth until she was satisfied with the result and then made a note of the numbers on the paperwork. She jerked her head to the other end of the hall. "Let me get you set up in a room."

Jenn followed her to an open exam room.

Reba pointed to a chair, and Jenn obediently sat down while Reba gathered her tools. She took Jenn's blood pressure and heart rate and made notes.

"How am I doing?" Jenn asked, her anxiety wrapped around her like a cloak.

"You're still here." Reba gave a harsh laugh. "Doc'll be with you in a few minutes." She left, closing the door behind her.

Jenn swallowed hard, experiencing a sudden sense of claustrophobia. The room was small but felt *too* small. She gazed at the supplies on the little counter. A jar of tongue depressors. A box of rubber gloves.

And then a brief knock and Dr. Cami was in the room with Reba on her heels. "Good to see you, Miss LaChance. You look better than the first time we met." She held the clipboard and seemed to be totally in charge.

"I do feel better, Dr. Ryan. I was just…overcome with emotion, and it was so very hot."

"It surely was." The doctor seated herself on a rolling stool and proceeded to examine Jenn, while Reba made notes.

Finally, the doctor frowned at Jenn and made little clucking noises. "I'm going to have Reba do a blood draw. You're quite pale, Jennifer, and your nail beds are too. I suspect you're anemic." She inspected Jenn's lower eyelid and continued with the clucking. "You're not vegan, are you?"

Jenn shook her head. Due to her financial woes, her nutritional status was probably in the toilet, but she didn't want to explain to these women that a steady diet of ramen noodles had been budget-friendly. "No. I don't pay much attention to what I eat."

Cami and Reba exchanged a dark glance.

Reba leaned toward Jenn in a conspiratorial manner. "Honey, you could use one of them posters about the food groups. You know, protein, grains, veggies, fruit, and don't forget about dairy."

Jenn blinked and drew back. "Well, I have to—to be able to afford all that...and there's just one of me. It's hard to have all that and not waste a lot of food." Her voice wound down to a whine. "When I was taking care of my parents, I made sure they had complete meals, but since they passed away, I've just been eating whatever's handy." *And cheap...*

Dr. Cami put her hand on Jenn's shoulder. "Maybe Reba overstated it, but you are seriously anemic. I suspect that your long-term diet has affected your overall health. Let's get your blood work." She smiled encouragement before leaving the room. "You're going to feel a lot less fatigue."

Jenn nodded, terrified of the items Reba was assembling. "Is this going to hurt?" She recalled all of the doctor appointments she had taken her parents to.

Reba snorted. "Nah! I'm a one-stick wonder. Just have to find a vein." She tied a rubber strip around Jenn's upper arm and then examined the inside of her elbow. Reba thumped the area several times and then smiled. "There you are." She slid a needle into Jenn's inner arm before she could even draw a breath. Blood flowed into glass tubes and Jenn immediately felt light-headed.

"Hang on," Reba ordered. "Don't you pass out on me." She filled the last vial and removed the needle, pressing a cotton ball against the puncture site.

Jenn sucked in a deep breath, trying to blink away the nausea. She had never been good with blood.

Dr. Cami was back with a small notebook. She opened it and held a pen at the ready. "Okay, what have you eaten so far today?"

"Today? I haven't eaten yet today."

They both stared at her, appearing to be somewhat horrified.

"You haven't eaten anything?" Reba's voice was harsh.

"Nu-uh," Jenn stammered.

"It's after one in the afternoon. Your body hasn't received any nourishment since whatever you ate for dinner." Cami raised her brows. "Doesn't that seem a bit extreme? Aren't you hungry now?"

"Well, I guess so. I could eat something, but I had to come here and then go to see your husband, the lawyer."

"I see," Cami said. "Reba, find out what's in the fridge."

Before she was allowed to leave, Jenn was practically force-fed. She was given a carton of orange juice and a tuna salad sandwich. The latter had been Reba's lunch, but she insisted that Jenn eat it. Reba said she would go to the drive-through at the Dairy Queen.

Jenn managed to eat half of the sandwich and washed it down with orange juice.

"Try to finish it," Reba said.

"I—I generally don't eat this much."

"Well, you're eating it today."

Jenn took another bite and chewed furiously.

Dr. Cami brandished the small notebook. "I want you to write down everything you eat for the next week and then bring it back. Even if it's only a bite, write it down."

Jenn was finally allowed to leave the doctor's office with the notebook and a sample bottle of multivitamins with iron. She drove to the lawyer's office, knowing she had distinctly fishy breath.

―∞―

Cade was early. Truth be told, Cade was usually early. His paternal grandmother had drummed it into him that being late was rude and a sign that you did not hold the person or event to which you were late to be important enough to trouble yourself to be on time, so he was habitually early.

"Hi, Cade. Mr. Ryan will be with you shortly," Misty assured him. She was married to Big Jim Garrett's oldest son, and she was Breck Ryan's secretary/office manager.

Cade nodded at her and took a seat, and in just a few minutes, he was shown into Breck's office. They shook hands, and Breck waved him to one of the seats across from his desk.

He took a sealed document out of his desk drawer and laid it reverently in front of him. "I'll start the reading as soon as Miss LaChance shows up."

Cade glanced at the antique clock on the wall. It had a brass pendulum swinging back and forth. *Three o' clock sharp.* "She's late."

"Not seriously late. We'll give her a little leeway." Breck shrugged. "Besides, you were early."

Cade was resigned to wait for Her Highness to arrive, the woman who was apparently always late.

Breck's mouth was tight as he drummed his fingers on his desk. He heaved a sigh and swiveled his chair to face Cade. "How are you doing? I know that losing Sara was quite a blow. She was a lovely young woman."

Cade drew a deep breath, bracing himself for the pain that ripped through his chest at the mention of her name. "She was the best."

"And I understand you've got the LaChance kids? How is that going?"

Cade made an exasperated growl. "They're so young and helpless. I—I feel really inept." He clasped and unclasped his hands. "Thank God for Mrs. Reynolds. I don't know what I would do without her."

Breck gave him a long, solemn stare. "But you have a ranch to run. How can you do that with two small children?"

"I owe it to Sara. She would have wanted me to step up." He shook his head. "Those kids have Garrett blood."

Misty knocked on the glass inset in the door. "Miss LaChance is here, gentlemen."

Breck growled something unintelligible and Misty opened the door to show the latecomer into the office.

Both men stood, but Cade couldn't summon a properly welcoming expression. He stared at her, feeling as though he'd been punched in the gut.

The sister looked amazing. Her eyes weren't puffy and she wasn't hiding behind oversize sunglasses. She was tall and had a very nice figure. Her dress was of some soft, pale-blue material that sort of fluttered when she walked, and her pale skin was sort of glowing, like a pearl.

He honestly didn't understand how she managed to affect him whenever he saw her, but she stirred something inside him… something he wasn't sure he wanted stirred.

Breck gestured for her to take the other chair and then seated himself.

Cade, too, dropped into his own chair, trying to ignore the scent of whatever made Jennifer LaChance smell so good.

"I'm sorry to be late," she said a bit breathlessly. She gave a smile that let Cade know, for the first time, that she had dimples. "I was visiting your wife, Mr. Ryan. She said for me to tell you it was all her fault." She blinked those wide-set eyes. "She was holding me prisoner."

Cade noted the Band-Aid taped to her inner arm, complete with a cotton ball. Obviously she'd given blood. He tried to reconcile his feelings that were warring over her tardiness and his reaction to her long legs and the fragrance she wore like an aura.

Breck lifted one side of his mouth in a knowing smile. "I'm sure she was." He began some kind of legal blather that sounded as though he had memorized it, or at least had said it a few times in the past. He reached for the large manila envelope on the desk and broke the seal.

Jenn crossed her legs, diverting Cade's attention once again.

Breck cleared his throat, rattled the pages in his hand, and began reading. "This is the last will and testament of Jason LaChance and Sara Garrett LaChance."

That sounded so final, but Cade was ready to get on with his life, which would now include the two little ones. Yes, he would manage. Maybe hire someone part-time to give Mrs. Reynolds a break.

Most of the language was above Cade's pay grade, but he sat up and wrenched his attention from Jenn's long legs.

He had been so deep in thought he hadn't heard all the legal-speak Breck was mumbling until he heard the sister cry out.

"Thank goodness," she gasped, half rising from the chair. "I've been so worried about them."

"Wait," Cade said. "Can you read that part over again?"

Breck scowled at each of them in turn. "I said, Jason and Sara gave their house and guardianship of their two children, Leo and Lissa LaChance, to his sister, Jennifer LaChance."

Jenn blinked rapidly. "Wait! I don't understand all that you said."

Breck carefully set the papers aside. "To put it simply, the two of you are to share in their business, the airfield north of town. Proceeds from their business are to be split between the two of you." Breck cleared his throat and glanced at each of them in turn. "By the way, I have been contacted by a party who is interested in purchasing the airstrip. If the two of you aren't willing to be involved in the day-to-day running of their business, you should know there is one interested party, and of course we can list it with a commercial Realtor."

Cade's insides were boiling. He felt as though he had been physically assaulted.

The sister appeared to be stunned as well. "Children!" Jenn's eyes opened as wide as eyes could possibly open and her voice sounded faint. "Where are the children?"

"No! I cannot accept this," Cade roared. "The children belong with me."

"We're talking about Jason's children. I'm so thankful they realized I'm the only logical person to raise them." She was frowning now. Or at least he thought she was. Maybe she just looked thoughtful.

Cade smacked his open palm on the desk. "Look here, Breck. Those kids belong with me. You know that." He felt his heart hammering in his chest.

"Settle down now, Cade." Breck's dark brows almost met in the middle of his face. "Don't blame me. I just gather the information that my clients tell me and try to deliver what they want." He pushed back from the desk. "In this case, your little sister and her husband wanted Jennifer here to raise their children."

That fact stunned him. Cade could hardly draw a breath.

Chapter 6

Jenn sat in Breck's office long after the will had been read. She felt numb.

She had hoped there might have been a bit of cash to tide her over until she obtained a job, whatever menial task she could find, but she had become the recipient of a house and two very young children. And she was to be partners with this Cade person in her brother's business.

The Cade person was standing near the door, with his hands on his hips, glowering in her direction. He had ranted at Breck for a while but appeared to have blown himself out.

To tell the truth, Jenn hadn't heard much of it. Her thoughts had overwhelmed her. She tried to wrap her head around everything she'd heard. Somehow, Jason and Sara wanted her to take care of their two children, and they must have intended for her to raise them right here in this small community. She was terrified. What if she made a mess of it? What if she couldn't do it? What would happen to the children then? *I'm not a small-town person. I need to go back to Dallas, so I can put my degrees to work. I need a real job.*

She swallowed hard and looked at Cade again. He seemed to feel he would be the better parent. But he was such a big, angry man. How could he take care of two sensitive children? They needed a mother.

Mother? They need me.

Jenn thought she might throw up. Would she have to fight this big cowboy for the guardianship of her niece and nephew?

She had taken excellent care of her parents and of Minnie. Could children be much more complicated? After all, kids could tell you how they were feeling, and you just had to guess with a dog.

But in the middle of all that self-doubt, a kernel of hope bloomed in her chest. Her brother wanted her to take care of his children. He had faith in her, as did Sara. They would not have trusted her with their children's upbringing if she wasn't up to the task. But did it have to be here in Langston? Maybe she could find a buyer for Jason's house and return to Dallas with the children.

"Okay," she said. "What do I need to do now?"

Breck gazed at her. "Well, next...we need to get you settled into the house and then we can transfer the care of Lissy and Leo to you."

"But they don't even know her," Cade protested. "You're asking me to just hand them over to a complete stranger."

Jenn was outraged that this clod was verbally attacking her. She knew the children and they knew her...probably not as well as they knew their uncle, but she was not a stranger. She crossed her arms over her chest and sat glaring at him. She had not visited while her parents were alive, but Jason had Skyped with her regularly. Sara sent photos of the children almost daily. Well, maybe she knew more about the children than they knew about her. *Not a problem. We'll get along fine.*

Breck raked his fingers through his hair. "Well, maybe you ought to get to know her, Cade. Your sister married her brother, and they both sat right across from me at my desk and directed me to make sure Jennifer here was the legal guardian of their minor children in the event that something happened to them."

"But their plane crashed in the canyon. Surely you don't think they expected to die, do you?"

Breck put his hand on Cade's shoulder. "Nobody does."

—∿∿—

Jenn returned to the inn and took Minnie for a walk. When she got back, she climbed onto the porch and sat on the porch swing with Minnie in her lap. That's where Ollie found her.

"You look like you're deep in thought." Ollie took a seat beside her. "What's up?"

"Um...I'm going to be taking care of children...my niece and nephew."

Ollie clasped her hands together. "Oh, that's wonderful. They're so cute." She looked at Jenn intently. "That's what you wanted, isn't it?"

"Well, as I understand it, I will be living in Jason's house with the children."

"Perfect. The kids will be in a familiar setting."

Jenn nodded. "That makes sense. I guess that's why they willed it to me."

Ollie sobered. "Oh, that means you'll be leaving me." She sighed. "I've really enjoyed getting to know you. I feel that we have become friends." She looked at Jenn hopefully.

"Of course we're friends. We'll still be friends when I move into the house." She shuddered as the reality hit her. "Oh, all of my brother's things are there. I don't know if I can handle that." She swallowed hard. "I thought I would be bringing the kids to my house in Dallas. It's the house Jason and I grew up in...and where my parents lived out their years together." She blinked against the tears. "Why does this have to be so hard?"

Ollie reached over to pat Jenn's arm. "Don't you worry about that, sweetie. I'll come over, and we can pack up the things you don't want to keep. I'm sure you can take their clothes to a thrift store or donate them if you don't want the bother."

"I—I haven't thought this through," Jenn admitted. "I'd appreciate the help."

"Sure thing." Ollie beamed at her.

"Mostly, I'm worried about getting a good job. I'm pretty sure nobody needs an art teacher here in Langston. And I want to be a good mother to the kids. I don't want them to develop a complex because of bad parenting."

Ollie shook her head. "I think there may be an art teacher at the high school and maybe at the middle school…but I can't think of anything else you might do." She brightened suddenly. "Maybe you could teach private lessons?"

Somehow, Jenn doubted that this would bring much in the way of financial support for her new family.

Minnie whined and put her paw on Jenn's arm. "Oh, am I neglecting you?" She scruffled the dog's ears. When she looked up, Ollie was smiling.

"I'm not worried about you becoming a mother to Lissy and Leo. Look at how you take care of Minnie."

"But that's easy. Dogs just want someone to love them."

"So do kids," Ollie said. "Just love them and everything else will fall into place."

Jenn considered this. She could see herself lavishing love on the children. It was an image that brought a smile to her face and warmth to her chest. "Do you have children, Ollie?"

"No…never married. But I was the oldest girl in my family, so I helped raise my younger brother and sister."

"I was the youngest, and it was Jason who took care of me."

"Sweet! My mom needed the help, so she had me cooking and cleaning from an early age."

Jenn sucked in a breath. "Cooking! I don't know how to cook much of anything. My parents were on a pretty bland diet, so there wasn't much variety. I mostly know how to nuke stuff and order in."

Ollie patted her on the arm. "Not a problem. Kids are easy. Just open a box of mac and cheese, add a can of Vienna sausages, and they're happy."

"Really? That sounds horrible."

Ollie chuckled. "Yes, it is."

The porch swing had a comforting creak to go with the motion.

Jenn relaxed, thinking she would figure out this parent thing. In the meantime, she was glad that she had one friend.

"I cannot believe my own sister thought that ditzy little flake would be a better parent than me." Cade was pacing around his kitchen, trying to keep his voice down.

"They probably knew you would be busy with the ranch." Mrs. Reynolds sat at his breakfast bar, her hands folded in front of her. She surveyed him calmly, a counterpoint to Cade's turmoil. "Maybe you ought to give her a chance. She might surprise you."

He raked his fingers through his hair. "Are you kidding me? It's Lissy and Leo we're talking about. No telling what she would think is appropriate. I can't take a chance with their safety."

Mrs. Reynolds rolled her eyes and crossed her arms over her chest. "Seriously? Cade Garrett, you have to get over yourself. I'm sure you'll be seeing the children. This woman is not going to lock them up in a tower."

Cade scowled at her. The words should have calmed him, but he felt as though she was refusing to acknowledge his fears.

She tilted her head to one side, staring him down.

"Okay, okay. I get your point. She's not a monster...just a little flaky."

Mrs. Reynolds gave a slight shake of her head. "By all accounts, she's a nice young woman. You liked Jason LaChance, didn't you?"

"Of course. Jason was a fine man. He and Sara were very happy."

"And Jennifer is his sister. She grew up with him. Stop judging her just because you got off to a bad start."

He heaved out a sigh. "I'll try, but you may have to sedate me when I have to turn the kids over to her."

"It's a deal."

The next day, Jenn ate breakfast with Ollie in the kitchen of the inn. Ollie made biscuits with sausage gravy and eggs over easy. The aroma was intoxicating. Jenn remembered that her grandmother had made biscuits and gravy when she was a little girl. She opened the notebook Dr. Ryan had given her and wrote down the date. She carefully listed a biscuit, an egg, and approximately three tablespoons of gravy.

"What's this?" Ollie asked, pointing to the notebook.

Jenn's lips pressed together for a moment. "Um, I went to see the doctor and she thinks I'm not eating right." She shrugged. "It seems I'm anemic. I haven't exactly been eating a well-balanced diet. I'm taking a multivitamin now too…with iron."

Ollie snorted. "I'm sure you're going to be just fine."

"All my life…well, since I was a kid, I've been a picky eater." Jenn knew she was pouting and sucked her lower lip back. "And now, the doctor is fussing at me. She thinks that if I start eating better…I won't be so exhausted all the time."

"Honey, honestly, I'm going to introduce you to a whole world of food. I read that eating berries and nuts is good for your brain."

Jenn felt tears gathering in her eyes and tried to blink them away. "It's my brain that has made my living for a number of years now…at least until—until…"

"Until what?" Ollie set her fork down and leaned forward. "What happened to kick the spirit plumb outta you?"

Jenn piled some egg on top of a wedge of gravy-covered biscuit and stuffed it in her mouth. She wasn't sure she was ready to discuss her life that had flatlined, but since it was completely over and done with, she realized it didn't matter. "I spent several years chasing after my degrees. I put everything else aside. I don't know how to explain it… It was like the university was a whole 'nother planet and everything revolved around getting those credits and making A's." She shook her head sadly. "Excelling in school was just everything to me. I was so happy…and then…" She reached for a napkin and carefully blotted her eyes.

Ollie's mouth was slightly agape. "And then what happened?"

"And then my parents became ill, and I realized I had neglected them. I was halfway to a doctorate, but I just walked away from everything and went home to take care of them."

"How horrible. You must have been so upset."

"Yes, and heartbroken. I couldn't believe that everything I had been working for felt so shallow…and it really broke my heart that I had neglected my family. I had my degrees, but instead of getting right out there with my résumé, I tried to make it up to my mother and father… At least they knew I loved them." Tears were running down her cheeks unchecked. She stared at a pretty transferware plate hanging on the wall in Ollie's kitchen but saw nothing.

"Oh, you poor dear," Ollie breathed. "I'm so sorry your parents were so ill, but things are okay now, aren't they?"

Jenn considered this question. Were things okay? A few days ago, she thought she was at the bottom. No job. No money coming in. No good news from résumés she'd sent out. Then she'd been informed that her brother was dead. How much lower could she go?

"I guess things are better. I'll have a place to stay here, and I'll have two little children to care about. And I'll have to figure out what to do with my house in Dallas. I really don't want to sell it."

"You could get with a Realtor and rent it out. That would give you some income, wouldn't it?"

The thought of having strangers living in her home was somehow repellent, but the idea of having income was not. She would have to consider this carefully.

Ollie passed the plate of biscuits. "I think you need another biscuit with my homemade peach preserves. That's always going to make things better."

—∿∿—

Jenn went to the office of Breckenridge T. Ryan. She was drowning in anxiety, mostly because all the legal business scared and confused her.

Breck had quite a few papers for Jenn to sign, and then he walked her over to the bank, where she signed more papers, opened checking and savings accounts, and the balances of Jason and Sara LaChance's accounts were transferred to hers. Her signature was also added to the business account of the airstrip.

"I don't know anything about running an airstrip, or any other kind of business for that matter."

Breck informed her that Cade would also be added to the account and gave her the number of a CPA who could examine the books and reconcile them and would be able to explain everything about the financials.

She left the bank with a checkbook, a debit card, and a brand-new pen. She was nervous, but thrilled to be solvent.

Breck instructed her to follow his truck in her car, and he would show her around the house she had inherited. "I thought it would be best to get you installed in the house before bringing the children over."

She fell in behind Breck's big truck. He drove down the main street and turned off into a residential area. A few blocks more and he turned again, eventually stopping in front of a bungalow that had been built in the fifties. It was well-kept, with a nice yard and front porch. The front door was painted red.

It was the house in which both Jason and Sara LaChance had lived and had been raising their two children. Now it was Jenn's responsibility.

Home…

Jenn pulled in behind Breck's truck and climbed out. "Oh, this was their own little house." She swallowed hard to keep the tears at bay. "They—they were so very happy here. I visited once when Leo was born, but then Mom and Dad needed me. I—I couldn't leave them."

"I'm surprised you didn't meet Cade or any of the Garretts when you visited," Breck said.

Jenn shook her head. "I remember there were a ton of Sara's relatives at the wedding, but I couldn't put names to faces. They all kind of looked alike. It was a hit-and-run trip for me." Her mouth tightened. "I was neck deep in my studies then, and so very serious about it."

"Your brother and sister-in-law took good care of the house. Jason made quite a few improvements. Let me show you around." He produced a set of keys and headed up the walkway, stepping up on the porch. He unlocked the red door and held it open for her.

Jenn's chest felt tight. This was where Jason had lived with his family. She had only visited once but hadn't really considered the house because she had been focused on the people who lived there. She stood in the middle of the living room and looked around, unable to speak. The walls were painted a soft gray, and all the woodwork was glossy white. It gave the impression of being clean and calming.

There was a fireplace with family pictures on the mantel.

Jenn gazed at the happy faces staring back at her. Jason looked so alive, a grin on his tanned face, his arm around his wife. In one, Leo was sitting on Jason's broad shoulders, while Lissy was in his arms. He looked every bit the proud father. And he'd entrusted those precious children to his sister.

I can do this, Jason. She swallowed hard. *I will do it.*

Breck cleared his throat. "Do you want to see the rest of the house?"

She turned back to him, nodding. "Yes, so much to take in." She followed him through a formal dining room that looked as though it wasn't used much to a cheery kitchen with a plastic-and-chrome dining set, a high chair, and a raised seat for the children. Very cozy. Jenn could envision her brother's family gathered there.

The appliances were new, and everything was gleaming. There

was a laundry room off the kitchen, and she glimpsed a fenced yard with a swing set. Everything was quite cozy.

Breck opened the door past the laundry room that led out to a garage. There were two vehicles parked inside. "The Jeep was your brother's, and the sedan was your sister-in-law's. They belong to you now. You just need to change the registrations and get them insured in your name."

Jenn couldn't believe her good fortune. She could sell her sometimes-unreliable sedan and not have to worry about transportation.

The knot in her stomach was loosening… Things were working out. Somehow, out of tragedy and despair, she could see a glimmer of hope. Was this the way her life was supposed to turn?

Breck held out two sets of keys. "These are the car and house keys, as well as a set of keys to the business. I'll be meeting with Cade shortly, to introduce him to the business. Why don't you pack up your things and pay your bill at the Langston Inn, then get settled in here?"

"Okay, I can do that."

"Then when you feel comfortable, Cade can bring the children home, and you can take over as guardian." Breck looked at her for confirmation, and she nodded.

"I'll do that right away and be ready for the children tomorrow." She had her doubts as to her ability to perform well as a parent, but she was damned if she would let Breck know that.

She locked up the house and returned to the inn, where she told Ollie about her meeting with Breck.

"That's fantastic. I'm so glad you're going to stay here in Langston." Ollie appeared to be delighted. "You go ahead and get your things packed up and I'll make us some lunch." She gave a wide grin. "Be sure to bring your little food notebook. We'll give Dr. Ryan some good, nutritious food to read about."

It took very little time for Jenn to repack her belongings and load them into the car. She knew the day was getting away from her and she wanted to follow Breck's instructions and get settled in the house.

Ollie rode with her, which was good because she was holding Minnie. The dog was not a good car traveler and stood in Ollie's lap while gazing out the window. Her long fur was blowing in the wind, and her big eyes were taking in the passing scenery.

Jenn was a little anxious to be moving into her brother's house. "I'm glad you're with me. I was feeling weird going into Jason's place, like I'm trespassing."

"You'll get over that. It's your house now." Ollie turned to look at Jenn. "Didn't you visit Jason and Sara?"

Jenn shook her head. "Just a couple of times. We Skyped or FaceTimed. For so long, I was working on my education. I mean, I was constantly in class or working on papers and projects. Then Mom and Dad went downhill and everything just went to hell." She heaved a huge sigh. "Jason and Sara brought Leo to visit Mom and Dad a couple of times. They were so delighted to be grandparents."

"Well, that was then and this is now." Ollie's voice sounded chipper. "You're living here. You have a house and two beautiful children. Things change. We just have to adapt."

"And cars. There are two cars in the garage. Breck said those belong to me too."

"Whoo-ee! Let's get rid of this money-sucking old automobile. You can put an ad in the local paper, and someone will snap it right up."

"That's wonderful. I'll be so relieved to sell this car." Jenn laughed. "I love the way you look at everything through those rose-colored shades, girl. You're cheering me up."

Ollie laughed. "Up. It's the only way to be."

Chapter 7

CADE DECIDED TO DEAL WITH STRESS THE WAY HE USUALLY dealt with it: on horseback. He saddled his favorite gelding and rode around his property. Something about surveying his domain from the back of a horse put everything in perspective.

He had thought he would be taking young Leo riding with him and, later, both children.

The bachelor rancher had embraced the idea of raising children and taking on the role of father. He hadn't realized how thoroughly he had taken to the idea of fatherhood, but now he felt as though the children were being wrenched from his arms.

He had no idea why Jason's city-living baby sister was willing to take on the role of substitute mother. She definitely didn't seem to be the type. Jennifer—or Jenn as she called herself—sure didn't look like any of the local mothers.

She was always way too well put-together, for sure. *Doesn't the danged woman have a pair of denims or some sneakers?*

He couldn't imagine her lifting and hauling the kids around like he did. When Lissy put her little arms around his neck, his surly old heart melted. And when Leo cried out in his sleep, Cade leapt out of bed to comfort the child.

He couldn't conceive of Her Highness interrupting her beauty sleep to ease the suffering of a toddler.

Cade blew out a breath and tried to focus on the beautiful countryside. A small herd of Hereford beef cattle was grazing in the easternmost pasture. He had always thought this breed was particularly attractive, with their large brown eyes and long white lashes. The red-and-white patterns were somehow especially pleasing to him. He couldn't help but smile when he counted the number of calves born in the past spring.

Cade also owned a much larger herd of Black Angus cattle that grazed in another pasture.

He gave his horse a gentle nudge and clucked his tongue to increase the pace. He wanted to feel the air brushing his face as he raced headlong into the future without his precious niece and nephew safe under his watchful eye.

Today, Cade needed more speed to outrun his demons.

"Are you sure you want to stay in the guest room?" Ollie asked. "I mean, it's your house now, and the master bedroom is lovely."

"Yes. I couldn't sleep in the same room where Jason and Sara slept." Jenn felt a shiver snaking around her spine. She swallowed hard. "It would just be too creepy."

"Aww, I understand." Ollie shrugged and spread her arms. "Well, this is a nice room too. A little masculine, maybe."

Jenn nodded. "Maybe the burgundy and hunter green is a bit dated."

"Y'think?" Ollie crossed her arms over her chest. "If you decide to redo this room, I guess I can help you. We could paint and maybe change out the drapes and bedspread."

"It looks okay to me right now. Breck wanted me to get settled before he brought the children over, so I guess I need to check things out."

"Let's nose around," Ollie said. She grabbed Jenn's hand and pulled her from the room. "So, the master bedroom is the one Jason and Sara occupied when they were alive, and the kids' room is next to it." She opened the latter, and both women leaned in to check it out.

"Cheery," Jenn commented. Indeed, the room was painted a light yellow with a row of white, lacy curtains flanking the windows. A crib and a low twin bed were arranged on opposite walls. The chest of drawers and closet were filled with clean kid clothes.

"Okay, that should make it easy. Both kids in one room."

"I'll find out." Jenn hoped that Ollie's enthusiasm would prove true. She had no idea why having the children together would be easy. What if one got sick?

The doorbell sounded, shattering the silence. The tone felt like a hammer blow.

Jenn and Ollie went to the door together. A tall, gaunt man with a very red face stood on the porch. He held his Western hat in his hand, baring his almost-bald head, except for a thin-strand comb-over of once red hair.

"Miz LaChance?" The man glanced from one woman to the other.

"That's me," Jenn said.

The man extended a hand to clasp hers and pump it several times. "I'm Edgar Wayne Pell. I'd been talkin' to your brother about buyin' the airstrip...afore his untimely demise."

Jenn stared at Mr. Pell. "I—I don't know anything about that."

His wrinkled face split into a frightening semblance of a grin that brought to mind a leering skull. "Yer brother and I was just about to reach an agreement. He was agreeable to my last offer. We were just working out some of the details."

The idea of getting out from under the responsibility of taking care of Jason's business sounded like a reprieve to her.

"You wanna come in and sit down?" Ollie offered, holding the screen open wider.

"Sure thing," he said, appearing to be eager. He pushed through the space between the two women, who both stepped back abruptly. He turned, still grinning.

"I jus' wanted yew ta know 'bout the deal we was workin' on, and I'm ready to complete tha transaction, Miss LaChance."

Jenn heaved a sigh. "That sounds good, Mr. Pell. I would be happy to work with you, but the airstrip was willed to me and Cade Garrett equally. Maybe you should talk to him because I'm totally ignorant about business matters." She watched his grin erode into a grimace. "Or maybe you should talk to the lawyer, Breckenridge Ryan. He's the one handling the inheritance."

Pell abruptly jammed his hat on his head and stepped toward the door. "Thanks." With that, he strode out the door, letting the screen slam behind him.

"Well!" Ollie stared after him, looking somewhat astonished. "That was odd, to say the least."

"It sure was. But it would be wonderful to sell the business. I certainly have no idea how to run an airstrip, and I'm sure this Cade fellow would rather spend his time out on his ranch, rather than trying to run Jason's business."

If Mr. Pell bought the airstrip, surely the money would be split between her and the big cowboy. Her first thought was that she would have funds to live on until she got a job...or perhaps she should pay for a more practical education...

The thought of returning to the world of academia quickly faded. That was her past.

Now she was settling in at a house in Langston. Thanks to Jason and Sara, she was the owner of her brother's home and a surrogate mother. Her future would be devoted to caring for those two children.

She swallowed hard. Her immediate future would be focused on learning how to care for the children. She turned to Ollie. "I don't suppose you would be willing to teach me how to cook, would you?"

Ollie's brows rose almost to her hairline. "You really don't know how to cook?"

Jenn chuckled. "I have an advanced degree in microwave and ordering in. My dad's favorite food was oatmeal with brown sugar and a little cinnamon. My mom loved cornbread from a mix. I think the kids need more from me."

Breckenridge T. Ryan was a man who knew how to hide his feelings. He could be the cool and controlled attorney in courtrooms and in his office, and even when presented with his clients' tears. But the one person who could read him like a large-print book was his wife, Dr. Camryn Ryan.

At the moment, she was gazing at him, her wide-set blue eyes giving him the third degree. "Well?"

He blew out his pent-up breath. "Okay, you're right. I've got to go to Cade Garrett's house and remove the children. He's going to blow like a volcano." He shook his head. "I just dread it. Cade is quite attached, and he's convinced that Jennifer LaChance is not competent to take care of kids."

Cami's mouth twisted into a wry grin. "And I suppose that Cade thinks he's the perfect parental choice? In my unbiased opinion, Jenn is a perfectly lovely young woman. She has some health issues, but not anything to rule her out as a stand-in parent."

Breck leaned closer. "Health issues?"

"You know I can't talk about a patient's information. She's going to be fine. Don't you breathe a word to anyone." The lovely blue eyes narrowed.

Breck's curiosity was enormously piqued. Now, he wondered if there was a physical reason that Cade might be the better parent.

"Just do what you need to do," Cami said. "Pick up the children and deliver them to the woman Sara and Jason chose to entrust them to. I'm sure Jenn will do a good job of caring for them."

Breck nodded and reached for his Stetson. Thanks to his beautiful wife, Breck was stoked and ready to carry out his difficult duties. He knew if his wife trusted the woman, the kids would be okay.

He kissed Cami goodbye and drove his pickup to the ranch where Cade lived. Cade had inherited the house, and his many acres of ranchland were pastures for his enormous herd of beef cattle and for growing grain crops to feed that herd.

When Breck knocked on the door, it was opened immediately, as though Cade had been waiting on the other side.

He looked ragged, as if his tension were strangling him. "Breck." He swung the door open wider. "I—I haven't told the kids. I just couldn't find the words to explain all this."

"It's okay, man. Let's just get this done and maybe you can come to my office for a little liquid therapy."

"This is killing me," Cade groaned.

Breck felt pity for the big fellow. Cade was a man who was always in charge, yet in one week's time, he had lost his beloved baby sister and now her children were being taken from him. "It's happening. You need to rip off the Band-Aid. Miss LaChance is ready for the children."

Cade huffed out a sigh. "We mustn't keep Her Highness waiting. I'll take the kids in my truck. Their car seats are already set up."

Breck watched as Cade gathered the children and arranged them in their safety seats before he climbed into his truck.

Breck followed in his own vehicle, drawing up behind him at the home Jenn had inherited.

Cade sat in his truck, but Breck was ready to make the transfer of custody happen. Prolonging the misery was not going to help anyone. He walked to Cade's vehicle and knocked on the window.

Cade climbed out and opened the door behind him. He lifted Lissy out of her seat, but Breck held out his hands.

"I'll take this little cutie." The young girl settled against his shoulder, drooling a bit.

Cade rounded the truck and released Leo from his restraints. He swung the boy up into his arms and carried him up onto the porch.

The front door was flung open, and they were greeted by Jenn with a wide grin on her face. "Oh, come right in. I've been waiting for you." She gestured for them to enter.

The house looked exceptionally neat, and Jenn was a trifle overdressed. She was wearing a slim dress that emphasized her figure, but her feet were bare. Her hands were clasped together, giving Breck a hint that she was very nervous.

Cade stared at her, frowning. "We brought the children."

"Yes, I see." Her voice sounded breathless. She reached out to touch Leo on the arm. "Hi, Leo. Remember me? I'm your Auntie Jenn."

Leo stared at her, his very distinctive Garrett-blue eyes assessing her warily.

"I made some cookies... Well, they came from a mix, but they're pretty tasty. Would you like to try one?"

Leo nodded and struggled to get down.

Cade looked as though he had been slapped but set the boy on his feet.

She held out her hand. "Want to come to the kitchen? I'll pour you a glass of milk."

After a moment of hesitation, Leo took her hand and started walking to the kitchen.

"Come on, gentlemen. I made enough cookies for you too." She let Leo pull her toward the back of the house.

Cade turned to Breck. "I don't understand," he whispered.

"She's trying. Give her a chance." Breck looked at Lissy, who was gnawing on her finger and drooling. "How about a cookie?"

Cade's insides were roiling. He didn't know whether to be angry or sad.

For his part, Breck seemed to be satisfied with the situation. He followed Jenn into the kitchen, holding Lissy high on his shoulder.

Cade lagged behind, but when he got to the kitchen, he felt another blow when he saw Jenn looking right at home in Sara's kitchen.

She was sitting at the table with Leo kneeling on a chair beside her. He was stuffing a big, puffy-looking cookie into his mouth. Breck arranged Lissy in her high chair and rolled it over to Jenn's other side.

"Hello, Lissy. Would you like a cookie too?" Jenn broke one of the cookies in half, and Lissy immediately picked it up and started munching. "I poured some milk in your sippy cup." She placed the two-handled cup with the lid on the high chair tray.

Cade couldn't believe this was the same woman. If she weren't the person Breck had greeted, he wouldn't have recognized her.

"Breck," she said, "a man named Pell showed up here. He said he wants to buy the airstrip." She gave a half shrug. "I told him to talk to you. I mean, I'm willing to sell. I have no idea what to do with the property. I'm a mess when it comes to business." She glanced from one man to the other.

Cade's back teeth gritted together. How could she be talking about selling off the business her brother had poured his life into?

Breck stroked his chin. "Edgar Pell, huh? Well, that makes two interested parties. If you two decide to sell, it looks like you're going to have some lively bidding."

She nudged the plate of cookies across the table. "Help yourselves, gentlemen. There is a pitcher of tea and some beer in the fridge."

"Delicious cookies, Jenn. You're doing a good job." Breck saluted her with the cookie, then went to rummage in the refrigerator.

She seemed pleased. "I'm trying to figure it out." She wiped Lissy's chin with a paper napkin. "Is it normal for kids to drool so much?"

"She's teething," Cade bit out. He immediately regretted speaking so sharply. Breck turned to frown at him, and Jenn sucked in her lower lip. "Sorry," he murmured.

Jenn nodded and her cheeks reddened. "I'll be the first to admit this is all new for me, so anything you can tell me will be appreciated."

"Unca Cade," Leo said, his eyes wide. "Where is my mommy an' daddy?"

Total silence.

Cade groped for words. Something to say...anything that would not cause pain to the ones he loved.

"Um, your mommy and daddy had to leave, but they wanted to make sure you would be taken care of." Jenn brushed Leo's hair away from his eyes. "They asked me to come stay with you and love you like they would."

Leo stared at her but took another bite of cookie.

"Is that okay with you?" She tilted her head to one side as though his response was the most important thing in the world.

He nodded his head. "Yeah, that's okay."

Cade heard her heave a sigh.

Jenn patted Leo on the arm. "Great. You'll have to help me get to know what you like to eat and show me the books you want me to read."

"Okay," Leo said.

Breck caught Cade's eye and gave a self-satisfied smirk. "We need to go. Is there anything you need from either of us, Jenn?"

She did that cute thing again, where she tilted her head to one side and grinned, complete with dimples. "Probably. But I don't know what it is yet. Just feeling my way here."

"I understand," Breck said. "But you're off to a good start. Just so you know, here's my cell, and Cami's too. You can call on either one of us any time of the day or night." He handed her his card with some handwritten numbers on the back. He looked at Cade pointedly.

"Oh yeah. You can call me anytime too." He felt around in his pocket for a pen and added his number to the ones on the card. Somehow, touching her hand to retrieve the card felt as though he'd touched a live wire. He swallowed hard. "I'll be available if you need me."

"Thanks a lot." She reached for the card and their fingers touched again.

Her smile caused his insides to do a tumble and roll. "Oh, and I have the children's car seats in my truck."

"You better keep them," she said. "I'm sure you're going to be a part of their lives. Besides, there are safety seats for both children in the car in the garage."

He exhaled slowly. Maybe things would work out okay. Maybe he would still have access to Leo and Lissy. "Good to know. How about if I pick you all up for church on Sunday?"

Her smile was like the sun breaking through on a cloudy day. "Why, Cade, that would be lovely."

―⁓―

When Breck and Cade had gone, Jenn was alone with the children.

She had changed Lissy's wet diaper but didn't get the new one on properly, and the minute Lissy stood up, the diaper fell down around her feet.

Okay, do-over.

She learned that the tape had to be really tight and stretched a bit so the diaper stayed in place.

Mostly, she was in awe of the children: the color of their hair, the texture of their skin, and especially the intense blue of their eyes...like Cade's...like Sara's. She swallowed hard, wishing she had her box of pastels and drawing pad.

Ollie showed up in the late afternoon to help with dinner. She brought some things she called "beanie-weenies" and "tater tots."

Jenn had never encountered either of these delicacies in her past life. She picked up her fork and stabbed one of the delectable, golden brown potato bundles and took a nibble. "Oh, this is heavenly. How come I never knew about this before?" She stuffed the entire tot in her mouth and chewed it blissfully.

Ollie let out a loud guffaw. "From what you've been telling

me, your former diet consisted of stuff that wouldn't keep a gnat alive. You've been missing out on anything that could remotely be called comfort food."

Jenn was examining the beanie-weenies now. She noted that Lissy was picking out the individual beans and weenies with her tiny fingers. Of course, she was covered with the tomatoey sauce, but she was eating, and that was all that mattered to Jenn. She tasted it herself and smiled. "Not bad. Probably about a thousand calories and I'm going to blimp out in all directions."

Ollie hooted with laughter. "You could stand to gain a little. Eat up, girl."

Jenn enjoyed the taste of this food. Her mouth was rejoicing and she was feeling…satisfied.

"It looks like this meal is a hit," Ollie commented. "But how about tomorrow?"

"Um, I'm going to make oatmeal for breakfast." Jenn looked to Ollie for approval. "I have pudding cups."

Ollie heaved a sigh. "So much work to do," she said dramatically. "I'll make a list for you to go to the grocery store."

"Hey, I learned how to apply a diaper to a squirmy one-year-old today." She scooped more food into her mouth.

"I better get going," Ollie said. "Since you moved out, I don't have any guests and no reservations. Business is slow."

"Oh no! How are you going to get by?"

Ollie flashed a smile. "I'm okay. I own the inn outright. I have some savings."

"That's good. I hope you get a ton of reservations soon."

"Me too." She pushed her chair back. "You enjoy all those beanie-weenies."

Chapter 8

THE HOUSE WAS UNNATURALLY QUIET.

Cade realized he'd gotten used to the noise of little children's voices and their footsteps running around on his hardwood floors.

He got a longneck out of the fridge and flipped the cap into the trash can. Heaving out a deep sigh, he lifted the bottle to his lips and let the cold liquid roll down his throat.

Things were going to be different now. He should be feeling relieved that someone else would be caring for the children. He should be eager to get back to his carefree bachelor life. But he wasn't.

He felt a huge void in his chest, as though his heart had been surgically removed.

At least his fears about Jenn LaChance had been somewhat allayed. She wasn't the bubble-headed little flake he had first thought.

An unwilling smile tugged at his lips. *Dang!* She was beautiful…and she seemed to be much more centered than when she'd first arrived in town.

Her infectious grin and flash of dimples always took him by surprise. Maybe because she'd looked so haunted at the funeral and afterward. Apparently, she had come out of her funk. She even looked healthier…better color… Her eyes sparkled with vivacity and had lost that semi-dead look.

After seeing Jenn with the kids, he figured she would do her best to provide for their needs. She was Jason LaChance's little sister, and Jason had been a great guy.

Surely she doesn't eat babies for breakfast.

He finished off the beer and put the bottle in the recycle bin. The day was pretty much used up, but there were hours to go before he could reasonably go to bed.

Tomorrow he should probably go to the airstrip, just to check in and see what was going on.

Cade was relieved that there were buyers lined up to purchase the business. He knew the area needed the airstrip, but since he didn't fly or own a plane, he didn't have any expertise to bring to the table. Thankfully, Jenn was apparently not interested in trying to run the business either.

Cade went into his den to watch the news from a television channel out of Amarillo. The world had not ended just because his house was devoid of children. Absently, he flipped channels, but his mind kept returning to the possibility of selling the airstrip.

He knew Edgar Wayne Pell but wasn't a fan. He had never done business with him but had a vague mistrust. There was talk among some of the ranchers. Something distinctly eerie about the man. A shiver played around his spine.

Cade shrugged off the feeling, hoping whoever the other prospective buyer was, it might be a less reprehensible person.

Perhaps Jenn LaChance might be willing to sell the airstrip and invest the proceeds of the sale in an annuity for the children's college fund. He was most concerned that the children have a secure future. But apparently, Jenn had no income, so he dismissed the idea of her contributing to an annuity. But he had no problem setting one up with his half of the proceeds.

Jenn had a hard time getting to sleep.

Surprisingly, Lissy had curled right up in her crib and gone to sleep in just a few minutes. It must have been because it was so familiar.

Jenn had stood beside the crib for a few moments, taking in the beautiful little face. Lissy resembled a Botticelli cherub with her round cheeks and softly curling hair. Jenn thought that she could make a lovely pastel study of the child…if only she had some art supplies with her. She heaved a deep sigh. It would all come together in time. *Just give it a little time…*

Leo was delighted that Minnie was now a part of the family. He had never had any contact with a dog and couldn't seem to keep his hands off of her. For her part, Minnie was content to snuggle up beside him and wallow in the affection he was lavishing on her. Jenn couldn't help but smile when she saw them together. Something about a boy and a dog.

Lissy, on the other hand, seemed to view Minnie as a great place to take a nap. Jenn kept having to rinse a patch of drool off Minnie's soft fur.

When Leo brought Jenn a picture book and crawled into her lap, Minnie stretched out by her feet. She knew this book routine was something Jason and Sara had done, and now the task had fallen to her. "Is this one of your favorite books, Leo?"

He nodded. "My mommy weads it to me."

Jenn ruffled his hair. "I'll try to do a good job of reading it."

She read the book and another after that, feeling pretty comfortable in her new role. At least, so far. She put Leo to bed in the same room as his sister. His bed was on the other side of the room and was a twin bed that sat pretty low to the floor.

Leo had scrambled between the covers Jenn held open for him. She snuggled the covers under his chin and gave him a kiss on his forehead.

This mothering gig wasn't so hard after all, and the kids were adorable. If anything, they were even cuter than ever.

Jenn felt a different kind of warmth swirl through her insides when she thought of Cade, the fierce rancher uncle. He had the same intense turquoise-blue eyes as the children. But when he'd first laid eyes on her, those eyes had drilled into her with disapproval…almost contempt.

Well, perhaps she had deserved it. She had not been at her best, but then again, she was bleeding from every pore over the death of her brother…but no one could see her invisible wounds. She'd been a wreck.

Although not much time had passed, she felt much more pulled together. She was no longer floating on a sea of uncertainty.

The thought that kept plaguing her was that this had not been her plan. She had inherited a great house in Dallas, but she needed to have a job to pay for its upkeep and the utilities. She had closed off most of the rooms and sealed the AC/heating vents, but still… most of her worldly possessions were locked up there.

On learning of Jason and Sara's accident, Jenn's main concern had been for the children. She had planned on returning to Dallas and raising her niece and nephew in the home where she and Jason had grown up.

But in the blink of an eye, things had changed. She still owned a house and generations of family treasures, but all that seemed less important now.

I have a home here. I have a family. A tight band seemed to be constricting her throat. *I have someone to love.*

Lissy was adorable. She didn't talk much, but the big blue eyes said a lot all on their own. When she reached up to Jenn with those chubby little arms, Jenn's heart just melted.

She had thought love was what she would feel for some future mate, but how would he find her here in the sticks?

But now, Jenn felt a rush of warmth in her chest every time she glanced at either of the children who were now hers. *Mine to love.*

She lay awake in the guest room, staring at the ceiling with a smile on her face. The door was open, so she could hear the children should they awaken and call out to her.

"Thanks, Jason," she whispered into the darkness.

—~~~—

Deputy Derrick Shelton was in a state of shock. He had just begun his shift and was still in the office. He planned to carry out several of his usual tasks, but when his boss, the sheriff, called to say he was about to go into surgery, he had been astonished. "Are you all right, Sheriff?" This struck him as an extremely dumb thing to say to the man who was calling from his hospital room.

"Hell no, boy. That's what I'm tryin' to tell yew." He made an exasperated noise. "I'm gonna be laid up for a while and I want yew ta take mah place."

"Me, Sheriff?" Derrick sat down on the hard wooden chair behind his desk. He swallowed hard, but it felt like a chunk of concrete in his throat.

"Yes, yew. I'm gonna be outta commission for a while. I already tole tha mayor that yew were mah choice. He's a-gonna make tha official announcement. Actin' Sheriff. How does that sound?"

Derrick tried to comprehend what was taking place. "Sounds great, Sheriff, but you've got some men who have been with you a lot longer."

The sheriff made a disparaging sound. "Yer tha one that's got good sense. I cain't leave none of them others in charge. I'm countin' on yew, boy. It's a done deal."

"Um…yes, sir. I'll do my best."

"These docs are gonna cut me open tomorrow mornin' so you're in charge until…until yew see me a-comin' in tha door."

"Yes, sir." Derrick heard the sheriff disconnect but sat gripping the phone, his stomach roiling. He wasn't sure he was up to the task. He'd lived in Langston his entire life and knew everyone, but still…

Another deputy leaned against the desk. "What's the matter, Derrick? You look like someone just punched you in the gut."

Derrick carefully placed the receiver back in its cradle and heaved a sigh. "Pretty much."

—~~~—

Jenn managed to get through the next couple of days without screwing anything up.

Ollie dropped by from time to time to help Jenn figure out what to make for meals. They had loaded the children into the car, and Ollie gave her a tour of the local grocery store. She showed her the foods that young children would like to eat and which would be grouped together to provide a balanced diet.

It was a whole new world of eating. Jenn learned about finger foods. Chicken strips quickly became a favorite. She learned to peel and section an orange like an expert.

Somehow, preparing the simple meals for the children became one of her favorite activities. It pleased her to please them.

Jenn was totally neurotic about letting Leo and Lissy out of her sight. She had heard that young children were apt to get into trouble unless they were properly supervised, so she was especially vigilant.

Ollie just laughed at her.

"Don't be such a Nervous Nelly. Kids are going to fall. They're going to get bumps and scrapes."

"Yeah, I guess…but…"

"Didn't you ever fall and scrape your knee or get a bump on the head? It's a rite of passage for children. They have to learn."

Jenn nodded. "You're right, but I can't help being a little nervous. This is all new to me."

Ollie flapped her hand in dismissal. "You'll get the hang of it. No new mother ever knows how to do it all. You got dunked right in the middle of everything with no prep time. You're doing great."

Jenn heaved a huge sigh, thankful that someone believed in her. Now all she had to do was survive the next few weeks and make sure the children were thriving while she got her mommy on.

Cade looked at himself in the mirror. Perhaps he had taken a little extra care when he'd shaved that morning, and he was wearing his favorite Western shirt, the one that was almost the color of his eyes. He centered the large metal buckle on his hand-tooled Western belt and smoothed his dark hair back. This was as presentable as he would be able to make himself.

He donned his Stetson and headed out the door. Once in his truck, he drove to the house that his sister had taken such pride in. Pulling into the driveway, he parked and strode up to the front door, trying to squelch his nerves. He didn't know why Jenn LaChance made him feel antsy.

Cade blew out a deep breath and raised his fist to knock on the door, but it was thrown open before he could connect.

Jenn greeted him with a wide smile and a gushy greeting. "Hi, Cade. I'm so glad you're here. We're all ready." She did a pretty turn and gestured for him to enter.

When he stepped over the threshold, he inhaled her fragrance...something sweet and naughty at the same time.

"Leo is excited that his Uncle Cade is taking him to Sunday school."

At that time, a small, blue-eyed tornado hit Cade, grabbing him around the knees. "Hey, Leo! How you doin', buddy?" He leaned down to lift the boy into his arms. A rush of warmth filled his chest.

"And here's Lissy. Doesn't she look adorable?" Jenn carried the girl to where Cade was standing.

He had to admit the children appeared to be well cared for. They were clean and dressed in fresh clothing. Leo's hair was combed and Lissy sported two ponytails adorned with tiny bows to match her dress.

He cleared his suddenly husky throat. "Ready?"

She nodded and grabbed a tiny handbag with a long chain strap. It wasn't big enough to stuff a tissue in, but she tossed it over her shoulder. Jenn was definitely color coordinated, the mini-purse the exact color of her shoes and picking up a color in the print of her dress. She preceded him to his truck, giving him an eyeful of her backfield in motion.

Cade installed Leo in his car seat and went around to take Lissy from Jenn. He fastened Lissy's buckles and closed the passenger side back door.

When he turned, Jenn was standing way too close. Her skin was like satin, smooth and looked touchable, but he restrained himself. He stepped back and opened the passenger door for her, offering a hand to help her up, but she looked at the height of the step and her perfect brows drew together.

Cade realized that she couldn't step up with her slim dress and heels. "Let me help you." He lifted her in his arms, hesitating when her arms circled his neck. It just felt too good.

"Thank you, Cade." Her wide-set eyes examined his features at extremely close quarters. "I—I didn't bring any casual clothes... I thought I would be taking the children back to Dallas." She gazed at him earnestly.

He had to hold himself in check to keep from kissing those luscious lips. With intense effort, he hefted her onto the seat, although she weighed practically nothing. "Seat belt," he said tersely. "I mean, fasten your seat belt." He closed the door and circled back around the truck, feeling shaken but determined to keep his actions honorable.

When they arrived at the church, he opened her door first and then set about releasing the children. Unfortunately, when she slid down to the street level, her dress hiked up and he glimpsed the entire length of her long, shapely legs.

Damn! There was only so much a man could be expected to take. Didn't she know what kind of effect she was having on him?

"I'll take Lissy." She stood behind him when he freed the baby girl from her safety seat and reached out to take her.

Cade got Leo and locked his truck with the remote. Together the four of them entered the church.

It was early. Some people were seated in the pews. Most were chatting with their neighbors.

Cade led the way through to the back of the church where a door opened to a hallway. Together they found the appropriate Sunday school for Leo and the nursery for Lissy. Leo was excited to join the other children and his Sunday school teachers greeted him by name.

"This is so nice," Jenn said. "I know why my brother was so happy here." She looked up at him. "He really loved Sara. You know that?"

Cade nodded. "Yes, I know that. She loved Jason right back."

She appeared to be a little sad. "That's the way it's supposed to be." Her lower lip trembled a bit, but she pressed her lips together, looking more resolute.

He realized he was growing to like this woman...the one he'd thought a bit flaky. The woman who wore high heels and smelled like heaven.

Together, they retraced their steps back to the nave. By this time, most of the pews were beginning to fill with church members.

Jenn looked around, as though searching for someone or something.

Ollie Enloe stood up, waving and gesturing for them to come to where she was sitting in the third row. "I saved your seats," she said breathlessly.

Jenn excused herself and stepped in front of several people in a family, to slide down the row to where Ollie stood, grinning.

She greeted Jenn with a hug. "You look so pretty. I saw you come in with the children."

Cade followed behind Jenn, trying not to stomp on anyone. His countenance, that had actually appeared pleasant, was back to Mr. Grumpy Face.

Ollie greeted Cade, and he nodded at her before taking a seat.

Ensconced between them, Jenn felt a bit more secure. This had been the church her brother and his family had attended. Now the parents were gone. No Jason or Sara. Just Jenn and Jason's children and Cade, his brother-in-law.

I'm the mom now. She settled into the hard wooden pew and laced her fingers together in her lap.

A plump woman wearing a floral tentlike dress climbed up on the dais and edged herself behind the organ. She looked over the music and finally began playing something light and lyrical.

This felt like church should feel.

Jenn looked around, surprised to note that quite a few people were staring at her. She leaned to whisper in Ollie's ear. "Why are people staring?"

Ollie grinned. "Because you look great and they're speculating about you and Cade. Tongues will wag, you know?" Ollie's breath was warm against Jenn's ear.

A rush of heat rose from her core. She knew she was blushing. Heaving a sigh, she looked down at her own hands. She just wanted to be a member of the community without anyone taking special notice.

Since she could no longer consider herself a part of the academic community, she realized she might be able to develop a new persona as a well-educated woman living in a small rural town. She could not go back to her academic life. No more endless learning. She could not be the brilliant student she had been, but she could reinvent herself, as a woman, as a mother, as a member of this close-knit community. Yes, she could hold her head up again. And in time, she hoped she would emerge as the talented artist she was born to be.

In a short time, the preacher took his place on the dais and led them in a prayer. He prayed for the well-being of his flock, for members now deployed in the military, for the firefighters and police officers who protected the community, for people who were sick or suffering from loss… He droned on and on. It was a wide-ranging prayer.

Jenn stared forward but was extremely aware of the large hunk of maleness sitting next to her. He had been a little grouchy when she had taken a seat beside Ollie. It was church. Everybody had to sit beside somebody else.

Slowly, Cade relaxed next to her. He rested his arm on the back of the pew. An embrace that was not quite an embrace.

She turned and gave him a brief smile and found those intense blue eyes riveted to hers. She felt a rush of heat that brought a blush to her cheeks.

Cade's gaze deepened and his lips curved up in a brief smile. His hand rested on her shoulder momentarily, then returned to the back of the pew. It was some kind of acknowledgment that they were on an even keel.

After the service, they gathered the children, and although Ollie wanted them to stay and visit with the churchgoers, Cade seemed anxious to leave. Jenn said goodbye and took one last look at the table filled with tasty goodies. Ollie had told her the church ladies vied to bring their best offerings to share on Sundays.

Once he had hefted her back into his truck and secured both children, he smiled. "That wasn't so bad, was it?"

"Not at all, Cade." Jenn fastened her seat belt. "Just the way Jason described it. He really enjoyed belonging to this church…" She pressed her lips together. "When Jason bought the airstrip and moved here, he seemed to become a different person. His value system changed."

He looked puzzled, but she quickly shrugged.

"I want to thank you for bringing the children and me to this service. You made it so much easier."

"I, uh…I thought we might have lunch at the steak house…if you're hungry."

Yes, she's hungry. "That would be very nice." She suddenly realized this gesture meant more than sharing a meal. Was this Cade's idea of a date?

When they were all ensconced in appropriate seating at the steak house, Cade commandeered the menus and ordered for everyone. Jenn would have ordered a much smaller portion, but she figured there would be leftovers. He ordered from the kiddie menu for the younger members.

When the food arrived, Jenn took her notebook out and jotted a quick note as to what she had been served.

"What's that?" Cade asked.

She tucked it away quickly. "Um, just making a note of what I eat. Dr. Ryan wants me to show her next week."

"Girl! You do not need to be on some screwy diet." His expression was intense. "I mean—you're just about perfect."

A blush crept up her cheeks. "Oh, no. No diets for me."

Chapter 9

CADE DROVE JENN AND THE CHILDREN TO THE LACHANCE house and reluctantly took his leave. When he arrived at his own home, he found a patrol car parked in front and the new acting sheriff waiting for him.

Derrick Shelton climbed out of the vehicle to meet him on the walkway. He huffed out a grunt in greeting, and Cade opened the front door, gesturing him inside.

"Good to see you, Derrick. How about some iced tea?" He started toward the kitchen, stopping when Derrick remained just inside the doorway.

The expression on the officer's face alarmed Cade, chasing away the high he had been on after spending the morning with Jenn and the children.

"What's going on, Derrick?"

"I wanted to ask you if you know of any enemies who might have had it in for Jason and Sara LaChance." His brows were almost drawn together in a V.

"Enemies?" Cade considered for a moment. "That's ridiculous. Sara was the sweetest woman on the planet, and Jason was a fine man."

Derrick took a wide stance and crossed his arms over his chest. "I've always thought so, but what about business? Was there anyone they had problems with at the airfield?"

"Problems?"

"Anyone who might want them dead?"

A sick feeling swirled through his gut. Cade tried to speak, but there were no words he could muster.

Derrick shook his head. "Sorry to inform you that the federal boys got through with their investigation of the crash and determined that the plane's fuel line had been cut."

Cade reeled backward, grabbing for a chair. He sank down on it and Derrick took a seat on the sofa. "I can't believe it. Who would want to hurt my baby sister? Who would hurt Jason?" He shook his head. "There must be some mistake."

"Sorry. The line was definitely cut. Someone wanted them to crash."

"I really cannot believe it. Everyone loved them."

Derrick heaved out a sigh. "Apparently, not everyone."

Jenn spent the next few days trying to establish some sort of routine. She relied on Leo for some basic information and felt that their relationship was growing stronger. The only problem was when he would gaze at her with his soulful eyes and ask when his mommy was coming home.

Lissy was easy. She was teething, so she was generally a little fussy and drooled all the time. Dr. Cami advised her to buy a couple of pacifiers and keep them in the freezer. Easy enough and now Lissy was chomping on the pacifiers instead of her forefinger.

Jenn was surprised when the landline rang and she heard Cade's deep voice greet her.

"Jennifer? This is Cade Garrett."

She swallowed hard. He was the only one who called her by her full name. Somehow this made it all the more special. "Hi, Cade." She sounded breathy, like a teenager.

"I, uh...I was wondering if you're busy tonight."

She managed to chuckle. "Of course I'm busy. There are two little creatures in this house that keep me on my toes."

"I was thinking I might bring dinner tonight…and get to spend some time with you and the kids…and you."

Jenn smiled, a flush of pleasure washing through her. "That would be very nice."

"I don't suppose you would allow me to bring my cousin and his wife? They're a great couple. You probably met them at your brother's wedding."

"Your cousin?" A note of hysteria pinged off her brain as she recalled the seemingly endless stream of Garretts she had shaken hands with on that day.

"Yeah, they wanted to visit with the kids. Is that all right?"

She glanced around the living room strewn with toys and discarded kid garments. "Um, sure. That would be great."

"Don't worry about a thing. We're bringing dinner. I know you have your hands full with the kids and everything."

Jenn had been pleased when he first invited himself over, but now it was going to be a big deal. She wasn't sure how she felt about Cade and another couple barging in on her. "Yeah, hands full and everything…"

By the time she disconnected, a knot the size of her fist was forming in her stomach. The house wasn't exactly set up for entertaining, and this had all been foisted on her out of the blue. She huffed out a sigh. Lissy was asleep facedown on the sofa, a big wet spot where she drooled. Minnie shared the sofa with Lissy, asleep with her paw on Lissy's leg.

Leo played with an electronic children's game that looked like something between a tablet and a phone. At least he was occupied and not asking her about his parents' whereabouts.

I can do this.

As quietly as possible, Jenn circled the room picking up toys and clothing and anything else that was out of place. She really didn't have time to find the right home for each of the items, so she rushed into the laundry room, her arms full. There was a small broom closet with shelves, so she shoved her armload onto a shelf and closed the door. A few more trips through the house and she had stuffed the closet full.

Jenn thought about running the vacuum but didn't want to wake Lissy, and she did want a little time to primp. She didn't intend to overdress, but she didn't have that many clothes to select from, so she chose a dark-green dress and plain black pumps. That should say entertaining at home...except they would be entertaining her by bringing the food.

She dusted and made sure the clutter was at a minimum. When she turned around, Leo was regarding her, his expression mournful. She dropped down to his level, gazing into his beautiful eyes the color of polished turquoise. "Hey, sweetheart. Is there something I can get for you?"

His hands were gripped together tight. "My mommy an' daddy?" He made a little whimpering sound. "Are my mommy an' daddy coming home?"

Jenn sat down on the carpet and regarded him solemnly. No way to dodge this direct little man. "No, Leo. Your mommy and daddy have gone home to heaven."

His face puckered, but he pressed his lips together.

"I know they didn't want to leave you, but they had to go... and they made sure you would be taken care of." She brushed his thick, light-brown hair back from his face. Except for those Garrett eyes, Leo was the spitting image of Jason. "Your daddy was my brother. I grew up with my big brother helping take care of me, just like you help Lissy."

The large blue eyes searched hers.

"And now I'm going to take care of you and Lissy. I'll never leave you."

The eyes became liquid. "But what if you go to heaven?" Tears rolled down his cheeks.

Jenn clasped him in a fierce hug. "Well, I hope I go to heaven someday, but I'm going to try to hang out here with you and Lissy for a long, long time." She felt Leo's tearful shudders as he wept, but she kept patting him and whispering against his hair, "It's okay. We'll be okay."

She sat holding Leo for some time. Eventually his shaking and sniffles abated, but still she held him tight, cooing comforting words against his hair. "We'll be fine. I love you and your sister. I won't let anything bad happen to you."

Leo pulled away, looking back over Jenn's shoulder. "Unca Cade."

Jenn turned to see a crowd of people standing in the open doorway. Cade's large form was flanked by two males who were as tall and broad-shouldered as he. One of the men held a blond woman in one arm and a baby in a carrier looped over the other. The blond woman had one arm around a tiny elderly woman and the other around a blond girl of school age.

Jenn sat, as if struck dumb, staring at the odd assemblage.

Then Leo wriggled out of Jenn's embrace and ran to throw his arms around Cade's leg.

Cade lifted Leo, a wide grin on his face. "Hey, boy. How you doin'?"

"Oh!" Jenn struggled to her feet with a minimum of grace. She could feel her face burning with embarrassment. The bodice of her dress was damp with Leo's tears and she was pretty sure there were smears of snot.

"Unca Cade, my mommy an' daddy has gone to heaven."

It was as though the room had been instantly frozen. No one moved. No one spoke.

There was silence as the newcomers stared at Jenn.

Then everyone began speaking at once.

"Um, Leo and I were just talking about…"

The older man stepped forward. "Good for you. Leo needed to know." He extended his hand to give hers a shake.

It felt as though her hand had been wrapped in a giant baseball glove, warm and rough in places. "Thank you. I had to be honest with him, but it was so hard." Her voice wavered.

Cade stepped forward, Leo in his arms. "Jennifer, this is my uncle Big Jim Garrett."

"Howdy, young lady." The mountain of a man pumped her hand with enthusiasm.

Jenn swallowed hard, staring up into the blue eyes that were a Garrett characteristic. This man had the same tall, broad-shouldered physique as Cade Garrett, same strong chin and handsome features, but this face had been weathered by time and the elements, and his thick head of dark hair had turned silver.

"I—I'm pleased to meet you, Mr. Garrett," she said.

Big Jim patted her hand. "Now, none of that 'Mr. Garrett' stuff. Just call me Big Jim. We actually met at Sara and Jason's wedding, but you had to meet a lot of Garretts."

"And this is my cousin Tyler and his wife, Leah, and their kids." Cade indicated the couple still standing in the doorway. "And that's Miz Fern. She's Leah's grandmother."

The small woman regarded Jenn solemnly through a pair of wire-rimmed glasses but raised one hand in a silent greeting.

"I'm happy to meet all of you. Won't you please come in? I didn't mean to ignore you." Jenn gestured for them to enter.

"You seemed to be busy," the woman named Leah said. She touched the infant in her husband's arms. "Children have to come first."

―――※―――

Big Jim Garrett checked out the woman who was creating such a stir in his extended family. Everyone was mourning the death of Jason and Sara LaChance, but it seemed that this very attractive young woman had a pretty good head on her shoulders, despite what his nephew had first intimated.

He liked that they had caught her in the act of comforting a small child. When she did not answer the door, Cade had twisted the knob and revealed this Jennifer woman sitting on the floor in her pretty dress with Leo in her lap.

Big Jim especially liked that she had been honest with Leo. She had found a way to break the bad news about his parents' deaths in a way that he could understand and also give him confidence that he and his sister would be well taken care of.

At that moment, Big Jim felt a slight pressure at his knee. He looked down to see a mass of long, white fur with a black nose. "And what is this?" He leaned down to pick it up. "Almost looks like a dog."

"Minnie is our doggy," Leo asserted.

"Is that so?" Big Jim squatted down to Leo's level still holding the fur ball named Minnie.

Leo nodded solemnly. "Minnie is a good doggy."

"Good. Every boy should have a good dog."

"I, uh, I set the table in the dining room," Jennifer said. "I'm still getting used to the house. I'm finding things in places I wouldn't have thought to look."

"Everything looks lovely," Leah offered. "I hope you're getting settled in okay."

Jennifer appeared to be a little shy, which surprised Big Jim, since from Cade's description she was a "bubble-headed little flake" who couldn't possibly be trusted with the children's welfare…but from what he could see, she appeared to be doing a bang-up job.

"Uh, we brought food," Cade said. For his part, he looked somewhat in awe of the woman. He gestured toward the front door. "I'll go bring it in."

"I'll help you," Tyler offered. He leaned over to give Leah the infant carrier and a kiss on the temple, and then he followed Cade out the door.

Big Jim gave Minnie a scruffle behind what he suspected were her ears and set her on the floor. He couldn't help smiling when the dog immediately zipped to the sofa and jumped up to settle next to the sleeping Lissy.

Big Jim turned back to gaze at Jennifer. "Well, let's get things set up, shall we?"

Suddenly, her big-eyed, serious expression morphed into a dimpled grin. "I think I'm pretty well set up, at least I hope so. Come and see." She took Leo by the hand. "Let's go see if Big Jim likes the way we set the table."

She led the way back to the dining room, where Big Jim was surprised to see the table was set for six with a high chair pulled up close. There was a pale-blue tablecloth, and it appeared that a leaf had been added to the table.

There was a bouquet in the center of the table with freshly clipped roses in a low bowl.

Big Jim couldn't suppress a smile. "Well, little lady, I haven't eaten at a table this nice since my dear wife was alive." He blinked a couple of times to keep from embarrassing himself by tearing up. "She loved to set some posies on the table. Looks real nice."

Jennifer dimpled again, and a little more color flushed her cheeks. "Thanks, Mister…Big Jim. Roses were my mother's hobby. She was an avid gardener." She gestured toward the back of the house. "I was really happy to see those old rose bushes growing by the back porch."

Cade and Tyler came into the room, each bearing a cooler.

"I've got the hot stuff," Cade announced.

"And I've got the cold stuff." Tyler lifted the cooler.

Leah brought up the rear with her grandmother and the young girl. "Gran closed the front door and I brought the baby."

Big Jim gave her a big grin. "Good work, ladies."

Jenn gestured toward the table. "Well, uh…I made sweet tea, but that's about all."

"We gots ice cweam," Leo announced solemnly.

Big Jim ruffled the boy's soft hair. "That's good 'cause I really like ice cream."

Cade and Tyler returned from the kitchen, having arranged the contents of the coolers on the kitchen countertops.

"Okay, we have a plan," Cade announced. "There's too much food to pile it all on the table, so why don't we dish up the food here in the kitchen?"

"Um, sure," Jennifer said. "That makes sense. I'm going to go wake Lissy and get her in her high chair." She walked away, leaving Big Jim with a big smile.

"I like her," he said.

"I do too," Leah said.

"She sure has a way with that little 'un," her grandmother commented.

Tyler shook his head before giving Cade a punch on his arm. "Yeah, what's the matter with you? She's Mary Poppins."

———— ∼ ————

What is the matter with me? Cade stared after Jenn's retreating form. It appeared she was doing a great job. Why was it when she walked away from him, he had to fight down a rush of pure lust?

He and Ty busied themselves in the kitchen. Big Jim poked his head in to tell them to pile his plate high.

"Your father's hungry," Cade said.

"Dad's always hungry. He could eat a side of beef in one sitting." Ty picked up a plate. "I'm going to make a plate for my wife and Miz Fern. You can shovel out some food for Big Jim."

"Sure thing." Cade began to pile meat and the sides on a plate for his uncle. Ty was giving him a weird look. "Okay, why the face?"

"You're such a jerk." Ty shook his head. "Jennifer is a beautiful woman. The way you described her, I was expecting a raving lunatic."

Cade's mouth tightened, and he heaved a huge sigh. "I know, but when she first came here, she was different…crazy."

Ty shot him another sharp glance, totally disbelieving. He balanced two plates and backed out of the kitchen, using his shoulder to open the swinging door. "Here you go, ladies. Only the best for my girls."

The door swung closed, cutting off the response from Leah and Fern, but when it opened again, it was Big Jim who pushed through.

"Gimme a plate for Leo. Maybe a chicken leg and some veggies." He picked up a plate and held it out for Cade to fill. "How 'bout Miss Jennifer. Ain't she a beaut?"

Cade kept his focus on the potato salad. "Um, yeah. She's a fine-looking woman."

Big Jim was grinning. "Not just another pretty face, huh? She's got this mama thing down pat. Kids look great."

"Yeah, they do." He added a spoonful of coleslaw to the plate.

"Now, don't get your panties in a wad," Big Jim said. "I just think you owe Jennifer an apology. She's doing a great job."

"I was too," Cade snarled, then took a deep breath and expelled it. Not a good idea to show disrespect to his uncle.

"Sure you were, son…but kids that young need a mama. You can be lots of things, but you sure ain't no mama."

That truth hit him like a punch to the gut. Big Jim was right. "I had visions of the kids growing up on the ranch. You know, teaching them to ride and doing 4-H projects."

Big Jim placed one of his big paws on Cade's shoulder. "You can still do lots of things with them, but, Cade…you just ain't equipped to be what those kids need most right now."

Cade swallowed hard. "I feel like I owe it to Sara to make sure her children are taken care of."

"Don't be such an asshole. It's not an either/or situation. You can still be a part of their lives. Do you think if your sister and her husband had any doubts as to whether little Miss Jennifer was up to the task, they would have entrusted her with their precious children?"

"I suppose you're right."

"Just give her a chance, Cade. It will all work out."

Cade turned and handed the plates he had filled to his uncle. "This one's for you and this is for Leo."

Big Jim's expression let Cade know that he could read everything he was feeling.

Chapter 10

JENN HAD CHANGED LISSY AND BRUSHED HER HAIR. SHE looked a little sleepy still, but when they entered the dining room, Lissy took one terrified look at all the people, buried her face against Jenn's neck, and began to whimper.

More kid snot. Jenn jiggled her a little and patted her back. "Are you hungry? Let's get you ready to eat something really good." She tried to put the child in the high chair, but Lissy clung to Jenn's neck and let out a loud wail. "Okay, don't cry. You can sit in my lap."

Big Jim pulled out a chair at one end of the table and held it while she was seated.

"Thanks," she said, settling Lissy in her lap.

For her part, Lissy was just whimpering and gnawing on her forefinger now, but her lashes were spangled with tears.

Big Jim touched Jenn's shoulder, and when she looked at him, he handed her a large white cotton handkerchief. "Thought you might be able to use this."

"Thank you." Jenn used the handkerchief to mop up Lissy's tears, drool, and snot. When she looked up, Leah and her grandmother were smiling at her, and Big Jim was too. *Maybe I'm doing something right.*

Big Jim seated himself at the opposite end of the table with Fern Davis, Leah's grandmother, on his left and Leah on his right. Tyler had brought in plates to both women, and Cade came to stand beside Jenn. He offered a plate, mumbling that it was for Leo, but Big Jim spoke up.

"Right here with that plate. My friend Leo is going to be my dining buddy tonight." Big Jim patted his knee.

Leo gazed up at him solemnly. "I a big boy now."

Big Jim looked at Jenn, obviously confused.

She smiled. "Leo's my big boy, so he sits right at the table beside me while I feed Lissy. It's our thing."

Big Jim busted out laughing. "Well, you go on, big boy. Do your thing."

Leo scrambled to drag his special chair right up to the table beside Jenn. This had been his high chair, but the tray had been removed so it brought the young boy right up to table height.

She looked up at Cade. "Could you please lock the brake on it...and maybe help him get situated." She smiled at Lissy. "Got my hands full here."

Cade placed the plate on the table and gave Leo a boost into the chair. He pushed it up close to the table and set the brake with his boot. "I'll bring you a plate, Jennifer."

Eventually, everyone had been served, and while Ty seated himself next to Leah, Cade slid onto the chair beside Jenn and Leo.

Jenn felt the weight of Cade's surreptitious observation, but she was confused. She had been the object of male interest since her teen years. This was different.

Cade was an enigma. He ran hot and cold. At first he had been positively vibrating with rage, but now he seemed tongue-tied around her, and yet she felt moments of admiration. He sat near her and kept sneaking shy glances at her.

This big cowboy was more than a little intimidating. Perhaps it was those intense, almost-turquoise eyes that seemed to cut into her soul like a laser. She was sure Cade could hold his own with any man, but she sensed that she might have somehow risen in his esteem.

As if...

But the meal went well. The food was delicious and there was conversation, mostly orchestrated by Leah and Tyler.

She was able to slide Lissy into her high chair, where she mostly ate cooked baby carrots and drank milk from her sippy cup.

Cade didn't say much, but he laughed at the appropriate times when others said something funny and responded when directly addressed.

After the main meal was eaten, Cade and Tyler jumped up, insisting they would clear the table and bring the aforementioned ice cream.

Jenn was amused by this. Apparently the two had been close friends growing up and quipped back and forth. She thought this was the only time she could actually see glimpses of the real Cade Garrett.

Ice-cream dishes were also cleared quickly, and Big Jim decided he should join the two younger men in the kitchen.

"Why don't you ladies relax and get to know each other while we take care of the clean-up?" Big Jim made a rising motion with his hands as though the women were supposed to leave the table.

"Well, this little one needs to be changed," Leah announced. "Where can I change him?"

"There's a changing table in the kids' room." Jenn lifted Lissy out of her high chair and led the way to the room the children shared. "Lissy is getting to be pretty big for it now, so I usually just throw her down wherever we are to make the change." Jenn checked Lissy and was relieved that her diaper didn't need to be changed.

Leah gave a little giggle. "I remember when Gracie was at that stage, but I was too broke to spend money on a changing table. I just threw her down anywhere too."

Leah laid the infant on top of the changing table and began unwrapping him. "Tyler adopted Gracie, and they're very close."

"She's a beautiful girl." Jenn felt a tightness in her chest. "That sounds lovely. And now you have this wonderful baby boy."

Leah leaned over to place a kiss on the baby's forehead. "I am so very blessed. The way my life was going, I never imagined that I could be so happy."

Tears stung Jenn's eyes, but she blinked rapidly. She wondered if she would ever experience this kind of happiness.

By the time the Garrett entourage took their leave, Jenn felt a lot more relaxed about this family.

Cade lingered behind, purportedly to say good night to Leo and Lissy, but as soon as his family members were out the door, he came to the door where Jenn stood waving.

"I don't suppose you like to ride," he asked. "Do you?"

She smiled and leaned back against the door frame. "I haven't been on a horse since I was a schoolgirl."

He looked disappointed.

"But I used to love riding. My brother and I spent a lot of time in the saddle."

That news seemed to bring Cade's spirits back up. He swallowed hard. "I don't suppose you might like to go for a ride with me…would you?"

Jenn giggled. "Sounds wonderful, but I have two little children to take care of. Can't exactly stuff them in saddlebags."

He laughed at that, and suddenly his face changed. He looked genuinely amused for the first time since their rocky first meeting. "I have a housekeeper. Mrs. Reynolds. I can pick you and the kids up and take you to my ranch. Mrs. Reynolds loves those children." He seemed to have warmed up without his relatives standing by.

"Sounds like fun. I'll think about it."

He leaned closer. "Well, how about lunch tomorrow? I'll bring Mrs. R to sit with the kids while we have a nice meal. I think we need to get to know each other a lot better."

"I—I guess we do."

He leaned even closer to brush a quick kiss across her lips.

This caught her off guard, and she drew back, staring up at him in surprise.

"I'm sorry," he said. "You just looked so damned kissable, I couldn't help myself." The blue eyes seemed to be devouring her.

She reached up to grab his face with both hands. "Well, you damned sure better kiss me then."

For just a moment, something feral flashed in his eyes. Then he slipped his arms around her, lowered his mouth to hers. This kiss was not so gentle, nor so fast. As his lips impacted hers, a spiral of lust twisted her insides. It had been so long since she had been kissed…and never with such unrestrained passion.

Cade drew back, gazing at her face with such intensity she thought her heart was going to beat its way out of her chest.

When his strong arms finally released her, she felt light-headed, as though she might fall.

"Well…I mean…well…"

He grinned, his face crinkling up in delight. "Yeah, me too."

—⁊⁊—

Cade drove back to his ranch, but he could hardly keep the grin off his face. He made a conscious effort to control it, but his head was filled with Jennifer. He pictured her sitting on the floor with a sobbing Leo on her lap, holding and comforting the heartbroken boy. Her kindness had given Leo some support when he needed it most. Lissy was too young to take it all in. But he felt confident that, when the time came, Jennifer would be there to give her the reinforcement she would need.

Big Jim was right. Cade knew in his heart that the children needed Jennifer in her role of surrogate mother more than they needed him right now…but he hoped that a time would come when he would play an important role in their lives.

He was glad she liked to ride, even if she had not been on a horse since she had been a teen. At least she knew which end of the horse was which.

And they had a date. Well, at least a lunch date. He would take what he could get at this point.

Cade turned off the highway onto the Farm-to-Market road

leading to his ranch house. He always felt a sense of pride as he drove past the pastures that had been in his family for generations, knowing that he had done his part to maintain and improve the property.

When he turned onto the road leading up to the house, he pulled to a stop close to the barns and outbuildings. He swung out of the truck and strode over to the fence. "Hello, Leroy." He greeted the red-and-white longhorn bull who waited patiently for his arrival. "I didn't forget you, boy."

He reached over the barbed wire to rub the massive bull's face and nose. "Good boy. I just got hung up on a really pretty little filly. Let me get you some grain."

Cade went to the barn and scooped grain into a wide bucket. Leroy did not need the extra feed, but it was part of the bond they shared. Leroy was the reigning alpha bull of Cade's small herd of prime Texas Longhorn cattle. He treated them like pets, gave them names, and enjoyed the hell out of looking at them.

When he climbed back into his truck and drove close to the house, he found another reason to admire his property. The house was quite well maintained and attractive.

For a moment, he felt a twinge of dread to walk into his empty house. Just one twenty-nine-year-old bachelor to rattle around inside. It had never felt lonely before, but after having the children with him, it was quiet as a tomb.

Cade entered, tossed his Stetson onto a peg near the door, and slipped out of his boots. Walking around in his stocking-clad feet was a secret pleasure. Mrs. Reynolds always kept the floors mopped or vacuumed.

He went to the refrigerator and pulled out a longneck, flipped the cap into the trash can, and let the icy liquid roll down his throat. He used the remote to turn on the wall-mounted television that took up a lot of the available wall space. Scrolling through the channels, he settled on a sports program but failed to really hear the announcer.

The picture was preempted by the vision of a beautiful face with flawless skin, a mass of blondish hair, wide-set blue eyes, and the most luscious, kissable lips on the planet.

Chapter 11

At 9:00 am, the phone rang. It was the landline.

Jenn shot into the kitchen to snatch the receiver off the wall phone. She had to untangle the curly cord before she could gasp, "Hello!"

"Kids chasing you, Miss LaChance?"

She recognized Breckenridge T. Ryan's deep, articulate voice immediately. "Um, no. I just had to run in here to grab the call." She stretched the cord and cautiously opened the swinging door to peek at the children playing with Minnie on the dining room floor.

"I called to see if I can get you to drive out to the airstrip this afternoon. You and Cade Garrett need to take over the business officially. The office has been closed, but maybe the two of you can figure out some way to keep the airstrip open. The community needs this business."

"Oh, I…uh…" Jenn drew a deep breath and blew it out forcefully. "I'm sure I can be there. I'll probably have the children with me."

"You can bring the kids over here if you want. My office manager is a Garrett by marriage."

"Oh? There seem to be a lot of Garretts around Langston."

"That's the truth." Breck let out a deep chuckle. "You can't throw a rock around here without hitting a Garrett. Misty is married to Colton Garrett, Big Jim's oldest son."

"I guess that will be okay. I'll see you at your office this afternoon."

"Great. I'm calling Cade next. We should be able to get things settled."

Jenn hung up thinking that her day had just gotten to be a whole lot more complicated. It seemed everyone had a plan to care for the children. She sat down beside Lissy, who was receiving lessons from her big brother on how to pat the dog.

"No, Lissy," Leo said. "Like dis." He demonstrated the fine art of dog patting by plopping his little hand up and down on Minnie's head. She didn't seem to mind, although his pats were somewhat rough. Lissy leaned over to kiss Minnie on her head.

Jenn started to interrupt, but it was over, and now Minnie was lying on her back, exposing her belly and begging for belly rubs. Jenn reached out to gently rub the dog's underside. "That's right. Just like this. So sweet. Minnie really likes that. Nice doggy."

Lissy reached out, and Jenn guided her hand to stroke instead of beat on the dog.

"Goggy!" Lissy exclaimed.

The phone rang again and Jenn scrambled to her feet. She made it back to the kitchen just slightly out of breath. "Hello?"

"Hello, Jennifer. It's Cade."

She found herself grinning, feeling suddenly flushed.

"I got a call from Breck Ryan. I told him to let Misty off the hook because I was bringing Mrs. R to look after the kids. She can stay while we have lunch and after, when we go to the airstrip. So we can have a nice meal and then meet up with Breck at his office."

"That sounds like a great plan," Jenn said.

"I'll be there about a quarter of twelve."

She hung up, oddly buoyant. She wasn't sure what in her minimal wardrobe would be appropriate to wear to lunch with a hunky cowboy in a small town. She finally settled on the blue dress. That should be okay for lunch and being indoctrinated into the world of airport management.

By eleven thirty, she had bathed and dressed the children and was dressed herself. She kept glancing out the front windows, anxious to be at her best when Cade arrived. She wanted to be calm and composed as opposed to her usual state of near hysteria. She would be cool and sophisticated.

She paced a little, keeping an eye on the children who were running around with Minnie, but she could not tell who was chasing whom.

There was a knock at the door and Jenn tried to ignore the herd of butterflies flying formation in her stomach. She fixed a smile on her face, trying to appear composed, and opened the door.

Cade stood beside an older woman who appeared to be friendly. Maybe he was a little nervous too. He stared at her and swallowed hard.

"Hello, Jennifer. I'm Maybelle Reynolds. I keep house for Cade here." She gave him a pat on the arm.

"Oh, yes... Please come inside. Of course you know the children." Jenn turned to gesture to the children, but the woman pushed past her and squealed when she saw Leo and Lissy.

"My babies! I've missed you." Mrs. R spread her arms and gathered a rather bewildered Leo and Lissy in her arms.

"Well, I guess you're all set." Jenn shrugged. "The children have eaten their lunch, but there are snacks in the refrigerator."

Mrs. R turned, a wide grin on her face. "You young folks go on to lunch. We'll be fine here."

Cade looked on proudly, Stetson in hand, as though he had single-handedly solved a major world problem. "Are you ready?" He nodded toward the door.

"Uh-huh." Jenn grabbed her small handbag and waved goodbye to the children. Cade took her hand and walked her to his truck. When he opened the passenger door for her, she remembered it was too high for her to climb into in her slim dress.

It took a moment for Cade to figure out why she was not climbing into his truck. "I...uh...I can help you up...if it's okay. It's a little higher than standard pickups."

She nodded and he picked her up as though she weighed nothing. Being held in Cade's very strong arms sent a thrill spiraling through her core. He gazed into her eyes intently, but then he glanced at her lips and she could read his desire. If she just lifted her chin a little, he would kiss her.

Jenn looked down. "Thank you," she said, and he slid her onto the seat. "I've been so busy with the children, I haven't had a chance to get back to Dallas for more clothes." She shrugged, hoping he understood that she had more than a few dresses in her wardrobe.

"Seat belt." He closed the door and hustled around to climb behind the steering wheel. He started the truck but let it sit idling. "Do you have a preference? I mean, would you prefer the steak house or Tio's?"

"Tio's, please. I really like Mexican food."

"Yes, ma'am." He flashed a remarkably boyish grin and put the truck into gear.

When he smiled like that, she couldn't remember why she had thought him grim and distant. He drove her to Tio's, smiling all the way. There was no conversation, making her wonder if their meal would be consumed in silence.

When he parked, he gave her a long look before jumping out of his truck and rounding the hood to open her door. He reached up to her, holding both hands out.

Jenn's heart fluttered, and her stomach was doing flip-flops. She wanted to throw herself down into his arms, but she held herself in check. *Be cool. Don't blow this.* She leaned down to him and allowed herself to be gathered and lifted gently down to the street. There was a moment when her feet first made contact with the pavement and she was gazing up into Cade's eyes when she ached to have his arms draw her closer, to have him lean down and kiss her. Her hands were on his shoulders, and she was locked onto his gaze.

"Thanks for the assistance." She dropped her hands and turned toward the restaurant. "I'm starving."

Cade gestured to the entrance of Tio's. "We better get you fed, then." He escorted her inside, where Milita Rios greeted them with a wide smile.

"Hello, Cade. And Jennifer, it's so nice to see you again." She picked up two menus and two napkin-wrapped sets of eating utensils. "Where would you like to sit?"

"Somewhere quiet," Cade said.

This struck Jenn as funny, since there was some lively Mexican music playing. But Milita showed them to a table against the far wall. When they were seated, Milita placed a menu and the utensils in front of each of them and left to attend another customer waiting at the cash register.

"What looks good?" Cade asked.

"Everything, but I'm thinking about the puffy tacos with a side of guacamole." She looked at him over the menu. "What about you?"

"I'm having the Tio's Special Platter. It's got a little bit of everything." He folded the menu and slid it to the edge of the table.

"Oh, I cannot eat that much in one sitting."

Milita returned to bring ice water and take their orders. She also placed a bowl of salsa and a basket of tortilla chips in the middle of the table. "Enjoy."

Jenn reached for a chip and dipped a small area in the salsa.

Cade watched as she tested the heat with her tongue. "How is it?" She nodded. "Tasty."

Cade scooped the salsa with a chip and managed to get it into his mouth without spilling any.

"I hope the children are doing okay," she said.

"I'm sure they are. Don't worry about Mrs. Reynolds. She was helping me with them before you—" He stopped abruptly. "I mean, right after Sara and Jason were—" He shook his head.

"Got it," she said.

"I just wanted you to know that Mrs. R is great with the kids." He sat scowling at her, reminding her of when they first met. "Sorry. I didn't mean to bring up…"

"It's okay. They're gone… I'm trying to deal with it." Jenn concentrated on unwrapping the eating utensils and spread the napkin in her lap. She made a quick note of what she had ordered in the food diary and replaced it in her small handbag. "We just have to get over losing our loved ones and go on without them. The children need both of us in their lives."

Cade's frown suddenly disappeared. He looked as though she had offered him a sandwich when he was starving. "Both of us?"

She huffed out a little sigh. "Of course they need both of us." She gave a little shake of her head. "No matter how much I love Leo, I cannot demonstrate to him how to become a good man."

Cade nodded furiously. "Yes, I was thinking that too."

"And Lissy… She needs a good man in her life to be there for her." Jenn shrugged. "You know, to look daggers at her boyfriends and make them quake in their boots," she finished with a grin.

Cade broke into a grin of his own. "I can do that. I'll scare the little weasels into oblivion."

Jenn picked up her ice water and saluted him with it. "So you're willing to co-parent with me?"

His face reflected his surprise. "Co-parent? Uh, yes. That sounds great. We can be parents together…I mean…"

She sat smiling at him, allowing him to gather his thoughts.

"Yes!" he said, lifting his glass to touch it to hers in a toast of sorts. "Yes, we can do a great job of parenting the children." He seemed to be greatly relieved.

She wondered what he had imagined she would demand of him. He was the children's uncle.

But she was the children's legal guardian.

—~~—

Breckenridge T. Ryan approached the Langston airstrip. It was a bright, sunny day, but he was on edge. He had to climb out of his truck to punch the code into the entry gates. The heavy barrier rolled completely open on wheels to the accompaniment of screeching metal scraping metal.

He stood in the roadway, surveying the ghost-town atmosphere. There were no other vehicles on the property that had formerly been abuzz with traffic and people. Rows of grounded aircraft gave silent testimony to the lack of activity in the installation.

Breck couldn't imagine how Cade Garrett and Jennifer LaChance would be able to run the airstrip.

Cade was a rancher. Plain and simple. He had no experience in working with the public. He didn't own an aircraft and had shown no interest in his younger sister's business.

Jennifer was a mystery. He had no idea what her background was. He guessed she knew nothing about managing an airstrip.

Breck shook his head and climbed back in his truck. He drove past the silent hangars and parked in front of the building where Jason LaChance had had an office. His wife had worked with him, bringing their baby son with her to keep up with the books, but the arrival of their daughter had caused the young couple to hire a couple of office workers, now laid off, waiting to find out the fate of the airstrip. Would it be sold? Would new owners bring their own staff or rehire the former employees?

When Breck unlocked the office, he thought it looked as though the owner had just stepped out for a moment and would return shortly. He turned on lights and tried to shake off the feeling of dread hanging over him.

There were two entities interested in buying the airstrip. He figured that neither of the heirs would be involved in or capable of running the business, so he hoped they made a decision that would serve the community. "Lord knows we need the airstrip." His voice hung in the silence like a shroud.

He stood in the open doorway and leaned his forearm against the doorjamb, gazing out at the open field. No planes in the sky. No aircraft being prepared. The total silence was like a vacuum.

Time did not exist.

And then another truck rolled through the gate and came to a stop beside his own. Cade and Jennifer appeared to be in high spirits. Breck could see them laughing and talking through the windshield.

He blew out a lungful of air before stepping out, waving both arms in greeting. "Come right in, folks. See what you two have inherited."

Cade glanced up to see Breckenridge Ryan waving his arms over his head. He was reluctant to let anyone else into this little interlude he had enjoyed with Jennifer. It seemed that the interior of his truck was a special environment that only the two of them shared. Now the sanctity would be broken. "Are you ready for this?"

Jennifer gave a little shake of her head. "Probably not. I've been dreading coming to this place that Jason built. Missing my brother is worse here because I know I should have come to see him in his own rarified environment, but I've never been to the airstrip. I mean, we communicated almost daily, but it was mostly digitally. I should have been more involved in his life, but with Mom and Dad, it just wasn't possible." Her lower lip trembled, and she caught it between her teeth.

For some reason, that gesture aroused something primal in Cade. He wanted to rise up and surround her—protect her with his very being.

She quirked her head to one side and gave a tight-lipped smile. "That's what I have to deal with." She raised a hand to wave at Breck. "There's our guide to Wonderland."

"Yeah, let's go find the Mad Hatter." He opened the door and climbed out. He had intended to open Jennifer's door, but she slid out on her own. He gave himself a mental head smack for feeling disappointed and fell into step behind her as she made her way to the airstrip office.

Breck spread his arms. "Welcome to your own domain. Let me show you around." He pointed out the hangars and the different kinds of aircraft whose owners were renting space for them.

Jennifer shrugged. "It's so big. I mean, how can we possibly get up to speed?"

Breck gave her a puzzled look. "It sounds as though you're considering keeping the place open."

"I—I don't know. I mean, the people we loved most built this place together and made a go of it." She shrugged again. "We could try."

Cade frowned down at her. "I don't know…"

Breck joined him in frowning. "Cade here has a sizable ranch to run. Lots of stock to take care of. I don't know how he would have time or energy to run the airstrip too."

She looked crushed. "Oh, well…I was hoping maybe we could learn to run the airstrip. I hate for it to pass out of the family." She raised her eyes to Cade as though pleading for understanding. "My brother put his whole life into this. It somehow feels as though I'm letting him down…" Her lips tightened. "I know it's improbable, but still…"

Cade nodded. "Um, I can see what you're thinking." He looked at Breck questioningly.

Breck huffed out a loud sigh. "Look, it's not my job to have an opinion. I just need to help transfer your inheritance to the two of you. If you think you can manage the airstrip, I would advise you to go over the financials with the person who was doing the bookkeeping for Jason after Sara became a stay-at-home mom. That's the best I can do for you."

Cade could hear the doubt in Breck's voice, which made him

doubt the wisdom of this line of reasoning...but Jennifer looked so sad. Might as well just check things out. At least they could learn more about the airstrip. Perhaps she was right.

They spent the next half hour inspecting the contents of Jason's desk. They found a roster of clients who rented space to store their aircraft, mostly outside but some inside the hangars. There were a couple of individuals who provided maintenance on the various aircraft. And they found the names and contact information of everyone who was employed by or contracted to the airstrip.

Just as they were winding up the tour and had walked through the hangars to inspect equipment whose function neither Cade nor Jennifer could identify, Cade saw an official Sheriff's Department vehicle pulling up in front of the office.

"Is he supposed to be here?" Jennifer asked.

"Not that I was aware," Breck said, but he strode across the tarmac to investigate with Cade and Jennifer trailing behind.

By the time the three of them reached the patrol car, Sheriff Derrick Shelton had climbed out and was waiting for them. He wasn't smiling.

"Miss LaChance, Cade Garrett, and Breck Ryan. Just the people I wanted to see."

Breck stuck his hand out to shake with Derrick. "I wasn't aware that we were to meet today."

"No, sir. I went by your office and Misty told me where you would be. Glad I could catch the three of you together."

Breck's brows drew together. "Let's go inside and you can tell us what this is all about."

"Sure." Derrick, always the gentleman, gestured for Jennifer to precede him. "Go ahead, folks." When they were all inside the office, he stood looking very grim, with his thumbs hooked through his belt loops. "I have to talk to you about the supposed accident that took the lives of Jason and Sara LaChance."

Jennifer let out a little gasp and Cade found himself clenching his jaw to the point of pain.

"What are you talking about?" Breck asked.

"The feds got done with inspecting the plane and gave us the news that there was a fuel line that had been tampered with. They have their own investigation going on, so I'm sure they will be poking around here, but I have to follow up. Can you tell me who was working here up to the time of the crash?"

Jennifer's color had drained right out of her face. She sat down heavily on one of the wooden folding chairs, her hand over her mouth.

Breck motioned to Derrick. "I'm not for sure. We found a roster of employees, but I have no idea how current it is." Breck rummaged around in the files, opening one drawer, rifling through it and slamming it shut. He opened another drawer and blew out a breath. "I think these are employee files." He swept his hand over the contents.

"I—I thought you said there were only a couple of employees." Jennifer's voice sounded small.

"I think this is the entire history of everyone who has ever worked here." Breck had poked through a few of the files. "Looks like this goes back to the first day Jason opened the doors here."

Derrick nodded. "I'm going to look through all the employee files." He cast a dark gaze at Jennifer and then Cade. "You two are the only heirs?"

Jennifer nodded, looking miserable.

Cade placed his hand on her shoulder. "I want you to do whatever it takes to find out who tampered with the fuel line, and when you do…" He swallowed hard. "I want you to bring them to justice." He gazed steadily at the sheriff, knowing in his heart he wanted the perpetrator to die.

Chapter 12

JENN SAT QUIETLY ON THE DRIVE BACK TO THE HOUSE. SHE FELT she had been assaulted, at least emotionally. It would never have occurred to her that Jason had been murdered. She had thought it was just a terrible accident. Who would have wanted to kill the kindest man on the planet?

Cade must have been dealing with his emotions as well, because he didn't appear to be in the mood for conversation either. When he pulled into the driveway of the house she had inherited, he turned off the motor and sat, staring straight ahead for some time. "I'm sorry."

Jenn turned to gaze at his profile sorrowfully.

"I'm sorry that our family members were murdered by some monster." He smacked the steering wheel with the heel of his hand. "They were so happy together. They had worked so hard to achieve their dream: two beautiful children, a home, and a business to support the dream."

Jenn couldn't respond. There were no words she could possibly say. How was it that her wonderful brother, who had done everything right, married his sweetheart, produced two perfect babies, and succeeded in business…how could he be gone while Jenn remained?

She put her hand on the door handle, but Cade sputtered something and jumped out of his truck. She watched him hustle around the front of the vehicle to open the passenger-side door and offer Jenn a hand.

She accepted Cade's hand, and when their skin connected, she felt a spark of electricity. Cade's eyes reached into her, sharing the pain he was feeling—the only other person really mourning the passing of their siblings. The only other person who was trying to pick up the pieces.

He must have been able to read her misery as well. His intense blue eyes offered a place she could go for comfort.

Jenn slid off the seat and into his arms. Cade clasped her to his very hard chest as she clung to him, finally letting the tears flow. His arms were the only safe place she could recall in recent times.

"I'm sorry. I'm sorry," she gasped out between sobs.

Cade's lips pressed a kiss against her temple. "Jennifer, you have nothing to be sorry for. You've done nothing wrong." He wiped her tears with his thumb.

"I was so stupid. I thought my brother and his family would always be here for me, while I kept my nose in books." She shook her head. "I neglected them and now they're all gone…except for the children. Oh no! The children will grow up without knowing their parents at all." That realization hit her like a physical slap.

When she drew back, he kissed her cheek, wet with tears. And when she lifted her chin, he kissed her lips. It was a good kiss—not in passion, but with comfort and companionship. This misery was what they shared…and two very adorable children.

Jenn rested her head against his chest, taking comfort in the strong arms that held her close. "I can't believe anyone would hate Jason and Sara enough to want them dead."

"I agree." His voice rumbled deep in his chest. "But there must have been a reason. What did their deaths mean to someone?"

She gazed into the depths of his remarkable blue eyes. "I don't understand."

He exhaled a deep breath. "I mean, what does someone stand to gain from the deaths of Sara and Jason LaChance? What did the killer profit from their deaths?"

Jenn felt as though the life was being squeezed out of her. What did someone have to gain if Jason and Sara were murdered?

-----~~~-----

Cade drove Mrs. Reynolds home and headed for his ranch. He'd tried to keep up an appearance of being confident in front of Jennifer, but he was anything but confident.

He was torn by the news that someone had deliberately sabotaged the plane in which his baby sister had died...had been murdered.

He pulled up close to the fence where Leroy stood, gazing at him with his wide-set brown eyes. If everything could be as simple as Leroy's life...

Cade's life was a total mess. First, he'd lost his sister. Then, he had jumped into his role of caretaker to Leo and Lissy. He heaved a sigh. And then, just as he thought he'd gotten things figured out, this crazy, beautiful woman barged into his life in her slinky dresses and high heels. Oh, and her perfume. She smelled better than Mrs. R's fresh apple pie. Better than new-cut hay and freshly tilled soil, two of his favorites.

Now, he knew the taste of her lips and the feel of her sweet body pressed up against him. He stroked his hand over Leroy's wide nose. "Face it, boy. I'm hooked on that little lady."

Leroy gazed at him, his wise brown eyes seemingly filled with compassion.

"Trouble is, I don't think Miss Jennifer feels the same way about me." He leaned up against the fence and let his mind travel over the small amount of information he had about Miss Jennifer LaChance. He had probably met Jennifer at the wedding, but he had been the one to give Sara away, since their father had passed, and he had been focused on being there for her. But Jennifer had totally knocked him out the moment he first laid eyes on her when she showed up at the funeral...late, of course. She had seemed so fidgety and flighty then, but now he understood that her emotions were strong and that her brother was the last link she had to her family.

Now, she had been left the house, which Cade reasoned was the right thing to do. And he supposed that was one of the reasons she had been named as the children's guardian. Sara and Jason had wanted their children to grow up in a familiar environment, and they felt that Jennifer was the best person to raise them.

Cade tried not to feel slighted about them choosing Jennifer over him. She for sure was doing a bang-up job of caring for them. And she seemed to be warming to the idea of him sharing parenting duties.

But he wanted more. He wanted Jennifer. He wanted her kisses, and he wanted her sweet body in his arms again.

―∞―

Jenn had been dropped off at her home. She had accepted that the place was hers now. This was the home the children's parents had built for their family. Now, she sat in the big leather recliner. It was in remarkably good shape, the burgundy leather a bit worn, but treated well.

She could envision her big brother lovingly caring for the chair he enjoyed. Now, it was hers. The chair. The house. The kids. She hoped she was up to the job. The load had seemed heavy enough when she thought her brother's death was an accident, but now that she knew he had been murdered, the weight was crushing.

How could anyone take the life of such a loving man? His generous spirit reached out to everyone in the community.

She stirred as a whisper of fear coiled down her spine. A murderer was out there in the relative darkness. Someone who had killed two people, maybe more. Was it over? Or would more people die?

―∞―

Derrick Shelton sat across the table from Breckenridge. They were in the back of Breck's office where a long folding table acted as a sorting surface.

Misty Garrett looked anxious. She sat at her desk in the front of the office, which had once been a storefront. Large glass show windows fronted the office and lent a lot of light to an otherwise dark interior. "Are you sure I can't help you?" she asked.

Breck shook his head, his brows drawn together. "We're not sure what we're looking for, Misty. So there's no way we can tell you about it."

Derrick felt sorry for her and tried to soften Breck's terse response. "We may not know what we're looking for, but I sure do hope it will jump right up and smack us in the face."

"Amen!" Breck thundered, slamming one file folder closed and reaching for another. "I'm not seeing anything suspicious so far."

"Me neither," Derrick growled. "And I've known most of these people all my life. Even the old-timers."

"Watch it, kid."

"No, sir." Derrick had to laugh at Breck's fierce expression, although the young lawyer was somewhere in his late thirties. "Don't people around here call you 'that young lawyer feller'?"

Breck let out a hearty and derisive snort. "Everything's relative."

"I'm not finding anything in these files of the earlier employees," Derrick said. "What about the current workers? Anything promising?"

"There are only three people currently on the payroll. There was a part-time bookkeeper and two part time mechanics." He spread his hands. "What do you think?"

"Well, the mechanics, of course. They had opportunity. The bookkeeper, not so much." Derrick heaved a sigh. "Anyone else? Someone fired recently?"

Breck scowled. "Digging back in." He pulled another file toward him.

—◊—

Jenn awoke with her heart trying to beat its way out of her chest. Her limbs were tangled in damp bedding, and she seemed to be moist in every place a woman could be moist. She opened her eyes and heaved a sigh, trying to snatch on to shreds of the dream that had put her through a strenuous workout.

And Cade Garrett had been the star.

She had tried so hard to ignore the tenuous moments when he'd held her and kissed her. When she had been so weak after learning that Jason's death had been murder, she had drawn strength from Cade's hard body and strong arms.

Cade's were the first lips to touch hers in a long time.

She was almost virginal…except that her hormones were raging and the source of all that raging was a most inappropriate cowboy.

She swallowed hard and brushed a lock of hair out of her eyes.

A big, strong cowboy with dark hair and devastating blue eyes.

He would be perfect if she were some sweet schoolgirl who had grown up here in Langston. Indeed, a relationship with a well-off rancher, who happened to be scrumptious to look at, would have been a grand coup.

But not for the forever college student. *Nerd… Loser… Laughingstock… No man could love me now.*

A tremor shook her from the inside. How could this country bumpkin shake her to the core? *He's never been to an art museum or a Broadway show.*

Jenn took a deep breath and blew it out forcefully. Maybe not a bumpkin. He did seem to be capable of expressing himself adequately, although at first his verbiage had been in the form of short, terse linguistic jabs.

Now, he seemed to have changed his opinion of her, defrosting quite a bit. Maybe it was the fact that she was caring for his niece and nephew. And yet he had held her and kissed her as though he truly had feelings for her.

She sucked in a deep breath and let it out slowly. No point in even dwelling on what happened between them. It was just a dream. But what a dream!

Jenn untangled herself sufficiently to throw the covers back and struggle to her feet. It was early, and she hadn't heard anything from the children's room, but she shrugged into her robe and peeked in on them just to be sure.

The little ones were fast asleep, Lissy clutching her favorite toy, and Leo had rolled onto his back, breathing with his mouth open.

Jenn felt a tingle of tears as she gazed at the sweet and innocent children who had come to mean so much to her. Now if she could just live up to the title of *Mom*.

Resolutely she opened the fridge and took out some of the ingredients for a hearty breakfast: milk, butter, eggs. She set them on the counter next to the stove. Oatmeal—kids liked oatmeal. She pawed through the pantry and lined the box of cereal up next to the cold items.

"What else?" She cast about for any other items needed for breakfast. *Toast? Yeah, they need toast… and jelly.*

When she had assembled all the components for a breakfast feast, she felt a bit more confident.

Jennifer LaChance had blown off her credentials as an artist in academia. Now she would build a new persona. She would be Super Mom to two adorable children. She would become a den mother for Leo and take Lissy to ballet lessons. She would make sure they got their homework done. Whatever they needed, she would help them achieve it. She would set her artistic talents free by painting landscapes and sketching the children.

Most of all, she would squeeze the big, beautiful cowboy out of her thoughts. No more steamy dreams of Cade Garrett.

Chapter 13

WHEN BRECKENRIDGE T. RYAN PULLED UP IN FRONT OF HIS storefront office in the old redbrick building, he was surprised to recognize Cade Garrett's truck parked right in front. He'd hoped Cade had made his peace with Jennifer LaChance and wasn't here to make any further complaints.

Breck climbed out of his own vehicle and stomped up onto the sidewalk with a determined set to his jaw. He didn't want to hear any more babble about the young lady. Unfortunately, he took his irritation out on the front door, slamming it so hard the beveled glass inset shook and setting off the little bell over the door.

Breck's secretary, Misty Garrett, stared at him, wide-eyed.

For his part, Cade had been sitting in one of the chairs by Misty's desk. He jumped to his feet, clutching his Stetson to his chest. "Good morning, Breck. I thought I would catch you early."

"You got me," Breck snapped, then softened his tone. "Anything else I need to tend to, Misty?" He removed his own Stetson and placed it on a peg near the front door.

"Quiet so far," she said. "Here are a couple of phone messages for you."

Breck accepted the papers and nodded his head toward Cade. "This fellow giving you a hard time?"

Misty laughed at that. "Just catching up with my hubby's favorite cousin."

Cade snorted. "All the Garrett cousins were a fearsome gang of renegades."

Breck waved him into his private office. "I never had to arrange bail for any of you, so your gang must not have been too bad."

"I'll never tell," Cade murmured as he entered the office.

Breck closed the door and took a seat behind his massive antique desk. He didn't consider it antique but acknowledged that it was old. "Make yourself comfortable." He gestured to the chairs on the other side of the desk.

Cade sat and crossed one of his long legs over his knee at his ankle. He appeared to be having trouble sharing what was on his mind.

But Breck was an expert at prying the truth from witnesses. "How's Jennifer doing?"

Cade's smile betrayed far more than he had expected. "Aw, she's great. Really loves the kids…and she's real sweet."

So it's like that, is it? Breck filed that little bit of information away for the future.

"I know she's taking her brother's death real hard," Cade said. "But when Derrick told us someone sabotaged the plane, it really broke her up. She idolized Jason."

Breck folded his hands on top of his desk, trying not to seem impatient. "Yeah, it's a big-brother thing."

Cade nodded. "Well, I wanted to know if you and Derrick came up with anything else. Does he have any suspects?"

"Not that I know of. We looked through all the employee files, and Derrick is going to check out the most recent people who worked at the airstrip. There were a couple of mechanics and a sort of glorified secretary who kept the books after Sara decided to stay home with the little ones."

Cade's brows drew together. "So I guess Derrick will let us know if there is any news." He sounded hopeful.

"Good idea to stay out of it. Let the sheriff's office deal with the investigation. I'm sure Derrick will keep us informed when there's a break in the case."

Cade's mouth tightened. He twirled his Stetson around in his hands. "I—I just wanted to make sure that Jennifer isn't in danger." He heaved a sigh. "I mean, I can pretty well take care of myself, but Jennifer is just a girl. If someone is after the airstrip, they might try to get rid of the heirs too." His gaze seemed to bore into Breck like a laser.

Breck frowned and unclasped his hands. "I must admit, I hadn't considered that the heirs could be in danger. Do you have any suggestions for keeping yourself and Miss LaChance safe?"

"Well, I kind of thought I'd see if she would come out to the ranch with me...and Mrs. Reynolds, of course." Cade was staring down at his hat. "And the children. I mean, we could all be together."

Breck regarded him intently. "So you want to sort of circle the wagons?"

Cade heaved a deep breath. "Exactly! I thought maybe I could keep Jennifer and the kids safe out at the ranch."

"Or maybe they would be more exposed out there." Breck leaned forward on his elbows. "You know, more open spaces."

"The main house is like a fortress. I just want Jennifer and the kids to stay out of the public eye until the sheriff's office can figure out who messed with the plane."

"Are you sure you can focus that much of your time and energy to acting as watchdog?"

"You realize I was willing to put everything aside and just work on raising the kids?" Cade's brows were drawn together. "I owe it to Sara to do everything I can to ensure the kids grow up safely and without any more pain."

"I don't doubt your motives, Cade. And I admire your enthusiasm, but you can't be everywhere. How do you think you can protect the children and Miss Jennifer twenty-four hours a day?

They might be safer staying in their home with some deputies to stand guard."

Surprisingly, Cade huffed out a laugh. "I'm a Garrett. When we circle the wagons, the wagons are Garrett."

"I see." Breck felt a little better. "I don't know if there is any threat at all, but I suppose it wouldn't hurt to play it safe."

"I'd appreciate it if you'll let Derrick know that I would like to be kept informed of any new details that come to light." With that, Cade stood and reached across Breck's desk to shake hands.

When he left, Breck and Misty stared after him.

"Do you know Cade well?" Breck asked.

Misty shook her head. "I don't, but my husband thinks the world of Cade. Colton said they grew up like a litter of puppies... all the cousins."

Breck knew that was right. There were plenty of Garretts around the Langston area. And he had to admit, all the Garretts he knew were genuinely good people. He was glad to know that Jennifer LaChance had a champion in Cade Garrett, even if he did appear to be completely smitten.

Breck grinned and shook his head before heading back to his office to return his phone calls.

Cade respected Breck Ryan. He was a very smart man. He knew things. Everyone around the Langston area felt the same.

He felt empowered by gaining Breck's approval. Now all he had to do was to convince Jennifer that it would be in her best interests to come with him to the ranch. He thought if she could spend some time with him in his own environment, he might be able to convince her to stay.

Cade wasn't kidding himself. He knew he wasn't glib enough to be able to win Jennifer's affections with his words. She was a beautiful, very feminine woman, and he was...well, he was only a guy.

He had called to ask her to lunch, thinking he would bring Mrs. R to sit with the children, but when he'd called, her friend Ollie Enloe had been visiting and offered to stay with the kids.

When he pulled up in front of the house—Sara's former house—he experienced a few moments of trepidation, wondering what he was doing there, mourning anew for his sister, and finally accepting that it was only right that the house had been given to Jennifer to raise the children.

Cade pulled the keys out of the ignition and tucked them in the pocket of his Wranglers. He strode up to the house purposefully, hoping he appeared confident. He raised his hand to knock, but the door opened to a smiling Jennifer.

"Hello, Cade," she said. "Come on in. The kids were excited to see you, but Lissy fell asleep."

Momentarily flustered, he gazed down at her soft, pretty mouth and took a deep breath before he stepped over the threshold.

He was immediately assaulted by a small guided missile by the name of Leo. "Hey, buddy," Cade said. "I gotcha now." He lifted the young boy high over his head, relishing the delighted giggles.

"Unca Cade. I misted you."

"Me too," Cade said. He took a moment to appreciate how gorgeous Jennifer looked, but she was busy giving instructions to Ollie Sue Enloe, who held a sleeping Lissy.

"We'll be back soon," Jennifer crooned, giving Leo's curls a tousle. "You be a good boy for Miss Ollie, y'hear?"

Leo nodded his head. He proudly pointed to himself with his thumbs-up thumb. "I a good boy."

"You're the best." Jennifer grabbed her purse and took Cade's arm. "Let's make our getaway while we can."

"Um, yes, ma'am." He dutifully walked her out to his truck and lifted her up to the seat on the passenger side.

"I swear, your truck gets taller every time I see it." She settled herself in the seat and fastened her seat belt.

Cade swung up into the driver's seat and grinned. "Did you ever think that maybe your legs are getting shorter?"

"Not for a second. I am a tall woman, I'll have you know."

He started the vehicle, enjoying the roar of the diesel motor. "If you say so."

He drove her to the steak house and scored a parking place right in front.

Cade helped Jennifer down and just holding her close for a moment was enough to rattle his brain.

"Oh, this looks good." Jennifer looked around the parking lot. "At least a lot of people around here seem to think so."

"I'm pretty sure you're going to find something tasty on the menu." He gestured toward the entrance, and she started in that direction with Cade following close behind, again wondering how one woman could raise his temperature just by prancing along ahead of him, in full sashay mode.

He leaned around to open the door for her and noticed that all heads turned to gape at Jennifer as she entered. She seemed to be totally unaffected by all the attention, or perhaps she hadn't noticed the stares. A waitress appeared to show them to a table, and more heads turned as she made her way through the crowded room.

Nonetheless, Cade felt a sense of pride as he followed her to a table. *Yeah, this little beauty is with me.* He held out a chair for her and managed to inhale the wonderful fragrance that seemed to be a part of her.

He seated himself and accepted the menu the waitress handed him, although he knew what he would order. But he pretended to peruse the offerings while surreptitiously observing Jennifer as she scanned through the restaurant's large selection.

The waitress brought ice water and took out her pad to record their selections. Jennifer ordered a small bacon-wrapped filet mignon with a salad and seasoned green beans, while Cade chose a heartier portion with a stuffed baked potato.

When the waitress had taken the menus, Jennifer leaned closer to Cade. "I was looking at the plates on the other tables. Huge! I couldn't eat that much food if I had to sit here all day."

"Sure you could. This is going to be the best slab of beef you ever tasted, and you're just going to want to gobble it all up. So just write that in your little food diary."

She laughed at that, throwing her head back to expose her creamy throat. The sound of her laughter caused a squeezing sensation in his chest. Impulsively, he reached to take her hand, and when she didn't pull away, he drew her hand to his lips and brushed a quick kiss across her knuckles.

Her expression softened, but she was still smiling.

Cade could not release her hand, so he held it while gazing into her eyes. "I was talking to Mr. Ryan..." He heaved a deep breath. "I was thinking...well, maybe you and the kids might be better off at my ranch."

She blinked and her brow furrowed. "Better off?"

"I mean safe. I want you to be safe."

Jennifer gazed at him, her expression unreadable. "I can't do that. It just wouldn't look right." She shrugged. "If you think we're in danger, I can take the kids and go back to Dallas. I do have a perfectly good home waiting for me."

"Oh." Cade clamped his mouth shut. He definitely did not want her to leave. "No, not danger... I just thought..." A man appeared beside their table and cleared his throat. A rough, hacking sound.

Jennifer withdrew her hand. Her expression changed abruptly. Her eyes were staring at the man, and her jaw had dropped open. "Mr., uh...?"

Cade tore his eyes off of Jennifer's lovely face to find a tall, gaunt man with his gaze fixed on Jennifer. The man had a very ruddy face with mottled skin. His skin was shiny, as though it had been stretched tight over his skull.

"Miss LaChance? 'Member me? Edgar Wayne Pell. Yew done any more thinkin' on that deal we discussed?"

Jennifer pressed her lips together. "Um, not really. I mean, things have just been happening so fast."

Pell was like ice—a frozen figure with an unreadable face. A muscle near his mouth twitched. Other than that, total ice.

Cade didn't know Pell but knew who he was. He couldn't recall anyone ever speaking well of him but tried not to form any judgments.

"Yes, I remember you, Mr. Pell." She gestured toward Cade. "This is Cade Garrett. He and I share ownership of the airstrip equally."

Cade stood and offered his hand.

Pell's eyes skewered Cade like daggers. He made a sound, something like a grunt or snort. He finally drew his knobby hand out of his jacket pocket and reached to give Cade's hand a firm shake. He managed to check Cade out, boots to hair, in the process, although Cade was a few inches taller and much broader of chest.

The waitress returned bearing their salads and a choice of salad dressings. She looked uncertain, but Jennifer gestured for her to set them down. The waitress complied and made a quick getaway.

"Well, I won't be botherin' yer dinner. I'll get back to ya in a few days. Yew be thinkin' on it." He turned and strode across the room to the door, pausing to glance back at them before exiting.

A visible shiver caused Jennifer to wrap her arms around herself.

"Are you okay?" Cade asked. "Is that Pell guy upsetting you?"

"I'm all right. Mr. Pell came to the house and said that Jason had been working with him on a deal to sell the airstrip. I told him before that I didn't know anything about it. I referred him to Breckenridge Ryan. I figured he could deal with Mr. Pell a lot better than me." She sucked in a breath. "I keep going back and forth, thinking we might be able to keep the airstrip open, and then reality smacks me on the head and I think we should sell."

Cade's brows drew together. "Yeah, I understand." He felt that this Pell character had intended to intimidate Jennifer. "I'll tell you what. If Pell shows up again, tell him to give me a call. I'll make sure he doesn't bother you again."

Jennifer drew a ragged breath and started to speak, but the waitress appeared, bringing their entrees. She unfolded her napkin and draped it across her lap. "I'm glad you were with me. That man— he's kind of scary."

"Definitely a creep. So let's forget about him and enjoy our meal." She nodded, saluting him with her iced tea.

Chapter 14

JENN FELT SHAKEN BUT TRIED TO BRUSH IT OFF. SHE HAD NO idea why this Edgar Wayne Pell seemed so scary. It would be a good thing if he bought the airstrip…or if someone else bought the property. For sure, she had no experience at all in any kind of business, let alone knowledge of the management of airstrips.

She looked at the big cowboy sitting beside her. He might know which end of the cow to milk, but she was pretty sure Cade Garrett had no hidden knowledge about running a small airstrip…but maybe she was wrong. Maybe there were layers of technological data stored behind those killer blue eyes.

"Didn't Breck Ryan say there was someone else interested in buying the airstrip?" She had been mulling over their options and realized her thoughts about keeping the airstrip in the family were not practical. Being a good businessman, she was sure Jason would have advised them to sell.

Cade nodded. "Maybe we should call on Mr. Ryan tomorrow. I'm certain he will have a better grasp on the situation than either of us." He took the plastic off a packet of saltines but sat tapping them against his salad plate. "But don't you think we should at least look into the way the airstrip has been run up to the point when Jason and Sara were killed?"

She speared some lettuce and shoved it into her mouth, mostly to keep from having to come up with an answer. In truth, she was torn between needing desperately to know what happened and wanting to hide from the ugly truth. Maybe someone else would discover why her brother had to die. Maybe Jenn could just continue to bury her head in the little bits of happiness she was discovering here in Langston, Texas. She would go on playing mom to the children and live in the dollhouse where they had been raised. And maybe she would continue to enjoy the company of this pillar of manhood quietly brooding beside her.

Yes, the appearance of Edgar Pell had brought Cade's mood way down. There was a furrow between his brows, but he still looked at her expectantly. She would be forced to respond.

Jenn swallowed her thoroughly chewed lettuce. "Um...I'm sure you're right." She shrugged and skewered another bite. "How do you propose we check out the business if we are both totally ignorant about it?"

"I think we should open the airstrip for business, hire the employees back, and see what we can find out. Maybe the people who worked there have their own theories."

Jenn nodded. That didn't sound too dangerous. Just meet the employees and poke around a little. Maybe Cade could dig in and find out what he needed to, and then he might be ready to sell to whoever had the money to buy them out.

"Okay. That sounds reasonable."

"Good, we can take a little drive out there after we finish our meal."

———

Jennifer tried to enjoy the excellent meal, but her stomach had been a little tied up in anticipation of going back to the place where Jason had worked. She was now tucked into Cade's truck and they were headed for the airstrip. She had no idea why he seemed to be in such a good mood, but Cade was zooming there like an arrow. Apparently, he had no idea how she felt about the enterprise Jason had so loved.

He had kept up a commentary, requiring very few responses from her. When he turned off the highway, her stomach was already in a knot. Cade got out and punched some numbers into the keypad and then drove through as the gate slowly closed behind them.

Jenn could hardly draw a breath.

"I'm going to make a loop of the property, just so we can check the layout. I wanted to know if anyone was making changes since the office had been closed. You know, like getting away with something. Is that okay with you?"

"Sure." She tried to make a smile happen on her face, but it felt more like a grimace. Taking a few deep breaths, she sat up a little straighter.

It seemed to her that the same small planes and helicopter that had been there before were sitting out on the tarmac. And there were several hangars still standing in their same locations. Only one had the overhead door open, and it appeared someone was inside because there was an old Jeep and a shiny silver BMW parked close to the building.

Cade slowed, and they both got a chance to peer inside.

Someone was on a ladder, situated near the front of the small plane, and someone else was standing below. They both turned to stare back.

Cade waved and the two people waved in return. He continued to drive slowly around the field but wound up parking at the small office building near the entrance. "Let's take a look." He took a set of keys out of the glove compartment and got out.

Jenn released her seat belt, resigned to the inevitable.

Cade opened her door and helped her get down, then walked purposefully to the office, used the key, and held the door wide open for her to pass through.

All the blinds had been drawn and the air conditioner was off, so it was dim and stuffy inside.

Cade set about opening the blinds and turned on a large window air conditioner.

"You've been here pretty often in the past?" she asked. "When—when they were alive?"

"Just came out sometimes to keep Sara company or to bring her lunch. After Leo was born, she brought him out here with her, but when he got to be up and running around, she stayed home with him. Mrs. Reynolds would go stay with him one day a week, and Sara managed to keep up with the bookkeeping, but when Lissy made her appearance, she had to give it up altogether. They hired a part-time person to keep books, answer the phone, things like that."

"I see." What she saw was the same grim-looking office with filing cabinets, a desk, and two chairs placed in front of it. Nothing had changed.

"Jason used the desk in the back." Cade indicated the desk half-hidden behind a tall bookcase at the far end of the office. "This one up front is the one Sara used, and then later, the woman they hired to keep books."

Just the sight of Jason's neatly arranged desk again caused a shiver to tease the back of Jenn's neck. He was always one to straighten things before he left. Apparently this habit had carried over to his own enterprise.

"Your brother was a neatnik," Cade said. "He always kept things shipshape."

Another tremor caused Jenn to gasp. She caught her lower lip in her teeth, taking deep breaths until the sensation passed.

Cade gazed down at her. "Hey, are you all right?"

She swallowed hard. "Just peachy."

There was a knock at the door. "Hallooo?"

She turned to find a very attractive woman framed in the doorway. She was smiling and stepped toward Jenn, her hand outstretched. "I'm Magdalena Swearingen. Just call me Maggie." She gave Jenn's hand an enthusiastic shake before reaching for Cade's.

"How do you do, ma'am?" Cade looked beyond the woman to the large man standing behind her.

"Oh, this is Butch. He works for me." Maggie made an elaborate gesture toward the man who towered over her. "Butch is the best airplane mechanic anywhere around here."

Butch looked a bit embarrassed but lurched forward to shake hands with both Cade and Jenn. "Good to meet you folks."

"I'm Jenn LaChance and this is Cade Garrett. We—we just inherited the airstrip."

Maggie's face contorted into a frown. "Yes, I heard. So sorry for your losses. I can imagine how you're feeling." Then she gave a wide smile. "But if you're ready to talk a little business, I wanted you to know that I'm interested in purchasing the property, lock, stock, and barrel. I lease hangar number five from you...for my personal plane...and sometimes the company aircraft."

"Miz Maggie owns the Swearingen Corporation," Butch offered. "Outta Dallas."

Maggie smiled in a deprecating matter and shook her head. "Oh, no. I'm just part of the family."

Jenn felt a suffocating pressure in her chest. Things were happening so quickly, and she had no idea what was the best choice. "Well, um, I don't think we know enough about the airstrip to discuss it with you. We just came out today to look around and get to know the place on our own."

Maggie's grin widened. "Well, no one expects you to become experts overnight. But we just wanted to meet you and let you know that the absolute minute you're ready to deal, we are too." She reached in her pocket and drew out a couple of business cards.

"Thanks," Cade said. He studied the card intently before tucking it in his shirt pocket.

"We'll get out of your hair so you can get your business straightened out," Maggie said. "C'mon, Butch. Let's go back to work."

She waggled her manicured fingers and turned to exit the building with Butch trailing behind her.

Jenn and Cade stared for a moment at the door and then began speaking at once.

Cade grinned. "I'm glad we have more than one prospective buyer for the airstrip."

Jenn nodded. "And I'm glad we don't have to sell to Mr. Pell." She shrugged. "He just seems so grim."

"We can talk to Breck Ryan about the sale. He probably has some good ideas. Maybe we should list the property with a Realtor. You know, the ones that deal with business properties."

"That sounds like a great idea." She looked around the office. "I suppose there are some financial ledgers around somewhere. Let's check and see if we're in the black."

"Yes, ma'am. Let's find that ledger."

They spent the next few minutes pawing through the desk drawers and the filing cabinets until Cade let out a whoop of discovery. "Aha! I think this is what we're looking for." He placed the blue clothbound book on the desktop. When he opened it, Jenn could see rows of entries.

"This is it!" Jenn settled in the chair behind the desk and started turning pages. "Oh, look at all these customers. These are the people who are leasing hangar space and these are the ones who pay to let their aircraft sit out on the tarmac."

After they had spent a few minutes perusing the ledger, they agreed that the airstrip was profitable.

"Unfortunately, neither of us knows a thing about running this business." Cade was leaning over her, his clean man smell drawing her attention away from the book. *He sure does clean up well.*

"Um, yeah. It looks like the airstrip is in the black. Maybe we can get this sold for some big bucks." She closed the ledger to, hopefully, end the discussion.

"I was hoping we could put some money into a trust for the

kids' education." He said it casually, just dropped it into the conversation, but she could tell it was important to him.

Jenn held her breath for a moment. "Yes, well, I am not independently wealthy, so I will need to have money to feed, clothe, and shelter them."

His blue eyes seemed to bore into her. He looked as if he had more to say but pressed his lips together.

"I swear, Miz Fern, this is the best pecan pie I've ever had the pleasure to eat in my entire life." Big Jim Garrett took another bite, savoring the taste on his tongue.

"Why, thankee, Big Jim." Fern Davis's face crinkled up in a pleased grin, and her cheeks took on a rosy tone. "It's a secret family recipe."

Big Jim gave her a look of mock surprise. "I'm family."

"Well, that's a fact." She peered at him over the top of her wire-rimmed glasses.

"And we harvested a huge crop of paper-shell pecans this past year. We have bags and bags in the freezers." Big Jim took another bite.

"Don't yew worry yoursel' one little bit. I'll be mighty happy ta make yew all the pecan pies yew can eat." She giggled, covering her mouth with both hands.

Big Jim leaned forward earnestly. "You consider my sons to be part of your family, don't you? They sure do think you're family."

Fern's eyes opened wide. "Why, I shore do. Them boys o' your'n are the salt o' tha earth. None better."

"And they think the world of you, Miz Fern." Big Jim scraped up the last bite of his pie but held off putting it in his mouth. "I sure do hope you plan to share that recipe with your lovely granddaughter Leah."

Fern's mouth puckered up in a scowl. "Well, of course. She's my own flesh an' blood."

"And little Gracie and your brand-new great-grandson James Tyler Garrett."

Fern planted her fists on her hips and glared at Big Jim. "Jist what are yew gittin' at, Big Jim Garrett?"

He assumed an innocent expression. "Why, Miz Fern, I'm just saying that family is family. We should share and share alike."

"That sounds 'bout right." She folded her arms but continued to give him a suspicious glare.

"So I'm sure you want Leah to be able to make this wonderful pie for Tyler and the children."

Her little head nodded, just once.

"And I'm sure you wouldn't withhold something this delicious from my other sons, Colton and Beau...and their wives, Misty and Dixie...Leah's sisters-in-law and the aunties for your own great-grandbabies."

Fern made a snorting sound. "Well, ain't yew somethin', Big Jim. I guess I'll have to make shore my secret family recipe for home-made pecan pie will have to be shared with everyone in my family."

Big Jim flashed a wide smile. "That's the spirit, Fern. Do you suppose I could have another slice of this excellent pie?"

Fern's lips twitched. "No."

Chapter 15

CADE DROVE JENNIFER TO THE HOUSE THAT WAS NOW HERS. HE walked her up to the door, wishing it had been a real date and that he could take her in his arms and kiss those luscious lips. But he sensed she had enjoyed his company enough for one day. "I…uh, I thank you for going with me today."

She gazed up at him. "Don't be silly. I'm the one thanking you for the time we had today. The lunch was great, and I never would have gutted up enough courage to go out to the airstrip without your urging. When Breck sort of made us show up there, I felt like crying… It was just as though Jason should be right around the corner."

Cade swallowed hard. "I know what you mean. It was tough."

"I was really dreading going there again, but now I'm feeling better about it. It's just a business…my brother's business." She drew a deep breath and blew it out forcefully. "I'm all confused now. Part of me wants to keep Jason's business in the family…but I'm so woefully ignorant of any business management expertise." She shook her head, looking sad.

Cade stroked her cheek with his fingertips. Her skin was as soft as Lissy's. He cleared his throat. "Whatever you decide to do is fine with me. If you want to take over the management of the airstrip, I'll do my best to learn."

"That's just it," she said. "I'm also thinking that we should just take the money and run, so we can concentrate on things that are more important, like the children."

Cade leaned one hand against the doorjamb, in effect fencing her in. "There's no hurry. It seems that both of our prospective buyers will wait on us. Just take it easy, and we'll figure it out together."

Jennifer reached up and took his face in both her hands. She pulled him down to her level and placed a firm but lingering kiss against his lips.

Cade wrapped both arms around her, drawing her close. He deepened the kiss, tasting her sweetness. All of his senses were going berserk. He felt hot, flushed with desire, yet consumed by the icy shiver circling his spine.

She pulled away abruptly. "I—I'm sorry. I shouldn't have done that."

He didn't release her, holding her clasped against his chest. "No, you did the right thing. I needed that." He lowered his mouth to claim another kiss.

This time it was warm and sweet. When he pulled away, she was smiling.

"I just don't know if we should be doing this," she said. "I mean, it might make things difficult if we were to become involved."

A wry grin spread across his face. "Or it might become wonderful if we were to become involved."

She smiled but cast her eyes down. "I—I should go in now. Ollie has been with the kids all day."

"I understand. I'll take the ledger to Breck tomorrow. Maybe he can help us come up with the right decision."

"Good idea." She hesitated and then stretched up for another kiss, heaved a sigh, and quickly entered the house, closing the door in his face.

She likes me.

<hr>

Jenn leaned against the door. *Oh, what have I done now?*

"You're back already?" Ollie said in a stage whisper. "Kids are asleep. I figured you would stay out for a long time with that hot cowboy. Dang! He's a babe."

Jenn let out a long, pent-up breath. "You're telling me."

Ollie patted the sofa beside her. "Come tell me all about it. Confession is good for the soul."

Jenn stowed her keys and jacket before going to sink down beside Ollie. "It was just lunch, and we went out to the airstrip to look around." She was aware that her voice quivered a little.

Ollie gave her a wry smile. "Oh, is that all?"

"Of course. What else would there be?"

Ollie chuckled. "Oh, I'm pretty sure there's more."

Jenn shifted under Ollie's scrutiny. "Not really. We had a great lunch at the steak house and then he drove me out to the airstrip. We were there when Breck handed over the keys, but we thought we should just go back there and look around." She shrugged. "We looked at the ledger in the office. Cade is going to take it to the lawyer's office tomorrow. Breck told us there were some possible buyers in the mix."

Ollie's eyes opened wide. "Oh, that sounds exciting. So you're planning on selling?"

"Maybe. I'm not an expert, so I'll go along with whatever Breck and Cade think is best." She clasped her hands together. "Although I really feel bad about getting rid of the business that Jason loved. I mean, he built it from scratch. He was always crazy about flying."

"I remember your brother. He was a charming man. I used to love watching him in church. He was a very manly man, but he was a pushover for his wife and children. I always thought they had the perfect family."

Jenn swallowed hard, the taste of tears burning her throat. "They were."

Ollie leaned over to pat Jenn's hands, clasped tight together in her lap. "I'm outta here. Have a great evening." She gathered her handbag and keys. "I'm pretty sure you're going to have cowboy dreams."

Jenn sucked in a breath. "Oh, no. I most certainly will not be dreaming about Cade Garrett." She jumped to her feet.

Ollie just chuckled as she headed to the front door. "I think you're protesting too much. Just sayin.'"

Jenn rushed to catch her before she left. "Wait! I didn't get a chance to thank you for staying with the children. I appreciate you so much."

"Not a problem. I love being a part of your happy little family, even a little bit. I'm glad we're friends."

"Me too." Jenn gave her a hug. "You're the best."

The next day, Cade took care of his stock at the crack of dawn, so he could clean up and go to Breckenridge T. Ryan's office early.

He didn't see Breck's truck outside, but he went inside anyway.

Misty Garrett, his cousin Colt's wife, sat at her desk, sipping coffee. "Good morning, Cade. What are you up to so early in the morning? Did you have an appointment that I didn't know about?"

Cade grinned and shook his head. "Not likely. You and Colt doing okay?"

Her face lit up like sunshine on a cloudy day. "The Colt man and I are totally fabulous. I never dreamed I could be so happy."

"Aw. You deserve it. I know you went through a lot to be together." He took a seat in one of the chairs in front of her desk.

"What about you, Cade? Anyone exciting on your playlist?"

"Um—" He felt blindsided by that simple question. "I...uh..."

Misty chortled and pushed back from her desk. "I'm going to get you a cup of coffee while you think up an answer. There's got to be someone special. You're a great guy and not too hard to look at." She went to the coffeepot on the console behind her desk and poured a cup of the dark, rich liquid. "Sugar, creamer?"

"Just plain, thanks." Cade accepted the cup, thankful to have something to do with his hands.

Misty settled behind her desk. "Well, if you're not going to dish about your love life, tell me what brings you in today."

Cade huffed out a sigh, relieved that she wasn't going to pry into his romantic relationship, although he was pretty sure he didn't have one. A few kisses didn't amount to much…but it was a start. He took the blue cloth ledger out from under his arm and placed it in front of Misty. "I wanted Breck to take a look at this. It's the financial ledger from the airstrip."

She gazed at it as if it might bite her. "Unfortunately, Breckenridge T. Ryan is in Amarillo, representing a local rancher's son in a DUI arrest that resulted in a motor accident with injuries. He may or may not be in today, but he'll call in when he can."

"Oh. Well, I guess I better make an appointment."

Misty arranged for him to come in the following day, late morning. She explained that Breckenridge T. Ryan considered himself a rancher first and an attorney second, so he still made his wife and his ranch his first priority. "You can leave the ledger with me, and I can make sure he has a chance to look it over before your appointment."

Cade pressed his lips together. "Um, no thanks. I think I need to keep this book close at hand, for a while at least." He took his leave and returned to his own ranch to continue his usual tasks and try to figure out how to convince Jennifer to fall in love with him.

—

Jenn had been awakened quite early.

Ollie had apparently given Lissy enough liquids to float a battleship because the diaper had not been able to contain the output.

Lissy's cries jerked Jenn out of a very passionate dream starring the very hot Cade Garrett.

Jenn took a moment to compose herself before yelling, "I'm coming, Lissy." She staggered to her feet and reached for a robe. By the time she reached the children's room, she had managed to close the garment around herself and tie the sash. "Oh, poor baby."

She lifted Lissy but held her away from her body, transporting the sopping-wet child into the bathroom, where she ran a few inches of warm water in the tub and managed to get her cleaned up in a relatively short time.

Lissy followed behind her as she stripped the child's bed and got the sheets into the washer. With that task underway, she set about preparing breakfast.

Leo was apparently not a morning person. He had slept through all the commotion but now appeared in the kitchen in his pajamas and with a grumpy expression on his face.

"Good morning, sleepyhead. Breakfast will be ready in a few minutes." She had made scrambled eggs and pushed two slices of bread into the toaster.

She helped Leo onto his booster seat and had just lifted Lissy, intending to put her in her high chair, but the doorbell sounded at that moment. "Oh, great!" she murmured.

Lissy started fussing, but Jenn arranged her on one hip and threw the door open, startled to find Edgar Pell on her doorstep.

He nodded curtly. "Miz LaChance, I jus' wanted to see if you'd given any more thought to my offer."

By this time, Lissy was in full voice, howling, drooling, and gnawing on her first and middle fingers. "Well, no. Actually, I—"

Pell leaned forward and held his arms out to Lissy. "Aww, poor little 'un."

Surprisingly, Lissy leaned toward him, and he cradled her against his chest.

Jenn noticed he was wearing a very nice and immaculately pressed Western shirt, which was quickly christened with a large blob of drool, but he didn't seem to mind. In fact, he was grinning.

Edgar Pell bounced a little, patting Lissy on the back and crooning to her. In a remarkably short time, she had quit crying and laid her head on his shoulder. "That's a good girl. Jus' settle down and let ole Uncle Ed sing yew a li'l song." With that, he began to croon about the itsy-bitsy spider.

Jenn realized her mouth was hanging open. She recovered, gesturing for him to enter. "Please come inside, Mr. Pell. I was just fixing the children's breakfast."

"Sorry, I didn't mean to interrupt yer mornin' routine, but I didn't have yer number." He stepped inside, still swaying with Lissy and patting her back.

Jenn emitted a short laugh. "Hah! We really don't have a routine. Just feeling my way here. Do you like scrambled eggs?"

He appeared to be startled by her question. "Uh, sure. Who don't like scrambled eggs?"

"Won't you please join us for breakfast?" Jenn returned to the kitchen, confident that Pell would follow. She gestured to the table. "Please, make yourself comfortable. I didn't have time to make coffee, but we have cold milk and orange juice."

"That's jus' fine. I'll take a glass o' milk, please." His voice still held a trace of puzzlement.

"You can put Lissy in her high chair now." Jenn busied herself with buttering toast and dishing up eggs onto serving plates. She poured milk into sippy cups and a tall glass for Mr. Pell. "Here we go." She brought a jar of strawberry jam to the table and seated herself.

Pell folded his hands and bowed his head.

"Oh!" Jenn realized she was expected to say grace. "Um...Lord, please bless us...and this food."

"Amen!" Pell said in a resounding voice.

Jenn was relieved that he recognized it as a prayer. She spooned a bite of eggs into Lissy's mouth, pleased that Leo was awake enough to feed himself.

"This is plumb nice, Miss LaChance." Pell waited until Jenn picked up her fork to raise his bite to his mouth. "I ain't had no home cookin' in...." He paused to chew, or perhaps to think. "Oh, heck. I can't recall."

"I'm glad you could join us, Mr. Pell. You sure do have a way with babies."

He grinned again, that skin-too-tight grimace. "I was tha oldest in a big family. There was always another little 'un to tend to."

"That must have been nice to have so much family. It was just Jason and me against the world." Jenn swallowed hard to keep tears from falling. "He was always my hero."

Pell's face crinkled into a smile, skin taut. "That's nice. Most o' my family is gone...or not speakin.'"

Jenn's chest tightened. The man, who had been singing to a one-year-old a few moments ago, seemed to have been swallowed into a morass of sadness. She cast about to find another topic of conversation. "Why don't you tell me about the airstrip? It was the reason that Jason came here in the first place. He was so happy following his passion."

Pell relaxed and proceeded to tell her about his small aircraft that resided in a shared hangar with some owned by other local veterans who were flying enthusiasts. He knew a great deal about the operation and appeared to be comfortable discussing it.

By the time Jenn had shoveled all of Lissy's breakfast into her mouth and mopped up both children, Pell had finished talking and seemed to be reminiscing.

"Well, I better be lettin' yew git on with your day." He drained his glass, leaving him with a slight milk mustache.

Jenn resisted the urge to mop up his face as well. "It's been a pleasure visiting with you, Mr. Pell. I'm sorry I don't have an answer for you regarding the airstrip. Cade and I are going to consult with Mr. Ryan, the lawyer. We figured his advice would help us make a decision. I think we're both torn as to whether to sell or keep it in the family."

Pell stood and gave her a little two-finger salute before donning his cowboy hat. "Yes'm, I understand. Well, just keep me in mind 'cause I sure am interested."

Jenn followed him to the door, making certain it was secured behind him. She stood, leaning with her back to the door, considering the morning's events. Somehow, the man she had considered scary had become so very mellow.

—⁓—

Cade dug his cell out of his shirt pocket. His caller ID told him his uncle, Big Jim Garrett, was on the line.

"Hello, Uncle Jim!"

"Hello, yourself." Big Jim's deep voice resonated. "How ya doin', boy?"

A grin painted itself across Cade's face. "Mighty fine, sir. What can I do for you today?"

Big Jim chortled. "You can make yourself available to come to the ranch for barbecue this Saturday. We're gonna char everything that don't move fast."

"Your special rub?"

"You betcha! We're gonna have us a feast."

"I'll be there. Say, Uncle Jim, I don't suppose I could bring a guest...or maybe three?"

"Whatcha got in mind, son?"

Cade drew a deep breath and huffed it out. *Time to man up.* "I would like to bring Miss Jennifer LaChance and my little niece and nephew."

There was a long silence. "So you're gettin' along okay?"

"Yes, sir. We sure are." He felt a little feathery feeling in his chest, recalling how Jennifer's lips tasted and how her slim body felt in his arms. "It's all about the kids, you know?" he added in a rush.

"I see," Big Jim said. "Please bring Miss LaChance and the children. We're all about family, you know that...and friends are welcome."

"I appreciate it, sir. I'll ask her for sure."

"She's a pretty little thing." Big Jim paused. "A mite fragile for a big strappin' cowboy like you."

Cade let out a roar of laughter. "Jennifer is a lot tougher than she looks."

~~~

Jennifer had wrestled both children into their car seats and driven the short distance to Cami Ryan's office.

"Well, looky here." Loretta stood up to peer at the children over the top of her desk. "I haven't seen these two for a while. Looks like you're taking to the job of mothering these little ones."

Jennifer felt a rush of pride. Maybe she was doing something right.

Reba came out of the back and squinted at Jennifer and her charges. "I don't think either one of them are due for any vaccines yet."

"I—I, uh…the doctor told me to come back with my food notebook." She flashed a nervous smile and dropped Leo's hand to reach for the little book. "I wrote down everything."

Reba let out a somewhat derisive snort. "Lemme see that thing." She held out her hand, reminding Jennifer of her second grade teacher—she who must be obeyed.

Jennifer handed it over, taking a deep breath as the eagle-eyed Reba scanned it, turning pages and muttering something unintelligible. "Looks much better. C'mon back here. Dr. Cami is in her office."

Jennifer carried Lissy and held Leo's hand as they fell in behind Reba, walking into the hallway leading to the office. There she saw Cami Ryan working on a computer. She looked up when Reba presented the trio and tossed the food notebook on her desk.

"Oh, this looks good. You're actually eating three meals a day. Perfect. How are you feeling?" Cami gestured to a chair.

Jennifer sat down, arranging Lissy on her lap and snugging an arm around Leo to keep him close. "I guess I feel better." She pressed her lips together. "I think part of my problem was emotional. I had just lost…" She glanced at Leo. "Someone very close."

Cami tilted her head to one side. "You admitted you weren't

eating much. You were anemic, but your color is much better." She reached toward Jennifer. "Let me see your hand."

Jennifer released Leo and complied.

"See how nice and pink your nail beds are? Much better."

Jennifer nodded. "I'm taking the vitamins and learning to cook. My friend Ollie is teaching me. And I eat what I'm feeding them, so lots of macaroni and other high-carb foods."

Cami chuckled. "For you that's a good thing. And I see you're eating from all the food groups. Good job."

"Gotta feed my kiddos." She sucked in a breath, realizing that she did indeed consider them her own children.

"Keep up the good work." Cami gave her a thumbs-up. "Reba, tell Loretta to make a follow-up appointment for thirty days."

Reba had been slouching against the doorframe, but she pushed away and sauntered down the hall.

"Thanks." Jennifer struggled to her feet with Lissy clinging to her neck. She adjusted the child and reached for Leo's hand. "I'll see you next month."

She left the office feeling that she was as least doing one thing right. *I've got this.*

Chapter 16

BIG JIM TUCKED HIS PHONE AWAY, THINKING ABOUT THE SLEN-der woman who was Jason LaChance's baby sister.

She brought to mind the term *arm candy*, although he had been informed in no uncertain terms by his daughter-in-law Misty that Jennifer was a brilliant student who had earned all kinds of awards and scholarships. Misty had done her research. Jennifer had gone on to earn several degrees.

Big Jim didn't know if he should address little Miss LaChance as *doctor* or just *professor*.

But he had been immensely impressed by how she had helped Leo accept the fact that his parents were gone. He was way too young to grasp the concept of death, but gone was something he could handle.

He walked into the kitchen and opened the door to the freezer. Plenty of meat for the barbecue. He would have two more young children, so he would ask his daughters-in-law to make a little something the kids might like.

In the meantime, he took a couple of racks of ribs, a couple of whole chickens, and a brisket out and placed them in the bottom of the fridge to thaw gently. He thought the Saturday get-together would show him a lot more about the relationship between his nephew Cade and this lovely young woman who had come to them from the world of universities.

And he would learn more about Jennifer. He hoped she was up to the task of raising two wild young children who were half Garrett.

When Cade showed up at Breckenridge T. Ryan's office, he was relieved to see Breck's truck already there. He climbed down from his own vehicle with the blue ledger tucked under his arm.

He opened the glass-paneled door to the old storefront office, jangling the metal bell overhead.

"Hey, Cade!" Misty hailed him from her desk. "You coming to the barbecue on Saturday?"

Cade gave her a salute. "Yes'm, Miss Scarlett. Wouldn't miss it for the world."

"And I heard you might be bringing a special guest?" She gave him a wink.

"I hope I'm bringing three of them."

"Hope?" She raised her brows, silently interrogating him. "What's this hope thing?"

"I, uh…I haven't asked Jennifer yet," he stammered.

Misty heaved a very dramatic sigh and crossed her arms over her chest. "Really? What are you waiting for? She might make other plans. The girl is gorgeous, you know."

"I know." Cade regarded her ruefully, wondering why he hadn't called Jennifer immediately after his Uncle Jim asked him. "I'm planning on it."

She started to add something, but Breck's office door opened and he stood in the doorway, a slight frown on his face. "I was under the impression that I had an appointment with this young man. Do you think you could break up this gabfest to let me find out why he's coming to seek my advice?"

Misty flushed a deep red. "Yes, sir. Cade, you can go in now," she murmured.

Cade figured Breck was teasing, but then again, a lawyer's time was valuable and he had wasted some of it horsing around with his cousin's wife. "Sorry, sir." He crossed to where Breck stood, but when he drew even with Breck, he was enveloped in a big hug.

"Just giving you two a hard time. Come on into the office and tell me about that blue book you're clutching." Breck took a seat behind his massive desk and gestured to one of the chairs on the other side.

Cade dropped into the chair, reluctant to let go of the ledger. "I know you're still working on the inheritance...the house and the airstrip."

Breck nodded. "That I am."

Cade took a deep breath and plunged right in. "Jennifer and I went out to the airstrip, just to check things out. We looked around and found this ledger in the office. It has all the financial information in it...up to the moment when..."

"Yeah. Up to that moment." Breck looked grim.

"And while we were out there, a lady and her mechanic came to the office to meet us...a Maggie Swearingen."

Breck nodded. "She's been in touch with me about purchasing the airstrip. Big, big money out of Dallas. Big old money."

"She seemed nice."

"Classy lady," Breck agreed. "I understand Edgar Pell is also interested in the property."

Cade grimaced. "He's kind of a spooky dude."

Breck's dark brows almost met in the middle. "He's had a hard life, that's for sure, but he should have the wherewithal to buy the property, if that's what he decides to do." He reached toward the ledger still clasped close to Cade's chest. "I'll take a look at that now."

Cade surrendered the book without further delay.

Breck found the last entries, perusing them with the same frown. "I'll keep this for a while to give it a more thorough examination...but it appears that the airstrip has been operating in the black. Good business. Good bottom line. Lots of area customers have their small planes stored in hangars or on the tarmac. Monthly fees are paid up." He closed the book and rested one hand on top of it. "I'll get back to you in a few days. If you're leaning toward selling the property, do you have any idea what you want to ask for it?"

"No idea what it's worth."

"Then I suggest you get a knowledgeable commercial Realtor to appraise the property and give advice. If you choose to list it, the Realtor will advertise it as well, so you may get a lot more interest."

Cade felt a bit overwhelmed by the possibilities, and he wasn't even certain he wanted to sell the property, but he had promised Jennifer he would support her decision...no matter what.

Jenn had just wrestled the children down for a nap and was sprawled on the sofa, with Minnie snuggled on top of her. She stroked the dog's fur, realizing that since she had become a surrogate mother, she had seriously neglected Minnie's grooming. "Poor baby. I'm such a bad doggy mom."

Perhaps there was a dog groomer in Langston, someone to give Minnie's toenails a trim. The small dog was easy to bathe and brush, but one had to take the time to perform these tasks. Plus, Lissy had a habit of decorating Minnie with whatever was on her hands at the time. But Minnie appeared to be devoted to Lissy, thriving under her ministrations.

Jenn wiggled her bare toes. The great thing about kids was that you didn't have to dress up for them. Earlier, she had climbed out of bed when Lissy first woke up and thrown on a T-shirt she had found that must have belonged to Jason. It was huge and had a hole on one side, showing the world her ribs, if the world had been on hand to check them out. She had kept her flannel pajama bottoms on to complete her extra-comfy outfit. Perfect for a lazy day at home.

The doorbell chimed, causing Jenn to leap up and hurry to the door, Minnie tucked under her arm. Above all, she didn't want someone to wake the children from their naps. When she threw the door open, Cade stood grinning down at her.

"Oh!" She gaped up at him, realizing she had no makeup on and had barely run a brush through her hair many hours ago. "Cade! I didn't know you were coming." She would have brushed her hair back out of her eyes, but Minnie was wiggling in delight, her attention riveted on Cade.

Cade reached to take the dog out of Jenn's arms. "I'm sorry. I should have called but I was just so anxious to see you." He flashed the boyish grin again. The grin that caused a squeezing sensation around her heart.

She moistened her lips. "Uh, well...come on in, then." She made a vague gesture to the interior of the house. "But please keep it down. The kids are napping...and I was..."

Cade stepped inside, inspecting her thoroughly in the process. "I see."

She sucked in a breath, a whisper of heat washing over her. "Um, well, come inside." She led the way to the sofa. "Would you like some iced tea?"

"No, don't go to any trouble. I just had some things to tell you and something to ask too." He seated himself on the sofa and settled Minnie in his lap before patting the cushion beside him.

Jenn swallowed and sat down as far as she could away from the very desirable hunk who was making her feel flustered. She ran her fingers through her disheveled hair.

"First, I wanted to let you know that I did take the ledger to Breck Ryan. He's going to look it over more thoroughly, but he did skim through and said the business was in good shape, at least financially."

"Oh, that's a good thing." Jenn clasped her hands together, delighted with the good news.

"Yes, it is. Breck and I talked about the two people who want to buy the place. He said that woman we met at the airstrip, Maggie Swearingen...well, she is rich as anything and has some kind of company in Dallas but keeps her small planes in a hangar on our property."

"And then there's Mr. Pell. He's interested, as well," she offered. "Breck said Pell could afford it too."

She thought about the man who had crooned a children's song to Lissy. "That's good to know."

"But Breck said he could arrange for a commercial Realtor to evaluate the property and that would bring more possible buyers to the table." Cade ended his speech and sat gazing at her expectantly.

"Um, all that sounds great, Cade. Pardon me if I'm still a little confused. Just too much happening. I haven't fully grasped it all yet."

"No hurry," he said. "Let's see what Breck has to say after he has a chance to take a more thorough look over the books."

She nodded, fidgeting with her hands, clasping and unclasping them. "Thanks. I appreciate you going to all this trouble to follow-up on our little visit to the airstrip." She paused. "I'm glad we have time to make an informed decision about the property. I would hate to jump to a hasty conclusion and live to regret it."

Cade shrugged. "We'll just figure it out at our own pace. Don't you worry your pretty little head about it."

Jenn couldn't keep from emitting a groan. It was such a trite thing to say, like something your grandpa might utter...but somehow she was both flattered and ashamed.

"What's the matter, Jennifer?" Cade leaned closer, allowing his clean man smell to invade her senses. "Did I say something wrong?"

"Nooo," she moaned. "I just look so awful today. I was embarrassed already that you caught me looking this bad. I almost didn't open the door to you." Her lower lip quivered, and she caught it in her teeth. "But I certainly don't deserve any kind of compliment, no matter how well meant."

He stammered something unintelligible and reached out to her. "I—I'm sorry. I think you look pretty all the time...really. You don't have to be dressed up to look good to me." He laid one of his big hands on her shoulder.

"Ooh, that is so sweet." Her voice had taken on a whiny, nasal quality. She bit the inside of her lip to keep from breaking down in a puddle of tears.

"Please don't cry," he said, scooting even closer. "I couldn't take it if you cried."

She shook her head rapidly. "Not gonna cry. Why would I cry?"

"That's my girl." He brushed her hair off her forehead and planted a kiss against it.

My girl? What does that mean?

"Just let me ask you what I wanted to ask you."

His face was so close to hers, she felt his breath on her cheek. "Okay," she whispered. "Ask."

"Um, will you go with me to my uncle's ranch this weekend for a barbecue?" He said it fast, as though he had memorized it.

"Sounds great, but I don't have anyone to sit with the kids."

He grinned. "That's the good news. The kids are invited. Big Jim is all about family, and he's related to Lissy and Leo too."

She let out a deep breath. "That sounds nice. I want the children to know family…to be a part of a real family."

"They are," he said. "We are. You and me…we're part of a family."

This struck her as funny and she began to laugh—laughed so much she couldn't catch her breath.

Cade drew back. He looked worried. "Jennifer? Are you all right?"

She wiped her eyes. "Sorry, it just hit me as hilarious…you and me as family."

He frowned. "But…"

"If we're family, what were those kisses about? Those were not the kisses you give to a relative."

Cade sighed. "You're right. I kissed you the way I would kiss a beautiful, desirable woman…not a relative." He slipped his arms around her and drew her closer before laying a kiss on her that made her glad they weren't related.

Jenn and Cade stayed on the sofa, a tangle of arms, sometimes with lips involved and sometimes just lying together, talking softly and listening to each other breathe. They stayed this way until Leo came in from the bedroom.

Leo's eyes were half-closed, and he was weaving as he walked across to the sofa. Without preamble, he climbed onto the sofa and onto Jenn and Cade, who scrambled to gather him in their arms. Cade and Jenn looked at each other, and Jenn released Leo to Cade.

"I'll go check on Lissy. She's probably about to wake up, and she'll need to be changed." She got up and went to follow through on her intentions.

When she returned she had a clean and fresh young girl in her arms. She found Cade stretched out on the floor with Leo sound asleep on top of him.

"I don't think this little one got enough nap."

Yes, her heart melted a little.

<hr />

Big Jim was excited.

Leah, the wife of his middle son, Tyler, was helping with his effort to entertain, while Misty, wife of his oldest son, Colton, was tending to the children.

His youngest son, Beau, his wife, Dixie, and their daughter would be over later. Dixie had called to see what she could bring and promised to make a dessert.

Big Jim hoped she was picking up a dessert from the Tasty Pastry, the local bakery, since Dixie was not known for her talents in the kitchen. She had many other talents, managing to run the local feed store she'd inherited from her father. Most of all, his son Beau was extremely happy, loving his role as husband and father.

With all three of his sons happily married, Big Jim considered that, as a grandpa, his job was to spoil all the kids and make sure there were plenty of opportunities for the brood to get together.

This usually occurred on Sundays, when they all showed up at the same church and sat together in the pew they had commandeered years ago. They usually managed to get together after church, either when Big Jim treated the whole brood to a meal at one of the nearby restaurants or a home-cooked meal at his ranch house.

Frequently, the entire Garrett clan gathered together over food. And food was Big Jim's arena. He was a big man with a big man's appetite. A big man who had raised three other big men, feeding their voracious appetites as well as his own.

Feeding his family was a part of the job. As patriarch of the family, he was bound to nurture them. Even the preparation was a family event.

Big Jim looked around the kitchen, a smile on his face and in his heart.

Leah and Misty had prepped side dishes. Leah's grandmother had made two of her famous pecan pies. Even Gracie and Mark had washed and chopped vegetables for a salad. Big Jim was rubbing his special blend of spices into the racks of ribs.

"Did you say that Cade was coming to dinner?" Leah asked.

"Sure is," Big Jim responded. "And he's bringing guests."

Misty clapped her hands. "The children?"

Big Jim nodded. "He's bringing Leo and Lissy...and another guest."

Leah and Misty both paused what they were doing to gaze at him expectantly.

He teased them by ignoring their expressions as he concentrated on seasoning the meat.

"Dad! C'mon. Who is Cade bringing to the barbecue?" It was Misty who demanded an answer. "He told me he was bringing three guests."

He looked up, assuming as innocent an expression as he could muster. "Cade? He's bringing Jennifer LaChance. What do you think about that?"

"Woohoo!" Leah hooted. "That's great. She's gorgeous."

"And she's really nice too. I think they'll make a great couple," Misty said.

"Who said they were a couple?" Big Jim asked. "Maybe he just felt sorry for her and thought she needed a meal. She is on the skinny side, you know."

"Big Jim! She's perfect." Leah stuck her fists on her hips. "I would kill to look like Jennifer. I gained so much baby weight with J.T., and it's not coming off fast."

Misty made a scoffing noise. "You look great. You just had the baby in December, and you're nursing, so you're all boob city." She blushed and glanced at Big Jim. "Sorry," she murmured.

Leah just laughed.

"I think you look very nice, Leah," Big Jim said. "My sons have very good taste in brides." He gave a wink. "Which means, of course, contributing my excellent gene pool will result in incredibly gorgeous babies."

Leah and Misty both laughed.

"Well, J.T. sure is a beautiful boy. I can't wait until Colt decides we're ready to have a baby of our own." Misty's face morphed into an exaggerated pout.

"Me too," Big Jim said. "What's the holdup?" He turned on the tap in the sink with his forearm and washed the spice rub off his hands.

"You know Colt. He wants everything to be perfect." Misty shrugged. "The house is coming along, so we should be able to get settled in a few months."

Big Jim slid the tray of seasoned meat back into the refrigerator to continue chilling. "It's going to be mighty lonely around this big ole place when you two and Mark move out."

"I'm pretty sure you'll be glad to get rid of us," she said. "But Mark is going to miss you a lot. He loves to get up early to make a trip to the stables with you, Big Jim. He idolizes you."

Big Jim had to take a quick breath to keep from blurting out how much he loved Misty's young brother. Mark had been through such a hard time. He'd lost his father and his older brother but had settled in at the Garrett ranch. The boy was faithful to his chore list but especially enjoyed caring for the horses, which was also Big Jim's favorite. He and Mark had spent a lot of time together over the past year.

Big Jim swallowed hard. "I sure will miss that rascal. He's a special young man."

Misty gazed at him. Her expression told him she knew exactly how he felt.

"Let's get this shindig goin'. I'm gonna go out and get the fire started." He grabbed a longneck from the fridge and flipped the cap into the trash.

He couldn't handle all this female emotion. He needed to get outside and do man things. *Start a fire. That's manly.* "Hey, Mark!" he called. "C'mon out back and help me with the fire."

There was a whoop, and Mark came running into the kitchen to hit the door right behind Big Jim.

Chapter 17

"Okay, Leo. Try to stay clean while I change your sister." Jenn gave Leo a long look, the look that says *I mean business*, and took Lissy to be cleaned up.

When she returned to the living room, Leo had indeed stayed clean. He was sitting on the sofa with his hands clasped. Minnie was lying beside him, showing her stomach in hopes of a belly rub.

"You are such a good boy, Leo. Thanks for being my helper." She sat down with Minnie between them, Lissy on her lap. She had placed a bib around Lissy's neck in hopes of catching some of the constant drool.

Jenn felt flutters of anxiety swirling around in her gut. She was going to mix and mingle with Cade's relatives. *The Garretts.*

They were a powerful local family. Lots of land. Lots of cattle. Lots of Garretts…but Cade was a Garrett, and he was so sweet… so kind…so damned hot.

In a few minutes, she heard the doorbell chime. The flutter turned into a whirlwind. She squashed down her nerves and gave the children a big smile.

"It's Uncle Cade! Are you ready to go?"

Both children nodded vigorously.

She went to open the door, holding Lissy in her arms, with Leo and Minnie on her heels. Throwing the door open, she figured Cade might be overwhelmed by their greeting, but no, he just stood grinning at her with his genuine pleasure shining through.

He caught Leo, who had thrown himself at Cade. Minnie circled around his boots, barking her cute little yips. And Lissy leaned toward him, reaching with her drool-covered fingers.

"Well, I'm glad to see you too." He shifted Leo to one arm and leaned close to take Lissy from Jenn. "I'll just get these two little ones in their car seats." He started to leave, but Minnie wanted to follow.

"Oh no! Minnie wants to go." Jenn leaned down and called the dog. "Come here, Minnie."

"Not a problem," Cade said. "Big Jim has lots of pets. Why don't you bring her?"

Jenn straightened. "Seriously?"

"Sure. Bring her along. It's a family thing." Cade turned toward his truck, a child in each arm.

Jenn thought her chest might burst wide open. She pressed her lips together as she grabbed Minnie and went into the house. She tucked her small handbag under her arm, donned her sunglasses, grabbed Minnie's leash, and locked up the house. By the time she made her way to the truck, Cade had secured the children in the back seat and stood beside the open passenger door.

"You sure do look pretty today," he said.

For some reason this simple compliment pleased her immensely. She felt her cheeks warm. "Thanks," she whispered. "Oh my!" She kept forgetting how high his truck was and how slim her skirt was. Maybe she could go back to Dallas to pick up some casual clothes... or she could just keep recycling the same three outfits.

"Here ya go." Cade scooped her up and lifted her onto the seat. She grinned, feeling breathless, although she had not exerted herself. Minnie settled in her lap.

"Seat belt," he reminded her before closing her door and rounding the truck. By the time he had climbed into the driver's seat and started the ignition, she was buckled up and ready to go.

"I think you're going to have a good time at my uncle Jim's

house. He's a great guy." He pulled out into the street. "I grew up with his three sons and a couple of other cousins."

"That sounds lovely," she said.

"We were wild boys growing up in the country. We all had chores, but when we got together, it was just so much fun."

"Are you still a wild boy?" She realized she was flirting, and this surprised her, since she hadn't felt this way since her early college years when her male classmates had swarmed around her like bees to a flower—*and look at how that turned out.*

He glanced at her with approval. "Not anymore." He shifted gears and made a turn onto the highway. "I'm a wild man."

When the doorbell rang, Misty's twelve-year-old brother, Mark, ran to throw the door open wide. "Oh wow! It's Cade," he yelled. "And he's got some people with him."

"Well, let them come on back," Big Jim shouted.

Almost immediately, Mark ushered Cade, who appeared to be ushering Jennifer LaChance. He carried his little niece, while Jennifer led the young nephew by the hand. There was a small, fluffy dog in her other arm.

Big Jim wiped his hands and stepped from behind the counter. "Good to see you, boy!" He reached to give Cade half of a man hug, keeping the space between them somewhat open so as not to squash the young girl. He tickled her on the tummy and she giggled, rewarding him with her wet fingers on his hand.

Big Jim turned to Jennifer. "Welcome to the Garrett casa, Jennifer. Please make yourself at home." He stopped short of hugging her, not because he didn't want to, but because she looked a little frightened.

He placed his hand in front of the dog's nose, letting it get to know him and not taking a chance on getting bitten by the little fluff ball. The dog's tail wagged, so he gave it a few strokes. *Cute little booger.*

He gestured to the people gathered in the large room, which consisted of the kitchen with a so-called "breakfast bar" separating it from the dining room and den beyond. "You know everyone?" he asked.

A weak smile flashed on her lips. "Um, not everyone." She looked around uncertainly.

Misty, kindhearted person that she was, got up from the table and came to greet Jennifer. "Hey, Jennifer. Why don't you come over and hang out with the girls? We've paid our dues, and now the menfolk are cookin' up the meat."

Leah waved her hand. "So we're just chillin' and spreadin' gossip."

Jennifer looked a bit confused. She gazed up at Cade.

Big Jim thought he could see real affection between the two of them.

Cade's expression told the whole story. "You get to know these ladies, and I'll help my uncle wrangle the meat." He reached to take the dog from Jennifer's arms. "I'll make sure she gets to play."

"Here," Misty said. "Let me take Lissy."

"Unhand that baby," Big Jim said. "I get dibs on getting to know these two little critters." He took Lissy from Cade and nodded to Leo. "C'mon, boy. Let's get the meat on the grill."

Jennifer looked alarmed and took a step forward, but Misty put a hand on her shoulder.

"Don't worry. Big Jim is magic with kids," Leah said. "He's like a big kid himself."

"C'mon, Cade. Tear yourself away from the beautiful young lady. We got meat to burn." Big Jim cocked his head at his nephew.

Cade grinned at Jennifer. "I'll be out back if you need anything."

Big Jim turned back to face them. "You ladies mind my corn-bread. I set the timer, but you might want to look in on it in a bit."

Cade leaned close to her ear. "I'll be back shortly." And he followed his uncle out the back door, the dog tucked under his arm.

Jenn stared at his retreating form. She felt abandoned but sucked in a deep breath and turned to the women sitting around the table.

"You might wanna peek in that there refrigerator," a small woman said. "There's cold drinks an' a big jug o' sweet tea."

The little woman had been with Leah and Tyler when Cade first brought some of his family to meet Jenn. She recalled that the woman was Leah's grandmother.

Misty smiled and led Jenn to the large double-door fridge. "Here, I'll help you. Would you like a soda or tea?"

"Tea is fine."

Misty took a tall glass and filled it with ice from the door before filling it with sweet tea from the jug with a spigot at the base. "Here you are." She handed the tall glass to Jenn, then motioned her to the table.

"Join us," Leah said.

Jenn knew she wasn't exactly the "girls club" kind of woman. Yet these women appeared to be harmless—friendly, in fact.

She had thought that her role at this family shindig would be to mind the kids, but the children were being doted upon by Cade and his uncle, Big Jim Garrett himself. How cool was that?

So Jenn took a seat at the table next to the little old lady, with Leah on the end, crocheting something. She had a baby monitor on the table and a cup of tea that must have become tepid by now.

"Jennifer, do you remember my grandmother, Fern Davis? She was with us when we all came to your house and brought food. She has a ranch on the other side of Langston, but she lives with us now." Leah gave the woman a loving smile. "She helps me so much with the baby. Don't know what we'd do without her."

"Of course I remember." Jenn smiled at both women. "It's good to see you again."

The little lady smiled, her face crinkling up in a thousand tiny lines. "I'm mighty pleased to see yew too, young lady." She offered her small and bony hand.

Jenn took it, surprised at the strength that little hand conveyed. "I hope you're doing well." She noted that Fern Davis also had a small crochet hook and some lacy sort of project that she was working on. "That looks complicated."

"Aw, I been makin' doilies since I wuz a li'l girl."

Misty sank onto the chair across from Jenn. "Leah is teaching me to crochet. I've just learned a couple of stitches, but I'm making baby blankets for a project at church." She held up a pale-blue square. "Thankfully, they don't demand perfection."

"That looks nice," Jenn said. "What is this project?"

Misty brushed her long, dark hair back, off her shoulder. "The blankets go to the hospitals in Amarillo and Wichita Falls. To the neonatal ICUs."

Fern chuckled. "I'm jus' makin' somethin' purty." She held up the lacy circle. "In my day, ladies had doilies on their furniture, not fer any particular reason…just to look purty."

"Very pretty indeed," Jenn said.

Misty looked around in a conspiratorial manner. "We call this our stitch-and-bitch session."

Jenn had to laugh at that. "Well, I have no such skills."

"That's what I said a few months ago, but when Leah was pregnant, she taught me the basics." She took another look at the project she was working on. "But it's kind of satisfying. I like to crochet at the end of the day, when it's just me and my honey."

"I see," Jenn said, though she didn't. "Which one are you married to?"

"Colton, the oldest. He…Colt is the best man on the planet." Misty's statement ended with a wide grin accompanied by a blush.

"Well, he couldn't be any more wonderful than my Tyler." Leah leaned closer to Jenn and whispered, "Ty is the middle brother. He's the wild man of the Garrett clan."

"Aw, Tyler is the sweetest an' the bravest fellah," Gran said. "He done saved my Leah and my li'l Gracie from some awful bad men."

Jenn sipped some sweet tea to keep from commenting. "Tasty."

A buzzer sounded and Misty tossed her yarn project on the table. She jumped up and went to the kitchen area. She turned off the timer and reached for a pair of oven mitts. "It's ready."

A delicious aroma permeated the kitchen. Jenn took a deep breath and emitted an involuntary groan. "That smells great. What is it?"

Misty placed a large, black cast-iron skillet on a trivet on the breakfast bar. The sound of metal on metal revealed that the skillet was heavy. Misty leaned over the pan and inhaled. "Heaven."

"Yummy," Leah said. "That is Big Jim's own version of Texas cornbread. He mixes it up himself."

Jenn's stomach twisted with a hunger pang. She hadn't been particularly hungry until that moment, but now she was salivating for a taste of that cornbread.

Misty had taken a stick of butter out of the refrigerator and was spreading a pat over the top of the cornbread.

Obviously, this woman had never heard the word *diet* before. But still...

Cade was delighted that Big Jim was so taken with the children. Indeed, the backyard seemed to be filled with happy, frolicking offspring. He knew the players. The blond girl, Gracie, was Leah's daughter, who had been adopted by Tyler. And the boy, Mark, was Misty's younger brother.

The sight of a little girl with red curls running wildly with the other children made Cade laugh. This child was like a replica of Dixie, his cousin Beau's unbridled childhood playmate, the woman he had ultimately married.

Tyler was manning the grill, with Colt supervising, while Big Jim and Cade kept an eye on the little ones.

Big Jim held Lissy in one arm and clasped a longneck in the other. She held the collar of Big Jim's Western shirt firmly in one chubby fist, with two fingers of her other hand in her mouth. She chewed those two fingers furiously, which caused copious amounts of drool to run down her chin.

Leo, on the other hand, appeared to be confused. He seemed to want to join the older children but stayed close to Cade. He kept his hand on Minnie, who seemed to offer him some comfort and confidence.

"Gracie," Big Jim called.

The girl immediately ran over to see what he wanted.

Big Jim asked her to take Leo to play with the others and to watch over him.

Cade had a moment of fear as he watched the girl lead Leo to the other kids. Leo looked so small, but he seemed to be trusting, walking hand in hand with Gracie.

The other two children came to meet him. Cade felt almost teary to see them accepting him. This was what family was all about.

"So, tell me, Cade." Big Jim shifted Lissy to his other shoulder. "What are you and Jennifer going to do about the airstrip? Are you keeping it in the family or selling it off?"

Cade shook his head. "We don't know yet, Uncle Jim. We're talking about it...and Breckenridge Ryan is looking into things. We trust his advice." He set Minnie down and she immediately settled at his feet but kept watching the children at play.

"Hmph!" Big Jim made a derisive sound in the back of his throat. "I don't suppose Ryan knows much more about the airstrip business than you do."

Cade shrugged. "At least he knows more about business in general than we do. I own a ranch. I know about land management and animal husbandry, but that's about the limit of my knowledge." He spread his hands, feeling helpless. "And Jennifer has been a student. She's got degrees out her ears, but no business experience. We're trusting that Mr. Ryan will research the possibilities and give us some options."

Big Jim appeared to be skeptical. "Well, good luck with that." He jiggled Lissy a bit.

"That's what we need."

Tyler lifted his longneck bottle in a salute, and Colt lifted the lid on the grill. Smoke roiled up to surround them both in an aromatic cloud, the scent every Garrett man recognized as the sacred rite of the barbecue grill. A manly pastime, and one that literally put food on the table for his loved ones. It was a genetically inbred part of being a Garrett man.

Cade felt a strong kinship with the other Garrett men. His cousins were like brothers to him.

"So you're thinking about selling the airstrip." Big Jim fixed him with a raised brow.

"We're considering all possibilities," Cade said. "Uncle Jim, we just don't know what we're going to do. We don't have enough information to make a good decision." Cade realized his uncle had some sort of opinion on the matter.

"We Garretts don't own any aircraft," Big Jim said. "But a lot of people around here do, and they need the airstrip to stay open. There are two different crop dusters who rent hangar space and keep all their chemicals stored there."

"What makes you think the new owners wouldn't keep the place open? It's a business after all." Cade couldn't follow his uncle's thought process.

"I dunno. I just got a bad feelin' about this. Something's not right."

Cade felt a tightness in his chest. "You're damned right something's not right. My sister and her husband were murdered, and apparently the sheriff has no idea who did it."

Big Jim placed his large hand on Cade's shoulder and gave it a squeeze. "That's what we all want to know, son."

Chapter 18

THE MEAL WAS WONDERFUL. JENN WAS STUFFED, BUT SHE KEPT eating because each item she placed in her mouth was incredibly delicious. The meat was tender and flavorful, the side dishes remarkably tasty, but it was the cornbread that she kept nibbling.

Beau Garrett had arrived late with Dixie, his redheaded wife. They had dropped their daughter, Ava, off earlier. They brought a pineapple upside-down cake in a long rectangular glass baking dish.

Jenn hadn't intended to partake, but when a big square of cake was placed before her, she automatically picked up a fork. "Oh, this is insane! I thought I couldn't eat another bite, but this is too good."

Dixie grinned. "Thanks. It's from a mix." She shrugged. "I'm not very good in the kitchen."

There was a general groan of denial around the table.

"You're doing great, Dixie," Leah said.

Beau leaned over to give her a kiss on the temple and whisper something in her ear. It must have been pleasant because Dixie's grin widened.

"Your daughter is beautiful." Jenn surprised herself by speaking up.

"Thank you, Jennifer. We're pretty fond of her."

Big Jim spoke up. "Me too. I'm quite fond of all the Garrett kids."

"We Garretts do good work," Tyler said. He was holding the baby son he and Leah had produced just a few months previously.

Leah gave him a smirk. "Seems to me I contributed half the genes, Mr. Garrett."

Ty laughed, but Big Jim set the record straight. "Leah brought the good-lookin' genes."

"It's the eyes, Dad," Ty said. "J.T. got the Garrett eyes."

"Course he did. It's our dominant gene. You marry a Garrett, you get blue-eyed kids." Big Jim waved a hand. "It's part o' the deal."

Jenn brushed her fingers over Lissy's cheek. "Not a bad deal at all."

Cade beamed at her, and so did Big Jim.

"Say, young lady, are you and Cade planning on keeping the airstrip, or are you gonna sell it to some stranger?"

Jenn felt as though the air was being crushed from her lungs. She looked to Cade for support.

"I told you, Uncle Jim," he said. "We're working with Breckenridge Ryan. He's looking up some information, since neither of us has any experience running a business like this."

Big Jim's bushy brows lifted. "I believe I was addressing the young lady."

"Oh, well…my answer is the same as Cade's," she stammered. "I certainly don't know a thing about managing an airstrip. We would probably go broke in a month."

"So, what is it you think Breck Ryan is going to be able to do for you?" Big Jim asked.

"Um, well…there are two entities interested in the property already," she said. "Breck said that a commercial real estate agent might be able to bring more interested parties to the table."

Big Jim was still frowning, but at least he appeared to be considering her words. "Who are these interested entities you have now?"

She shrugged. "I really don't know these people." She looked at Cade again.

"It's a Mr. Pell and a Ms. Swearingen."

Big Jim stroked his chin and stared up at the ceiling. "Hmm…I don't know any Swearingens, but the name Pell is vaguely familiar."

Leah's grandmother spoke up. "Aw, I know Edgar Wayne Pell. Known him since he was a little bitty boy."

Somehow those words gave Jenn a little confidence. "He–he seemed nice when we were talking."

Fern Davis flapped her hand. "Edgar Wayne has been through a lot, but I'm right certain he's still a good man."

"Good to know." Jenn filed that little tidbit away for future reference. Pell scored high on the little-old-lady scale.

When they adjourned from the table to the den, Tyler entertained them by playing his guitar and singing some of the songs he had recorded. He was quite good, and Jenn came to understand he was somewhat famous.

When they got ready to leave, Jenn thanked everyone for their hospitality.

"Cade, you be sure to bring Jennifer and the children back to see us." Leah gave both of them a hug and planted a kiss on both children's cheeks. She reached out to take the baby from her husband who had fastened him in a carrying apparatus.

"Yeah, don't be a stranger." Ty clapped Cade on the shoulder. He put an arm around Leah and Gracie and ushered them out to a waiting vehicle. He assisted Leah up into his truck and secured Gracie and the baby in the back seat.

Big Jim assisted Fern Davis into the back seat and helped her fasten the seat belt.

They all waved as Ty backed out of the drive.

"Thanks again, Big Jim," Jenn said. "This was really wonderful."

"You, young lady, are always welcome in my home." Big Jim beamed at her.

When Cade had loaded the children into his truck, he held the door open for her and swept her up in his arms and deposited her on the passenger side. For some reason, this action always sent a thrill roiling deep in her belly. She swallowed and tried to compose herself while Cade took his place behind the wheel. He gave his uncle a wave and pulled away, eventually stopping in front of the LaChance house.

Lights were on inside, giving the house a warm, welcoming appearance. When Cade helped Jenn down, she slipped her arms around his neck. "Thanks for everything. This was a really wonderful way to spend the day. I—I felt like I was a part of something."

His gaze was riveting. "That's called family."

She lifted her chin, and he took the hint, pressing a warm kiss against her lips. Then the kiss deepened, setting fire to her senses. "Cade," she whispered, her voice ragged. "Help me get the kids inside and into bed."

"Sure." He gave her another kiss and started to unfasten Lissy, while Jenn went to unlock the house.

She left the door wide-open and hurried to open the door to the kids room, quickly turning down Leo's bed and lowering the rail on Lissy's crib.

Cade brought Lissy first, laying her gently on the crib surface.

Jenn loosened her clothing and arranged her comfortably, smiling when Lissy emitted a big sigh and curled up.

Cade brought Leo next. The tot's face was pressed to Cade's shoulder, and he was drooling a little. He was able to slide Leo into bed, remove his shoes, and pull the cover over him. "They look so sweet."

She drew him by the arm out the door and closed it gently.

Cade gazed down into her eyes and slipped his arms around her. "I'm glad you came with me. It meant a lot to me to have you get to know the Garrett family."

She placed her hands on his chest, appreciating the hard muscles, warm under her touch. "I loved it. Spending time with your family was great. I really liked everyone."

"I hope we can be all be friends and hang out, you know?"

"Mmm…that sounds nice." She gazed up at him, wanting more kisses…wanting more.

"I…uh… It's late. I guess I better go."

Jenn thought he didn't realize how much she wanted him. She swallowed hard. *Here goes nothing.* "Cade, you don't have to leave."

He hesitated a second and then realization showed on his face. "Oh, well, sure."

Cade felt as though he'd been punched in the gut. Did she mean what he thought she meant? She was gazing up at him with her lips parted, inviting his kisses.

Cade couldn't deny his urges any longer. "Um...where...?"

"I was thinking we would be more comfortable in my bedroom." She turned and took a couple of steps toward the back of the house, then glanced back over her shoulder. "Coming?" Her voice was low and sexy, sending shock waves to his libido.

"Um, yes." He swallowed. "Right behind you."

She led him to the room that had been used as a guest room and silently twisted the knob. "Let's try and be as quiet as possible. Don't want to wake the children."

"Oh, yeah...the kids."

She turned on a small lamp on the bedside table, giving the space a little light but not too much. "Would you help me with this?" She turned her back, indicating he was to unzip her slim dress.

He fumbled with the tiny zipper tab. His big fingers felt clumsy and incompetent to deal with something as delicate as helping this beautiful woman undress. He did manage to get the long zipper all the way down, and the dress fell to the floor, puddling around her ankles.

She stepped out of the fallen garment, giving a little shake of her foot. Jennifer, clad only in a lacy pale-blue bra with matching panties, was prettier than most of the centerfolds tacked up on the wall of the pool hall. In truth, she was making it hard for Cade to breathe...hard on everything.

Jenn sat on the edge of her bed and slipped out of the stilettos. She looked up at him, taking in his boots, Wranglers, belt, and shirt. "One of us is wearing entirely too much clothing. Would you like me to help you?"

Cade moistened his lips, momentarily frozen. "Oh, no. I got this." In a matter of seconds, he managed to shed his shirt, the snaps popping as he tore it off. He stripped his hand-tooled leather belt with the big metal buckle from his belt loops and unzipped his Wranglers. Then he realized he had to get out of his boots, a task he usually accomplished with the aid of the wooden bootjack stored under the edge of his bed.

He stood in his briefs, with an enormous erection and his pants around his ankles. Heaving a sigh, he sat on the edge of Jennifer's bed and tried to wrestle each of his boots off, but his jeans had slipped down to cover each boot.

"Would you like some help?"

Jenn's soft inquiry did nothing to deflate his erection. He heaved a deep sigh. "Yes, please."

But when she leaned over to grab one of his boots, the mere touch of her warm flesh on his leg was enough to cause his senses to riot. He pulled her onto his lap and kissed her with all the passion raging through him.

In the next moment, her arms were around his neck and he unfastened her bra. It fell away, revealing her pert breasts. She shrugged out of the straps and wriggled away from him, dropping the bra beside the bed.

At first he thought she was rejecting his clumsy attempt to make love to her, but when she stood before him, slipped out of her panties, and climbed onto the bed, he had to act.

Cade managed to get his briefs down and crawl onto the bed, boots and Wranglers still hobbling him.

Jennifer stroked her hand over his chest and scooted closer. "Let's do this."

With no further preliminaries, she drew him down and wrapped her silken thighs around his torso.

She was wet and rubbed herself against his erection, inviting him to enter. Their coupling was fast and hard and delicious. In a very short time, she arched against him, making a soft moaning sound. He tried to match her sensuous rhythm with his thrusts until they both exploded in a blaze of passion.

He held her tight. They were both breathing hard, but Jennifer trilled out a little giggle. "Oh, I needed that."

"Me too," he huffed in her ear.

Cade hardly slept. He was accustomed to being alone. Sleeping alone.

Now, there was a soft bundle of femininity cuddled against his side, her pretty face on his shoulder. He was in no way a prude, but his sexual experiences had been sporadic—high school and college girlfriends for the most part. Moving back to Langston had put a kink in his love life, because all the local girls were looking for husbands. He'd felt like a prize piece of chum in a shark tank. As a Garrett, his name alone gave him stature as a prime candidate for holy matrimony. Then there was his ranch. Yeah, he wasn't deluded enough to think the feeding frenzy among unmarried females was due to his outgoing personality.

Just about any place he happened to visit in the town of Langston, he would be greeted by a female with a particular lyrical quality to her voice. He had become used to tensing up when he heard the words "Why, hello, Cade" drawled out with an almost musical cadence. He would lock eyes with some local lovely who was weighing his worth. Nothing personal. Just the same way he sized up a beef cow for possible addition to his herd. Breeding possibilities were checked out. What characteristics would this heifer or bull bring to the herd?

But his unplanned coupling with Jennifer LaChance had been overwhelming. Her slender body had been a surprise. He had thought her slight stature indicated weakness, but little Miss Jennifer was solid muscle. He had no idea what she did to stay in such good shape, but he was properly impressed. When she'd wrapped her satiny thighs around him, he'd been consumed in a wildfire of pure lust. The first round of lovemaking had been phenomenal and started without preamble. It hadn't lasted long. But the second time…

Jenn awoke slowly, like she was rising to the surface after a deep dive. She just floated up into wakefulness.

Every molecule of her being was hypersensitive, aware of the incredible man holding her. Her skin touching his skin felt as though they had melded together. Her blood was flowing through the thin membrane separating them and connecting with Cade's very hot blood.

He had amazed her with his strength, his ardor, and his technique. Not what she had expected from a loner cowboy.

She could feel him watching her. If she opened her eyes, it would break the spell. He would go all strong and silent on her, and she was enjoying the feel of his soft breath against her skin, his strong arms cradling her, and the sensory experience of their flesh pressed together.

She wondered what time it was, but she would have to open her eyes to check the digital clock.

There was the sound of something smacking against the bedroom door. Cade tensed and then drew away.

Reluctantly, she opened her eyes, realizing that the sound she was hearing was one of the children trying to get in. Thankfully, they had locked the door.

Jenn gazed into Cade's eyes. "Good morning." She smiled.

His face split into a wide grin. "Good morning, beautiful. Last night was…"

"Yes it was," she said. "But our little family is expecting me to make breakfast and, of course, change diapers." Reluctantly, she peeled herself off him but swept her palm across his chest. "You were wonderful." Jenn dropped a quick kiss on his lips just before she rolled to the side of the bed and stood. She wrapped a robe around herself and tied the sash. "Be back soon."

She unlocked the door and slipped out. Leo was standing in the hall, gazing up at her. "Hello, Leo. Are you hungry?"

Leo nodded his little head and turned back to the room he shared with his sister.

Jenn recognized the need to have a change of underwear. Thankfully, his were disposable. He had obviously sucked down too much liquid the night before and hadn't been able to hold it. It didn't take long for her to change Leo and then she awoke the sleeping Lissy, giving her a similar treatment. She led the two youngsters to the kitchen, where she got them seated in their appropriate chairs, and when she turned back, she found that Cade had recovered his clothing and was standing in front of the stove.

"What does everyone want for breakfast?" He winked at Jenn. "I'm pretty good in the kitchen."

Jenn giggled. "Really? We'll have to try that out sometime." She was delighted when he blushed. *Good. Not an overconfident Romeo. A man who did good work. A man who—*

"Eggs? Bacon? What can I fix for you?" He gazed at her earnestly.

His expression caused a squeezing sensation in her chest. "That would be wonderful. I was thinking I would make oatmeal in the microwave."

He just grinned and opened the fridge. "This is not an oatmeal day." He took eggs and bacon out of the fridge and set them on the counter. "What are you hungry for, Leo?"

Leo sat up straight. "I want ice cweam."

Cade looked perplexed. "Um, no. I meant what do you want for breakfast?"

Leo cocked his head to one side. "Ice cweam."

Jenn chuckled. "Uncle Cade means would you like your eggs scrambled or over easy?"

Leo sank back against the seat, appearing to be crestfallen.

"How about scrambled all around?" Jenn asked.

Cade saluted her with the spatula and began laying strips of bacon in the pan.

Something about a man in the kitchen was very endearing. A hot, sexy man in the kitchen? *Oh my!*

In no time at all, Cade had served up a plate piled high with crispy bacon and another with a pile of fluffy scrambled eggs. He set about making toast while Jenn poured milk into sippy cups.

"Good job, Mr. Garrett," she whispered in passing. The expression on his face told her exactly how he was feeling.

Suddenly, she realized she was completely and comfortably in love with the man. Not a roller-coaster thrill ride, but good and solid love that she hoped would be there for a while. She sat down at the table and viewed the tall, broad-shouldered cowboy contentedly buttering toast for her and the children. *Like a real family.*

She swallowed hard. *Are we a family?* That thought hit her like a slap in the face. Somehow, just acting as surrogate mother to these two adorable children had changed her—changed her goals and dreams…changed her life.

Grinning broadly, Cade set a plate in front of her. He was obviously proud of his accomplishments.

Leo reached for a spoon and Lissy reached with her fingers.

"Oh, hot!" Jenn said. "Wait just a minute for your eggs to cool a little." She moved the bowl out of Lissy's reach and gave a warning glare to Leo.

Leo looked disappointed, blowing out a deep sigh.

"Sorry," Cade said. "I didn't know."

"No problem. I usually dish up their food at the counter, and by the time I set it in front of them, it's cooled a little." She flashed a warm smile to soften the rebuff. "It smells wonderful."

Cade scraped the rest of the eggs onto his own plate and slid the skillet into the sink. His demeanor didn't seem to be as upbeat as it had before her intervention over the hot food.

After breakfast, Jenn cleared the table while Cade spent a little extra time with Leo. She knew her brother would want his son to have a good role model, and if Jason couldn't be there for Leo, she was sure glad Cade was standing in.

Cade hung around for most of the morning, but he left to take care of tasks on his ranch. He recovered his good humor quickly after spending time with the children.

Jenn saw him to the door, lingering for a few moments until he took the hint and cupped her face in both hands, delivering a discreet kiss that nevertheless caused her toes to curl.

"Bye," she sighed.

He gave her a one-sided grin and loped down the steps to climb into his truck.

Okay, now he's gone. And I want him to come back…now.

Chapter 19

"Now this is my special spot." Big Jim lowered his voice, speaking in a conspiratorial manner. "It's my secret place." He put his finger to his lips, although he and the boy were the only ones within two miles.

Mark's eyes were shining, and he bore a wide grin. "Don't worry, Big Jim. I won't tell anybody."

Big Jim nodded. "Good, because this is our spot now. Yours and mine." He handed Mark a fishing pole and settled the can of worms between them. "Do you want me to bait your hook?"

"If you can just show me, sir, I'll try to do it right."

Big Jim's heart squeezed. He had learned that this wonderful young man had never been fishing. Not with his deceased father, and not with his deceased brother. This had ticked Big Jim off considerably, since he had done everything within his power to make sure his three sons had plenty of father-and-son time, sometimes as a group and sometimes one-on-one. He was proud that his boys had grown up to be fine men, and he was determined to make it up to Mark for the shortsightedness of his male relatives. "Looky here, boy," he said. "You hold the hook this way. Don't want to get your fingers stuck on the barbs."

Mark inspected Big Jim's demonstration carefully.

"And then you reach in and get a worm with your other hand… and you slide him on the hook this-a-way."

"I see," Mark said. "I think I can do it now."

Big Jim made encouraging sounds as Mark baited his hook. "Well, look at you. That was a first rate job, son. Let's get our hooks in the water and see if we can pull some fish outta this here creek."

They cast their lines in the gently rippling water and settled comfortably against the trunk of an old oak that had spread its branches like an umbrella, sheltering those below.

"How you doin' in school, Mark? I know your grades are pretty good, but how is everything else goin'?"

Mark shrugged. "Okay, I guess." He kept his gaze on the water, his dark lashes hiding his eyes.

Big Jim sensed Mark was keeping his schoolhouse problems to himself. His own sons had never had to deal with bullies. They were big. They were tough. They had each other. And they were Garretts.

But Mark Dalton was the son of a rancher who drank his property away, and then died while it was being foreclosed on. Mark's older brother had fallen in with some bad company and been murdered. Lots of things for this amazing young lad to be sensitive about. Fuel for bullies.

When Big Jim's oldest son, Colt, had married Misty Dalton, Mark's big sister, he brought Mark along with him. Now Mark was a part of the Garrett clan.

Big Jim considered Mark part of the family and treated him as though he was. But Mark was also the last male Dalton left to carry on the name. Big Jim wondered how Mark felt about that status. Was it a badge of honor to be the namesake, or was it a painful burden?

"Beautiful day, ain't it, son?"

"Um, yes, sir. It is."

Big Jim decided to try a different tactic, changing the subject to something he knew Mark was passionate about: horses.

"You think that new foal Magic Lady dropped will amount to anything?"

Mark turned to him, eyes alight with enthusiasm. "He's a beauty, ain't he?"

"You think?" Big Jim eased back on one elbow, leaving his fishing rod propped against his knee.

"Oh, yeah. He's got the most beautiful blaze on his face, and white stockings. He's gonna be a gorgeous mount."

"So you think he's worthy of the Garrett Ranch name?"

Mark slanted him a questioning gaze. "Sure. He's a beautiful animal."

"I agree. And I think you're right...so I'm giving you the task of coming up with a name for him. Can you do that for me?"

A wide grin spread across Mark's face. "Me? I get to name him?"

Big Jim nodded his silvery head. "You betcha. I can't think of a single person more deserving of the honor. Having you come live on the ranch has been a real pleasure for me. You love horses the way I love horses."

The tips of Mark's ears reddened. He was grinning but perhaps a little embarrassed as well.

Big Jim cleared his throat. "You love horses the way Colton loves horses—the way he did when he was a little bitty boy and the way he did as he was growin' up. Now he loves your sister, Misty, and he loves you, y'know?"

Mark nodded. "I love him too. He's like a big brother." His eyes were cast down now, perhaps remembering his real big brother and how different that relationship had been.

Big Jim had cracked the door open, and now he was weighing the merit of going forward. He cleared his throat again. "You could be his little brother, if you wanted to."

Mark gazed at him, dark eyes filled with questions.

Big Jim struggled to retain a casual tone to his voice. "You know...I could adopt you, and you could become my son and Colt's brother."

Silence.

"But only if you want, of course. No rush. Just think about it and let me know if this is something you might like to happen." Big Jim sat up abruptly. "Oops! I think I got a bite."

—∿∿—

"I just don't feel confident about advising them, Cami." Breckenridge T. Ryan tilted his favorite coffee mug up and drained the last of the liquid.

His wife, Camryn, the local doctor, was headed into Langston, expecting a full day of caring for the locals. But because her husband had a frown on his face and she suspected he needed to use her as a sounding board, she lingered at their home, hoping to provide some of that care to him.

She poured him a second cup of coffee and one for herself. "I can't recall a time when you've claimed to lack confidence." She reached for a packet of sweetener. "Tell me what's got you buffaloed."

Breck blew out a deep breath. "It's the airstrip. The kids who inherited it haven't got a clue."

Cami gave out a little chortle and took a sip of her brew. "And they think you do?"

"They're thinking about selling out, and I told them I would help." Breck raked his fingers through his thick, dark hair.

"Help them sell? Are you crazy? We need that airstrip."

"Well, I know that, but I have to represent the heirs' best interests." He paused. "I honestly don't see either Cade Garrett or Jennifer LaChance having the chops to be able to manage the business or have the knowledge to support the community interests."

Cami's brows drew together. "Breck, we have to have that airstrip open. The medevac helicopter is stationed there. Everyone in the area needs to have this service available in case of an emergency. I'm in that helicopter at least a couple of times a month. There are lives at stake here." She was aware her voice had risen in timbre.

Breck reached over to cover her hand with his own. "I understand how you feel, honey. Maybe the sale will bring about an improvement. Maybe the new owner will be competent and care about the community."

"Hmph!" Cami swirled the coffee remaining in the bottom of her cup. "Maybe that land will go to someone who doesn't give a flip about the residents of Langston. Maybe they just want that huge tract of land."

Breck's steady gaze had a calming effect. "Maybe you're right."

"Oh, Breck. That's a horrible thing to even contemplate."

"I know. I contacted a commercial real estate broker in Dallas, and while he doesn't have the property listed, he's discreetly offering the possibility that it may come on the market. He said he has multiple interested parties immediately."

Cami pushed back from the table and took her cup to the sink. She fought the tightness in her chest by rinsing the cup under the running water. She knew that Breck would value her opinion, but at the moment, she felt like screaming.

Breck brought his cup to the sink, and Cami rinsed it, putting both in the top rack of the dishwasher. He kissed her temple and her jaw tightened.

"I didn't mean to upset you. I just needed your input."

She turned and reached up to embrace him. "I know, and I'm sorry to be so irritable about it, but this community must keep that airport open. It's important for locals to have that medevac chopper ready to go." She gazed up at him earnestly. "It's a matter of life and death."

Breck kissed her and caressed her cheek with his fingers. "You're the strongest person I've ever known. I promise you that I will do my best to research any prospective buyers and try to guide Cade and Jennifer to make a decision that will not be detrimental to the community of Langston."

Cami gave a mock pout. "You better."

—◆—

Cade had driven to his ranch and jumped right into his usual chores. He made sure every living thing on his ranch had feed and water. Then he released his three horses into the corral and set about mucking out the horse stalls. Not one of the most pleasant tasks, but nonetheless, he found himself grinning for no reason.

Well, okay. There was a reason.

The image of Jennifer LaChance as he'd last seen her rose in his mind. As he shoveled horse manure and pushed a broom through the stable, his brain was entertaining the beautiful woman who had invited him to stay over last night.

He didn't know what he had done to deserve such a gorgeous and talented woman, but he wasn't going to question his great good luck.

Cade had remained a bachelor when most of his cohorts were happily married—most with children. Somehow, he had been focused on the ranch and kept his head down for the most part.

Sure, he had slicked up and gone to town to dance at the Eagles Hall when they hosted a country band. He had joined his friends and relatives, sipping a beer and dancing to a few songs, but at the end of the night, he had gone home alone. Well, most of the time. The women he'd bedded had never been more than a momentary fling.

But that was before he'd met Miss Jennifer LaChance.

He had shoveled the manure into a wheelbarrow and now he wheeled it to the mulch pile. A rivulet of sweat rolled down his brow, and he wiped it away on his sleeve. He shoveled the contents of the wheelbarrow onto the pile and worked to turn it under the vegetation and other elements. Good rich mulch.

He removed his hat and gazed up at the beautiful, clear blue sky. "I'm a farmer. I'm a rancher. And I'm in love with Jennifer LaChance."

Jenn spent the day with the children, playing games, reading stories, changing diapers, and thinking about Cade Garrett.

Every time Cade's image had appeared in her mind, she had felt a rush of heat, and an involuntary grin had graced her face.

Damn! Hottest man on the planet.

Well, here she was, living the good life in a small town, sur-rounded by good-hearted people, playing mama to two adorable children, and her heart was going pitty-pat over the long, lean cowboy with the bluest eyes in Texas.

"I am so totally a goner."

Leo looked at her curiously.

"Nothing, sweetie." She placed a kiss on his forehead.

Minnie wagged her tail, looking as though she too deserved a treat. Jenn scruffled the dog's ears.

Funny how life takes a turn.

She had spent years preparing for a professional career, earn-ing a Master of Fine Arts degree and another master's in education. She was extremely qualified to be an art teacher, but she was sure there was one art teacher at the high school and that that person would die with his or her boots on, so to speak. Jenn could wait for years for an art job to open up. Other than that, there were no other employment opportunities in the Langston area that she was quali-fied for. She was pretty sure she would make a really awful waitress.

She knew there was money in the bank that Jason had earned, but it would run out at some point in time, and she would have to find a way to support the children.

Jenn heaved a deep sigh. Of course, there was the airstrip. Jason's passion. The passion that had gotten him murdered. She presumed that a competent person could pick up the reins and make a go of it. Too bad neither she nor Cade were that person.

Still…

She had to wonder what it would take to run the airstrip. In her heart, she thought that Jason would not have wanted his beloved business to pass out of the family. Maybe he would have visualized Leo and Lissy working by his side, maybe eventually taking over.

She heaved a sigh. She knew she was flipping and flopping back and forth about whether the airstrip should be sold or kept in the family.

Jenn's chest felt tight. *My poor brother*.

The doorbell chimed, startling Jenn out of her reverie.

When she opened it, Ollie was on the porch bearing a glass baking dish covered with aluminum foil and a wide smile. "I missed you, girl."

"Oh, Ollie! I've missed you too. There is just so much to do with the children and all." She opened the screen and ushered her friend inside.

"I'm taking a break from the inn. My only boarder is some woman who seems to be more interested in driving around the countryside, checking out property, than sitting down for a good gossip." She shook her head. "I swear, this Dallas lady has more money than brains."

"Come on in the kitchen and let me pour you a cup of coffee to go with whatever is under that tinfoil. I haven't smelled anything that scrumptious in a long time." Jenn led the way to the kitchen with Ollie, Leo, and Minnie trailing behind.

Ollie made herself comfortable at the table and busied herself uncovering the baking dish. She revealed a cakelike creation with peaches. The aroma was divine. "This is my grandmother's recipe for peach kuchen. It's an old German recipe handed down in my family."

Jenn selected plates for the dessert and cups for coffee. As she placed the dishes on the table, she gave Ollie a knife to cut the cake. "That is really a lovely dessert, Ollie."

"I picked these peaches off my very own trees," she said proudly. "They're so sweet."

Leo was trying to climb up in his chair, so Jenn lifted him in and scooted the chair close to the table. Lissy was looking at her high chair too, since she expected that food would be forthcoming. Jenn settled her in her chair, securing her in place with both belt and tray.

Jenn turned around and found that Minnie was standing on her hind legs, looking particularly attentive. "I suppose you want to be seated too?"

Ollie threw her head back and laughed. "I swear, I would never have figured that you would just settle right in here like a little hen on your nest. You look happy, Jennifer. Really happy."

Jenn brought the coffeepot to the table, a slight frown on her face as she considered Ollie's words. "Yes, I really am happy. Happier than I ever thought I could be…unless you serve me up a slice of kuchen." She filled Ollie's cup and one for herself. Then brought milk to the table in two sippy cups.

"Here you go." Ollie pushed a saucer across the table toward Jenn.

"Looks great," Jenn said. "Thanks for sharing this treat with me." She looked at the children. "Do you think maybe we can share a little with the kids?"

"Oh, of course," Ollie said. "How much?"

"Just a spoonful for Lissy and a little more for Leo. We'll see how they like it." Jenn fastened a bib around Lissy and another for Leo, while Ollie placed a dab of the kuchen on each saucer. Lissy did not hesitate to sink her fingers into the goodies in front of her and immediately suck it off.

Leo picked up his spoon and chased the kuchen around his saucer before using his hand to nudge it into the utensil. Both children seemed to be delighted with their treat.

Finally, Jenn picked up her fork and scooped a bite into her mouth. "Yum. This is heaven. It's a peachy, custardy orgasm on a plate."

Ollie appeared to be enormously pleased. "I knew you would love it. I'm known for my cooking."

"Well, this is fabulous."

Ollie leaned forward in a conspiratorial manner. "I've never shared this recipe since it's a family thing, but I don't have any children to pass it on to, so I'll share it with you."

Jenn tried to envision herself baking. Couldn't. "That would be wonderful, Ollie. I'm honored."

Ollie beamed with pleasure. "I wrote it out for you." She pushed a piece of paper across the table to Jennifer.

Chapter 20

AFTER THEIR SNACK, JENN LED OLLIE BACK TO THE LIVING room and they enjoyed a nice long chat. When Ollie left, she seemed to be in a very happy state.

Jenn had re-covered the peach kuchen with the aluminum foil and stored it in the refrigerator, promising to return the glass baking dish when it was empty.

She felt oddly elated that the treat was safely stored in her refrigerator and she might be able to share it with Cade. She carefully folded the recipe and put it in a cookbook in Sara's collection.

Maybe she would learn how to cook. Jenn hummed a little tune, thinking that she might become a great cook, given the chance. Surely she could follow written instructions?

Cade had worked and worked. Then he had saddled one of his horses and taken a ride out to the creek and back. He tried to ride one of his horses each day so they would get exercise and so they would retain their relationship with him.

When he went back to the ranch house, he took a quick shower and toweled off. He wanted to see Jennifer again, but he didn't want to crowd her. She might not be willing to see him two nights in a row. And he didn't want to assume that she would want a repeat performance of their stellar night of lovemaking. He had to take it easy and let her call the shots. *Don't want to spook her.*

He thought he might call her and see how she had spent her day. *Taking care of kids, dumb ass!* He shook his head. What else could he say to her?

He had his phone in hand but couldn't quite come up with any good reason to call her.

He wished they could be together at that moment. And for many days and nights to follow. *Serious courtship.* That was what it would take.

Cade selected Jennifer's number on his phone and waited for her to answer. When he heard her voice, he groped for something to say.

"Hello?"

"Um, uh…I mean…" he stammered.

"Cade, is that you?"

"Uh, yes. It's me." He wanted to smack himself on the head. *She must think I'm a total idiot.*

"I'm so glad you called." She sounded genuinely pleased.

"Oh, well, uh…"

"I was thinking about the airstrip. Do you really think we should sell it?" She paused to heave an audible sigh. "I mean, Jason worked so hard to make it successful, and I hate to just throw away his dreams."

Cade could tell she was really wound up about it. "Well, I never said we should sell." He swallowed hard. "I was just worried that we might not be capable of running the business. I mean, I'm not a businessman. I know about running my ranch, but I grew up learning about ranching every single day."

"I just thought maybe Jason would want his children to inherit his business eventually."

"I'm sure he did, but he didn't know he and my sister were going to die in a plane crash."

"They were murdered, Cade. Don't you ever forget that." Her voice took on a hard edge.

"Um, no. I didn't forget."

She was silent, and Cade had no idea how to change the subject. "Listen, Jennifer. I don't have the answers, but I'm pretty sure Breckenridge Ryan will be able to advise us. He's pretty smart."

"I'm sure he is. I'm just frustrated."

More silence.

"Um, do you like to dance?" He cringed in anticipation of her response.

"Of course," she said. "Doesn't everybody?"

He felt the first hint of a smile twitch the corners of his lips. "Well, I'd like to invite you to go with me to the Eagles Hall on Saturday. We can have dinner first, and then go to dance. The Eagles has some great live bands come through."

"Sure. I love to dance." He could hear the change in her voice. The terse edge was gone and she sounded happy.

"I can get Mrs. Reynolds to babysit for us."

"Great. The kids love her. I'll have to see what I have to wear."

"Just throw on a pair of jeans and your dancing shoes. We'll have a great time." Cade couldn't wait to hold her in his arms. Perhaps she would invite him to stay over again.

"Oh, that is a problem."

"A problem?"

"Um, you see…I don't have anything like that. I left things in my house in Dallas. I thought I would just be here a few days… and…and I was so upset over Jason's death, I just threw things in a suitcase."

Cade chuckled. "You could always go shopping. I thought you ladies liked to go clothes shopping?"

There was a long pause. He thought perhaps the call had been dropped.

"Well…I don't have any income at the moment. I don't want to spend the money in Jason's account on myself. That rightly belongs to the children, so I'm just out of luck."

Cade's face morphed into a frown. He could only admire

Jennifer for refusing to spend the inheritance on herself. "Whatever you wear will be fine. Don't worry about it."

"Aren't we supposed to go meet with Mr. Ryan tomorrow?"

"You're right. Want me to pick you up?"

"That would be nice. Ollie is coming to stay with the children while I'm out."

"Thought she had to stay at the inn to admit new boarders."

"She told me she only has one woman staying there at the moment and she spends her days driving around looking at property."

"That's great. Maybe we can grab lunch somewhere?"

"Lovely. I'll be ready at ten."

Cade disconnected, grinning. He would get to spend time with Jennifer the next day, and she would haunt his dreams tonight.

Jenn was dressed and waiting when Cade pulled up in front of the house. "He's here," she called to Ollie and gave a wave as she stepped outside.

Cade left the motor running but got out to help her up into his way-too-high truck.

She figured she would eventually get the rest of her wardrobe from the house in Dallas and would be able to climb up under her own steam without exposing anything. Of course, he had already seen everything. She stifled a grin as Cade lifted her up. *Oh, those strong arms...*

Cade climbed up and revved the motor. Maybe he was excited to be with her. She knew she was really charged up. *Just keep breathing, girl.*

They chatted about the children, the beautiful day, and in no time at all, he was pulling into a parking spot in front of Breckenridge Ryan's office.

When she slid out of the truck and into Cade's arms, she

wanted to embrace him and never let go…but managed to control her primal urges.

Her feet reached the ground and she found herself gazing up at him. She swallowed hard. "Well, we better go inside."

For his part, Cade was staring at her as though she were the last chocolate doughnut on the plate. He said nothing, but gestured toward the law office.

When they entered, a tiny metal bell clanked against the beveled glass insert in the door, and Misty Garrett looked up and smiled.

"Hi, Jennifer. Hi, Cade." She motioned them to her desk. "Breck is expecting you. I'll let him know you're here." She punched a button and spoke into an intercom.

"Send 'em in here," Breck bellowed.

Cade opened the door to Breck's office for Jenn and followed her inside.

Breck sat behind a big mahogany desk, gesturing to the chairs in front of his desk. "Have a seat, folks."

When they were sitting down, Jenn realized she was quite nervous. She had no idea how to manage or take part in the management of the airstrip, yet she was reluctant to let it go.

"Here's what I've found for you." Breck slid a piece of paper across the desk for them to share. "I contacted a large commercial real estate firm and dealt with the broker. He made some discreet inquiries and thinks he could get you up to this amount for the sale of the airstrip. That's way more than the Swearingen corporation has offered, and of course, the local man, Edgar Wayne Pell, doesn't have that kind of money."

Jenn stared at the paper, her eyes locked on the amount of money the Realtor claimed he could get them for the property. Her mouth felt dry.

"Well, there you go," Cade said. "This amount of money would sure provide for the kids."

Breck leaned back in his chair, propping his boots on the edge of his desk. "That's for sure. In fact, with some wise investment, you could support the next couple of generations."

Jenn blinked. "Could I please have some water?"

Breck dropped his boots to the hardwood floor and leaned forward to punch the intercom. "Misty, do we have some bottled water in the fridge?"

In a few minutes, Misty brought three bottles of water in and handed them out.

"Thanks a lot." Jenn uncapped the water and took a long drink. She couldn't fathom that amount of money. Now she was feeling guilty for her reluctance to let go of the property that Jason had built.

Cade and Breck were staring at her.

"I—I'm just overwhelmed," she said. "That's so much money."

"That's for damned sure." Cade looked dazed. "So, what do you think, Jennifer? We should go ahead and list the property to sell to the highest bidder?"

"Um, well, I guess so, but—"

"Fine," Breck said. "I'll get in touch with the broker on Monday and get the ball rolling. You're making a good decision, for the present and for the future."

Jenn nodded absently. She was being promised huge bucks and wouldn't have to worry about how to support the children...ever.

Breck leaned forward, looking each of them in the eye. "Well, if you're both agreed, I can contact the broker and set up a listing contract for you to sign. I would think the offers will come pouring in quickly."

"Hot dang!" Cade said. "We might as well get it over with, right, Jennifer?"

She nodded, her stomach caught in a tight clench. "Yeah, right." She felt as though she had been dealt a physical blow. As she left Breck's office, she took long, slow breaths. *Let it go. Let it all go.*

Cade, on the other hand, was elated. He couldn't stop grinning.

When they were on the sidewalk, he let out a little whoop of plea-sure. "That's about the best news we could get. The kids will be set for life."

"Um, yeah…for life." She didn't know what was wrong with her. She should be elated. She stepped down off the sidewalk and almost fell. She flailed her arms like a windmill and grabbed for the front of the truck. She had twisted her ankle and broken the heel off her shoe. "Guh-rate! Just what I needed."

Cade stepped down to steady her. "Are you hurt?"

She huffed out a sigh. "Only my pride…"

Cade helped her up into the passenger seat.

She slipped off the remains of her shoe and examined the heel, hanging on one side by a few threads.

Cade climbed into the driver's seat and started the motor. "It's a little early for lunch. I need to stop at Sunny's Western Wear."

"Sure," she said, aware that she sounded grumpy as she cradled her broken shoe in her arms.

He stopped the truck two blocks away and climbed out.

"I'll just wait here," she said as he opened her door.

"Nope. Not gonna happen." He unhooked her seat belt and scooped her out of the truck.

Jenn grabbed Cade's neck, almost decking him with her sti-letto. "No, I could wait for you."

"Nope. I need you inside." He stomped up the steps and into the store.

She glanced around, seeing a store filled with Western shirts, cowboy hats, boots, and a whole wall of jeans. There were racks of hand-tooled leather belts and, of course, boots.

A big cowboy with a belly protruding over his large belt buckle ambled over to help them. "Whut kin ah dew fer yew?"

"She needs everything," Cade said.

"Oh, for goodness' sake. I do not need everything." She frowned at Cade, who completely ignored her protests.

The big guy grinned and turned, gesturing for them to follow. "Start at the top or at the bottom?"

"Bottom," Cade said. "Here. This is her shoe size."

The big guy reached for her stiletto, but she clasped it to her bosom. "No! I wear a size seven."

"She needs socks, boots, blue jeans, a belt, and some tops."

"We got ladies' underwear too," the man said.

"Oh hell no!" Jenn glowered at him, which was largely ineffective as she was being carried to the back of the store.

"Here we go." Cade set her on her feet…well, on one foot and one shoe.

"What are we doing here?" she demanded.

"Jennifer, you need to adapt to your environment. I hope you're gonna stay here forever, but you dress like you're going to a fancy dress ball. This is Langston, Texas. And I'm taking you to the Eagles Hall tomorrow night…and we're gonna dance." His laser-blue eyes penetrated all her defenses.

"I see." She backed off her annoyance, suddenly realizing that Cade was sincerely trying to solve one of her problems. She had nothing to wear.

"So, Freddie here"—he gestured to the big guy—"is gonna help you find a good pair of boots that you like. Make sure they're comfortable because we're gonna dance the soles off your brand-new boots tomorrow night." A flash of dimples softened his words.

Jenn swallowed hard. "Okay," she breathed.

What followed was an onslaught of offerings displayed for her pleasure. Boots in brown and black. Boots with colorful stitching and boots with flowers and butterflies.

At first she thought the boots were clunky and unattractive, but most were very comfortable and looked remarkably good on her long, slim legs, even with a dress. In the end, she settled on basic black with a squared-off toe.

Cade then insisted she try on jeans and tops.

She had to admit she was having fun with this country fashion show. It was a whole new look for her. The jeans she liked were Lees, and they made her butt look stellar.

Cade was grinning. "I must say, Miss Jennifer, you're looking mighty fine all dressed up in your Western wear."

Jenn drew in a breath. Cade's admiration made her chest swell with pride. "And all this is just so I don't embarrass you at the Eagles Hall tomorrow night?"

Cade's dimples flashed. "Aw, honey. I'm always proud to be seen in your company. I just thought you would be more comfortable…" He stroked her cheek with the back of his hand. "And to be fair, I have been known to step on my dance partner's feet…so be forewarned."

Jenn gave him a coy smile. "Why, Cade Garrett. I cannot believe you would mangle my tootsies."

"Those boots should keep you safe."

She glanced down at the shiny black leather. "Good to know."

When they left the store, Jenn was wearing her new cowboy boots with her dress, and Cade had an armload of packages.

They dropped her broken shoe at the local shoe repair shop, where Jenn asked the owner to have them ready for her to wear the following Sunday.

———

On Saturday morning, Jenn loaded both children into the car and drove out to the airfield. She knew that she could have called Cade and he would have been happy to accompany them, but she wanted to get the feel of the place without any pressure from him. He seemed anxious to sell the property, and she was unsure if this was the best move. It was probably just guilt over the idea of selling off the property that Jason had worked so hard to build. She felt as though she would be betraying him if she shirked her responsibility. If there was a way to manage the facility, she thought that she should be strong enough to take it on.

Now she sat in the car with both children strapped into their car seats behind her. She stared at the office, feeling totally inept. How could she have thought that she was up to this task?

Jenn heaved a huge sigh. *Ridiculous.*

She had just turned the motor back on, preparing to drive back to the house, when someone knocked on the driver's side window. She about jumped out of her skin but turned the motor off when she saw an attractive, dark-haired woman who was probably in her forties. The woman was smiling, and her hair was blowing in the breeze. Jenn remembered that this was one of the interested parties—the woman from Dallas with all the money.

Jenn lowered the window. "Yes, can I help you?"

"You sure can. You're Jennifer LaChance, aren't you?"

Jenn nodded.

"Do you remember when we met? I'm Maggie Swearingen and I really want to buy this property." She gazed at Jenn with what appeared to be sincerity.

Jenn glanced in the back seat, noting that Lissy and Leo had fallen asleep. She opened the door as silently as possible and stepped out of the vehicle. She reached to shake the woman's proffered hand.

"Do you mind my asking why you're interested in the airstrip?"

"It's in my blood," Maggie said. "My family has rented a hangar from your brother for years. We all fly our own planes, and I would love to be the owner."

Jenn swallowed hard. "So you're not going to close the airstrip and turn it into an apartment complex or a strip mall?"

Maggie threw her head back and laughed so loud Jenn was afraid she would wake up the children. "Heavens, no. We want the airstrip to remain a viable business. I'm told that it's important to the community, and it's certainly important to me." She stood, hands on hips, staring at Jenn encouragingly.

Jenn drew a deep breath and let it out. "I see. Well, I know it's important that the airstrip stays open. I totally do not understand anything about the business, but my brother worked so hard to make it successful, I'm feeling a little guilty for even thinking of selling everything off."

"Oh, I understand, but you can be sure that my family and I will be very responsible and manage everything just the way Jason would have. He was a great guy."

Jenn leaned back against the fender of the car. "I hate to tell you that our lawyer wants us to list the property with a commercial real estate broker. He says we owe it to the children to get top dollar for it." She shrugged, detecting a glimmer of anger in Maggie's eyes.

"Well—well, that's to be expected." Maggie's lips tightened. "Just promise me you won't agree to any sale before you talk to me. I'm willing to beat any offer you receive." She dug in her hip pocket and drew out a business card. "You can reach me at this number any hour of the day or night. Don't let me down." Her smile was soft again.

"Sure, I'll do that." Jenn put the card in her pocket and watched Maggie drive away in her silver BMW.

The children were still fast asleep in the back seat, so Jenn opened the windows and stepped up to the office door. She unlocked it and entered the building, leaving the door wide open so she could keep an eye on the children.

The office had a musty, closed-up feel. It seemed that Jason had just stepped out, giving her an even more eerie feeling.

There was a barrier with a counter, which apparently functioned as a workspace, and a small desk. Then, the desk in the rear of the office that had been where Jason worked. She touched the desk surface and gave the chair a twirl.

"Oh, Jason. I wish you could tell me what to do." She opened the top drawer and found a date book calendar shoved in the back.

Jenn stared at it for a moment before reaching to scoop it out of the drawer. Just touching the leather-bound volume caused a shiver to coil around her spine.

She glanced out the doorway and saw that Lissy was rubbing her eyes furiously. Tucking the date book under her arm, she strode out the door and locked the office up again. Sucking in a deep breath of fresh air, she vowed that the next time she came here, she would open all the windows to air the place out. She wanted to sit in Jason's chair and go through everything tucked away in that desk.

"I don't want to let you go, Jason." She slid behind the wheel and turned on the ignition. "We're going home now," she announced.

Chapter 21

BIG JIM AND MOST OF HIS FAMILY WERE PLANNING TO GO TO the Eagles Hall that evening, eager to dance to a live band and kick up their heels after a hard workweek. The entire family would be there, even his youngest son, Beau; his wife, Dixie; and their daughter, Ava, who usually holed up on Saturday nights to read together and engage in other family pursuits.

But this weekend, all three of his boys would be in attendance, along with their families, plus a couple of cousins to boot.

Each of his sons would be arriving in his own truck, but Mark Dalton and Gracie, Leah's daughter, would ride with Big Jim. He enjoyed spending time with the young ones. And he wanted to give his sons some private time with their wives as well.

Big Jim and Mark were polishing their boots. It was a ritual for the Garrett men to polish their boots before stepping foot on a dance floor.

"Them boots are lookin' good, boy."

Mark appeared to be pleased. "Thanks, Big Jim."

"Now, I picked out our Wranglers and dress shirts, so we can get dressed and head to town ahead of the others. That a-way we can stake out the very best table for the family." Big Jim reached for Gracie's boots to dab a little more polish on the scuff marks. That girl was growing like a weed. She was eight but would have her ninth birthday in a couple of months. He was glad his middle son, Tyler, had married Leah and adopted Gracie. Now they had a son, delivered a few months ago just before Christmas. Big Jim was thrilled that Tyler's son was being raised in such a loving family. "Mark, you might want to grab your shower now so you can get started on gettin' dressed."

"Yes, sir," Mark said, and got up from the table. His boots had been placed on a couple of sheets of newspaper. He stood, gazing at Big Jim as though he wanted to say something but couldn't seem to find the words.

Big Jim set Gracie's boot down and wiped his hands on a paper towel. "What can I do for you, son?"

"It's just…I've been thinking about what you said…about being a Garrett."

Big Jim held his tongue, trying to keep his expression neutral, not wanting to influence the boy.

"You and Colt have been so good to me. I want to do what you want me to do, but I'm just not sure what the right thing is."

Big Jim laid his big paw on the boy's shoulder. "The right thing is whatever you want. There is no right or wrong answer. Whatever you decide is right for you is right for me." He gave Mark's shoulder a pat and drew his hand back. "You have all the time in the world, so no hurry."

Mark looked relieved. "Yes, sir. I'll think about it some more."

"Good boy. Now run and get your shower, and save me some hot water."

–––~~~–––

Jenn was nervous.

"You look great," Ollie said. "What's the problem?"

Jenn was pacing around, checking the front window to see if Cade's truck was out there. "No problem. It's just that there are so many Garretts…and just one LaChance."

"You know what I think?" Ollie arched her brows.

"No, what do you think?" Jenn sat down at the dining table beside Ollie, glad her friend was willing to babysit for the children.

"I think Cade Garrett is a very nice man, and he is truly a pleasure to look at."

Jenn drew a deep breath and expelled it. "I agree. He's a babe."

"And he seems to be crazy about you, girl."

"I'm pretty crazy about him, y'know?" Jenn felt a little tightness in her chest when she visualized Cade's handsome face.

"But I can't believe how good you look now." Ollie waved her hand, indicating Jenn's new Western wear. "You look more... down-to-earth."

"Cade said he bought the boots because he was going to step on my toes tonight."

Ollie guffawed. "I've seen that sucker dance. I would be very shocked if he stepped on your toes."

Well, that was comforting...somewhat. Jenn was envisioning Cade with his arms around someone else, and that was not comforting. She cleared her throat. "So has Cade had a lot of girlfriends?"

Ollie put her finger against her cheek, pantomiming confusion. "Define 'a lot.' I'm not sure how to quantify that."

Jenn rolled her eyes. "That bad, huh?"

"Why, whatever do you mean, dearie?"

"Brat! You know what I mean." Jenn fisted her hands on her hips. "Is Cade a playboy? Does he have girlfriends waiting in the wings to pull my hair out? Is he going to break my heart?"

"I've seen Cade with different females over the years," Ollie said, suddenly earnest. "But I don't think I've heard about anything serious. He seems to have been spending most of his time working on his ranch and building his herd. Everybody likes him, as far as I know."

There was a knock on her door, and Jenn's stomach grabbed. "It's him."

Ollie smiled. "Well, go let the man in."

Jenn could hear her heart pounding in her ears as she hurried to the door. When she threw it open, Cade was standing on her porch with an armload of roses.

"Oh, Cade! How lovely. I haven't gotten flowers in a long time." She blinked fast to avoid tearing up.

"Well, that's too long." He handed off the bouquet and stepped inside.

Jenn brought the roses to the table and went to look for a vase, while Cade and Ollie chatted. "I think this will do." She returned to the table with a glass vase, but Ollie took it from her hands.

"You two run along. I'll take care of the roses. You have to cut the stems on an angle, underwater, so they will last a long time." She made a shooing motion with her free hand.

"Thanks, Ollie," Jenn said. "I really appreciate you taking care of the kids."

"Don't be silly." She beamed at them. "I adore these two. I get to play mom and then walk away. Just enough diaper changing to let me know how nice it is to be single."

Cade ushered Jenn out to his truck and opened the passenger door. When he started to lift her, she waved him off.

"I can do this." Jenn put her booted foot on the lower step and grabbed for the handhold inside the door and hoisted herself up and into the seat. Yes, it was a strain, but she was proud that she could at least lift her own weight. *Small victories.*

Cade stared up at her, admiration in his expression. "Awesome, but I really liked holding you in my arms."

Jenn's heart clutched. She held out her arms to him and slid down to the ground.

Cade's kiss was stellar, transporting her into a high altitude of euphoria. *Man, can this guy kiss.* She heaved a satisfied sigh, and he lifted her into his truck as though she were the helpless little female in high heels and short skirts. Some things did not need to change.

He closed the door and rounded the vehicle, a wide grin in place.

They drove in silence, but Jenn's hand was resting on his thigh. His hard, warm thigh.

When he turned in at the Eagles Hall, the parking lot was packed. Pickup trucks lined up as far as the eye could see.

"I'll let you out at the door," he said and put the truck in gear.

"I can walk with you." She could not imagine walking into this huge, packed building by herself.

"You can wait for me at the front door. I'll be right there."

"Okay, I'll just slide out." She accomplished this and closed the door, but he waited until she had climbed the steps before he took off. Feeling somewhat out of her element, Jenn waited for her guide to return.

Two couples came up to the door. They were laughing and talking amongst themselves. The women were dressed much as Jenn was and seemed to be completely comfortable in their garb, but Jenn still felt that she was participating in some Western cosplay. *Not my gig...yet.*

But as long as Cade and the children were in her story, she would be there, trying to fit in.

In a few minutes, she spotted Cade's long-legged stride coming through the maze of trucks. She immediately felt safe again.

"There's my girl," he said, loping up the steps to take her hand. "Let me take you inside and show you off."

My girl? That sounded promising. It flashed through her brain that it was odd that her brother had fallen in love with a Garrett and she had too.

When they stepped inside, a barrage of noise assailed her ears. People were milling around, talking, and some screaming with laughter. She heard glass clinking and metal scraping. Canned country music was playing, but nobody was dancing.

"Two, please." Cade handed cash to a lady behind a card table at the door. She inked a stamp and rolled it across the backs of their hands.

Jenn recognized the image of an eagle with spread wings. *How appropriate.*

Cade tucked her hand in the crook of his arm and led her inside. "Let's find a seat."

There were long tables fitted with folding chairs all around, circling the large dance floor. Cade was obviously searching for someone, and when he spotted Big Jim at a table, his grin went wall to wall. He steered through the crowd and made it to the long table next to the dance floor. "Hey, Uncle Jim. I told you we'd make it this time."

Big Jim Garrett stood up and gave Cade a man hug plus a couple of hearty shoulder slaps. "Good to see you, boy. And, Miss Jennifer, you sure are lookin' purty this evenin.'"

"Why, thank you, Mr. Garrett…Big Jim." She felt her cheeks burn under his obvious admiration.

"You folks sit right down here with us." He gestured to the family members spaced around the table.

"Here, come sit by me," Leah called.

Jenn was surprised to see that Leah was holding her infant son. Cade escorted her to the other side of the table and held her chair, then placed his straw cowboy hat on the table next to her to save his place.

"Tyler and Colt went up to get us some food. Line's so very long, and I didn't feel like standing in it." Leah placed the baby in an infant seat on the table and turned to give Jenn a hug. "So good to see you."

"I better see about finding our dinner," Cade said. "What are you hungry for?" He pointed to a menu board posted on the far side of the room. It appeared to be mostly hamburgers and hot dogs with a variety of sides.

"Anything. I'm not particular." Jenn wasn't especially hungry but was willing to partake of whatever Cade chose for her.

Cade gave a little wink and took off in the direction of the food lines.

"I'm so glad to see the two of you together," Leah said. "You make a perfect couple."

"Really?" Jenn felt a bit uncomfortable discussing their relationship when she was just trying to figure out if they had one. "Cade is a very nice man."

Leah let out a giggle. "That's an understatement. He's also a babe."

Jenn had to laugh at that. "You're right. He is, and I'm still trying to figure out what we're doing together."

Leah slipped her arm around Jenn's shoulder for a quick embrace. "Because you're a very nice person and you are also lovely. Cade is lucky to have you."

"That is so nice of you to say." Jenn shrugged. "I'm just trying so hard to be a good mom to the children. I love them so much."

"How is that going for you? If you need any help with anything, just let me know. I think I've been through about everything raising Gracie and now the baby."

Jenn glanced across the table to where Gracie was chatting with Mark, Misty's young brother. They seemed to be very comfortable here, although the Eagles Hall was a sort of glorified bar. She noticed lots of children and teens in the property.

"I'm sure it's nice for you to leave the kids at home, but if you ever decide to bring them, they will be welcome here. We can help you with them."

Jenn stared around her. She had never considered bringing the children, but it seemed that many other people had. "I don't know. Lissy is teething, and she tends to be a little whiny."

"Aren't they all?" Leah winked at her.

"There she is!" Misty Garrett nodded at Jenn and came to the table bearing food. "This is for you and the kids, Big Jim." She set a stack of containers on the table beside him and handed off one box to Gracie and another to her brother, Mark. "Colt is juggling the drinks." She sat down beside Big Jim and placed the two remaining containers in front of herself and the chair next to her, obviously reserved for her husband.

In moments, Colton came to join them with three soft drink cans and a pitcher of beer with a stack of plastic cups. He set the pitcher of beer in front of his dad and dealt the sodas to the two young people as well as Misty.

Tyler came next with containers of food for his wife and daughter, and finally, Cade strode across the floor similarly laden. He slid into the chair next to Jenn and served her a carton of food and a soft drink. "I would have gotten you a beer, but I didn't know if you wanted one. The hamburgers are great."

"Thanks." Jenn opened the container and almost swooned when the aroma of freshly grilled beef rose up to meet her. "Oh, this smells wonderful."

"Hope you like it." Cade wrapped his big hand around the bun and took a bite of one of his burgers. Jenn noted that he had gotten two for himself, although they were plenty large. There were french fries in her container, as well as a plastic cup of coleslaw. What more could a girl ask?

Jenn picked up her burger with both hands and leaned over the carton to take the first bite. An explosion of flavors burst on her taste buds. The meat was delicious. A crispy lettuce leaf and sliced tomato were layered with a thin-sliced onion ring. There was cheese melting everything together. She realized she was moaning in appreciation.

Leah leaned closer and whispered, "I only make those sounds when I'm horizontal."

Jenn almost strangled on her burger.

Fortunately for her, the younger of the Garrett sons chose that moment to enter with his family.

"Hey, here comes our little brother," Colton said.

Tyler snorted. "Late as usual."

Beau Garrett held his redheaded daughter, Ava, in one arm and had his other arm around his equally redheaded wife, Dixie. He shot a dark look at his brothers that clearly said *If there weren't children present. . .*

"Sit right down, Son. Make Miz Dixie comfortable and let me see my precious Ava." Big Jim held his arms out to remove Ava from Beau's arms, while Beau held a chair for his wife and then went to forage for food.

Jenn waved at Dixie. She was a stunning woman and maybe a little less friendly than Leah and Misty. Maybe it was because they didn't live on the Garrett ranch itself, but on the land Dixie had inherited from her father.

But Big Jim and Ava seemed to have a very close relationship. He had seated himself and was sharing his french fries with her.

Jenn found herself smiling, but she got back to her dinner quickly. There was time to socialize when the delicious hamburger had been devoured.

Cade had finished his first one and was reaching for the second. Good thing this big boy worked hard every day. *No gut on this one.*

As soon as she had finished, a young boy not much older than Mark came by the table and picked up all the disposables, depositing them in a large rolling trash can. He moved down the line, picking up anything that was empty.

Her facial expression must have revealed her surprise.

"His father is an Eagle and runs the grill on weekends." Big Jim nodded his head toward the boy. "His mom is at the door taking the admittance money."

It seemed this was a family affair for families other than the Garretts.

"Nice," she said.

Cade reached for her hand, and they sat with their hands clasped right on top of the table. He certainly wasn't hiding his feelings. The phrase *my girl* kept reverberating in her brain as she contemplated her new life and the changes she was going through.

She glanced at the hand holding hers. It was comforting and exciting at the same time. She felt safe for the first time in a long time. She knew what tomorrow would bring and that made her happy.

The throng of people seemed to have cleared off the dance floor. Most were seated, having eaten, and were now watching as the band was setting up. In a short time, one of the Eagles took the stage and made some announcements about upcoming events hosted by the Eagles, and then he introduced the band members.

The band started off the first set with a lively, fast-paced song, and the dance floor was quickly filled with dancers spinning around.

Jenn felt a moment of terror. She had no idea what the steps were to whatever dance they were doing. *What have I done? I'm going to embarrass Cade and myself.*

But Cade was holding her hand and lightly stroking his fingers over it. It was somewhat calming, but she dreaded when he would want to dance.

Cade lifted her hand to his lips and brushed a kiss across her fingers.

Jenn felt a rush of lust swirl through her lady parts. That others in the Garrett family were surreptitiously observing his actions and exchanging glances was adding to her discomfort.

The music changed to a lively two-step and the dancers geared down a bit but still swirled around and around.

When the next song began, the lights dimmed a little and the band started a slower tempo number.

"This is our song," Cade announced. He pushed back from the table and held her chair.

Jenn sucked in a deep breath and let it out all at once. "I'm not really a very good dancer." Nonetheless, she stood and turned toward Cade.

He smiled encouragement and gestured to the dance floor.

Jenn took a few steps and stopped, but Cade took her hand and led her to the center of the large dance floor. She assumed a dance position with one hand on his shoulder and the other hand in his.

He whispered, "It's a two-step."

That meant nothing to Jenn, but surprisingly, she was able to follow his strong lead. After they circled the floor once, she began to relax, almost enjoying the music and being in his arms.

The two-step morphed into another song, a country classic that even Jenn had heard before. They danced and Cade drew her closer. This felt good. Maybe he could hold her even closer.

When the song ended, Cade took her back to the table. She noticed that all of the Garretts were staring at them and smiling.

Jenn took her place beside Leah, who gave her a nod and a wink. "You two looked really good out there."

"We did?"

"Sure. Weren't you enjoying yourself?"

Jenn considered for a second. "Well, yes. It was great."

"You gotta relax, Jennifer. We're all here for you." She rocked the baby in his carrying seat, but Big Jim scooted the baby's seat closer to him.

"You two get up there and dance. I got this little one." He was smiling as he gazed at his grandson, the first member of the generation to carry on the Garrett name. He was especially proud that this little one bore the name James Tyler Garrett, or J.T. as he was called.

With Leah and Tyler on the dance floor, Jenn got a chance to observe Big Jim in his natural state. He was in love with his grandchildren. All of them. The man was building their future by creating opportunities for the family to stick together, to become stronger, to prosper.

Big Jim glanced up and caught her staring. "Ain't nothin' like family, Jennifer."

She returned his smile. "I suspect you're right. Unfortunately, the only family I have left are just babies."

His bushy brows drew together. "Not so. You got all of us

Garretts. You're one of us now. Just relax and know that you are a part of the family."

"That's really nice," she said, but she wasn't sure she believed it.

Jenn and Cade danced again…and again. The steps to the two-step were indeed simple and varied by the tempo of the music. It could be a very fast two-step, or it could be a close and cuddly two-step. But the very simple steps remained the same.

She found herself grinning over nothing at all, throwing her head back and enjoying a hearty laugh. Cade appeared to be enjoying himself as well.

In between dances he was properly attentive, including her in conversations with his family about topics she barely knew. He made sure that she was properly hydrated and exercised.

They shared the floor with other members of the Garrett family. Tyler danced with Leah. Colton danced with Misty. Misty danced with her brother, Mark, and Tyler danced with Gracie.

The singer announced a ladies' choice dance, and Cade looked at Jenn expectantly.

Jenn pushed her chair back and walked a few paces to tap Big Jim on the shoulder.

He looked up, surprised. "Me? You're askin' me to dance?"

"I certainly am," she said, assuming a dance pose.

"Well, you asked for it, little lady." He pushed his chair back and unfolded his long legs to loom over her. "I'm gonna dance your little toes off."

"It's a deal." She practically ran out onto the dance floor, Big Jim on her heels.

Although she considered herself tall, she could not see over Big Jim's shoulder and felt a moment of claustrophobia. To her delight, Big Jim Garrett was as smooth on the dance floor as he was gruff on the outside. After the dance ended, Big Jim spun her around and around with a hearty polka. When he walked her back to the table, he was grinning. "Thanks for the dances, Miss Jennifer."

"My pleasure, Big Jim. I'll be your partner anytime." She collapsed into her seat beside Cade.

Big Jim clapped Cade on the shoulder. "Don't let this one get away, son. You got yourself a live one."

Cade shook his head, grinning. "Y'think?"

The Garretts stayed until the band played the last dance. Apparently, Jenn was with the cool kids because, time after time, groups of people came by the table to say good night, mostly to Big Jim, but also to the Garrett family in general. Big Jim was standing up over and over again, leaning over the table to shake hands with departing locals.

Ava was asleep in her daddy's arms, but Big Jim bent to drop a gentle kiss on her temple. Dixie, who had always seemed cool, spread her arms and gave Big Jim a hug. "Good night, Dad."

Big Jim kissed Dixie's cheek. "Good night, my beautiful daughter-in-law. Take good care of these two."

The next to leave were Colt and Misty, with her brother. Big Jim gave hugs to all and seemed to be especially in tune with Mark. "See you all in church tomorrow morning, late service."

"Amen," Colt said and shepherded his family out the door.

Tyler and Leah had been gathering the baby's things. Gracie's eyes were half-closed.

"I'm going to pull the truck up to the front. You stay right here with Dad."

"I'll keep 'em safe, Ty. Don't you worry." Big Jim grinned as his middle son gave him a thumbs-up. He picked Gracie up, and she put her arms around his neck. "Let's go wait for your daddy up front."

When only Cade and Jenn were left at the table, she started to push back, but Cade stopped her. "I hope you had a good time." His voice sounded wistful.

"Of course I'm having a great time. I learned to two-step, and I got to know your family a bit better." She stroked his cheek with her fingertips. "And I got to be with you."

"Jennifer…I'm pretty sure you know how I feel about you…"
His voice trailed off, and he leaned close to kiss her.

Her eyes remained closed after the kiss ended. "Words, Cade.
We females want to hear the words." She opened her eyes to fall,
headfirst, into the depths of his gaze. *I'm a goner*.

"You want words?"

"Only if they're true."

"In that case, I'll have to confess that I am truly and deeply in
love with you, Jennifer LaChance."

"Oh yes. Those are the words I was hoping to hear."

He brushed a stray strand of hair away from her face, then
trailed his fingers gently down her cheek. "I want to know where
it's written that the man has to say I love you first. I've been trying
to get it out for days."

"It's a rule," she insisted. "The man must declare his love first.
Every woman knows that."

His lips twitched, as though stifling a smile. "Oh, really? Well,
when does the woman declare her love?"

She considered several smart-assed responses that might make
him laugh but nixed that idea right away. The big guy looked so
vulnerable. She swallowed hard. "Well, I suppose it would be right
about now. I love you right back."

Blue fire flickered in Cade's eyes. "We need to leave."

"Yes, we do."

Chapter 22

BIG JIM WAS STANDING ON THE TOP STEP, WAVING GOODBYE TO Tyler and Leah. He had made sure the baby and Gracie were properly secured in the back seat and then promised to have meat ready for the barbecue grill Sunday after church.

"I'll bring potato salad," Leah had said.

Big Jim stood gazing after them when his nephew Cade came out, his arm around the pretty woman he had brought with him to dance and hang out with the family.

"So glad you brought this lovely little lady to have a good time with the family, Cade. I'm sure I'll see you two at church tomorrow, won't I?"

Smiling, Cade turned to Jennifer. "Are we going to church tomorrow?"

"I think that would be lovely," she said.

"Late service, of course," Big Jim said.

"Of course." Cade stepped down onto the hard-packed dirt of the parking area.

"I'll see you tomorrow, Big Jim," Jenn said.

Big Jim's craggy face split into a wide grin. "It's already tomorrow, young lady." He watched as they found their way to Cade's truck, one of only about a dozen remaining in front of Eagles Hall.

Big Jim turned around, gave a quick wave to the woman still sitting behind the table at the door. *Don't let anyone in without paying. Good job.*

He reached in his pocket to retrieve his keys and hit the remote. The big silver double dually came to life with a chirp. Lights on and ready to roll by the time he reached for the door.

"Mr. Garrett."

Big Jim spun around, his hands fisted.

It was Pell... Edgar Wayne Pell, standing with his hands slightly raised and open.

"What do you want, Pell?"

"Easy, man. I was having a few drinks inside and I saw you were leaving. Thought I would say hello."

Big Jim's heart was pounding and he was on high alert. He had never particularly liked Pell, especially now that he had been ambushed by the weirdo. Big Jim had a rifle and a shotgun in the rack that spanned his rear window, but he could hardly reach for one when Pell was standing there with his hands raised.

Big Jim cleared his throat and spat into the dirt. "Well, hello then. I got to be gettin' home now. We can talk some other time."

"Okay, I just wanted to know if you have any idea what that nephew of yours plans to do with the airstrip. I told Breckenridge Ryan that I am interested in buying it."

Big Jim reached for the door handle and hoisted himself up into his vehicle. "No idea. You might want to talk to Ryan. I'm sure he has a handle on it."

Pell raised a hand in farewell. "Sure. I'll give him a call on Monday."

Big Jim closed the door and watched as Pell made his way to his own truck. It was not a top of the line truck and not new, Big Jim wondered where Pell thought he would get the money to buy the airstrip. He revved the powerful motor of his own vehicle and shifted into gear. All the way home, he visualized Pell's reddened face as it had appeared in the headlights. Scary dude, as his sons would say.

—∿∿—

Cade drove through the heart of town, all the way to the house Jennifer had inherited. The house where his niece and nephew lay sleeping... where Ollie Sue Enloe was probably passed out on the sofa. He heaved a sigh. So much for spending the night with Jennifer...who loved him.

But he would pick her up for church the next morning and maybe get to spend the day with her. Maybe take her to his uncle's ranch for barbecue.

He liked the way she rested her hand on his thigh when they were traveling along. He liked everything about her. At the moment, he ached to hold her naked body against his.

He shook his head. *Cool down, lover boy.* He realized that Jennifer's head had dropped onto his shoulder, and she was breathing rhythmically through her slightly open lips.

Nice. He felt a surge of connection to this woman. He wanted to protect her, to watch over her while she slept. Most of all, he wanted to remain in her life.

The moon was bright, almost full, and it seemed to be following the truck, lighting the way. He drove through the familiar streets of Langston, his hometown, pleasantly tired after spending a great evening dancing with the woman he loved.

And she loves me right back.

He pulled up in front of her house as quietly as possible and turned off the motor.

Jennifer stirred and straightened. "Oh, I'm sorry. I didn't mean to conk out on you." She stifled a yawn.

"It's okay. You even look pretty while you're sleeping." He swung out of the truck and went around to open the passenger side door. "Let me help you down." He held out his arms to her and scooped her off the seat.

She let out a little whoop and then a giggle. "You always surprise me with your strength." She circled his neck with her arms and rested her head against his shoulder.

He wished he could stand there all night with most everything he held dear wrapped in his arms. He kissed her forehead and carried her up the front steps.

Ollie had been watching and threw the door open. "What did you do to her?" she demanded.

Jennifer raised her head. "I'm all right, Ollie. Just falling asleep."

Ollie placed one hand over her heart and fanned herself with the other one. "Whoo! I saw this big fellah carryin' you up the walk and I thought he'd got you drunk."

"No way." She let out a little giggle. "How did the kids behave for you?" Jennifer asked.

"Aw, they were little angels. They're fast asleep." She turned to Cade. "It's a good thing you didn't do anything bad, Cade Garrett." She gathered her purse and keys. "I'll just be going back to the inn now. Good night."

"Night, Ollie, and thanks again." Jennifer stumbled a little as she headed back to her bedroom.

"Miss Enloe, I'm going to follow you home. It's really late, and a lotta drunks are out on the road now."

Ollie drew herself up to her full height, which wasn't very tall at all. "I'm perfectly capable of driving myself back to the inn without you riding herd on me."

Cade took a step back and gestured for her to precede him out the door. "Yes, ma'am." She sailed past him, and he twisted the lock in the door before closing it behind himself.

However, when Ollie Enloe started her car and headed out, Cade followed at a respectful distance.

The evening had not ended the way he'd hoped, but at least he knew he was doing the right thing. When he saw that Ollie had parked in front of the inn and was unlocking the front door, he turned toward the highway and found that same bright moon lighting his way back to his ranch.

The sound of a small voice raised in a loud wail brought Jenn fully awake. She sat up straight in bed, still clad in panties and her new Western shirt, half-unbuttoned. At least she had gotten out of the boots and jeans. They had been tossed on the floor beside the bed, but she managed to step over them and grab her robe on the way to the children's room. "I'm coming. Hold on."

Their door was open and both children were awake, and Lissy was standing up in her crib, red-faced and blubbering snot. Leo lay in his low bed with his fingers in his ears.

"Lissy won't be quiet," he said.

"It's okay. I'm here." She reached for Lissy and changed her diaper. She tried comforting the child, but Lissy continued to sniffle and frown. "How about some breakfast?"

"I want Fwoot Loops," Leo announced.

"Fwoot Loops," Lissy echoed.

"Okay, I can do that." She got the children secured in their seating and poured the cereal into two plastic bowls and milk into sippy cups. They both preferred their cereal dry and milk as an accompaniment. "Here you go. Enjoy."

Jennifer looked at the time and felt panic nipping at her heels. She didn't have time for a shower and couldn't leave the children, so she gave herself a quick once-over at the kitchen sink and dabbed on a little makeup while the kids were eating cereal with their fingers.

Cade gave her a call when he was on his way to pick her up.

The panic quit nipping at her heels and climbed up her spine to strangle her. She was mostly dressed, but the children were covered in sticky stuff and both needed a bath desperately.

She managed to wash both children off and get them mostly dressed. Leo was running barefoot through the house, waving his shoes and socks, when the doorbell sounded. Jenn captured Lissy by one arm and threw the door open. "Come in. I'm sorry but I'm running late."

Cade scooped Leo up and sat down on the sofa to help him with his socks and shoes.

Leo lay on his back kicking his feet in the air.

"Well, Leo sure is wound up."

"Yeah…tell me about it." Jenn had dressed Lissy, but she was also wound up and vigorously resisting being picked up.

Cade stood and took Lissy, giving her a toss in the air before holding her close. Lissy was giggling when he headed for the door. "I'm going to put her in her car seat. Bring Leo out and I'll get him fixed up too."

Jenn heaved a sigh, watching him calmly take charge as he walked out the door. "C'mon, Leo. Let's get this show on the road."

Leo was doing his pony imitation and let out a whinny. He then galloped after Cade.

Jenn grabbed her purse and keys, locked the front door, and chased Leo all the way to the truck.

"Whoa, horsey," Cade said. "Let me get you in the corral."

Leo whinnied again and stomped one of his feet as a horse would, but Cade gathered him and managed to fasten him in the car seat.

"All saddled up," Cade announced. "Just one more pony to get in the corral." Then he opened the passenger door to lift her onto the seat.

Since she was dressed for church, she was glad to have his assistance. She smoothed her dress and fastened her seat belt as he started the truck and got underway.

At the church, he helped her alight and released Leo, who was still in full horse mode, prancing and tossing his head. Jenn grabbed his hand and tried to get him to walk into the church quietly, while Cade brought Lissy.

People were finding their seats, but Jenn and Cade dropped the children off at two different nursery rooms.

Jenn felt a bit guilty for feeling such relief to have pawned off

222   JUNE FAVER

the hyper youngsters on the nice church ladies, but maybe they were old pros at handling wild kids.

When they were returning to the sanctuary, Cade took her hand. As an outsider, having Cade's hand wrapped around hers was quite comforting, and it was especially heartening since they had both declared their love to each other. He seemed to be proclaiming to the locals that they were an item.

Leah Garrett was just taking a seat when she spotted Jenn and waved them over.

Jenn felt very gratified to be warmly welcomed by the Garretts. Cade kept his hand at her waist as she was hugged and greeted by Leah and Tyler, and then Big Jim and the others.

Leah insisted that Jenn sit beside her, with Cade on the aisle. The entire length of the pew was taken up with members of this wonderful, warm Garrett family...and one LaChance.

The choir members climbed into their tier of chairs, but they remained standing, leafing through pages of the hymnals. The choir master held up his hands to gain their attention, and the organist played a couple of chords before the choir began belting out a heartfelt rendition of "How Great Thou Art."

The churchgoers immediately took their seats and groped for the church bulletins and hymnals.

Cade began singing in a remarkably clear bass voice. Jenn, who was not very confident about her singing ability, just mouthed the words.

The preacher took his place and delivered a sermon that Jenn could relate to. She thought that she could apply the lesson to her life and hoped she was getting the hang of being a churchgoer again. Something she had not been since she went with Jason and her parents, years ago. Now it seemed normal for her to expect to attend church services every Sunday and even more important since Cade and the Garretts were a part of her life.

Jenn was feeling something she had not felt in a long time—happy...secure.

This frightened her. When she had felt happy in the past, it was just before the rug had been pulled out from under her and she had crashed. Was it possible to be too happy?

———

Cade was feeling quite satisfied with himself. He and Jennifer made a handsome couple, or so he had been told. She sure did feel right, as though their relationship was meant to be.

Now, he had Jennifer in the passenger seat and both kids strapped in behind them. Apparently, the burst of energy both children had experienced had worn off, because Lissy's head was lolled back against the child seat and her eyes were closed, while Leo had slumped down in his seat and his eyes seemed to have glazed over. Cade was certain they would wake up with renewed energy.

Cade turned onto the highway, headed to his uncle's ranch. The promise of Big Jim's barbecue was an invitation he couldn't pass up. Fortunately, Jennifer was agreeable.

Most of all, he wanted the children to be thoroughly entrenched in the Garrett family with all the accompanying values and traditions. It was good to be a Garrett.

Jennifer stifled a big yawn.

"Are you okay?" he asked.

"Just sleepy. I usually get a little more sleep." She shrugged. "And the kids were a handful this morning. I was really rushed."

"Sorry," he said. "You could have called me. I could have given you a pass on the church thing."

"No, it's a good habit to get into, and I'm always glad I went."

He reached to take her hand. "Just think about the feast we're going to score at Uncle Jim's. Everyone always makes sure the table is overflowing with goodies."

"Tell me about it. I'm going to have to buy bigger clothes if I keep eating with the Garretts."

He kissed her hand. "More to love."

"Hah!"

Cade slowed down to turn in at the Garrett ranch, bumping over the cattle guard and through the big horseshoe-shaped entrance. There were pecan trees bordering the drive. Trees that yielded a bumper crop of pecans for pies and other delights.

Both sides of the drive were lined with good pastureland. Black Angus grazed on one side, but Cade knew that his uncle's passion was his family. Like the well-bred animals he raised, his three sons were his pride and joy. Now he had grandchildren too, so he was in his element with the young ones.

Cade and the other cousins had been welcomed into Big Jim's everyday family events, so he had grown up having the run of the ranch property.

Now, he felt as though he was bringing his own family to blend his past with his present and, hopefully, his future.

"This is such a pretty place," she said. "And those big black cows have such pretty eyes."

He smiled at that. "Yes, they do. I have some Black Angus, Herefords, and a few pet Longhorns, but most of my herd is Charolais and Brangus. That's a blend of Brahma and Angus. Very hardy beef cattle."

"When I look in their eyes, I think I could become a vegetarian."

Cade glanced at her earnest expression. "My job as a rancher is to ensure that there is beef on the tables of families across the United States. I'm a farmer, and it's my job to feed people." He pulled up close to the Garrett ranch house. Quite a few other trucks were parked nearby. He told her there was a truck for Big Jim and each of his sons.

"We're here," he announced.

Leo rubbed his face fiercely, but Lissy slept soundly, her mouth still open.

Cade feared the children would not be at their best but released them from their car seats. He carried Lissy, who drooled on his shoulder, and Jennifer led Leo by the hand, but he appeared to be sleepwalking.

"Y'all come right in." It was Misty who held the door open for them. "Aw, look at these little angels."

"Sleepy little angels," Jennifer said. "Maybe we should just take them home?" She looked at Cade doubtfully.

"Oh, no," Misty said. "Come on back and let them get a little rest." She led them to the bedroom wing and knocked softly on one of the doors.

"Come in." It was Leah, who was gently rocking her new son in a bentwood rocking chair. She had a receiving blanket thrown over her shoulder to cover the baby.

Leo was rubbing his face again, so Jennifer took off his shoes and let him climb onto the bed, which he accomplished with his eyes closed.

Jennifer gestured to Cade to place Lissy beside Leo. When he had done that, she slipped Lissy's shoes off. "Why don't you go check in with your uncle? I'm going to stay here with Leah while the kids get a little nap." She waved him off with a smile.

Not sure why he was being dismissed, Cade gave her a little two-finger salute and backed out of the room, closing the door behind him.

Chapter 23

"THANKS FOR GETTING RID OF CADE," LEAH SAID.

"Men just don't have a clue." Jenn shook her head.

Leah slipped the baby's blanket down off her shoulder to reveal the infant suckling at her breast. "I've got the rest of the Garrett men trained not to bother me when I bring the baby in here." She gave a little laugh, patting the baby's back.

"Well, it's a beautiful thing to be able to nurse your baby."

"I'm pretty sure you'll have the chance when you have children of your own."

Jenn shook her head. "These two are my own, and I don't think I would be able to handle another one. I only have two hands." She gave a little giggle. "I honestly don't see how the moms with big families ever get their kids across the street safely."

"I'm sure they have their tricks." Leah nodded to where the two children slept. "You're doing a great job with Leo and Lissy. They seem to be thriving in your care."

Jenn felt a blush of pride. "I'm trying. Just want my brother's kids to have a loving home."

Leah adjusted herself after removing her son from her breast. "I'm sure Jason and Sara would approve. But if there's ever anything I can do to make your job easier, just let me know." She gave a wink. "I've got a few tricks up my sleeve."

Jenn grinned. "Feel free to share any of them because I'm fresh out."

"My greatest helper is my Gracie. She is always so cheerful and really loves her little brother."

"That's a blessing. Don't suppose you rent her out, do you?" Jenn thought she could use a little help.

"Of course, she's in school during the week, but when the bus drops her off, the first thing she wants to do is hold little J.T. He seems to know her and really perks up when she's talking to him."

"How sweet," Jenn said. "What does Gracie talk to him about?"

"She usually just tells him about her day at school, things that her friends did, or what she's going to do for homework."

"I hope they always stay close." Jenn thought about her own big brother and how he had always been her champion. Now she envisioned him as being her guardian angel and hoped Jason would be watching over her and the children.

Big Jim motioned for Cade to follow him into his office, the room where he kept the ranch accounts and records. He went behind the big mahogany desk and gestured for Cade to take a seat opposite him.

When both men had settled comfortably, Big Jim sat frowning at Cade.

"Hey, Uncle Jim. Is there a problem? Have I done something to tick you off?"

Big Jim waved off this idea. "Oh, hell no. Son, if I had a problem with you I wouldn't save it up. I'd get you on the phone right off the bat."

Cade relaxed a little, but Big Jim's expression kept him on alert.

"It's this Edgar Wayne Pell fellah. Does he actually have the funds to make an offer for the airstrip?"

Cade swallowed hard. "I don't really know the man, sir. I do know that he told Breck Ryan that he wanted to make an offer on the property. He and some woman outta Dallas, so far."

Big Jim drummed his fingers on the desk top. "So far?"

"Well, sir…you know that neither Jennifer nor I know a damned thing about running a business, much less an airstrip. We're just not equipped to take up the reins of Jason LaChance's pet enterprise."

Big Jim heaved a sigh. "No, I suppose not."

"Why did you ask about Pell, sir?"

Big Jim's brows almost met in the middle of his face. "He came up on me when I was on my way to my truck last night." He shook his head. "Damned idiot! Scared the hell outta me. It's a wonder I didn't pound the fool outta him."

Cade figured his uncle could pound the fool out of almost anyone if riled. "What did he want, Uncle Jim?"

"He wanted to know if you had considered his interest in the airstrip." His mouth tightened. "He doesn't appear to have the resources to make a real bid on the property."

"I'm not sure of anything, Uncle Jim. I know Mr. Ryan has contacted some commercial real estate broker in Dallas. That person told him that the airstrip would get more interest if we listed it through him."

Big Jim leaned back in his chair. "Everyone wants to get something out of it. Well, just listen to Breck Ryan. I think he's a pretty smart man, so you and Jennifer can trust what he says."

"Sure…but I'm not sure Jennifer really wants to sell. I mean, she knows neither of us are qualified to run the place, but she is emotionally involved because she really worshiped her big brother. It's like she's losing him all over again."

"Whoa!" Big Jim leaned forward, clasping his hands together on the desktop. "You gotta expect that she would be more emotional, I mean, her being a girl and all. But maybe Breck can help her see that selling the airstrip would be the best thing for everyone. The community needs the airstrip."

"Yes, we do. But we need the right people to manage it. I would prefer someone who is actually a part of the community." Cade shrugged. "It's hard to imagine that some outsider would have the best interests of the locals."

Big Jim huffed out a breath. "I can see what you're thinkin', boy. Nobody loves Langston like we locals do."

"Amen."

Leah and Jenn joined the others when Leo and Lissy were fully awake. Jenn was so happy to have someone to talk to who could actually give her some levelheaded advice. She was grateful to have a friendship with a young woman close to her own age who had gone through the same things Jenn was going through with her niece and nephew.

When they joined the menfolk, Cade came forward to take Lissy off her hands. "Thanks," she whispered.

The loving expression on his face was as good as an embrace. How could he convey such caring with a single glance?

Leo spotted Big Jim and took off at a run, aiming straight for his arms. Big Jim bent down and lifted Leo high in the air, making appropriate noises as though Leo were a plane.

Jenn bit her lower lip. She had forgotten what it felt like to be a part of a family.

The evening was filled with laughter and friendly chatter. The casual meal involved fat, juicy hamburgers with hot dogs as well. Lots of sides, including Leah's potato salad, which she made with tiny red-skinned potatoes.

Jenn was embarrassed to ask for a second helping, but Cade plopped a big serving spoonful on her plate when he caught her scraping up the last of it.

Leah caught her eye and grinned.

Yes, I love this potato salad. She gave Leah a wink.

After the dinner, Misty and Colt volunteered to clear the table, and Big Jim moved over to sit next to Jenn.

Cade took Leo to the bathroom, which she found a little convenient. *Conspiracy?*

"Look here, Jennifer. I don't want to get in your business, but I was wondering what your plans are for the airstrip."

Then stay out of my business. Jenn couldn't think of a way to evade the question without being rude, and she didn't want to be rude to this man.

"I don't have an answer for you right now," she said. "I don't know enough to be able to make a decision this important."

Big Jim's brows knit together in a fierce frown, but she sensed he was genuinely concerned.

"I understand you were pretty close to your brother, Jason."

Jenn felt her throat tighten up. She blinked, hoping to avert tears over just the mention of Jason's name. "My brother was always good to me."

"I'm sure he was. My older son always looked after his younger brothers."

She nodded, unable to speak.

"I know your brother would want you to make the best decision about the airstrip, but he's not here to advise you."

"I just don't know what to do," she said, clasping her hands together.

Big Jim reached to place his big hand on top of hers. He gave them a couple of pats. "I'm sure you'll make the best decision when the time comes. Just take your time and learn everything you can."

"Thank you, Big Jim," she said. "Cade and I are supposed to go see Mr. Ryan tomorrow. He's doing some research for us."

"That's all well and good, but you and Cade gotta come up with a decision you can live with."

"Oh, yes. I'm really glad you understand." She was so relieved, she felt like hugging the man.

"I do. I understand loyalty to family. I just have to ask you to consider the well-being of the community. We need the airstrip to stay open and be run by people who give a damn about their neighbors." He gave her hands a squeeze. "I don't mean to put any more pressure on you, but there's more at stake than you can possibly know at this point." He pushed back from the table and took his dishes to the kitchen to be rinsed.

"He's ready for you." Misty Garrett swung out from behind her desk and gave a quick knock on Breckenridge T. Ryan's private office door, then opened it wide. "Go right in."

Breck was ensconced behind his wide desk, but he gestured to the two chairs across from him. "Make yourselves comfortable," he invited. "I've got some great news for you."

Cade held the chair for Jenn and then seated himself. "That's good to hear."

Breck tapped a file that was open in front of him. "The commercial real estate broker I've been in touch with has come back with some very impressive offers from his contacts. I think we need to seriously consider them."

Cade slipped his arm around Jennifer's shoulders and gave her a little squeeze. "Sounds good to us, right, Jennifer?"

She pressed her lips together and nodded.

Perplexed, Cade looked at Breck for some kind of clarification. From what Breck had said, he thought Jennifer should be thrilled—ecstatic, in fact—but no... She looked all closed up and pinched, as though bracing for bad news.

Breck gave her a sharp glance. "You all right, Jennifer? Do you need some water?"

She gave a stiff little nod, and Breck punched the intercom, asking Misty to bring in some water for Miss LaChance.

In a few minutes, Misty brought a small tray with three bottles of water. She placed it on the edge of the desk close to where Cade and Jennifer were sitting.

"Thanks," Jennifer whispered. She uncapped one of the bottles and took a sip.

Cade smiled at her encouragingly. He couldn't interact as he would have liked in front of Breckenridge Ryan, but he hoped she could feel his support without words. He remembered that she'd said women need words. *What to say?* "Hey, Jennifer. We got this." *Dumb...dumb...dumb!*

She appeared to be confused by his statement. "Got what?"

"I mean, we're together in this. You and me."

That seemed to give her some kind of comfort. "Yes. You and me," she said.

"We'll figure out the best thing to do," Cade said. "With Mr. Ryan's help, of course."

She nodded again. "Yes, of course." Still closed up tight.

"Miss LaChance, I'm sure this all sounds confusing right now, but if you'll allow me to lay it all out for you?" Breck fixed her with a solemn gaze.

"Yes, please do." She folded her hands in her lap, appearing to be open to whatever he had to share.

"First, the broker came up with several other prospective buyers. These are the top three offers." Breck handed each of them a sheet of paper with the names of the individuals or corporations interested in acquiring the property.

Cade swallowed hard. "That is a whole lot of money."

"It is," Breck agreed. "There is a condensed paragraph about each one, since you may need more than the cash offer to make your decision."

Cade gave out a low whistle. "Big bucks, for sure...but Big Jim is urging us to make sure the buyer will be an asset to the community. He wants what's best for Langston and the residents." He looked at Jennifer. "That's the way my uncle thinks. He's all about family and community."

"He's a very good man," she said.

Breck cleared his throat, apparently trying to direct them back to the decision at hand. "Please look over the information and let me know what you want to do. I'll contact the broker and let him draw up a contact."

"Maybe we can show this list to your uncle?" Jennifer folded the paper. She was done.

Breckenridge Ryan closed the file and spread his hands. "You folks get back to me when you have a decision."

Jennifer gnawed her lower lip. "What about the first two people who wanted to buy the property? Mr. Pell and that lady from Dallas?"

Breck looked at her intently. "Their offers were nowhere near the three on the list. Is there a reason you would prefer to sell to one of them?"

"N-no... I just think they deserve to be kept in the loop." She shrugged. "I mean, Mr. Pell is local, and the woman has leased hangar space from my brother for years. At least they have a vested interest in the airstrip."

Breck smiled for the first time. "Good point."

Chapter 24

"I JUST CANNOT BELIEVE YOUR FATHER DID THIS." MISTY Garrett paced around her living room. "I mean, Mark is such an impressionable boy, and he idolizes Big Jim."

"Honey, settle down." Colt was torn between comforting his wife and defending his father. "You know the feeling is mutual. My dad thinks the world of your little brother."

Misty folded her arms and glowered at Colt. "Well, he sure doesn't think much of the Dalton name."

Colt heaved a sigh, not wanting to remind Misty of her drunken father and unscrupulous brother who had been murdered by his equally dishonorable running mates. "I'm sure Dad just wanted to make Mark feel like part of the family."

"Hmph! Mark is a part of the family. My family...and now our family." A tear slid down her cheek. "And he is the last Dalton. The last one to carry on the name."

"I understand, honey. Really, I do." Colt raised a hand to touch her, but she shrugged him away.

"No, you don't. Would you ever consider changing your precious Garrett name?" Misty's dark eyes narrowed.

"Of course not, but it's not the same thing." Colt held up both hands in supplication. "Honey, I don't have any idea what's going on or what caused my dad to offer to adopt your brother, but I'm sure he had good intentions. You know my dad would never want to hurt Mark, or you for that matter. Why don't you just settle down and let them work this out?"

Misty let out a little shriek of annoyance. "Because Mark is just a little boy!"

Colt reached for the Stetson perched on a hook by the front door and jammed it on his head. "I'm gonna go for a little ride to clear my head." He opened the front door, taking in a chestful of fresh Texas air. "But I will say that I think Mark has a lot of sense. He's going to be in middle school next year, and he's got a good head on his shoulders."

"So you think that earns him the right to be called a Garrett?" Misty's lips clamped together in a straight line.

Colt shot her a sharp glance before he stepped outside. "Yes, ma'am, I do."

———

Jenn was silent on the ride home. Thankfully, Cade seemed to be caught up in his thoughts as well.

When they arrived at the house, Mrs. Reynolds was reading to the children. It was such a sweet picture to see this nice, motherly woman ensconced in the recliner with both young ones, who were enraptured by the picture book.

Cade greeted both children warmly and then escorted Mrs. Reynolds to his truck. He came back to give Jenn a quick kiss by the door. "I'll tell you what: I can take this list to my uncle and see what he thinks, or if you want to come along and talk to him, I can pick you up."

Jenn shrugged, feeling deflated for some reason. "That's okay. You go ahead and talk to him. I'm sure his opinion will matter."

Cade walked away looking puzzled.

Jenn spent the afternoon caring for the children and cooking one of the recipes that Leah had shared with her. Leah said it was her favorite meatloaf recipe that she rolled into little meatballs and baked, so Gracie could pick them up with her hands. That sounded like something Leo and Lissy would enjoy.

———

"Damn!" Big Jim tried to wrap his brain around the amount of money written on the paper Cade had handed him. "That's plenty of money, for sure." He motioned for Cade to follow him to the rear of the ranch house. "You want some sweet tea? Just made some."

"You bet, Uncle Jim." Cade slipped onto a stool in front of the counter that separated the Garrett kitchen from the cavernous dining and family room. He watched as Big Jim filled two tall glasses with ice and then poured tea from a pitcher in the refrigerator. "Thanks."

"You kids could do a lot with the money from the sale of the airstrip. I mean, that is a whole helluva lotta greenbacks they're talkin' about."

Cade shook his head. "Sure is. I had no idea the airstrip was worth that kind of money." He took a long drink of the sweet, icy liquid.

Big Jim's eyes narrowed. "It may be about the airstrip, and it may be about the land. You know God's not making any more prime Texas ranchland…at least not on this planet." He scratched his chin thoughtfully. "Kinda makes you wonder what these folks really want it for."

Cade's brow furrowed. "I hadn't thought of that. You said the community needs the airstrip, so I thought that would be the purpose the buyer would want to develop it for. What else are you thinking, Uncle Jim?"

Big Jim set his tea glass down on the counter and took the stool next to Cade. "Well, if I was some big Dallas businessman, I'd be thinking about all the land surrounding the airstrip and about how I could develop it to best advantage."

"Such as?" Cade thought he must have been very naive not to

have questioned the motives of the prospective buyers. He had just seen the dollar amount and been ready to sell to the highest bidder.

"How about if they used the land to build a ritzy little housing development? You know? The kind where they build large houses right one on top of another, with barely enough room to walk between. Those places make me claustrophobic. Like the walls are closin' in on me. Places like that won't have septic systems like the rest of us. They will change the way the town of Langston does business, needin' more roads and utility systems, which will raise the taxes for everyone."

Cade tried to think how this would impact the area, but his uncle was in rare form.

"You know that would also impact the ecology of this area." Big Jim's face had reddened and the vein in his forehead was bulging. "Worst of all, they might build a strip mall. That would run the local small business owners right outta their businesses. We don't need no Wally World here in Langston."

"Um, no, sir." Cade concentrated on sipping his iced tea and keeping his mouth shut.

Big Jim glowered at him fiercely. "Would you want Langston to become another suburb of Dallas?"

Cade did not mention that Dallas would have to annex Amarillo first. "No, sir."

"Well, I think you oughta look into each of these companies and see what they're up to. Do a little research and find out what their business interests really are." Big Jim slugged down the rest of his iced tea and set the glass down on the counter with a clink.

"Yes, sir. I'll do that."

He left his uncle's ranch feeling even more confused than he had before.

When Mark got off the bus that afternoon, he went straight to his room and closed the door.

Misty intended to have it out with him right then and there. She was not going to allow him to just kick the Dalton name out the door.

She was proud of being a Dalton, although now she was a Garrett. The Dalton spread had been a very profitable ranch. They had raised beef cattle and grown feed crops for the animals.

Well, it had been thriving until her mother died and her father took to drinking instead of working his ranch.

Misty pressed her lips together.

The truth was the ranch had been in foreclosure when her father died of liver disease and heart failure. If Colt hadn't paid off the loan, the property would have been lost, along with their stock and farm equipment.

But still…

Misty knocked on Mark's door.

"What do you want?" came the gruff reply.

She huffed out a sigh. "Well, I want to talk to you."

"So talk," he said.

"Not through this door, I'm not. Now open up and let me in."

There was silence and then, just when she was going to knock again, the door opened and she got a look at Mark's face.

"Oh no! Mark, what happened to you?" Her gut roiled as she saw the dark bruise on one side of his face and his lip with a big cut in it.

He turned away, removing books from his backpack. "Nothin.'"

She put her hand on his shoulder, but he shrugged it off. "Please, Mark. Talk to me."

"Talk? 'Bout what?"

She took a seat on his bed, hoping to get some response from him. "Tell me what happened to your face."

He shrugged. "I got jumped on the bus. No big deal."

"Who did this to you? Please tell me, and we can go to the school and—"

"Forget it. I don't want any more trouble." He grabbed a tissue and blew his nose, but when he tossed it, the tissue was bloody. "Can you drive me over to Big Jim's? I want to take care of the horses."

Misty could not find the words to reply. She tried to moisten her dry lips, but still, no words. Silently she got up and went to get her keys. The least she could do was to drive her brother to the man who seemed to be able to reach him when she couldn't. As she led Mark out to her truck, she realized why he wanted to be a Garrett.

————

Cade drove back to his ranch. He wasn't sure how to go about doing what his Uncle Jim had suggested. He hadn't even considered the impact that selling the airstrip to the wrong buyer might have on Langston and the surrounding area ranchers.

He entered his house and tossed his hat on a nearby coatrack. Then he went straight to the refrigerator, choosing a longneck beer from the shelf. Flipping off the cap, he opened the back door and stepped outside. Cade took a seat, propped his boots on the porch railing, and surveyed the view. The barn and stables were in good repair, as were the other outbuildings where some equipment was stored. There were trees close to the house, a few pecans and a couple of oaks. Beyond that were pastures where beef cattle grazed and some fields planted with grain to feed his herd.

It was a simple life.

The only factors he had to deal with were the weather and issues in the market.

It was a good life.

He enjoyed working the land and cattle, and considered his role as provider of food for the American people.

It was a solitary life.

Just Cade and Mother Nature, most of the time.

And now there was Jennifer LaChance…and the two little children.

He sucked in a deep breath and let it out all at once.

Oh, how his life had changed. He was in love with Jennifer and loved the little ones as well. He knew there were changes coming, and he hoped he was man enough to take them on.

He figured Jennifer was smarter than he was. For sure, she had concerns about the big businesses willing to offer so much money to acquire the airstrip. For his part, he would have jumped at the highest offer and made sure the children's future was solid...and Jennifer's. Although he had an equal share in the property, he had enough assets to his name to live comfortably forever and then some. So he had thought that the profits from the sale would buy the children a great future, and Jennifer as well, since she was the conservator for the minors.

But now that his uncle had opened his eyes, he needed to view this proposed sale with microvision. He had to consider the long-range effects on the community.

He finished off the longneck and slipped the bottle into a bucket he kept just for such time as he made the trek to the recycle point that sent trucks to Langston once a month. Cade was glad to see that many of the older ranchers were getting on board with the recycling movement. Before, he and most of the area ranchers burned their refuse when conditions would allow. Cade couldn't recall the last time he had burned trash. After the recycle bin was filled and dropped off each month, all he had to deal with were kitchen scraps, and those went on the mulch pile.

Yes, it was a good life.

Chapter 25

BIG JIM OPENED THE DOOR, SURPRISED TO SEE MISTY WITH HER hand on Mark's shoulder. She looked grim.

"Come on in, you two. Mark, you know I leave the door unlocked. You could just bring your sister right in." He stepped back to allow them to pass.

"I'm just dropping him off," Misty said tersely.

Big Jim wondered what had her panties in a wad. "You can stay long enough for a glass of sweet tea, can't you?"

Her mouth tightened, but she nodded and followed him into the kitchen, where he gestured for them to sit at the table and brought glasses with ice and the tea pitcher. He noticed that Mark hung his head and was uncharacteristically silent.

"What's up, son?" He ruffled Mark's thick, dark hair, and the boy raised his head. "Damnation!" Big Jim thundered. "What the hell happened to you?"

"Some kid beat him up on the bus," Misty interjected. "I'm so upset. I don't know what to do."

"Tell me who did this to you," Big Jim demanded, still examining the extent of Mark's injuries.

"Just a couple of boys in my class. They always give me a hard time." He sniffled and a single tear rolled down his cheek.

Big Jim felt his back teeth grind together. This had never happened with his sons, but then, they'd had each other. "This is more than a hard time. What happened today?"

Mark was struggling to control his tears. "I was just sitting there, by myself, and Ken Robey got on the bus and jammed into the seat beside me. He really jammed his shoulder into me, and my backpack fell onto the floor of the bus."

Big Jim wanted to gather the boy in his arms, but he thought that would not be welcomed. He waited until Mark was able to add to his story.

"When Jay Sattler got on, he swung his backpack in my face and then Ken punched me in the mouth before the two of them went to sit in the back. They were laughing at me."

Big Jim's chest was so tight he could hardly draw a breath. "I'll be talking to the principal, son. Don't you worry." He couldn't resist any longer and leaned down to wrap his arms around Mark. "Don't worry. I'll take care of this."

Big Jim looked up to find that Misty's eyes were filled with tears as well. "Things are gonna be okay. Don't you worry either."

She nodded and said she had to be going, practically running out to her truck.

Big Jim stood, his arms around Mark, wondering what the hellfire had gotten into his daughter-in-law.

~~~

Misty cried all the way home, which wasn't all that far, considering she and Colt had built their home on the huge Garrett ranch property. Big Jim had given a significant plot to them as a wedding gift. Now she sat in front of the new house, crying in her truck.

Suddenly, she got it.

She understood why Mark needed Big Jim Garrett. Why he would trade the Dalton name in for Garrett.

Misty groped in her purse for a tissue. She wiped her eyes and gave her nose a blow.

Might as well face it: being a Dalton had not been such a good deal. When she was Mark's age, it had been a good name. Her mom and dad had taken them to church and attended all the school meetings with Misty and her older brother. But by the time her mom died, her father had crawled into the bottle and totally ignored those parental duties. Mark needed a father, or at least a father figure, and it appeared that Big Jim Garrett was willing to step in.

He seemed to really care about Mark. And he had not done such a bad job of raising her husband, or either of his brothers, to be a fine man. They were all good men. Maybe Mark would get some of that Garrett man varnish with Big Jim's guidance.

Misty climbed out of the truck, took a deep breath, and straightened her shoulders. *Well, if Mark needs a champion, I need to support him.*

She went into the house and splashed some cold water on her face. No point in spreading the gloom to Colt when he got home.

She opened the refrigerator and took out the ingredients for a hearty meal for her menfolk. In man-speak, she figured a plate full of hearty food would indicate she was on board with whatever Mark chose to call himself.

Jenn almost didn't hear the soft knock when Cade showed up at her door. She had just come out of the bathroom wearing her terry robe after she had showered and blown her hair dry. She was putting some moisturizer on her face when she realized there was someone out there.

When she peeked through the peephole, she saw Cade, his handsome face shadowed by the overhead light.

She closed her eyes and huffed out a sigh. *Why does he have to show up when I look so awful?*

Jenn opened the door a crack. "Cade? What are you doing here?"

"Sorry I didn't call first. I thought I would take a chance, and I saw a light on, so I thought..." He gave a little smile. "I thought maybe you might want to spend some time with me."

She opened the door a little wider. *Might as well let him see me at my ugliest.* "Sure, I always like to spend time with you." She gestured for him to come inside. "Um, you'll have to forgive the way I look. I was just getting ready for bed."

He turned and gave her an appraising look. "You look just fine to me." He reached to gather her in his arms, drawing her against his hard chest. Slowly, he lowered his lips to hers.

The kiss he delivered turned her nether regions to liquid fire. She wrapped her arms around his neck and he lifted her off her feet. Without any direction, Jenn's thighs circled Cade's torso and she found herself being carried to the bedroom.

Without turning on the light, he managed to find the bed and deposit her on top of it.

"The door," she whispered. "Don't want to wake up the children."

He quietly closed the door and began shedding his clothes as he approached the bed. His shirt was open, and his muscles rippled as he removed it and draped it over a chair. The belt was next. He sat down and wrestled his boots off, setting them neatly beside the chair. He gazed at her, a half smile on his lips, as he stripped out of his Wranglers.

By this time, Jenn's heart was doing triple time. *Oh my!*

"One of us is wearing too many clothes." He sat on the bed beside her and reached to untie her robe, revealing her state of nakedness. "I guess I was wrong."

She shrugged out of the robe, letting it fall beside the bed. Under his intense scrutiny, her nipples tautened.

"You're so beautiful," he breathed. "I don't deserve you, but I'm happy you think that I'm worthy."

She wrapped her arms around his neck, drawing him close. "Oh, Cade. You're the best man I have ever known."

Cade's lips caressed her cheek and grazed down her neck to her shoulder. Then he gave his full attention to her breasts, caressing them tenderly. He paid special homage to her nipples, circling each with his tongue before she broke into giggles and pulled him closer.

He ran his fingertips down, over her ribs, gently stroking her flat stomach, and then kissed his way down her body, stopping at her navel to explore with his tongue. He kneed her legs apart and trailed his kisses lower.

He caressed her mound with his fingers before he continued with his tongue.

She gasped as his tongue made contact with her most sensitive core. Waves of intense pleasure swirled through her, and she longed to cry out but did not want to wake the children, so she clamped her lips together and made little whimpering noises throughout his performance, ending with a low and sustained moan.

He looked at her so tenderly, she felt the power of his love. He produced a small packet. "Protection. I grabbed some at the store the other day." He applied the condom to his erection and pressed into her wetness.

Jennifer wrapped her thighs around him as he began to rhythmically stroke into her. She rose up to meet his thrusts. His passion thrilled her. As their bodies fused, she lost herself in the moment, forgetting everything but the strong man holding her in his arms. Everything but the sweetness of their coupling.

When at last they lay spent, limbs and damp sheets still twisted together, she hated that he would leave her.

He rolled onto his back and carried her with him. Kissing her damp temple, he grinned. "You just don't have any idea how much I love you and how much I hate to go back to my place."

Jennifer lay atop Cade, her heart still beating fast. "I would like it if you would hold me all night long."

The next morning, Big Jim called the elementary school principal. He knew the woman, who had lived in the community all her life.

He explained to her what Mark had been going through and informed her of the incident that had occurred the previous day on the bus.

"Now, I want to make sure this don't ever happen again."

The woman expressed her assurance that she would take care of it.

"Do I need to call the parents of the young bullies?" He tried to temper the hostility in his own voice.

"Oh, no, Mr. Garrett. That won't be necessary. We'll take care of the matter. It's a school issue."

"Well, it's a family matter to me, so you make sure there's not a repeat performance. Don't let those bullies off the hook." He hung up after receiving assurances that she would act immediately and that Mark would not be in danger.

Somehow, he didn't feel that he had done enough for Mark. He wanted to support him without emasculating him. While he would like to pick up the young bullies by their ears and give them a shake, he knew that could not happen.

He wished his dear wife, Elizabeth, were alive. He had always treasured her counsel. Now he was on his own.

Big Jim considered the parents of the two boys who had attacked Mark. The Robeys and the Sattlers were both longtime area residents. The Robeys had a local land-clearing business and apparently did fairly well. The Sattlers lived on a small farm on the other side of the highway from the Garrett ranch. He presumed they were doing all right as well. At least, both families dressed up their little hellions and brought them to church on Sundays. Apparently, it didn't take.

What made those boys think they could gang up on another boy and get away with it?

At 2:42 that afternoon, Big Jim parked his big silver double dually truck in the parking lot of the Langston Elementary School. There were large yellow buses lined up along one side of the building. *Not today.*

Big Jim swung out of the pickup and strode purposefully into the building. At the office, he didn't bother the principal, but instead asked the secretary which classroom Mark Dalton was in.

Armed with that information, Big Jim found the room and peeked inside. The door was open and the students had their heads bent over some task. He found Mark easily, his eyes on his paper, but Big Jim could see the darkening bruise on the side of his face even from his vantage point.

The teacher looked up and saw Big Jim. She went to the door and asked if she could help him.

"Thank you, ma'am. I just need to give young Mark Dalton a message, if you don't mind."

By this time, most of the class had noticed the big man standing in the doorway. When the teacher asked Mark to go to the doorway, a buzz of talk roiled through the classroom.

Mark had a smile on his face as he laid down his work and went to greet Big Jim.

The teacher went back to her desk, leaving Big Jim and Mark together in the hallway but in full view of the entire class.

"Big Jim!" Mark said. "I didn't know you would be here."

"I just thought I'd give you a ride home. Maybe we can stop and get an ice cream on the way?"

Mark grinned. "Wow! That's great."

"Now I want you to do something for me," Big Jim said, his voice low and confidential. He leaned down close to Mark's level. "I want you to point to the two boys who beat on you yesterday. Don't need to say a word. Just point."

Mark looked a little surprised but turned and pointed first to one young man and then to the other.

Big Jim gave both a stern look and then patted Mark on the shoulder. "I'll be waiting outside for you after the bell rings."

"Yes, sir." Mark's face was wreathed in a smile as he went back to his seat.

Big Jim continued to stare at the two young bullies in turn, giving them each the full force of his intense gaze, before pivoting abruptly and returning to his truck. When the bell rang, he climbed out and waited close to the door for Mark to come out. A rush of children spewed from the building, but Mark spotted Big Jim and ran to where he waited. Big Jim leaned down to give him a one-armed hug, then relieved the boy of his backpack and walked back to his truck, his hand on Mark's shoulder.

It pleased him to see the expression on Mark's face—his bruised face with the split lip. But it radiated happiness and that was all that mattered at the moment.

Before they headed to the ranch, Big Jim and Mark enjoyed a milkshake at the Dairy Queen and took one to Misty at the law office.

The little metal bell clanked against the glass in the door as they entered, and Misty looked up from the keyboard. Her face registered surprise when she saw them. "Well, what are you two rascals up to?"

Mark rushed up to her desk to present her with the milkshake. "We brought you a chocolate shake." He turned around to gesture toward Big Jim. "And Big Jim picked me up so I didn't have to ride the bus."

Misty swallowed hard. It was easy to read her emotions.

"I just got lonesome and figured I would get Mark to help me give the horses some attention. I thought maybe a ride would give me and the horses some exercise."

She grinned and reached to take the paper off her straw. "Thanks a lot, gentlemen. I appreciate the treat." She stabbed the straw through the top of the container. "I appreciate you, Big Jim, for giving my little brother a ride home, and I appreciate the friendship between the two of you."

Big Jim beamed. "You got a great young man here. Glad to have him in the family."

After a night of vigorous lovemaking, Cade awoke just as the first rays of the sun were sending vibrant colors across the eastern sky.

Jennifer was clasped to his chest and she had one long, lovely leg thrown across his lower torso, covering his manhood with her warm flesh. Warm flesh that was causing a serious reaction to that very interested manhood.

He figured the kids would be awake soon, so he was reluctant to start something he wouldn't have time to finish.

Gently, he rolled Jennifer onto her back, wondering how this woman could be so gorgeous without a speck of makeup. Her skin glowed with wellness and her long lashes fanned out on her cheeks.

Reluctantly, Cade climbed out of bed and began gathering his clothing. He managed to get everything on but his boots, and he carried those, silently slipping out the door.

He peeked into the children's room. Lissy was on her back, her mouth open and both arms and legs flung wide. She had wadded the light blanket into a ball at the foot of her crib.

Leo was curled up on one side, his fists clasped together under his cheek. He made a pretty tight package.

Cade tiptoed to the living room and stepped outside, making sure to lock the door behind him. *Keep them safe.*

He climbed into the truck to pull on his boots, leaving the door open as he needed room to stretch his legs to accomplish this task. He glanced back at the house, warmed by the morning sunshine. So many people he loved were inside.

Cade started the truck and headed to Tio's, the Mexican restaurant in the heart of Langston. He had worked up quite an appetite making certain Miss Jennifer had no unfulfilled yearnings.

When he entered the restaurant, the aroma of good food assailed his senses.

Milita Rios greeted him with a menu in her hand. "Good morning, Cade. All by yourself today, or meeting someone?"

"I'm alone," he said, but he saw Breckenridge T. Ryan motioning for him to join him. "Looks like I'm not alone." He followed Milita to the corner table where Breck held sway.

"Sit right down, Cade. Tell me what you and Jennifer are thinking."

Milita slid the menu onto the table and started to walk away, but Cade stopped her.

"I want an order of *migas* and coffee."

She smiled and took the menu. "Right away."

"Looks like you've eaten here a lot," Breck said.

"Enough." Cade smiled at Breck. "Thought you and the lovely Dr. Ryan would have breakfast together."

Breck tilted his head to one side and raised his cup of coffee in a mock salute. "You would think, wouldn't you? But no. My beautiful wife made a house call to deliver a baby way early this morning. So I ate my breakfast right here."

Milita brought a cup for Cade and filled it at the table, then gave Breck a refill. "Enjoy, gentlemen."

"Have you and Jennifer made a decision as to which buyer you're going to sell to?"

"Not yet. I think we need to investigate more, and neither one of us is really qualified to do the research. I had a talk with Big Jim, and he had a lot of insights. He only wants the best for this community."

Breck nodded. "Big Jim Garrett is a fine man. Glad you sought his advice."

"Now I just need to find a computer genius to do a little more digging into the prospective buyers. Research into all their interests."

Milita set the plate of *migas*, a combination of eggs, salsa, and crisp corn tortilla chips with lots of melted cheese, in front of Cade, and he dug into them. "Haven't had this for a while."

"Looks good." Breck clapped him on the shoulder and rose from the table. "About that computer genius…come by my office when you're done here, and I'll unleash my own computer genius on your research."

Chapter 26

Leah had told Jennifer that she could find good child-care for the children at the church.

Jennifer hadn't realized there was a prekindergarten and nursery available during the week, but she was glad to drop the children off after she had given them a good breakfast and cleaned them up.

Now she was driving through the entrance gates to the airstrip feeling a little antsy. She just wanted to take one last look around before giving in to the inevitable. Everyone was urging her to make a decision on the sale of the property, and she could not give one solid reason not to sell.

She took a slow drive around the place, noting that several hangars had their doors open and people were moving around inside. Quite a few small planes were lined up in rows along one side of the strip, with lots of room for them to taxi onto the runway.

The hangar leased by Magdalena Swearingen's company was open, and there was some kind of activity going on inside. The sleek Gulfstream aircraft had a company logo on the side, but Jenn was not sure what enterprise the organization was involved in.

As she idled outside the hangar, Maggie appeared and flashed a big, toothy grin and waved. She came to Jenn's car and greeted her as though they were old friends. "Hey, Jennifer. I'm so glad to see you. I was going to give you a call and see if you wanted to do lunch sometime."

"Um, that would be nice. Your plane sure is big."

Maggie laughed. "Well, I have big ideas." She leaned her elbows against Jenn's door and lowered her voice. "I was hoping you were ready to accept my offer to purchase this property. So, how is it going? Can I count on you to be in my corner?"

Jenn groped for words. "Well, we haven't really come to any decision yet. There's another local man who has an offer on the table, and—"

Maggie huffed out a derisive snort. "Oh, yes… Mr. Edgar Wayne Pell. I don't think you should bother with him. I'm certain he's not serious about the purchase." She straightened and fisted her hands on her hips. "Frankly, Pell doesn't have the resources to follow through." Suddenly the radiant smile was back. "So, can we get on with this business? I'm ready to transfer the money."

Jenn shrugged. "Well, I suppose you could say that I'm the speed bump. My brother put so much of himself into this place, and I'm just not sure we should sell." She swallowed hard. "I know I'm not qualified to run the business, and everyone is urging me to get it over with…but…"

Maggie's lips tightened. "Just make sure that my offer is the one you choose. I'll make it worth your while. I have a lot riding on this." She turned and strode back into the hangar and yelled something to one of the men working inside.

Jenn was stunned. She had no idea what Maggie was talking about and hadn't considered that Maggie had become a loyal ally. Was this woman trying to buy Jenn's vote on the sale of the property? Could Jenn be influenced by money?

Jenn put the car in gear and continued her circuit of the airstrip.

She was driving slowly, trying to notice everything, when Edgar Wayne Pell emerged from one of the hangars and waved her down. "Hello, Miss Jennifer. How are you doing this fine day?"

She shifted into park and let the window down. "Hello, Mr. Pell. I'm doing okay. Just thought I would look around."

He grinned, his reddened and scarred face twisting into a

somewhat pleasant expression. "Does this mean you've decided to sell the airstrip to me? I'm ready to rock and roll."

She had to laugh at that. "I'm afraid there is no decision yet. Our lawyer contacted a real estate broker in Dallas and stirred up some interest. There are some huge offers in the works, and I'm sure I will have to agree to one of them soon." She shrugged. "Sorry."

"Aww, bad news. I would have really loved to be working here every day. It's what I love." He wiped his hands on an oily rag and stuffed it in his back pocket. "Wanna go for a spin?"

Surprised, she furrowed her brows. "Spin?"

He pointed up to the sky. "In the air. I was just getting ready to take 'er up. How about I show you the Palo Duro Canyon the way Jason would have shown you?"

Jennifer swallowed hard. "In the sky?"

"C'mon. You'll love it." He put his hand on the car door and opened it, offering his hand.

"Okay. I would love to see the canyon, especially as Jason would have shown it to me." She accepted his hand and gave it a shake when she stepped out of the vehicle.

"This is my plane right here." Pell led her to where his plane was sitting in front of the hangar he leased. He showed her where to put her foot to step up into the interior. It was small but comfortable enough for maybe five or six people at the most. Pell closed it up and took his place in the cockpit. "Sit up here with me. You can see the sights."

Jennifer slipped into the seat beside him. Her stomach was doing flip-flops, but she reasoned that this was an opportunity she would probably not ever have again.

"Don't you have to call in to a tower or something?" she asked.

He laughed, a single syllable. "Do you see a tower? I don't."

Jennifer felt her face flush. "No, but…"

"Relax. We're not going to be flying at a high altitude. Just cruising over the canyon. It's really beautiful at this time of day."

Pell was busy getting ready for takeoff, and Jenn was steeling herself for that very same thing. She didn't want this man to realize what a complete wuss she was about flying. Even a big passenger plane caused her to grip the armrests on takeoff, and she had no idea how she was going to get through this new experience, but she was willing to stanch her fear to see the world her brother had loved, the way he'd loved it. "I can't wait," she breathed.

Pell grinned at her. "All right then. Let's get this baby in the air." He flipped some switches and fiddled with a few dials and the plane began rolling toward the runway. Pell turned the plane, and they sat for a minute while he made a couple of adjustments, then the plane went straight down the runway, the nose lifting as they neared the end.

Jenn's stomach was in a clench and she couldn't draw a breath. She wanted to close her eyes but forced herself not to flinch. She let out the breath she hadn't even known she was holding.

"Perfect day for a flight." Pell was grinning broadly. "Not a cloud in the sky. You can see all the way to Amarillo." He was in a great mood, and it was infectious.

Jenn found herself looking at the scenery below as Pell described it. "That's the Garrett ranch. Biggest spread around here. Nice folks, though. You wouldn't know they was richer than shit." His face twisted. "Oh, pardon me, ma'am. I didn't mean to offend."

"I'm not offended," she said.

He nodded. "Glad of that. I've been a lonesome old coot so long, I forget the niceties."

"No problem. Thanks for taking me to see the canyon. I know Jason would appreciate it."

"I was hoping I could continue the aerial tours over the Palo Duro. It's a beautiful place, and I wish I could share it with more folks. It's the second largest canyon in the United States. Only the Grand Canyon is bigger." He pointed out more sites, but then they were over the canyon.

Suddenly, the deep and colorful gorge was below them, and Jenn was enraptured. As the plane flew lower, she made comments on the thrilling colors.

The plane gave a little shake. Nothing big, but it scared her just the same. "What was that?" she asked.

"Not sure." He leaned forward, peering at the instruments before him. Another shudder and the plane started descending... fast. "Brace yourself!"

—◆—

After Cade had devoured his plate of *migas*, he went to Breck's office. He didn't see Breck's truck in front when he pulled in but hoped he was in his office.

The little metal bell over the door clanked against the glass of the inset pane. He saw Misty at her desk, intent upon something on her computer screen.

"Hi, Cade. Come on in." She waved him inside. "Breck had to go to Amarillo for a bail hearing, but he gave me my orders before he left."

Cade felt a little ill at ease, as apparently his cousin's wife was to help him gather information on the companies that had put in offers on the airstrip. He approached Misty's desk and stood awkwardly. "I—I'm not sure what Breck asked you to do, but he told me to come to his office."

"Sit down here. Let me show you what I've found so far." Misty handed him a file folder. "I'm still doing research, but this can keep you entertained."

He sat down in front of her desk and opened the folder. "I'm not sure what I'm looking at."

"I started on the list of prospective buyers. Breck said you want to know what other interests these companies have. This is just the beginning. I have so much more to wade through."

He noted that the first name on the list was Edgar Wayne Pell.

The paragraph below his name was short. Pell was a veteran who had served as a pilot in the U.S. Air Force until his plane was shot down. Pell sustained serious injuries and burns over a large part of his body.

Cade swallowed hard. This accounted for the taut, red skin on Pell's face. Apparently, Pell had recovered and returned to his place of birth to live on a small farm and enjoyed flying his small plane.

Cade picked up the next page in the folder. This one was much longer. Magdalena Swearingen came from old money in Dallas. The list of companies owned by this family was impressive, to say the least. Cade wasn't sure he could grasp the information about the company, but he was certain of one thing: this Maggie lady could afford to buy the airstrip.

"I'm working on them in the order that we received information that these companies were interested in the property." She sighed. "I'll have the rest for you by the end of the day."

"That's awesome, Misty. I'll take them to Big Jim's to look over. I appreciate your working on this, and I'm sure Big Jim will too."

"Hey, I get paid by the hour." Misty grinned at him. "This is more interesting than most of the work I do."

Cade stood and took his leave. "I owe you, Misty."

"Not a thing. As it happens, I owe Big Jim Garrett more than I could ever repay."

The plane shuddered and sputtered.

Jenn's heart raced as she gripped the seat, her jaw tight. Her feet pushed against the floorboard so hard it seemed she would push all the way through.

"C'mon, baby. You can do it." Pell spoke in a soft, coaxing voice. He clutched the wheel with both hands. "We're gonna make it. Don't you worry."

Jenn wasn't sure if he was speaking to her or the plane.

Pell dodged the steep edges of the canyon, zigzagging as they lost altitude. "Hold on!"

With a screech, the plane slid to a rough landing among dense brush and kicked up a lot of sand in the process.

Jenn opened her eyes but couldn't see out the front due to the sand and dust swirling in the air. Her heart tried to beat its way out of her chest, thundering in her ears. She leaned her head back against the headrest, gasping for air.

Pell had collapsed forward, grasping the wheel with both hands and wheezing. "Thank you, sweet Jesus!" he rasped out.

When she was finally able to draw a deep breath, she turned to face him. "What happened? I don't understand."

"Beats me. I gave her a complete overhaul yesterday. She was in great shape."

"I can't believe you managed to land. I thought for sure we were done for."

Pell reached to touch her arm. "Are you hurt?"

She shook her head. "No. I'm okay. Are you hurt?"

"Not this time." He shook his head ruefully. "Not like the last time. I almost burned up."

Jenn had her cell in hand and made a quick call to Cade, but it went to voicemail. She called the sheriff's office next.

They both jumped when they heard pounding on the outside of the plane.

"Let's get out of here." Pell pulled himself out of his seat and held out a hand to Jennifer. He managed to get the door open, and Jenn could see several people wearing shorts and bicycle helmets.

"We saw the whole thing," one woman shouted. "Are you folks all right?"

"We called 911," a man said. "Is anyone hurt?"

Pell climbed down and reached up to assist Jenn. "We seem to be okay."

"Man! That was some masterful flying, mister. I can't believe you didn't crash."

Pell gave a nod and a two-fingered salute. "Been there, done that. Got the medals to prove it."

Jenn felt nothing but respect for the man. She couldn't believe she had been so shallow as to judge him by his appearance when first they met.

The sound of sirens in the distance alerted them to the sheriff's vehicles fast approaching with a cloud of dust kicking up behind them.

"Well, Miss Jennifer," Pell said, "don't let it be said I don't know how to show a lady a good time."

~~~

That evening, Misty greeted Colton with a kiss. "Hey, big guy. How would you feel about having another brother?"

Colt drew back with his brow furrowed. "What? Do you know something I don't know?"

"I'm pretty sure I do." She grinned up at him as his face registered something close to shock.

"What are you trying to tell me?" He made an exaggerated surprised face. "You don't mean my dad…"

"I think your dad is going to adopt my little brother."

To her surprise, Colt burst out laughing. "Good one! I thought you were hinting that Dad had a girlfriend."

"Stop teasing me." She cocked her head to one side and folded her arms across her body. "Colt, I am serious." Misty turned and went out onto the porch. She sank onto the glider and set it in motion. A chorus of katydids were performing a concert in the field behind the barn. It was strangely comforting after the day she had endured—too much emotion for a woman who liked things to roll out easily.

Colt followed her and stood staring down at her. "Honey, I'm sorry. I'm glad you decided to embrace this idea. What changed your mind?"

She patted the seat next to her, and he slid onto the space. "I have to tell you that Mark has been bullied at school. He didn't tell me, but it's been going on for some time."

Colt's brows drew together. "Bullied? Why didn't he say something?"

Misty heaved a sigh. "Apparently, he was ashamed. These boys in his class were giving him a hard time about things that he had no part in." She blinked hard to keep the tears at bay. "Things that our brother did...so maybe being a Dalton is not such a great thing."

Colt wrapped his arms around her and kissed her hair. "Sorry. I didn't have a clue... Do I need to go up to the school and have a talk with the principal?"

Misty let out a huff of air. "Too late. Big Jim went to the school to pick Mark up today. I'm sure he made an impact."

Colt was silent for a few minutes, apparently letting this news set in. Finally, he nodded. "So my dad is going to adopt Mark?"

She shrugged. "I guess so."

Colt planted another kiss on her, this time on her cheek. "Well, Mark is already my little bro by marriage, so I'm okay if Dad makes it official."

"Better let your other brothers know." Misty leaned her head against Colt's shoulder, glad she could give Mark so many good role models.

Chapter 27

WHEN CADE GOT THE CALL FROM JENNIFER, HE WAS IN HIS truck before she disconnected. She sounded shaken but insisted she was all right.

"I think I'm fine. The EMTs are going to see if I'm okay."

"You went flying with Edgar Wayne Pell? Are you crazy?"

She gave a weak-sounding laugh. "Probably. I just wanted to see the canyon from the air, and he offered to show me."

"And he crashed the plane down in the canyon? Damn! You could have been killed."

"I've got to go. The medics want to check me out." She disconnected before he could get the exact location, but he figured he could find her or call back when he got to the canyon.

To say that Cade may have broken the speed limit would have been an understatement. As he flew toward the Palo Duro Canyon, he was alternately furious and panic-stricken over Jennifer's actions. How could she have even thought of going up in a small plane with a man like Edgar Wayne Pell?

The man's twisted, red face had always seemed to make Cade suspicious. Of course, that alone was no solid reason to mistrust the man. It was the way he was rarely seen in town. Maybe he was just a hermit? Maybe he was up to something in his hideaway?

And why had he targeted Jennifer?

Cade's back teeth were clenched so tight his jaw hurt. He

opened the window, hoping the fresh air would help clear his brain. He needed to be calm for Jennifer. She needed him to be strong.

Once he was down in the canyon, it was quite easy to find the site of the plane crash, as a cloud of red dust hovered over the area and several emergency vehicles still had their lights flashing.

A highway patrol officer waved him to one side of the path and kept him from parking near the small aircraft. There was an ambulance and several law enforcement vehicles barring the road, but when he approached the officer and asked where Jennifer was, he was told to check the ambulance.

He saw that the back doors of the ambulance stood open. Jennifer sat next to Pell, wrapped in a blanket and sipping water from a bottle. Her skin looked ashen and she appeared to be exhausted.

"Jennifer? Are you all right?"

When she saw him, she threw back the blanket and reached for him.

"Hold on, mister." A glaring sheriff's deputy stopped him, a firm hand to Cade's chest.

Jennifer's face crumpled and she began to cry. "But he's my boyfriend." Her voice sounded so small and fearful, it tore at his heart.

The officer stepped back, and Cade folded Jennifer in his arms as best he could.

"Try to stay still, sir." The EMT was pumping a blood pressure cuff around Pell's upper arm, and he appeared to be uncomfortable.

"Oh, Cade. It was so scary." Jenn buried her face against his chest. "But Mr. Pell here—he was incredible."

Cade cast a suspicious glance at Pell. "Oh?"

"When the plane started conking out, he managed to land it and save our lives." She shook her head as in disbelief. "I thought we were dead for sure."

Cade heaved a deep sigh, trying to expel all the mistrust and suspicion he had harbored against the man. He regarded Pell as the EMT removed the blood pressure cuff.

"Your blood pressure is way up there, Mr. Pell." The EMT rolled up the cuff.

"I took my meds this morning," Pell replied.

"Doc Ryan says she wants you checked out in the ER."

"Aww." Pell tried to protest, but the EMT was adamant.

"Doc Ryan will chew me a new one if I don't get you to Amarillo. She's at the hospital and wants to see you as soon as possible. Those were her exact words."

Pell shrugged. "Well, since you put it that way."

Cade cleared his throat. "I owe you a debt of gratitude, Mr. Pell. This woman means the world to me." Cade cradled Jennifer in one arm but extended his hand toward Pell.

"You're a lucky man." Pell clasped his hand for a hearty shake. "I just couldn't let this plane crash." He heaved a deep sigh. "I don't understand. I gave her a complete overhaul recently."

One of the sheriff's deputies approached and gave a nod to Pell. "The fuel line has a cut in it, Mr. Pell. Your plane was sabotaged."

Jenn stood in the safety of Cade's arms and watched as the ambulance took Edgar Wayne Pell to the hospital in Amarillo. She felt a strange sense of loss as the vehicle disappeared in a cloud of red dust—as though she was losing sight of a real friend.

"I hope he's okay," she said.

"Me too." Cade hadn't released her from his grip since the moment he had arrived on the scene.

Jennifer was glad. She was still trying to process everything that had happened. Earlier, she had decided to go to the airstrip by herself—to check things out, she had told herself. In truth, she had just wanted to feel closer to Jason.

"C'mon," Cade said. "Let's get you home."

"M-my car is by Mr. Pell's hangar. I need to get it."

Like a zombie, she allowed herself to be ushered to Cade's truck and loaded inside. He returned her to the airstrip, where she climbed into the sedan and followed Cade back to Langston.

When she was on the road, she felt her muscles start to relax. She hadn't noticed how tense she'd been, but now that she was removed from the scene, she began to release the horror.

She could not believe someone would cut Mr. Pell's fuel line the same way they had Jason's. It had to be related.

When they hit the edge of town, she flashed her lights at Cade and turned toward the church. He had to make a U-turn to follow her. When she stopped in front of the church, he pulled up behind her and leapt out to open her door. "What are we doing here at the church?"

"The children are being cared for in the Mothers' Day Out program. I needed to have some time to—to..." Her voice sounded a little curt.

His brows knit together. "You know you can call me if you need a break."

"Are you complaining because I brought the kids here?" She couldn't believe he was so upset. "For your information, I wanted them to be able to play with other children their age. It's called socialization."

His jaw was tight. "Stay here. I'll go get them." He turned abruptly and stomped up the steps to the church. When he returned, he carried both children and secured them in their car seats. He closed the back door and heaved a sigh.

"What are you so upset about?" she asked. "I'm the one who survived a plane crash."

"Yeah, and what are you doing getting yourself involved? You could have been killed."

"Involved? I am involved. Someone murdered my brother. That isn't going to go away." Jenn felt the stirring of anger in her gut. She couldn't believe he was angry with her. She started the car. "Why can't you understand that I will not rest until whoever is responsible for tampering with both planes is behind bars?"

"Because I don't want you to get killed. I love you, dammit!" He turned and climbed into his truck. He started the engine and may have revved it too hard.

Cade followed her to the house and helped get the children into the house and then took his leave.

She sensed he wanted her to invite him to stay, but she thanked him for picking her up at the crash site and for following her home with the children. She was exhausted as well as frightened.

Was she being targeted by her brother's killer, or was Edgar Wayne Pell? Although it was still daylight, Jenn locked the doors and closed the drapes. Fortunately, the children were exhausted from their playday and were willing to go to bed right after she fed them.

Jenn settled down in front of the television, holding the remote while characters played out stories on the screen, but the visions in her head were far more frightening.

⁓

Cade drove home feeling as though his insides had been sucked out through his heart. He had driven away from the family he loved and would give his life for, but Jenn didn't seem to have any use for him tonight.

When he arrived at his ranch, he went through the motions of closing the barn and making sure the horses were taken care of. He shut them in the stable and headed for the ranch house. It was time for dinner, but he had no appetite at all.

He settled for opening a can of chili and nuking it in a bowl. It didn't taste like much of anything, much less chili—not the chili his uncle made and served with cornbread he baked in a big iron skillet.

Cade understood. Big Jim cooked out of love. He cooked for the people he loved. For family. He had stepped up to be the sole provider after his wife died. And his sons and other relatives had thrived thanks to his efforts. Big Jim was the universal father figure.

That's what Cade yearned to be. He hadn't known he needed to be the man of the family. "Husband." He tried out the word, but it sounded foreign to his ears. "Father." He could embrace that role easier. The kids just needed someone to provide them with the basics: food, clothing, and shelter…and love.

Cade swallowed hard. What would he need to provide to Jennifer?

The next morning, Jenn called the hospital in Amarillo and asked for Edgar Wayne Pell's room. She found that he had not been admitted but spent the night in the emergency room, being monitored by Dr. Ryan and the staff.

"Please tell him I called." She disconnected and went to prepare the children's breakfast.

The best thing about kids was that no matter what awful event had taken place in one's life, the children would always need to be cared for. She could focus her attention on giving baths and preparing kid-favored food.

If her life could go on this way, where she didn't have to think about bad things like who killed Jason and who tried to kill her and Mr. Pell, she might be able to function.

But all too soon, the horror of the near crash returned, bombarding her mind with images of the canyon growing closer and closer…and then the impact.

She flinched as the memory flashed in her brain.

"Gotta do something else." Jenn took out her phone and called Leah.

When Leah heard about the plane going down, she was horrified.

"Why don't you throw the kids in the car and come out to the ranch? I could use some company, and I can offer a kid-friendly lunch."

Jenn heaved a grateful breath. "I'll be there as soon as possible. Thanks."

In no time at all, she had the kids clean and dressed and secured in their car seats.

"We're going to visit your aunt Leah. You'll have a good time."

"I wanna go to Miss Mary's place," Leo whined. Miss Mary was the pre-K teacher at the church.

Jenn glanced at him in the rearview mirror.

His lower lip jutted out, and he was frowning.

"Um…not today, Leo. You can go to see Miss Mary on Sunday." She changed the subject quickly and kept him occupied counting trucks on the highway. When she pulled in at the Garrett ranch, she called Leah to get directions to the new house Colt had built for his family on the huge property.

Leah and her infant son were outside waiting for them when Jenn pulled up close to the house. "Come on up on the porch. I made some lemonade and goodies for lunch, and I thought we could enjoy this beautiful day right here."

Jenn released the children and ushered them up onto the porch, which was a wooden deck with a wide roof overhang. A large oak tree provided even more shade, and there was a slight breeze, so it was quite pleasant. "This is really lovely."

Leah grinned and gestured for Jenn to join her at the table. "I have a macaroni casserole in the warming oven and I made a shrimp salad for the big girls."

Jenn seated herself, pulling Lissy onto her lap. "Yum! I haven't had shrimp salad since I moved here."

"Frozen shrimp, but it's pretty tasty." Leah stood up and placed the baby in a swing just his size. She gave it a little push and him a tickle on the tummy. "If you can keep an eye on him, I'll bring the rest of the food to the table."

"Sure thing." Jenn leaned to touch the soft fuzz on the baby's head. "See the baby, Lissy?"

For her part, Lissy regarded James Tyler Garrett in silence while gnawing on her index finger. A moment later, Leah reappeared bearing a tray. "I have cold drinks in the cooler. Take your pick."

When Jenn opened the cooler, she found it filled with several longneck bottles of beer, various sodas, bottled water, and juice boxes. "Wow! Quite a selection." She pulled out two juice boxes for the little ones and a soda for herself. It was hard to believe that Leah could throw all this together on the spur of the moment. There were disposable dinnerware and utensils on the table, as well as a bouquet that looked as if it had been freshly picked from the yard.

Leah placed the tray on the table and passed around bowls. "I thought I would make it easy on everyone, so I dished up our food in the kitchen."

"Great idea." Jenn watched as Leah hauled Leo up onto a chair and scooted a bowl of very cheesy macaroni in front of him.

"What is those gween things?" Leo asked.

Leah bent down to his level. "Those are peas. My great big husband swears that he grew so big because he loved to eat peas." She looked around in a conspiratorial manner. "I took some for you from his private pea collection… Don't tell anyone. It's our secret."

Leo stared at her open-mouthed, and then scooped the pea-laden macaroni into his mouth.

Jenn realized that if she served peas to Leo, he would have cried, pouted, and refused to eat them, while Jenn begged and bargained. *Leah is Wonder Woman.*

Lissy reached for her macaroni with her fingers and jammed it into her mouth. Leah fastened a large terry bib around her, which was just in time to catch what spilled down her chin.

Jenn reached for a napkin, but Leah waved her off. "We can clean her up later. Eat your salad and tell me what's going on with you and Cade. You said he came out to where the plane went down?"

Jenn took a bite of the salad and let out an involuntary moan. "This is delicious, Leah. You should open a restaurant...or maybe cater events."

Leah beamed with pleasure. "I would love that. You know I really enjoy feeding people...but you're avoiding the subject. Tell me how you and Cade are doing. Please tell me there's romance."

Jenn felt the blush creeping up her cheeks. "Um...yes. We care for each other." She took another bite and reached for a cracker. "I think I'm in love with the man, but he's really mad at me right now. He can't understand why I took a ride with Mr. Pell over the canyon."

Leah's brows rose. "Oh, wow! Is he jealous?"

That hadn't occurred to Jenn, but she rejected the idea. "I don't think so. He doesn't seem to like Mr. Pell for some reason."

Leah shrugged. "He is rather odd-looking."

Jenn laid her fork down, regarding Leah solemnly. "Edgar Wayne Pell is a war veteran. He was wounded when his plane was shot down."

Leah swallowed hard. "I didn't know that. Poor man."

"He was amazing. He managed to land the plane even though someone cut the fuel line...just like they did when they murdered my brother and sister-in-law."

"Oh my!" Leah pressed her napkin to her mouth. "That is so frightening."

Jenn picked up her fork again and resumed eating. "I don't think the killer was after me because it was a spur-of-the-moment decision to fly with him."

"So you're saying someone is trying to kill Mr. Pell?" Leah looked appalled. "You have to stay away from him."

"Well, it was sort of a fluke that we met." Jenn took a long drink of her soda. "I've just been dragging my feet about selling the airstrip. I know that I'm not equipped to run the place. I have no business skills at all." She shrugged. "So it would be incredibly dumb of me to hold on to it out of sentiment."

"I can understand. Your brother was important to you, so the airstrip has to mean a lot too."

A gentle breeze lifted Jenn's hair. "But I have to let go. Jason is dead, and I have his two kids to raise. In the long run, I'll need the money from the sale to put these children through college."

"Good plan." Leah saluted her with her soda can. "It sounds like you've made a decision."

"Not me," Jenn protested. "I'll leave the choice of buyer to Cade and Breckenridge Ryan. Breck seems to have a commercial real estate broker in his back pocket. I'll settle for signing my name to the paperwork."

Chapter 28

"Hey, Dad!" Misty greeted Big Jim Garrett with a hug. "What are you doing here? Breck didn't mention that you were coming in."

Big Jim took his Stetson off and placed it on the edge of her desk before taking a seat across from her. "Well, I called him earlier, and he said he had to go to the courthouse in the county seat before he got to the office. Thought I would have a little talk with you before he arrives."

Misty folded her hands on top of her desk. "What's up?"

Big Jim gave her a long look. "I bet you have that all figured out, little missy."

She smiled. "It's about adopting my little brother, isn't it?"

He nodded. "You're too smart for your own good. I sure am glad you married my oldest son."

"Me too."

"So, are you okay with this adoption thing?"

She heaved a big sigh. "Yes, I am. It took a little getting used to, but when Mark came home with cuts and bruises, I was so hurt for him." She spread her hands. "He looks up to you so much. You're the father he's never had."

Much to Big Jim's consternation, tears welled up in her large, dark eyes. As in most things female, he felt totally incapable of dealing with tears, especially with someone he loved. Her pain was his pain. "Uh…I'm sorry. I didn't mean to…"

"Nooo, I'm not really upset. I was just thinking of my father. He was such a good man when my mother was alive…but he just sort of fell apart after…"

Big Jim could understand that. His own dear wife, Elizabeth, had been killed when the church bus rolled over returning from a retreat. Big Jim had wished it was he who had died. Too much pain. But when he saw his three young sons mourning their mother, he had to be strong. Unfortunately, Misty's father had not been able to step up and be strong for his children. Poor Mark, the youngest, had not fared so well.

"It ain't easy to survive the death of a loved one." He gave her a nod. "You know that 'death do us part' stuff? Some of us take it real serious."

Misty mopped at her eyes, smiling through her tears. "Thanks. I know you're trying to give my dad an excuse for virtually abandoning us when Mom died. I appreciate your efforts."

Big Jim tried to deny her assertions, but in his heart, he knew it was true. He had held the Dalton family in low regard due to the father's usually drunken state. Now, he was trying to comfort Misty…who was his daughter too.

And there was Mark.

Just then, Breckenridge T. Ryan came through the front door, setting the little bell over the door clanking against the glass inset. "Sorry to keep you waiting, Big Jim. I trust that my intrepid office manager kept you entertained." He tossed his hat on a bent-wood coatrack near the door and crossed the room to clasp Big Jim's hand and pump it firmly. "Come on in my office and tell me what's on your mind." He breezed into his private office, removing his jacket as he walked.

Big Jim stood and reached across the desk for Misty's hand. He raised it to his lips and delivered a soft kiss. "I am so glad Colton won your heart. You are a treasured part of my family… and so is Mark."

Misty jumped out of her chair and came around the desk to throw her arms around his neck. She didn't speak, but Big Jim shared her feelings.

He went into Breck's office and took a chair. "What do I need to do to be able to legally adopt Misty's little brother?"

Breck's brows rose almost to his hairline. "You want to adopt?"

"Mark is a good kid. He needs to be a Garrett." Big Jim raked a hand through his silvery hair. "What's it gonna take to make it happen?"

Breck was still frowning. "To change his name will just involve a little paperwork and a few hundred dollars." He reached for a legal pad and began making notes. "To actually adopt will take longer and involve more."

"Well, why don't you get started with the name change, and we can work on the adoption?" That made perfect sense to Big Jim. Take care of the boy and make sure he never got bullied again. His three sons had each other when they were in school; now, Mark needed strong family ties to give him the support he needed.

Breckenridge started taking notes, writing down full names and dates of birth. "So the boy will become Mark Alan Garrett and give up being Mark Alan Dalton?"

They spent a few minutes discussing the changes and then Big Jim left the office. He climbed in his truck, feeling that he had made the right decision. The family could always use another good man, even if he was only a boy.

When Jenn got back from her visit with Leah, she found Cade waiting for her. He was sitting on the steps to the front porch.

Seeing him caused a crushing sensation in her chest.

He got up and strode to Jenn's car, his long legs taking him across the yard quickly. He opened her door and, without a word, leaned in for a kiss.

Apparently he was over his annoyance. He pulled her to her feet and delivered another soul-searing kiss. "Oh, babe. I'm sorry I was such an ass. I was just scared and took it out on you. Can you forgive me?" His amazing eyes, a smoky-turquoise blue with a darker blue around the edges, were fixed on her, as if she was the most precious thing in his life.

"No, I'm sorry. I was so rattled after the plane went down. I should have realized you were worried about me."

"Let me help you with the kids." He removed Lissy from her car seat and lifted her into his arms, while Jenn helped Leo climb out of his seat.

Once in the house, he helped her deal with the children, and when they had finally put them to bed, Cade pulled her into his arms. "Tired?"

"Yeah, a bit. I guess I've been a little fatigued after the plane went down. It was like all of my energy sort of got used up when I was so frightened."

He brushed a strand of hair away from her face. "I'll bet. I'll go back to the ranch and let you get some rest." He placed a kiss against her temple.

She wrapped her arms around his torso. "I was kind of hoping you would stay over."

A wide grin spread across his face. "I was kind of hoping you would say that. I brought a brand-new toothbrush with me."

Jenn stared at the plastic wrapped toothbrush, realizing it was a symbol of so much more. "You can put it right next to mine."

The next morning, Cade left shortly after breakfast. Starting the day in the arms of the man she loved was the very best way, as far as Jenn knew. The children were so comfortable with him, it made Jenn realize they had created a family of sorts.

If only he would make it real. He didn't have to get down on bended knee. All he needed to do was hint that he would like to marry her, and Jenn would jump on it. *Confirmed bachelor?* Maybe she was just a handy and willing sexual partner. Maybe he loved her, as he claimed. Was it a forever love?

Jenn and the children were on the wide front porch, playing with Minnie, when Pell drove up in his pickup truck. He was grinning as he swung out of the cab.

"Hey, Miss Jennifer. How are you doing this fine day?"

"You're released from the hospital? That must be good news."

He scruffled behind Minnie's ears as he came up onto the porch. "I'm a hard man to kill."

She gestured for him to sit beside her on the glider. "You must be. Come on up and have a glass of iced tea with me."

"Sounds good. The sheriff confirmed that the fuel line had been cut, so it was sabotage." He seated himself next to Jenn.

"I can't tell you how grateful I am that you were able to land the plane." She poured him a glass of tea and twisted a leaf of mint in it.

"Thanks. You know, I've been thinking. Maybe we could work together to run the airstrip. I know all about the mechanics, and you could run the office." He looked at her hopefully.

"That sounds great, except I know nothing about running an office…and I have these two little charmers to tend to. Wish I had some talents to add to the mix." She shrugged. "Maybe Cade has some secretarial skills."

Pell laughed at that. "Maybe."

"So, when you're not flying around, what do you do?"

"I got a little farm. Nothin' much, but it suits me and my herd."

"You raise cattle?"

"Nope. I raise Angora goats. I shear them and take their wool to a lady over in Amarillo who spins it into yarn and sells it. She's my partner in an online shop." Lissy had crawled over to inspect his boots, and he lifted her into his lap. "It's a nice little business."

"Sounds like you enjoy it." Jenn took a sip of her lemonade.

"Sounds like it keeps you busy. Are you sure you would want to take on an airstrip?"

He snorted. "The goats get sheared once or twice a year. Other than that, I'm at loose ends. So, what do you think? Can we be partners too?"

Jenn pursed her lips. She knew there were some high-dollar offers on the table, and she was sure it would be best to choose the best offer and be done with it. But she thought Edgar Wayne Pell had the same kind of passion for the airstrip that her brother had. It would be nice to let it go to another avid airman.

———

When the school bell rang, Tyler Garrett was waiting outside the door of Mark's classroom. He had been observing the boy through the glass inset in the door. He watched as Mark gathered his backpack and streamed out with the others when the door opened. Ty watched Mark's face morph as he recognized the large person by the door.

"Tyler!"

"Hey, boy. You ready to head for the ranch?" Ty noted that the other children filing out were taking notice. He put his hand on Mark's shoulder and the two of them were swept out the front doors by the crowd of emerging students.

When they were on the road, Tyler let Mark know that Big Jim had been to see Breckenridge Ryan and the options were to change Mark's name to Garrett, which could happen right away, but the option to be adopted was also on the table. "So, it's up to you, Mark. Big Jim can adopt you, and you will officially be my brother."

"Just like Colt and Beau?" Mark's large, dark eyes were shining.

"Just like them," Tyler assured him.

"My sister said it's okay." Mark's brow furrowed. "She and Colt said I need a father."

"It's all up to you. You just think about it and let me know."

When Tyler turned in at the Garrett ranch, he knew that he and Mark and Big Jim would talk it out over chores in the stable.

―⁓―

The next day, Jenn dropped the children off at the church day care and planned to drive out to Cade's ranch. It was about time she made a booty call.

On her return to the house, she made sure she had the proper bait to land a confirmed bachelor cowboy.

She was looking particularly gorgeous and wearing the clothing he found most appealing: boots, jeans, and a knit T-shirt. She spritzed herself with a lovely scent, and her hair was soft and free.

When she heard a knock at her front door, she thought perhaps the object of her affection had flown into her web. Jenn wore a wide grin when she threw the door open. Her grin froze on her face when she recognized her caller. "Maggie?"

Magdalena Swearingen stood on her front porch looking irritated. "You are messing with the wrong woman, Jennifer LaChance. I told you that it would be in your best interests to make sure I could buy the airstrip, but apparently you didn't believe me."

Jenn stared at the irate woman, unable to comprehend the source of her anger. "I have no idea what you're talking about. Would you like to come inside and tell me what has you so upset?"

Maggie stormed inside, huffing as she entered. "Upset? You call this upset? You haven't seen upset yet." She turned abruptly, glaring at Jenn with venom in her eyes.

Jenn's stomach did a tumble and roll. "Um…would you like to sit down and have some iced tea?"

"Oh, hell no! This is not a social call."

Jenn was a woman who knew anger, and hers was heating up fast. "Look, I have no idea why you're here and what has your panties in a twist, but I was just going out."

Maggie tilted her head to one side and made a face, mocking

Jenn. "Oh, you were just going out, were you?" She jabbed her finger at Jenn. "You are not going to ruin my deal. I have a lot riding on it."

Jenn took a step back. "What deal are you talking about? We have no deal. The decision about the airstrip will be made by Cade and the lawyer. I'm going to go with their recommendation."

"Not what I heard," Maggie said. "I heard that you were all sentimental about the property and didn't plan to sell."

Jenn pressed her lips tight together. "Who told you that?"

Maggie's eyes were slits, glowering spitefully. "Your dear friend Edgar Wayne Pell. He said he asked you to partner with him. You're too attached to the place because of your dear brother, Jason." She practically spat out his name. "I tried to make a deal with Jason too, but he wasn't interested in selling at any price."

A tingling sensation coiled around Jenn's spine. "You tried to buy the airstrip from Jason?"

Maggie paced around Jenn's living room, hands on her hips. "I made him a very generous offer, but he wasn't at all interested. Said it was the family business and he wanted to hand it down to his children."

Jenn could see Jason telling her that. He was proud of the enterprise he had built, and he was all about family. It seemed her heart was about to squeeze out of her chest. She realized this woman was the incarnation of evil. "What did you do to my brother?"

"Me?" Maggie placed her hand on her chest. "I did nothing... but my mechanic did a little alteration to Jason's plane. I didn't know his wife would be with him. I figured she would be a pushover and sell out immediately."

Jenn had wanted to know the truth about her brother's death, and now it was staring her in the face...or rather, glaring. "And you tried to kill Mr. Pell."

Maggie shrugged. "Get rid of the local competition. No one in the community would miss him."

Jenn felt her lip quivering. "Why are you telling me this? You know I will go straight to the sheriff."

Maggie's face morphed from anger to amusement. "You think?" She let out a huff of laughter. "You are the single impediment standing between me and the deal that will make my father respect me."

"I don't know what makes you think I can make your father respect you, but you need to get out of my house. You need to go now!" Jenn took a few steps to the door and wrenched it open, hoping Maggie would take her leave with no further incident.

"Yeah, I'm ready to leave, but you're coming with me." She produced a small handgun, pointing it at Jenn's midsection. "Go on out to my car."

"I'm not going anywhere with you."

The corners of Maggie's mouth turned up in a wry semblance of a smile. "Really? I was hoping you wouldn't get blood all over my car. I just had it detailed. Now start walking."

Slowly, Jenn raised her hands and stepped out onto the porch.

Maggie gestured with the gun for her to go down the steps and toward the silver BMW waiting at the curb.

"Get in," Maggie said. "No, not in the car. Get in the trunk."

Chapter 29

JENN'S HEART THUDDED AGAINST HER RIBS. SHE COULDN'T TELL where they were going, but they were definitely on the highway. The difference between the poorly maintained streets of Langston and the smooth interstate was easy to identify. Now she was being held in the trunk of a crazy women who was definitely speeding down the highway. She tried to straighten her legs, but there was a full-size tire in the trunk, and it was wedged against her back.

Jenn was cramped, to say the least. She had no idea what Maggie planned to do with her, but it wasn't good. If her captor had killed Jason and admitted it to Jenn, she was pretty sure she wouldn't make it out of this situation alive.

What would happen to Leo and Lissy if she wasn't around to care for them?

She swallowed hard. She knew that Cade would take over quite capably. He had Mrs. Reynolds to provide day-to-day care, and Cade himself would be a perfect father figure. Strong, honest, loving.

A tear slipped out of the corner of her eye and trickled through her scalp. *Oh no! I can't break down. I have to fight to the last—*

Her thoughts broke off suddenly. *I must not even entertain the thought that I won't survive.*

The car turned off the highway, and for the next half hour or so, Jenn was jarred all over the trunk as Maggie drove on some unpaved road. It was getting warm inside the small, confined space and there was no air circulating.

Finally, the car ground to a stop and she heard another vehicle pull up behind the BMW. The BMW's door slammed, and she heard voices. Maggie was speaking to a man who responded in single-syllable words.

Jenn let out a scream and banged her fists against the inside of the trunk. Maggie slammed her fists on the outside. "You can yell all you want. No one will hear you."

"Wait!" Jenn shrieked. "Tell me why you're so driven to own the airstrip. I have to know."

"You think you deserve to know?" Maggie laughed again. "I guess I owe you that much. My father has always treated me as his little darling, while my brothers made the business deals. Lots of Dallas suburbs were built by Swearingen Construction. This totally undeveloped area is all farmland and none of the farmers around here are willing to give up a freaking acre, no matter how much I offered."

Jenn winced as Maggie smacked the trunk again. "But when I realized your stupid brother owned almost a thousand acres and all he had on it was that tiny, small-town airstrip… Honestly, he had no vision. I could have made him rich, but nooo. He wouldn't budge."

"Please," Jenn begged. "Please let me go. I can't see how my death will get you what you want."

"I'm sure that farmer, Cade Garrett, will be easier to work with. He for sure doesn't want to run an airstrip."

Jenn realized Maggie was right. He would sell to the highest bidder so the children would have an assured future.

"Wait! What about me?"

Another laugh. "You, my dear, will die. When you are thoroughly cooked, we'll come back and leave your remains artfully displayed here on the trail. You will be found in a couple of days, out here in the canyon, dehydrated and dead from the heat. Poor, silly girl. Nobody will miss you."

Jenn heard the sound of a powerful motor starting up and a door slam, then the other vehicle pulled away, spewing gravel as it departed.

Jenn stared into the darkness. There was nothing but silence all around her. Silence and heat and very little air.

—◆◆◆—

Cade had driven by Jenn's house, surprised to find no one at home. He didn't recall her telling him about any appointments or meetings. He peeked in the garage and found both vehicles parked inside.

He must have had some sense of foreboding because he wasn't content to drive away. He called her cell phone, but heard its funny little song tinkling inside the house.

Jenn had gone somewhere with the children and without her phone...but she wasn't driving. He called the Langston Inn and Ollie Sue Enloe answered immediately, sounding perky and professional.

"Ollie, is Jennifer LaChance with you?"

"Um, no. Is this Cade?"

"Yes, sorry. I'm worried about her. She and the kids are gone, but both cars are in the garage. I was hoping you might know where they are."

Ollie gave a sort of snort of amusement. "I thought you were getting to be pretty sweet on Jennifer."

Cade blew out a breath. "Sweet on her? I'm in love with her... and I'm worried. Who would she leave with, especially with the kids?" He realized his hand was fisted.

"Well, you might check the church. She has been taking the kids to the pre-kinder program at least one day a week, so they'll have someone their own age to play with, and the church ladies are teaching them things too."

"Uh, that's nice, but it doesn't help me find Jennifer."

"You might try Leah Garrett. Those two are thick as thieves," Ollie said.

Cade disconnected, his concern growing. *Where would she go?*

"Young man?" An elderly woman across the street was leaning on her walker, but she let go with one hand and waved at him.

Cade crossed the street, trying to mask his fear. "Yes, ma'am. Can I help you?"

"If you're looking for that pretty girl who lives there with the two babies...the poor little orphans..."

Cade's chest felt as though it might explode. "Yes, ma'am. That's who I'm looking for. Have you seen her today?"

The woman smiled, her face wreathed in a thousand wrinkles. "I've seen your truck outside. I was thinking maybe you two were courting."

Cade tried to be patient. "Yes, ma'am. She's my girlfriend. I'm worried about her because I can't reach her by phone. Do you know where she might be?"

"Well, I was sitting on my porch this morning, having a nice cup of decaf, and I saw this silver car come up with a screech. I know the driver was speeding." The woman gazed up at him earnestly. "And a dark-haired woman went rushing up to knock on the door. I couldn't hear what she said, but she was yelling at your sweetheart."

Cade swallowed hard. "Yelling?"

The woman nodded. "Your girlfriend let her in, but I could hear the mad woman yelling after she went inside. Then, in a very short time, the door opened and the dark-haired woman came out with the young lady and made her get in the trunk. Then she drove away."

"What? Why did Jennifer get in the trunk?" Cade couldn't imagine.

"Oh, didn't I tell you? The dark-haired woman had a little gun."

—<small>∞</small>—

It was getting hotter. Jenn was sweating and felt weak. There was very little air in the BMW's trunk, and what air remained was like an oven. She groped around for something to use to pry the trunk open, but of course there was nothing. It seemed Maggie had cleaned out her trunk before forcing Jenn to climb inside.

What else?

Reaching in her pocket, she drew out the key chain that Jason had always carried, the one with the children's pictures. The hard plastic disk and keys were the only tools available.

Jenn gritted her teeth and pried the covering off the taillight, pulling the tiny bulb out of its setting and using the key to crack the red plastic outer covering. She poked it again and again until finally the plastic shattered and fell outside the trunk. Jenn could see the sandy, dry scenery that could only be the canyon. At least there was a little air in the void. She pressed her lips together. *Damned if I'm going to go easy.*

She could not reach the other taillight by her feet, but she was wearing the boots Cade had purchased for her. She kicked the second taillight out in one single thrust. Yes, there was air. It was hot air, but at least it was air.

Surely someone will find me. Cade, where are you?

She cradled her head in her arms and tried to be as comfortable as possible in her cramped position. She envisioned Cade's handsome face. The way he told her he loved her. And the kisses he delivered. He had to find her so they could get married and live happily ever after.

Cade returned to his truck and made a call to the sheriff's department. His friend Sheriff Derrick Shelton answered. "Derrick, my girlfriend has been abducted. You have to find her."

He hadn't heard the old truck pull up behind him, but when he turned, Edgar Wayne Pell was glaring at him. He listened while Cade explained to Derrick what had happened.

"The neighbor across the street said it was a dark-haired woman in a silver car, and that she had a gun when she forced Jennifer into her trunk."

"That's gotta be Maggie Swearingen. She's got a slick silver BMW." Pell was rubbing the side of his very red face. "She's tryin' to buy the airstrip."

"Did you hear that, Derrick? It's a woman who has a hangar out at the airstrip. Silver BMW. Her name is Swearingen."

"Swearingen?" Derrick asked. "Like Swearingen Industries?"

"I guess," Cade said.

"Big money. Big old money." Derrick said he was putting out an APB on the silver BMW and would be going out to the airstrip to see if he could locate Maggie Swearingen.

Cade disconnected. He stood, frozen with indecision.

"Well, what are you waitin' for? Let's get to moving." Pell gestured to Cade's truck. "We gotta save Miss Jennifer. Let's go to the airstrip."

Cade nodded and the two men, who had not been friends before, were united in a single mission: find Jennifer LaChance.

On the drive, Cade called his uncle, Big Jim Garrett, to get the rest of the family stirred into action. The more people looking for Jennifer, the better, and Big Jim was capable of bringing a lot of force to the search.

At the same time, Pell had his cell out and was making calls. Cade had no idea who he was talking to, but the more the merrier.

When they arrived at the airstrip, there was no silver BMW to be found. Pell pointed out the hangar rented by the Swearingen Corporation. But it appeared to be closed up and uninhabited.

The two men peered inside, seeing the two planes.

Just then, Big Jim Garrett pulled up behind Cade's truck. And behind him came Tyler and Colton. The Garrett men looked very grim.

"What do you need us to do?" Big Jim said.

Pell looked him over critically. "Well, Mr. Garrett, how do you feel about a little breaking and entering?"

Cade was gripping the armrests of the shiny blue plane that Pell had gotten airborne. Stolen, actually.

He had no faith in Pell's abilities, especially after he'd crashed his own plane with Jennifer in it. But she had complete faith in Pell, extolling his abilities. So Cade had climbed in with Pell.

Big Jim showed no such fear and seated himself behind Pell. He did deny his two sons seating on the plane. "Just sayin'…better to have some Garretts to carry on the name. You know, in case…"

Now they were airborne and peering out the windows.

"This sure has a quiet motor," Big Jim said. "What do you suppose a little plane like this one costs?"

"This little beauty is an Eclipse 550," Pell said. "It runs just under three million and is one of the most fuel-efficient twin engines on the market."

"Holy crap!" Big Jim exploded. "What's it made of? Pure platinum?"

"No, sir," Pell replied. "Just some of the most advanced design in aeronautics available today."

"Well, what the hell is that woman doing flying around in this thing?" Big Jim growled.

"Whatever she wants," Pell said. "Keep looking out both sides for the silver BMW. I put a call out to some of my veteran flyboys, and there are a lot of small planes in the air right now lookin' for Miss Jennifer."

Cade sucked in a deep breath. Jennifer was right. Edgar Wayne Pell was a good man. Cade stared out the window, hoping to spot a silver BMW on the ground below—hoping to find Jennifer alive and well.

Chapter 30

JENN WASN'T AWARE THAT SHE SLEPT. SHE HAD ALMOST GIVEN UP on being found. She was dreaming of Cade Garrett and he was looking at her in that way he had, the way that made her insides turn to jelly. And he was saying her name... No, he was yelling her name.

"Jennifer! Jennifer, baby! Please wake up!"

She heard him, but he was calling her from somewhere overhead and far away. She didn't know how she had sunk to the depths of wherever she was, but her skin was damp and now a breeze was cooling it.

"Come on, babe. Please look at me."

She opened her eyes, blinking in the bright sunlight. Cade held her in both arms and he appeared to be very stressed. She tried to speak, but no words came forth—just a sound between a moan and a grunt.

"It's okay. Don't worry. We got you."

Who got me? She struggled to regain full consciousness.

Big Jim Garrett leaned over her. "Here, try this." He mopped at her face with something wet and cool.

It all came back to her in a rush. "Oh!"

Big Jim handed a bottle of water to Cade, who held it to her very dry lips. She tried to peel her tongue off the roof of her mouth, but it felt like a strip of leather. Slowly, enough water trickled into her mouth to allow her to swallow.

A breeze lifted her hair. Her other senses gradually awakened.

Gasping, she took in big gulps of the dusty air. Although there was still plenty of light, she realized it must be late in the day because the sun was sending big smears of brilliant color across the skies from a westerly direction.

"Cade, I—I…"

He pulled her closer. "Don't try to talk. We know about that Swearingen woman. I'm just glad that we found you."

She managed a smile. "I had no doubt that you would find me."

He brushed a strand of hair off her forehead. "What made you so sure I would find you?"

Jenn stifled a giggle. "Because you haven't proposed to me yet."

Jennifer was taken to the hospital with a retinue of trucks behind the ambulance. When she was delivered to the emergency room of the regional hospital in Amarillo, she found Dr. Cami Ryan waiting for her.

"You have a lot of cowboys in your fan club," Dr. Ryan said. "It looks like most of the Garrett clan is camped out in the waiting room."

Jenn let her head loll back onto the pillow on the gurney. "Aren't they wonderful?" Her words were a little slurred. "They found me…Cade found me."

The nurse had started an IV to rehydrate her, and Dr. Ryan was taking her vital signs.

"And you were very lucky, my friend. You would have cooked in that trunk without water." She finished her preliminary examination and said she was keeping her overnight.

"I have to talk to Cade," Jenn said. "Please let me see him."

In a matter of minutes, Cade was standing beside her in the emergency room cubicle. He kissed her forehead and clasped her hand.

"Cade, you have to go get the children. I left them in the church day care program. They must be closed down by now." She felt tears gather in her eyes.

Cade leaned close and whispered, "The kids are just fine. Misty picked them up and is taking care of them at her home." He kissed her temple this time. "Don't worry about a thing. We're all here for you and everything is going to be all right."

Jenn felt all of the tension leave her body. She took in several deep breaths and exhaled them forcefully. Everything was going to be all right. "There's one more thing, Cade." She gazed up into the intense blue eyes. "Did I propose to you?"

A wide grin spread across his face. "Yes, you did suggest that I should get on the ball and propose to you, but I was planning on a more romantic setting. I mean this place smells like antiseptic, and—"

"Yes. I accept," she said. "I will marry you."

Cade just grinned and said, "That's good enough for me."

In the morning, Cade was awakened when a hospital attendant stopped outside Jennifer's room, pushing a very noisy cart. Cade stretched, trying to unkink his very sore muscles that had tightened up after he'd spent the night cramped in a chair.

The hospital aide sorted around, moving glassware and metal utensils, then gave a brisk knock on the doorframe and brought a covered tray to Jennifer's over-bed table.

"Just leave it," Cade ordered, sending the man from the room with a nod.

Jennifer, for her part, slept on in a nicely medicated state. The nurses had checked on her all night and replenished her fluids, but Jennifer had slept through all the noise and activity.

Cade settled back in his chair, content to stand watch over the woman he loved, glad she had survived and that she had taken the initiative when it came to the proposal. He had been thinking about it for some time, but never seemed to find the right moment. But now, it was done. He would figure out what needed to be accomplished and follow through: the church...and they needed a license... He was deep in thought when a knock at the door jerked him out of his concentration.

It was Sheriff Derrick Shelton, peering into the room. "Hey, Cade. Can I come in?"

Cade glanced at Jennifer and motioned for him to enter but indicated he was to be quiet. "Hey, Derrick. Jennifer's out of it. They've got her medicated."

The sheriff stepped into the room, casting a glance at the woman sleeping in the bed. "Sorry to see that. I was supposed to question her about the event. I understand that this Swearingen woman kidnapped her."

Cade motioned Derrick to the other chair, speaking in a low tone. "I didn't get to ask her much when we found her, but the lady across the street from the LaChance house was the one who informed me that Maggie Swearingen had forced Jennifer to get into the trunk of her silver BMW."

Derrick's eyes widened. "She said all that?"

"Well, no. She described the dark-haired woman and the silver car. It was Edgar Wayne Pell who put it all together."

Derrick was making notes. "I'll talk to both of them, but I really need to interview Jennifer to document this correctly. You know... tie it up with a bow?"

Cade shrugged. "Don't have any idea when she will be able to talk with you. She was pretty loopy last night."

"Give me a call when she's available." Derrick folded his notebook and slipped it back in his jacket pocket. "We located this Swearingen woman, but she lawyered up immediately. She's being held for questioning in Dallas." He pulled himself to his feet. "But her airplane mechanic is here in our Langston Sheriff's office and is talking up a storm."

Cade felt a great weight lift off his shoulders. If Maggie Swearingen and her mechanic were in custody, they could pose no threat to Jennifer or anyone else.

Jenn stayed in the hospital another day. Dr. Ryan was being careful, and Derrick was able to interview her the next afternoon. Having her recount Maggie Swearingen's admission that she had ordered her mechanic to tamper with the fuel lines of both her brother Jason's plane and that of Mr. Pell had caused Jenn to relive the horror anew.

Jenn tried to understand why she was hospitalized an extra day, since she seemed to bounce back quickly.

Cade said he was just glad she was back to her usual perky self.

When he drove her home, she was quite chipper. She thought it had to do with the fact that they were unofficially engaged, but it was also a combination of all the evidence concerning Jason's death and the sabotage of Pell's plane coming together. She had needed closure, and although the truth was not pleasant, at least she could close the door on it.

Leo and Lissy were being taken care of by Big Jim, with the help of his daughter-in-law, Misty. Leah had her hands full with her new infant, but Jenn had no doubt that the children were receiving the best of care.

When Cade pulled off the highway at the entrance to Big Jim's ranch, the tires bumped over the cattle guard.

"I can't wait to see the children," Jennifer said. "I've really missed the little rascals."

There seemed to be a gathering at the ranch, because a collection of pickup trucks were lined up in front of the ranch house.

"Wonder what's going on at Big Jim's?" Jenn said. "I don't want to interrupt some family function."

Cade opened her door and helped her alight. "Not a problem. We can just pick up the kids and run."

When they reached the front door, Big Jim was waiting for them. "You folks come right on in here. There are some people been waitin' on you."

Jenn stepped inside eagerly, thinking the children were the people he was referring to. But it seemed the entire Garrett family was grinning at her. "Oh my!"

Leah rushed forward to give her a hug. "We're so glad you're out of the woods and out of the hospital."

Jenn returned her hug but felt her color rising. "I—I'm glad I survived."

"We fixed you a little lunch," Misty said. "We've got lots to celebrate."

"Let's go back to the kitchen," Big Jim suggested. "We got a fine spread back there just waitin' for you. I hope you're hungry."

Jenn flashed him a grin. "Starving. I've been eating hospital food for a couple of days and very little of it."

Big Jim tucked her hand in the crook of his arm and escorted her to the rear of his home.

When they rounded the corner, the aroma of good food assailed Jenn's senses. Her stomach growled, reminding her how scant her breakfast had been. She was seated at the large table with Cade beside her and the rest of the family gathered around. Lissy was in her high chair and Leo sat on a stack of thick books.

The table was laden with platters and large serving bowls, all filled with food. Big Jim took a seat at the opposite end and began to fill plates with meat before passing them down the line. It was as though all the family members knew to keep passing plates before they filled their own.

Jenn followed suit, keeping up the rhythm until her plate arrived. The next step in the event was for the diners to help themselves to whatever was in front of them and pass that around.

Big Jim clinked his spoon against his glass of iced tea. "I'd like to take a moment to acknowledge some very good news for our family. We have several things to celebrate today. First off, I'm so happy Miss Jennifer LaChance is with us today and that she survived the attempt on her life." He raised his tea glass to

Jenn as did the others at the table, including some encouraging comments.

"And I believe my nephew has an announcement to make." Big Jim nodded to Cade, who stood up.

"I would like everyone to know that Jennifer has agreed to be my bride." There was an explosion of applause and chatter.

"Oh, that's wonderful!" Leah exclaimed. "You two make a wonderful couple."

Tyler and Beau slapped Cade on the back and congratulated their cousin.

When the din had quieted down, Big Jim remained standing. "There's one more announcement and then we can enjoy this fine meal and each other's company." He put his big hand on Mark's shoulder. "I would like to announce that the adoption process has begun. In time, Mark here will be my son."

Another burst of applause and chatter.

Big Jim held up his hand to settle them down. "But in the meantime…" Mark stood up and clasped Big Jim around the waist. "In the meantime, Mark has legally changed his name. I'm proud to introduce my soon to be son, Mark Dalton Garrett."

Misty gasped, covering her mouth with both hands. "Oh, that's perfect!" Tears sprang to her eyes. "Thanks so much, Dad."

Big Jim and Mark appeared to be very proud of each other, hugging for a long moment.

"Now, let's enjoy this fine meal and be happy for each other." Big Jim settled back into his seat. "Ain't nothin' like family."

―⁓―

It was just a little over a month later when the wedding was to take place.

She had not been able to let go of the house where she and Jason had grown up, but Cade had helped her pack up and transport the contents back to Langston. She stored everything in the smallest hangar at the airstrip, opting to take her time in dealing with her memories. Now, the house was in the hands of a Realtor, who would oversee its rental. She reasoned that the income would come in handy.

Leah and Misty were delighted to help with wedding plans, taking care of details Jenn hadn't considered. Nevertheless, when the day arrived, she was delivered to the church feeling totally inadequate for the occasion.

Jenn was filled with anxiety and her hands were shaking as she gazed at herself in the full-length mirror at the church. She and the rest of the bridal party were sequestered in a small dressing room, and she believed Cade and the groomsmen were similarly holed up in their own dressing room. "Oh my goodness. I look awful," she declared.

"Oh, pshaw! Yew are one real purty young lady." Fern Davis was watching the preparations with great amusement. "Young Cade is a-gonna keel right over when he lays eyes on his bride."

"Gran is right," Leah said. "You look lovely, Jennifer. I'm sure Cade is having his own anxiety attack right along with you."

Jenn nodded. "I guess so. I think everything will be okay right after we do this thing. This—"

"Wedding." Misty gave a little giggle. "It's your wedding and you should just be enjoying all the fuss. You got a great guy."

Jenn had to smile at that. "Yes, Cade is wonderful." She smoothed the skirt of her white lace dress. It had cost more than she would have spent, but Big Jim had given his platinum card to his daughters-in-law, instructing them to take Jennifer to Amarillo and make sure she and they were all properly decked out for the wedding.

Turning away from the mirror, she smiled at her bridesmaids: the two Garrett wives who had taken her under their wings. "I appreciate you so much."

Both Misty and Leah gave her careful hugs, making sure not to smudge her makeup or muss her carefully arranged hair.

"I'm so happy to have you in the family," Leah said.

"I know you and Cade will be so happy together."

Gran chuckled. "Well, I'm plumb tickled yew picked my friend Edgar Wayne Pell to walk yew down the aisle. He sure is a fine fellah."

Jenn blinked rapidly to keep from tearing up. "Yes, he is a hero in my book. He saved my life twice."

"An' I heard him say yew was gonna be pardners with him."

"What?" Misty gazed at Jenn, openmouthed. "Why haven't I heard about this?"

Jenn shrugged and spread her hands wide. "We just decided, and with all the excitement of the wedding, we thought we would wait to make any announcements."

Leah was grinning from ear to ear. "That's fantastic. Mr. Pell knows so much about airplanes and he is familiar with the airstrip, so he should be able to do the heavy lifting."

"We think so. He's retired military but still very active, so he will take on the day-to-day management." Jenn still felt anxious about the bookkeeping aspect, but Big Jim assured her he would give them a hand.

He was just glad that the property would not be developed by some "underhanded big-city crooks." Big Jim was certain that the Swearingens would not consider the ecology of the community or the welfare of neighboring ranches in their thirst to ravage the land.

There was a soft knock at the door. "Ready, ladies?" It was Tyler on the other side.

"We're coming," Leah said. "Please escort Gran to her seat." She opened the door just wide enough to let Gran through and give her husband a kiss.

Jenn could hear the organist playing something classical. Her heart fluttered when she realized the next few minutes would change her life forever.

"Ready?" Misty asked.

Jenn took a deep breath and exhaled. "Yes! I'm ready." Leah

handed her the bridal bouquet before Jenn followed her two bridesmaids through the open door and took her place in line behind them.

"Well, you sure do look like an angel straight from heaven." Edgar Wayne Pell took his place by her side. "And I sure am proud that you chose me to give you away."

She placed a kiss on his scarred cheek. "I'm so proud to have our very heroic partner by my side. You're the perfect choice. Thanks for walking me down the aisle."

He patted her hand as Leah nodded at her and began the bridal parade, with Misty following her. When they had taken their places up by the altar, the music changed and the organist struck the beginning chords to the traditional wedding march.

Everyone in the church stood and turned to stare at them. A wave of timidity washed over her, but Pell patted her hand again. *Yes, I can do this.*

There, at the altar, Cade and his three cousins stood in a line. He looked so happy and so proud.

"You okay?" Pell whispered.

"Better than okay," she whispered, and took the first step into her future. Into the arms of the man she loved.

If you love June Faver's Texas cowboys, don't miss her brand-new Texas romance series set in the Hill Country!

Welcome Back to Rambling, Texas

Coming June 2021 from Sourcebooks Casablanca

REGGIE LEE STAFFORD GLANCED OUT THE WINDOW OF HER daddy's Hill Country convenience store just northwest of Austin, Texas. She looked out in time to see the silver BMW cruise by slowly. The top was down, and the driver looked as divine as the vehicle.

A bronzed god with sun-streaked, longish blond hair. He radiated the attitude of a celebrity, hiding behind the lenses of his designer sunglasses. Driving with his elbow stuck out the window, he craned his neck to peer into the small store.

He gazed up at the fading sign that proudly proclaimed the establishment to be Stafford's Mercantile, a name Reggie's grandparents had selected in 1949 when they'd first opened their doors in Rambling, Texas, and when the wares had included yard goods and hardware.

Reggie leaned over the counter to stare at the hunk in the sports car, surprised when he pulled into the parking lot and climbed out.

He shoved the keys in the pocket of his faded denims and continued to gaze through the plateglass window with an air of indecision.

She noted that the denims were well filled with 100 percent prime American beef. *Well well well. Eye candy from the city. My lucky day.* She surreptitiously glanced at her reflection in the mirror behind the counter and ran her fingers through her tousled hair. She took a deep breath as the stranger pushed through the entrance, clanking the metal cowbell against the glass. Her dimples flashed as she wrapped her soft Texas drawl around the words of greeting. "Good afternoon. How can I help you?"

The stranger pushed his sunglasses up on his head and grinned back at her. He laughed, a single derisive snort. "Is that really you, Regina Vagina? Still here after all these years?"

A claustrophobic strangling sensation reached up from her gut and threatened to suffocate the life out of her. "Nooo!" she wailed. "Franklinstein!"

She stared in dismay at the grown-up version of the boy who had made her early adolescence a living hell. From the day he had arrived in town, Franklin Bell had been crossways with her, and he had remained so until the day he'd left.

A clutch of something other than dismay seized her as he continued to inspect her with unmistakably mischievous green eyes. "You got anything cold to drink, Regina?" He pronounced her name as he always had, rhyming with *vagina*.

Color flamed her cheeks. "Any fool can see the whole back wall is lined with reach-in coolers," she bit out tersely. "Serve yourself."

Seemingly undaunted by her scathing remark, he had the nerve to chuckle before turning to inspect the contents of the coolers. All too soon, he returned with his selection and slid it across the counter toward her.

Reggie rang up his purchase and murmured, "That will be a dollar sixty-nine." Her words came out all husky, and she pressed her lips together as she reached for the two singles he offered. Their fingers brushed, sending a tingling sensation to the pit of her stomach.

"You're looking good, Regina." His voice sounded smoky as his gaze lingered on the curve of her breast.

"Would you stop calling me that? We're not kids anymore, Franklin." She slammed his change down on the counter.

"Yes, ma'am," he said, seemingly contrite.

She took a deep breath and let it out all at once. "Reggie—my friends call me Reggie."

He gave her a strange little smile. "I know that. Only you would never let me be your friend." He twisted the lid off his soda and took a long guzzle.

"My friend!" she exploded. "You never wanted to be my friend. Your sole purpose in life was to make me miserable."

"If you say so." He smirked and took another swig.

She swallowed hard as she watched his mouth caress the soda bottle. She wet her own dry lips, trying to appear casual. "Just passing through?"

"Not this time," he said. "I'm here to tie up some loose ends and take care of a little business."

Reggie sniffed. "What kind of business?"

He leaned his elbows on the counter and gazed up at her. "My great-aunt, Miss Rosie Bell Grady... She passed and left me all her considerable property."

She glanced out the storefront at the silver Beemer sitting on the roasting hot asphalt. "It doesn't look as if you need it."

He smiled, unperturbed by her withering commentary. "That could be, but I always liked this town. Believe it or not, I do have some fond memories of Rambling, Texas."

Reggie stifled a curt rejoinder. "I didn't see you at Miss Rosie's funeral."

His brash humor faded abruptly. "I was, uh, out of the country."

She eyed him with uncompromising candor. "I sincerely hope that your business dealings proceed without delay."

He pushed away from the counter. "So I can get the hell out of town as fast as possible?" He raised an eyebrow, glaring at her, although she refused to be baited. "Sorry to disappoint you, Regina, but I'll be staying on a while." He tilted the bottle and drained the contents.

"I swear, if you call me that one more time, I'm going to climb across this counter and smack you one."

He opened his eyes wide in mock disbelief. "You would assault me on my very first day back in town?"

She glowered, crossing her arms across her chest. "Assault? You sound like a freakin' asshole lawyer or something."

"Guilty as charged."

Reggie experienced the choking sensation again. "Guh-reat!"

He replaced the bottle cap and flipped the empty into the trash container behind the counter. "See ya around, Regina."

--~~--

That didn't go well. But it never did with Regina... *Reggie*, he reminded himself.

He didn't know why he thought she would treat him any different from how she had in the past. Always had hated him. Always would. *Snotty bitch.* He sighed. *Beautiful, exciting, desirable, snotty bitch.*

Frank dug the keys out of his pocket, and with a last glance over his shoulder at the storefront, he climbed into his car and turned the ignition.

Still, she had smiled at him before she realized who he was. And how much she hated him.

He pulled out of the parking space, knowing Reggie was watching him.

Expelling the breath he'd been holding, he headed for Aunt Rosie's sprawling Victorian house by the river.

Rambling was located in the beautiful Texas Hill Country, the so-called Heart of Texas. There were two rivers and a lake, so it was a mecca for retirees and vacationers. For a prolonged period, visitors and residents alike took to the rivers to float with the currents on oversize inner tubes. The lake, on the other hand, offered the opportunity for motorboats to piss off the owners of sailboats, who preferred the much quieter and far less bumpy method. There were also canoes and kayaks on the lake and rivers, so most people had a means of assaulting the water on a regular basis. Frank had been an accomplished sailor, preferring the wind to power his boat, which had been moored at one of the marinas.

As he drove through town, he recalled his first encounter with Reggie Lee Stafford, the dark-eyed beauty who had laughed when he'd stumbled, dropping his books at her feet.

"Watch it, new boy. You almost ran me down."

In truth, he'd stumbled when he'd done a double take to get another look at her dancing eyes and flash of dimples. But he'd blushed when she'd chided him and gathered his belongings in anger. That meeting had been the first of many disastrous encounters where Reggie Lee and her friends had taunted him as the "new boy."

Later that day, when a teacher called on her in class using her full name, he'd seized upon the opportunity to get revenge. He'd enjoyed her discomfort when he'd first called her "Regina Vagina." His timing had been perfect. He'd chosen the moment just before class was dismissed while the teacher was distracted to call out to her, just loud enough to carry, "Hey, Regina Vagina. Why are you so stuck up?"

A wave of raucous laughter swept the classroom. Several boys who were to become his friends gave him thumbs-ups and nods of approval. It was the validation he needed. A way to fit in.

Reggie had turned red and her eyes teared. Grabbing her books, she'd rushed out of class, her covey of girlfriends clustered around her.

He'd felt a moment of remorse for hurting her feelings but had enjoyed bonding with the guys.

She'd retaliated in kind, dubbing him "Franklinstein," but her taunt had fallen short. Nothing could have equaled naming aloud the female body part that so fascinated the entire male student body.

The wind whipped Frank's hair as he picked up speed outside the city limits. Within a few minutes, he turned onto the shady lane that led to Aunt Rosie's house. It was lined with old pecan trees, their branches reaching across to one another like the arms of lovers forever separated by the winding dirt road.

Parked in front of the house, he turned off the ignition and sat for a moment before stepping out. The house had fallen into disrepair, but a feeling of warmth flooded his chest as he gazed up at the old structure.

The porch completely circled the house. He recalled the sound of his young footsteps as he ran around and around irreverently, playing games with other rowdy boys. He could still see Aunt Rosie rocking on the porch, a bit of needlework or a crossword puzzle and pencil in her hands.

Climbing the porch, he set one of the dusty wicker rockers into motion, giving it a push as he passed.

When he inserted the skeleton key in the old-fashioned lock, it turned with difficulty. He couldn't remember the house ever being locked, but the lawyer had mailed him a key along with a copy of Aunt Rosie's will. When he'd seen her spidery signature, he was overwhelmed with sadness. He'd been traveling in Europe and hadn't known of her passing until after the funeral. Sucking in a deep breath, he blew it out, puffing his cheeks in the process. He would have to find out where she was buried and pay his overdue respects. *Another sin to atone for.*

The door opened with a creak, and he stepped across the threshold, entering a treasure trove of memories: mostly pleasant, some bittersweet.

His footsteps sounded hollow. They echoed off the wooden floors and up the stairs to rebound from the hard surface of the stained-glass window on the landing and back down to impact him again.

Walking back to the kitchen, he experienced a feeling of remorse when he saw the layer of dust on Aunt Rosie's usually immaculate surfaces. His throat tightened with sorrow.

I should have been here more.

He opened the back door, stepped out onto the porch, and gazed across the fields and the orchards. The air was heavy with the smell of fruit trees in blossom and the drone of honeybees harvesting nectar and going about their business of pollinating the blossoms. He took in deep lungfuls of the fragrance.

This is mine now. He wasn't sure how he felt about owning so much land. He had scrupulously avoided entanglements, and this felt like a major commitment.

In the city, he leased a spacious condo, but he wasn't particularly attached to it. The furniture, even the paintings hanging on his walls, were all leased.

Frank stuck his hands in his pockets and sighed. Although he tried to live in the moment and be flexible enough to seize any opportunity that presented itself, he hoped this legacy wouldn't require too much of his attention. Up until now, he'd been able to leave the country and travel whenever the notion hit him, and it hit him quite frequently.

He realized that owning this property would infringe upon his ability to go with the flow, to change directions on a whim, celebrate his spontaneity. Now he was a landowner, and with that came certain responsibilities.

He knew Aunt Rosie had derived some of her income from the harvest of peaches and apples from the orchards and the grapes from the vineyard, where they produced a superb pinot grigio, all suitable to be grown in the moderate climate.

Her other income had come from rental properties her husband had left her. They were located all around the small town. Most were residential, but there were several businesses as well. She'd held the local Dairy Queen franchise, although there had always been a manager to handle the day-to-day transactions. Also the small flower shop that handled all the local weddings and funerals.

A smile formed on Frank's lips. There was one more property. The *Rambling Gazette*.

After her husband died, Aunt Rosie inherited the building housing the weekly newspaper. As owner, she maintained a very loose control over the building, and in return for free rent, the publication guaranteed to maintain the building. Miss Rosie didn't have to deal with it, and the community got their news.

Now the building had passed to Frank. He released a deep chuckle. The *Rambling Gazette*, where Miss Reggie Lee Stafford worked as reporter and columnist...when she wasn't babysitting her daddy's convenience store.

Frank had a feeling he was going to enjoy checking out that old building. It was four stories of red brick, and as far as he knew, the *Gazette* only occupied the ground floor. It seemed he'd developed a sudden interest in the publishing business. What else did that old building contain?

———

Reggie Lee stared out the window of the store but saw nothing. She shivered as she recalled the look in Frank Bell's green eyes. He was definitely up to something...and it had to be no good.

From the first moment Franklin Bell had arrived in Rambling, he'd been nothing but trouble with a capital T.

She recalled when he'd been introduced to her ninth-grade class. She'd thought he was cute in a green-eyed, dark-blondish sort of way. Way cuter than the other boys. He'd come from some prep school in Arlington, up near Dallas. He was pretty stiff at first. He couldn't take a joke, and he'd almost gotten into a fight with Kenny Landers his first day.

His temper didn't improve in the weeks to follow. He'd rushed right smack into her the next day and didn't even apologize. Just turned all shades of red as he'd gathered up his books and hustled off. Of course, a few people had laughed, but that was nothing. You have to be able to laugh at yourself once in a while.

As if!

Mr. Perfect would never be able to laugh at himself. Not when he could be ridiculing others. Reggie Lee to be specific.

How could a lady as sweet as Miss Rosie Bell Grady even be distantly related to Frank Bell? Their kinship was beyond Reggie Lee's wildest imagination. She couldn't conceive that they shared the same gene pool, except for the green eyes.

Miss Rosie had been the kindest person on the planet. If it

weren't for her, Reggie might not have been given an opportunity to become a member of the *Gazette* staff at such a young age. Miss Rosie had suggested Reggie might like to submit something for the "younger crowd," as she'd put it. Miss Rosie must have put in a good word for her because that led to Reggie being hired on to cover all school athletic events and later assigned her to write a weekly column titled "Around Town." Reggie also took her turn at writing obituaries and birth and wedding announcements.

Sadly, she had written Miss Rosie's obituary, cringing when she'd typed in the name of her nephew, Franklin Bell, as her sole living relative.

Miss Rosie's funeral had been attended by governors, the current and a couple past. Countless senators and congressional representatives came to pay their respects. But there was no member of the family to pay their respects to, because her only surviving relative was out of the country and couldn't be bothered to fly back to say a final goodbye to the wonderful lady who had taken over the role of parenting him.

Reggie sniffed, remembering that the loss of his own parents was what had brought Frank to Rambling in the first place. Maybe he'd been depressed when he'd first arrived, but it came across as a big, fat chip on his shoulder.

Now he'd come back to claim all of Miss Rosie's property. The lovely old Victorian house. The verdant orchards and the vineyard. The businesses...

A cold lump settled in the pit of Reggie's stomach. The *Gazette*. Frank Bell inherited the redbrick building that housed the *Gazette*. The building had stood in place for more than a hundred years. It was a monument to the community.

Frank Bell now owns the property. What will that smug bastard do to our building?

About the Author

June Faver loves Texas, from the Gulf Coast to the Panhandle, from the Mexican border to the Piney Woods. Her novels embrace the heart and soul of the state and the larger-than-life Texans who romp across her pages. A former teacher and healthcare professional, she lives and writes in the Texas Hill Country.

Also by June Faver

DARK HORSE COWBOYS
Do or Die Cowboy
Hot Target Cowboy
When to Call a Cowboy
Cowboy Christmas Homecoming

GARRETT FAMILY SAGA
The Best Cowboy Christmas Ever